HALF THE WORLD AWAY

Newly graduated photography student Lori Maddox takes a gap year after university and finds a job in China as a private English tutor. Back in Manchester, her parents Jo and Tom, who separated when Lori was a toddler, follow her adventures on her blog, 'Lori in the Orient'. Suddenly communication stops and when the silence persists, a frantic Jo and Tom report her missing. It is impossible to find out anything from 5,000 miles away so they travel out to Chengdu, a city in the south-western province of Sichuan, to search for their daughter. But in an unfamiliar country and with very little help, it's an unbearably difficult challenge...

HALF THE WORLD AWAY

HALF THE WORLD AWAY

by

Cath Staincliffe

Magna Large Print Books
Long Preston, North Yorkshire,
BD23 4ND, England.

British Library Cataloguing in Publication Data.

A catalogue record of this book is
available from the British Library

ISBN   978-0-7505-4436-8

First published in Great Britain in 2015 by Constable

Cover illustration © Xuesong Liao by arrangement with
Arcangel Images

The moral right of the author has been asserted

Published in Large Print 2017 by arrangement with
Little, Brown Book Group Limited

Magna Large Print is an imprint of Library Magna Books Ltd.

Printed and bound in Great Britain by
T.J. (International) Ltd., Cornwall, PL28 8RW

For Daniel
Fēi cháng găn xiè.
Yòng wǒ quánbù de ài.

CHAPTER ONE

Lorelei is leaving. Tom, my ex, and I drive her to the airport. A bright, blustery September afternoon. The sky a high dome of blue, chalk-marked with jet trails, the trees along the roadside heavy with leaves.

A cold, jittery feeling in my stomach, my jaw tense.

'You've got your passport?' I turn round from the front seat, an excuse as much as anything to see her, to see more of her.

'Yes.'

'Money?' Tom says.

'Da-ad.'

'Well, it has been known, babe,' he says.

'Once,' she huffs, 'once I forgot things.'

'Everything,' he says. 'Not so hot on the house keys either, as I recall.'

Lorelei laughs, a sudden peal of delight, then mock-outrage. 'Like, you're so organized,' she says to him.

'I'm here.'

'Late,' Lorelei says.

'Ten minutes,' he says. 'You've got plenty of time – your flight's not till eight.'

'Eight forty-five,' she says.

'Jo – you said eight.' He glances at me.

'I lied,' I say, 'to account for your pitiful time-keeping.'

Lori laughs again.

The short-stay car park is busy; we find space on the very top, open to the elements. Lori insists on carrying her rucksack herself. It is nearly as big as she is. She looks like she'll topple backwards, be stuck like a turtle. Tom takes her hand luggage.

'Photo,' I say.

She poses, hands on the rucksack straps. Her hair chocolate, shoulder length, with shocking-pink tips, choppy fringe. Leather jacket, pink T-shirt, skinny black jeans on skinny legs, purple Doc Marten boots. I take some pictures.

'Tom?'

He stands beside her, dwarfing her. Hard to believe they're related. Tom as fair-haired as she is dark, but they both have olive skin that tans easily. Down to some Maltese ancestor of his. I burn and peel at any lick of sunshine. Her dark hair, her petite frame, she's inherited from me. Though I'm no longer skinny after having three kids and many years in a sedentary occupation.

'Now you, Mum,' Lori says.

We swap places. Tom does the honours. I chat away, fighting an urge to weep that makes my cheekbones ache.

'You got your tickets?' Tom says, in the lift down to the terminal.

She sticks her tongue out at him.

I promise myself I will not cry. It isn't the first time she's left home, after all: she's been away at uni for three years. Back every ten weeks with washing and empty pockets and a ravenous appe-tite. Nocturnal, living in a different time zone from

12

the rest of us.

But she has never been so far away. Tom is all for it. Big adventure, he says. And he's lent her the airfare, with no expectation he'll be getting it back anytime soon. His latest venture is doing well.

I'd wondered if it might be better for her to try to get some work experience first. Lori wasn't having it. 'If I go now, I can travel with Jake and Amy. I don't want to go on my own later.'

As we wait at Check-in, the departures hall teems with travellers, queues snaking around the pillars, the clamour of conversation, of crying children and Tannoy announcements. Thailand, her first stop. Then Vietnam and Hong Kong.

Her phone trills. She reads it. 'Amy.' She grins. 'They'll meet me at the airport.'

Her bag is two kilos over.

'Shit,' she says, looking at me in panic.

'I thought you'd weighed it,' I say.

'I did. Those scales don't work.'

'How much?' Tom asks the check-in clerk.

'That'll be eighty-eight pounds.'

'God,' says Lori.

Tom has the cash. Crisis averted.

'Thanks,' Lori says.

'Make sure it's lighter coming back,' I say.

'I will.'

'Yeah, no Christmas presents,' Tom says.

'We could get a cuppa?' I nod towards the café, eager to delay our parting.

Lori screws up her nose. 'I'll go through,' she says.

The pressure rises in my chest. Don't go, I want

13

to say. Stay, come home with me, don't leave. Why can't I just be pleased for her, excited?

Tom opens his arms and she walks into them. He bends and kisses the top of her head. 'It'll be great, Lollydoll. You'll kill it, yeah?'

I look away, swallowing hard, eyes skimming the crowds.

'Bye, Dad.'

He lets her go and she turns to me. I hug her tight. When I try to speak my voice turns husky: 'Have a wonderful time.' I want to say more. *I love you. Be careful. Keep your money out of sight. Stay safe.* But my throat is locked, my head full of tears. So I just hug her tighter, sniffing hard, breathing in the smell of her – orange-blossom shampoo and mint chewing gum and something like salt.

'Bye-bye.' She does that funny wave, like her hand and arm are rigid, no wrist joint. And all I can do is nod vigorously and smile, lips closed, teeth clamped together.

We watch her walk away, her tote bag over one shoulder, a quick stride as if she'll break into a run at any moment.

She pauses where the ramp leads down to Departures and waves again. I wave back. Tom gives her a thumbs-up and a peace sign. Then she is gone.

'Oh, God.' I let my breath out.

'She'll be fine,' he says.

'It's not her I'm worried about,' I try to joke but it comes out all squeaky. I find a tissue, dab at my eyes

'Jo?'

14

I shake my head. 'It's OK.'

Back on the top of the car park, the sky is changing: a red blush tints shreds of cloud to the west. The end of the day is coming. The hotels around the airport are visible, as is the railway station and, further away, the skyline of the city.

'It's just–' I get no further. Tears come hot on my cheeks, making my ribs heave.

Tom puts his arms around me. I stiffen momentarily, the contact unfamiliar. Then I let go. The release helps, easing the heaviness in my chest, leaving me feeling raw and exposed.

'Sorry.' I blow my nose.

'Home?'

We drive back into the city, against the flow of commuters leaving after their day's work, the sunset a blaze of copper, the sky to the east darkening purple.

Tom drops me at mine, and once he's gone, I sit on the front step for a moment, readying myself to go in to Nick and the boys.

Almost dark, and the insects are still busy among the carnations, cosmos and honeysuckle. The perfume from the flowers is sweet above the city smells of stone, exhaust fumes and food cooking. The evening star is rising. Higher above, I see a moving light, white then a flash of red. A plane. Not Lori's, not yet. She'll be through security control now, waiting in the departure lounge. Maybe doing some shopping.

A cat yowls in the back gardens and I hear Benji answer with a bark from inside. Further away there is the sound of glass breaking, then a slam. Someone putting their bottles in the recycling.

15

All I want to do is indulge my sadness, get drunk and pine for Lorelei, weep and eat more than I need to, sleep late.

Fat chance.

So I go back in to my husband and help get Finn and Isaac settled in bed and answer all their questions about their big sister's big adventure for the umpteenth time.

And lie awake all night like an idiot.

CHAPTER TWO

Lori texts just as I'm starting work. *All good. Just got thru Customs. Knacked. Love you L xxx* I'm relieved. I can't imagine Thailand, only images culled from pictures in the weekend magazines or movies like *The Beach.* All vegetation, palm-fringed sands, endless hills and deep diving pools. What it might be like, the atmosphere, the day-to-day life, the cities, socializing – I'll be relying on Lori to broaden my horizons.

This morning I listened to the first jets taking off every few minutes from the airport, growls climbing to a roar, then fading. I'm still bereft. Lori going seems to fuel the grief I've been coping with since my mother died in June. The two things are muddled up.

The alarm went at seven, and Nick got the boys up while I made their packed lunches. The news about chemical weapons being used in Syria made my mood seem like an indulgence. Then came breakfast. No matter how well prepared I try to be, there is always a sense of impending chaos at breakfast time. Finn or Isaac will be missing some crucial item of clothing, their book bag or PE kit. There is a disaster with the food, one of them finishing the milk before the other has any, a cup of juice ruining a precious drawing (usually Finn's juice and Isaac's drawing). There is a squabble about toys. Or a sudden inability to reach the toilet in time. Things can get messy so I dress after breakfast, then chivvy the boys into footwear and coats, then herd them out of the door. Benji tries to come with us – he always tries it on even though he knows that Nick will take him for a turn around the park before going into work. And the boys and I will walk him again after school.

Finn is seven, Isaac two years younger and they both have places at the primary school where I work. It's a C of E school attached to a parish church, which wouldn't have been my choice (we're not religious) if I hadn't worked there. But sending them to another local school would've made all the taking and collecting so much more complicated. And, to be fair, I like the school: the head-teacher, Grace, puts her life and soul into it. She's a good manager and most of the staff respect her. I've been secretary there since Lori was eight when I gave up child-minding. She was already at a secular school and I didn't like to move her so we managed the hour before and after the school day when I was still at work with a patchwork of arrangements. I relied on other parents, the after-school club, child-minders, my mum and, when I

17

ran out of all other options, Tom. These days, the pressures on parents seem even greater and our school, like many others, has a breakfast club as well as the after-school club where Finn and Isaac go.

Having Lori so young – I was twenty. – put paid to any travel plans back then. While friends of mine were discovering Goa and Machu Picchu, I was by turns bewildered, exhausted and exhilarated in the world of nappies, baby sick and sleep deprivation.

I discovered I was pregnant partway through my second year but I was determined to complete my degree on time. It seemed important to prove to the world that I could do it all. And I did. Just. It was horrendous.

Now the phone is ringing with notices of absence, the mail is arriving and I've a tray full of work to get going on and a backlog of emails to deal with. It helps being busy: the demands of routine drive a juggernaut through any inclination to dwell on Lori leaving.

In the staffroom at break people ask me if Lori got off all right – everyone has been sharing in the build-up to her trip. We're a close team and I know the problems other people are dealing with. Henry's father has dementia – he's become restless and agitated and hostile; Zoë had a miscarriage last term; Pam is going through a really acrimonious divorce; and Sunita has just been diagnosed with diabetes. It puts things in perspective.

As we walk back from school Finn holds my hand, swinging his arm to and fro and singing.

18

He loves to sing but he makes an awful racket.

Isaac runs ahead and back, like Benji, a sheepdog driving his charges. He stops to examine anything of interest, a sock in the gutter, conkers, a worm stranded on the paving. He always finds something to bring home for his special box (currently the one that our microwave came in). Today it is a throwaway lighter. I check it doesn't work and is empty of fuel before letting him keep it.

Even though we have Benji, Isaac is scared of dogs. As we near what he calls the Dog House, he runs back and takes my free hand. The yappy terrier there barks furiously on cue and Isaac flinches, his fingers tightening around mine.

'Wait at the lights,' I remind him, once we leave the danger zone and he lets go. He zigzags along the pavement, holding the lighter out as if it's a lightsaber or a remote control or a magic wand, muttering something I can't catch. He's slight and dark-haired, skinny like Lori, pale like me. Both he and Finn have inherited Nick's deep blue eyes with those flecks of gold. I never tire of staring at them. Mind you, with the lads that depends on them sitting still long enough, which is especially rare for Finn.

We collect Benji and head straight back out. Stopping for a snack invariably descends into a rerun of the morning's mission to leave the house intact – things unravel so quickly – so I leave the boys in the drive and fetch the dog and his ball.

Finn throws the ball over and over, not necessarily in the direction he intends it to go but that doesn't matter to Benji. We stop at the playground and tie Benji up at the railings while the boys mess about on the slide and swings. Isaac wants to go on the stepping stones but he isn't quite brave enough to leap from one wooden block to the next so he jumps down onto the mulch between them, then clambers up again.

'See the heron?' I say. The bird is almost overhead, coming from the pond. Isaac looks up.

'Hey, Finn,' I call across. He's on his back, on the roundabout, his feet dangling over the edge onto the ground, slowly walking it around. 'See the heron?'

We watch it fly out of sight. 'Time to go,' I say.

'It flies high,' Finn says, as I'm untying Benji.

'Yes.'

'Like Lori in an airplane.'

'Aeroplane. That's right. And where's Lori gone?'

'Thailand.'

'Why's it called Thailand?' says Isaac. 'Do they all wear ties?'

'No. Nice idea but it's a different spelling, a different word.'

'I made a card for her,' Finn says, 'with all of us on, me and Daddy and you and Isaac and Lori and Benji.' He grasps my hand. 'Did she like it?'

'She will. She'll open the case and there it will be. And there's a picture from Isaac, too,' I say.

Isaac is crouched at the edge of the path. 'A feather.' He holds it out to me. Black with a metallic glint in the light.

'That's lovely.'

Nick gets back later than usual, staying at the office to make up the hours he missed the day before. I'll wait to eat with him, feed the boys first. While the pair of them watch television and Isaac draws herons and pterodactyls over and over again, I go up to strip Lori's bed.

The carpet is littered with scraps of paper, items of clothing, spent matches and torn Rizla packets. Several dirty cups stand on her bedside table, with a half-empty bottle of Coca-Cola and biscuit wrappers. I can smell the perfume she wears – Marc Jacobs's Daisy that we got her for Christmas. The room is decorated in the deep green she chose a few years ago and one wall is a collage of photographs. Some of her own and others from magazines and websites. She's built it up, sticking the pictures on with glue, and it now fills the whole wall. There's never been any theme to it, as far as I know. It's a mix of portraits, landscapes, nature photography and action scenes. I find it too busy, overwhelming the space, but it's not my space. Not yet. If she moves out when she's back from her travels then maybe we'll redecorate. See what she wants to do with the photos. They'll have to be stripped off the wall and they'll likely be damaged in the process.

Finn and Isaac are happy with the bunk beds for now but eventually I think they'll want their own rooms – at least, Isaac will. Before then it'll be nice to have a guest room. But who knows what Lori will choose to do? Her plans extend only as far as Christmas when her travels end and it'll be back to the harsh realities of job-hunting in a recession.

'You got her text?' The first thing Nick says when he gets back.

21

'Yes.'

He studies me for a moment.

'I'm OK. Just getting used to it. Hate goodbyes. And after my mum...' The sadness is still there, close to the surface.

He nods, gives a small smile. 'They asleep?'

'Yes. And Isaac wants to know what feathers are made of. I'll leave that one to you, something an environmental engineer should know.'

'We know everything.'

I fetch the salad from the fridge, dole out lasagne. Nick pours wine.

'She might not live here again,' I say.

'Jo, you said that when she went to Glasgow. If she moves out, new phase,' he says, 'that's life.' He raises his glass. 'To life.'

I share the toast, comforted by his reassurance.

CHAPTER THREE

'And how is Tom?' Nick says.

It's a few days later. We've not heard from Lori since she landed and I've just sent an email. A couple of lines. Hoping she'll not feel I'm pestering her. Remembering my own experience when I was away at uni and duty-bound to phone home every week, knowing my parents worried if I didn't.

'Same as ever,' I tell Nick, scrolling through the TV guide. 'He always lands on his feet. The apartments are going great guns. So he'll probably chuck it in soon,' I add.

'Getting bored,' Nick says.

'Lori told him off for being late,' I say.

Nick laughs. 'Seriously?'

'I kid you not. I didn't say anything.'

'Pot, kettle, apple from tree?'

'Not a peep. *Game of Thrones* or *True Detective?*' I waggle the remote.

Nick shakes his head. 'I'm going up. Site visit tomorrow. I'll reset the alarm.'

Left on my own, I wonder why Nick asked about Tom or, more specifically, why he waited four days to ask about him. Nick and I have been together for eleven years and we've gone through a lot of manoeuvring to make sure Lori spends time with her dad. It's been a rocky road but easier as Lori grew old enough to make her own arrangements with him. Nick still resents Tom, hasn't forgiven him for the hurt he's caused with his lack of organization, and the times his chaotic approach to life left us in the lurch or Lori disappointed. Nick is protective of me too. He's been witness to me raging about Tom's latest fuck-ups too many times.

Perhaps there's some jealousy as well. Much as Nick is a great stepdad to Lori, she and Tom are even closer.

Tom and I were never a good match. It was his difference that caught my attention. He was flamboyant and opinionated and impulsive.

Our first encounter ended in a blazing row. I was staffing a stall signing people up to a petition and vigil in support of the Chinese students on hunger strike in Tiananmen Square.

'What's the point?' he said. 'Nothing we do here will affect what happens.'

'With enough support and attention–'

'It's all over the telly – the whole world's watching anyway. A few names on a petition is a waste of time.'

'So we do nothing?' I said. 'This is a mass movement, a real chance at democracy.'

'When the Chinese government have had enough, they'll clear the lot of them out. Water cannon or whatever. None of this,' he waved his hand at the stall, 'will make a bit of difference.'

'You're talking crap,' I said.

'Put money on it – the protest is quashed, the Commies carry on and you have a drink with me.' His eyes were dancing. He was enjoying it, winding me up.

'You want me to bet on people's lives? Talk about shallow.'

His mouth twitched. I could tell he was fighting a smile. My face felt hot.

'You wait and see,' he said.

He wore a long duster-type coat, which emphasized his height, black denims, and I could see his jumper was shrunken and had holes in it. He'd sharp cheekbones, long hair the colour of honey, eyes of the palest blue.

I ignored him after that, feeling a smart of irritation each time I saw him in the union or a lecture hall. He'd always smile. Sometimes I felt I was the mouse to his cat.

Then came the massacre. We all watched in horror as the Chinese tanks fired on the protesters, mostly young students. Hundreds died. The world condemned the brutality but China's leaders remained unrepentant.

About a week afterwards Tom came up to me in the corridor.

'Come to gloat?' I said.

'I won the bet.'

'I never accepted your stupid bet.'

He sighed, stuck his hands into his pockets, as if I was boring him.

I moved to walk around him and he stood in my way. My face grew warm.

'What are you scared of?' he said.

'I'm not scared.'

'You seeing someone?'

'No,' I said.

'So?'

'Why would I want to go out with you? We don't agree on anything, I don't even–'

'What?' I wished he'd wipe the smirk off his face.

Like you, I was going to say but that felt unkind.

'It's just a drink,' he said.

'Why?'

'Might be fun,' he said. 'Tonight, the Lass o' Gowrie at eight.' He walked off without waiting for an answer.

I turned up feeling intensely awkward. We argued all evening.

I had a ball.

Lori in the Ori-ent

What's in a Name?
Posted on 15 October 2013 by Lori

Hello, and welcome to my new blog.

A bit of background – I'm a Brit, from Manchester, photography graduate (yay, Glasgow!), taking a few months out with my trusty camera to see something of this amazing planet and report back. In my former life I never made it beyond Tenerife so for me writing this from a guesthouse in Thailand is beyond cool.

(Hi Mum *waves* still alive. Sorry I've not replied to your texts – bit of hassle sorting phones out.)

Lori in the Ori-ent will be my working title. I was going to be Lori on the Lam but someone got there first, heads up to www.manonthelam.com. Then I came up with Lori's Big Adventure but that's been well and truly snaffled by many bloggers. So we are where we are. In my case Thailand. Whoop-de-doo!

My given name is Lorelei. It's not very common, though Marvel comic aficionados and the fans of Gentlemen Prefer Blondes will know it. The name means either 'alluring rock' or 'murmuring rock' or 'alluring temptress'. There is an actual rock called the Lorelei on the Rhine river in Germany. The story goes that it's inhabited by a siren whose singing lures mariners to their death. In my defence I'd like to point out that

26

a) No one asked me

b) I'm really not the alluring type

c) If I am called after a rock then so are the Jades and Rubys and Ambers out there, and maybe my rock has a little bit more character than theirs. Maybe. Granite, anyone? Millstone grit?

d) My singing may drive people to distraction but I have never drowned a soul, mariner or otherwise.

Most people call me Lori, not to be confused with lorry (a.k.a. truck, for any US visitors).

And here are my favourite photos so far, most from Ko Samet, where we stayed in a cabin above the bay and lounged like lizards. The island gets its name from the Cajeput tree – related to the Tea Tree – and also called a paper-bark tree. You can see why in the pictures.

Next week we head for Vietnam. Come and see me there. Lxxx

CHAPTER FOUR

Four weeks after her departure we have an email from Lori with a link to a blog she's started, where she's posted some photos. Pictures of her, Jake, Amy and a couple of others, at the beach, having a meal in a beachside restaurant. She looks happy, laughing at the table, grinning on the sand, her skin already darker from the sun. The new friends are Australians, Suze and Dawn. Several more photos show off the landscape.

'Still got her camera, then,' Nick says. He thought she shouldn't take it with her. We'd splashed out and bought it when she started at Glasgow. He worried it'd get stolen.

'Don't stress,' Lori said. 'I'll be careful.'

That's a first, I thought, but I didn't join in.

Nick raised his eyebrows.

'I'll be insured,' she said. 'Anyway, I've had it for three years and I've not lost it yet.'

She has a wonderful eye for colour and composition. The sweeping beaches and vivid seascapes she's posted might have come from a glossy brochure. Just looking gives me itchy feet. 'We ought to book somewhere for next summer,' I say to Nick. 'What about those French campsites with all mod cons? Are they expensive?' With my job we always have to take holidays when school's closed and the prices are at their highest.

'Find out,' he says.

'Finn and Isaac would love it.'

We've had a succession of wet summer holidays in Wales and the Lakes. The thought of another damp fortnight trying to entertain the kids, traipsing around petting zoos, going to unfamiliar swimming pools or sitting in family rooms in pubs with steamed-up windows and the stink of chips makes my heart sink. The prospect of fine weather day after day, the kids roaming free and making friends, four of us swimming in the sea, and watching the stars with no need for jumpers or waterproofs has the opposite effect.

'Either that,' I say, 'or a cheap and cheerful package somewhere like the Algarve or Menorca.'

'Be hotter there,' he warns.

28

'I'll wear my hat.'

I reread Lori's blog, which makes me laugh, and then we look up the places she's photographed on Wikipedia, Chon Buri and Ko Samet. It looks like she's having the time of her life.

Lori in the Ori-ent

Rule Number One: Don't drink the water
Posted on 28 November 2013 by Lori

Everyone says this. It's up there in travel advice for all Westerners entering Vietnam. But the water has a way of sneaking up on you. That apple you eat, the tomato, the pak choi – they need washing first. But NOT in the water.

And what about the bean sprouts? They grow in the water, they are full of the stuff. So avoid all water-based veg. In fact, ditch salads altogether.

Make sure everything you eat is cooked until it is unrecognizable. Not hard here. Below I've posted a selection of dishes we've had over the last week or so. Can you identify anything? (Rice doesn't count.)

Another thing to remember is that water can be disguised – as ice. So sling the cubes. And don't suck up steam either if the opportunity presents itself. The heat might make the vapour sterile, but a scalded face is so not a good look.

Don't use water to brush your teeth. Duh, right? You need to use bottled water for that too. This was my downfall. The habit of turning on the tap is so deeply ingrained that after making this mistake, following a suitable period of illness and recuperation, I found the safest thing to do is brush my teeth far from any sinks. It can get messy but not half so messy as the results of breaking the rule. I won't dwell too much on that except to say it was like a cross between the movies The Lost Weekend *and* Cabin Fever *interspersed with outtakes from the UK show* Embarrassing Bodies *(does what it says on the tin), that I lost eight pounds, four days of my life and that I LEARNED MY LESSON. Lxxx*

PS Some people will tell you the water is fine. They lie.

PPS Mum, don't worry, I'm fine. Just a lot thinner than you remember. #Notdeadyet.

CHAPTER FIVE

Autumn is the busiest term in school – new admissions, appeals over school places as well as all the celebrations harvest festival, Diwali, Hallowe'en, the Christmas fair and then the Christmas show. The tradition in our school is to involve all the junior children in the performance so it is usually an all-singing all-dancing version of the Nativity story. The infants learn the songs so, although they're in the audience, they can sing along.

It is early December and most of the children have gone home. I'm printing out song sheets, just two waifs and strays with me: James Porringer, whose mother relies on the bus to get here and is often late when the service is delayed, and Court-ney Collier, who can't remember who is picking her up today, Dad, Mum or Nana. I suspect one of them has forgotten too. Courtney has gone very quiet, and looks close to tears, so I ask her and James to count out some song sheets into piles of thirty.

I like, the feel of the place outside hours: it's not spooky, like some old buildings can be, but has a warm, slightly worn, homely feel to it. As though it's soaked up the affection and energy of all the generations of children it has seen come and go.

I'm sending another batch to the printer when my phone beeps: email. It's from Lori.

From: loreleimx@gmail.com
Date: 6 December 2013 23:08
To:joannamaddox70@hotmail.com;
 NickMyers@firenet.co.uk;
 tombolmaddox@aol.com
Subject: New Plans

Hi, I've had an awesome offer to go to China with Dawn. She's really nice and she's been once before so she can show me the ropes. The plan is to go on to Hong Kong from here, have Xmas and New Year there and get our visas then get to Chengdu sometime in January (it's near where they have the pandas). It's a really big city, but supposed to be laid-back compared to Beijing. We'll have a month there. It means I won't get back until Feb so tell Finn and Isaac I will bring them special late presents then.

I'm a bit low on money so Dad is there any way you

can send me some via Western Union? I need to buy plane tickets soon. We've found some for £700 – Dawn says that's cheap because it's three flights altogether (includes my return from China). Tomorrow would be good. Thanks soooo much!!!

Suze had to go back to Oz her dad is very ill so she can't go with Dawn as they planned. Dawn did journalism at home and she's hoping to make documentaries in the longer term. I told her she should do some pieces for my blog.

Lxxx

I feel a clutch of disappointment that Lori won't be here for Christmas, that it'll be another month after that. And then a flare of irritation: everything was arranged, agreed – why couldn't she just stick to that? Impulsive. The words 'like her father' hover in my mind. Maybe Tom won't send her the money. As soon as I think it, I feel ashamed. If Tom can't or won't then we'll find it, increase our overdraft if need be.

There's the noise of someone arriving: James's mum, red-faced and breathless. 'Sorry,' she calls to me.

'Don't worry,' I say. 'He's been helping me.'

James goes pink and his mum smiles, kisses his head and bundles him off.

Then the office phone rings and it's Courtney's grandmother full of apologies and promising to be there in five minutes.

The first chance I get to call Tom is after tea. We haven't spoken since the day we took Lori to the airport.

'It's all a bit last-minute,' I say to him. 'Anyway, can you transfer the money?'

'Sure, there's a place up the road does it nowadays,' he says. 'Have you been reading her blog?'

'Yes. You heard anything else about this Dawn?'

'Only what she said in the email.'

I wonder if Dawn is more than just a friend but don't particularly want to speculate with Tom. Lori's impulsiveness sometimes extends to relationships. She falls hard and fast and can get hurt. The worst was a girlfriend she had at school. Saskia went on to a different sixth form and broke up with Lori soon after. Lori messed up that school year and had to repeat it. There were a couple of relationships at uni but they seemed fairly casual. As if she was protecting herself from anything too deep.

'Be strange not seeing her at Christmas,' I say.

Tom grunts.

'What are you doing?'

'Nothing fixed yet,' he says. 'Got a couple of offers.'

Of course he has. He's never short of friends, or invitations. I don't know if he's seeing anyone new – Lori used to keep me up to date and the last I heard, in July, he'd broken up with his latest girlfriend. I don't know if Tom will ever settle down. He has lived with a few women since we were together but never for very long. I don't know whether that's something he hankers after or not. We're just not that close any more.

CHAPTER SIX

We Skype Lori on Christmas Day. Isaac is exhausted – he's been up since four, desperate for his big presents. I sent him back to bed but he didn't sleep. We've had our ritual opening and the boys clutch their gifts to show Lori. Finn has a mini-scooter and Isaac another Lego kit, City Coast Guard Patrol.

'Hi, guys.' She waves. She looks relaxed: she has a turquoise vest on and cargos, her hair is shorter – the pink has gone – and she's sitting on a single bed. I can see the metal bars of the headboard.

The lag between speaking and hearing adds to the chaos of four people trying to talk to one.

Lori makes a fuss of the boys, responding with appropriate excitement to their presents. Isaac wants to list all of his, including the trinkets in his stocking, but Finn keeps butting in. Eventually Isaac loses it, shouts and shoves his brother off his chair.

Nick pulls the boys aside for a talking-to and I get a chance to concentrate.

'What did you do today?' I ask her.

'A meal, then cocktails.' It is seven o'clock in Hong Kong. 'We're going out to a bar in a bit – there's a party.'

'It's going well?'

'Brilliant. See the room?' She swoops her laptop up and swerves it round. Green-painted walls, piles of her clothes, her backpack, a lamp and a mirror. Her face again.

'Is Dawn staying there?'

'Yeah, next door. She's sleeping. Heavy night.' Lori laughs.

Isaac yelling afresh at Finn makes further conversation impossible. I twist round. 'Isaac, do you want to talk to Lori or do you want to go to bed?'

'Talk to Lori.'

'Right. Two minutes.' I swing him up and plonk him on the chair directly in front of the webcam. 'And then Finn two minutes,' I say. Finn nods.

Isaac goes through his list, then Lori tells him about the aeroplane she's been on, the snakes she's seen and the flying squirrels.

'Time's up,' I say.

Isaac and Finn swap over and Finn shows her his scooter, then asks Lori when she'll be home.

'A few weeks,' she says.

'I miss you,' he says.

'I miss you, too, but it won't be long. Have you got any new certificates?'

'Yes!' He flies out of the room.

Nick sits down. 'Missing anything apart from us?'

'My bed,' she says. 'They're all like concrete here.'

'We like the blog,' Nick says.

'It's fun.'

'And the photos,' he says. 'Lovely stuff.'

'Here!' Finn is holding his latest swimming badge. He waves it at Lori.

'Awesome,' she says. 'You're a champion, Finn.'

A howl goes up from Isaac who, down on the floor, has managed to clout his head on one of the chair corners. Lori pulls a face, 'So, I'd better go.' She smiles, a dimple on each cheek.

I pick up Isaac so his face is against my shoulder and rub the back of his head with my hand. It comforts him but it also muffles the crying.

'Anyone special on the scene?' I say, before we get to goodbyes.

Lori grins. 'Maybe.'

'Dawn?' I say.

'Maybe. It's–' Then she's tongue-tied.

'Jo,' Nick chides me, 'leave her be.'

'Only asking.'

'Digging.'

'I'm going now,' Lori says. 'Happy Christmas.' She waves both arms and Finn copies her. Isaac digs deeper into my neck.

'Bye-bye, Isaac,' she calls. He glances back to the laptop, shakes his hand.

'Happy new year,' Nick says.

'Love you,' I say. 'Have fun.'

'Will do. Love you too.'

She waves again, blows kisses and cuts the connection.

'You going to have a nap?' I murmur in Isaac's ear. He shakes his head.

'OK.' I swap a glance with Nick. 'Milkshakes and Kung Fu Panda, then.'

'Whooo!' Finn dances, his approximation of martial-art shapes.

'I want to play Angry Birds,' Isaac says.

'You can do that after the movie or you can do it on my phone now.'

'I don't want to do it on your phone,' he whimpers.

'That's fine. After the movie.' I brace myself for more crying or a full-on tantrum but he gives a sigh of resignation.

The day stretches ahead. I work out we have another seven hours until they'll be in bed. Another three till the turkey will be done.

'Lori had cocktails,' I say to Nick, as I line up the DVD player.

'Cocktails.' He catches on immediately. 'Now there's an idea. Not sure what we've got, spirit wise.'

'Surprise me,' I say.

Lori in the Ori-ent

China
Posted on 20 January 2014 by Lori

First impressions. It is big. It is incredibly busy. Everyone is Chinese – does that sound daft? It's just there are very, very few non-Chinese faces in the crowds. I can't understand anything. At all. It is really, really noisy. Like everything is turned up to eleven.

Everyone stares at me. It's like living in one of those embarrassing dreams where you're onstage and have no clothes on, except you're awake and it's happening even though you're dressed. People laugh at me too.

Thailand and Vietnam felt new and totally different from home but China – it's like another planet, not just another country.

And I am the alien.

The most important thing I have learned is how to say 'No – don't want it'. Loud and proud. 'Bú yào.' Because everyone is hustling and you can't walk along the pavement without getting hassled to buy stuff.

In these first photos you can see the view from my room. There are three ring roads in Chengdu and this is the middle one. The tower blocks around are enormous, over thirty storeys high, and at street level there are shops and bars and street stalls. I love the old architecture, the teahouses along the river, the beautiful pagodas and bridges. There are lots of parks but there's also loads of building work everywhere (more tower blocks). The pictures of the park make it look old and peaceful. Maybe I'll add a soundtrack sometime so you can hear how loud it all is. It's a bit overwhelming but my travel mate Dawn says to go with the flow. So that's what I'm doing.

Lxxx

CHAPTER SEVEN

The new year doesn't bring all those things we hope for – health, wealth and happiness. Things start to unravel at the end of January. Nick is standing in the kitchen, his face several shades paler than usual, his eyes darker, inky, angry.

'They say there's no need to panic,' he says, 'but everyone's tarting up their CVs and rediscovering

LinkedIn. Fuck, Jo.' He refills his whisky glass.

'They'll keep some people on,' I say, 'surely, even if the merger goes ahead. The project will still need finishing.'

'I don't know. Andy's not giving anyone straight answers.' Andy is his boss, the project manager. 'He probably doesn't know himself,' he adds, still anxious to be fair, even though he might be getting shafted. 'It's an awful time to be looking for jobs.'

'It might not come to that. We'll manage,' I say.

'How? On what you earn? On bloody benefits?'

'We'll have to,' I say. 'People do.' I'm being optimistic. I've seen families at school go through the mill, plunged into free school dinners, shocked at the reality of life on the welfare system. And others who, despite all their efforts, have never been able to escape from it, now shamed and hounded by the rhetoric of blaming the poor for poverty. But I'm determined to remain positive, ignore the way my stomach dropped when he announced the risk of redundancy.

'Besides,' I say, 'you'll get some money.'

'Yes,' Nick says, 'twenty grand.'

'Breathing space. Then you could look for–'

He holds up his hands, he doesn't need any more blithe reassurances.

A week later I get a call from Sunita, Isaac's teacher. Can I come to the classroom?

She sounds strained, or am I imagining it?

The rest of the class are playing out. Isaac is there and his best friend Sebastian. Sebastian is in tears.

39

'What's the matter?' I say.

'I'm afraid Isaac bit Sebastian,' Sunita says.

'I didn't,' Isaac says.

Crouching down so I'm level with the two boys, I say to Isaac, 'What happened?'

His face is tight, a scowl scored deep on his brow. 'He's stupid,' Isaac says.

'Calling people names is naughty. What happened, Sebastian?' I say.

Sebastian's lower lip is quivering and his eyes well up again. He talks in hiccups. 'He bit me.' He shows me the evidence, tooth-marks on his forearm.

'You need to say sorry,' I tell Isaac, 'and you'll have to go to time-out.'

Isaac looks murderous. If he could bite me too, he would.

'He said Benji was a pig,' Isaac says.

'I did not,' Sebastian retorts. 'I said he was big. You didn't listen.'

'It doesn't matter what he said,' Sunita tells Isaac. 'You do not hurt other people. If someone is mean to you, you tell a teacher.'

Thank God it was Sebastian, I think. His mum, Freya, won't make a big deal of it. I hope the boys' friendship will last. Isaac needs all the friends he can get.

'Say sorry,' I say.

Isaacs spits out a 'sorry'.

'Isaac,' Sunita says, 'that doesn't sound like you mean it.'

It takes two more attempts but we get a halfway decent apology and Isaac spends the rest of the morning in time-out.

There's a darkness in Isaac I don't understand. It's not just the biting – that's one of the ways he expresses it. While the world is Lori's oyster and Finn's happy home, for Isaac it often seems to be a place of treachery and shadows. Glass half empty and witches under the bed. Where does it come from?

Lori in the Ori-ent

Food: the good, the bad and the... What is that?
Posted on 12 February 2014 by Lori

Sichuan province, and Chengdu in particular, is known for its spicy food. If you are lucky enough to stumble upon a waiter who has any English you might be able to negotiate a mild version of the day's dish. For mild read fiery.

The cuisine comes in three levels of spiciness. Spiciness is a bit of a euphemism. We're talking chilli at industrial concentrations. But also Sichuan peppers – little round peppercorns that are like culinary grenades, zapping the nerve endings and destroying all sensation in the mouth. Raised in Manchester, I am quite familiar with the delights of the curry house, and can scarf down a vindaloo with the best of them. I had no idea.

Here the meals are

1) hot
2) blazing hot

3) scorching.

It would be handy to have some sort of rating system on the menus, sticks of dynamite, maybe, or little bonfires. Until that is introduced (don't hold your breath) the dining-out experience can best be described as a minefield. One advantage of this custom of drenching everything in fiery, sweat-inducing chilli sauce is that while I am trying to tell if my tongue has melted or there's any enamel left on my teeth I am less anxious about what lurks within the sauce. Whether it is lamb or pork or chicken or, to be more precise, a bit of the animal I have ever allowed past my lips before. Armpits, eyeballs, testicles, toes? Or any of those inside bits I prefer not to think about? Nothing is wasted.

There is no bread. There are no chips, no mash or jacket potatoes. There is always rice or noodles – as long as you ask for it. I have never been so hungry in my life. You'd think three honey buns would fill up a girl with an appetite but the effect lasts for about ten minutes.

On Saturday I was out with friends (you can see us in the last picture). Bradley, Dawn and Shona. Bradley has better Mandarin than me (hah! everyone has better Mandarin than me), and by the end of our meal, with a little help from an app on his phone, he'd worked out that among our dishes of baby lamb and big pig we had also enjoyed sea slug.

I could've lived without knowing that. Lxxx

PS Mum, send cheese. And baguettes. Now. *joke*

CHAPTER EIGHT

Saturday, and Nick has taken Finn to his swimming practice. Benji and Isaac are lying sprawled on the floor. Isaac has been drawing – his pictures are astonishing for his age: intense, accurate, forensic in their detail. This morning it's been pirates, pirates and their ships, cutlasses and earrings, rigging and sharks in the water. Now he has one hand on Benji's chest and is murmuring.

I am ironing.

'What are you saying, Isaac?'

'A story.'

'He likes it,' I say.

My phone sounds an email. Lori.

'Mummy,' Isaac says, 'I feel sick.'

'Oh, no – come on.'

There are no false alarms with Isaac. We reach the downstairs toilet just in time.

When he's done I clean his face, give him water to drink. His forehead is dry and very hot.

'Bed,' I say.

He doesn't argue or even ask for any toys.

'Isaac's poorly,' I tell Finn when they get in, 'so play down here.'

'Why?'

'So he can sleep.'

'What's wrong with him?' Finn says.

'I don't know. He's been sick.'

Finn grimaces. 'Yuck.'

'How was swimming?'

'Good,' he says.

'He was great,' Nick says. 'The teacher says he's good enough to try out for the shrimps but he has to be eight.'

I pick up Lori's message.

From: loreleimx@gmail.com
Date: 21 February 2014 01:08
To: joannamaddox70@hotmail.com;
*   NickMyers@firenet.co.uk;*
*   tombolmaddox@aol.com*
Subject: News

Hi guys, amazing news. I've got a job! I'm working for an agency – Five Star English – as a private English tutor. They sorted out my visa, I had to fly to Hong Kong and back, but it's all done and. I can stay for a year. And so many people want lessons that I'll soon have enough money to get a decent place to live. The only thing is I can't get a refund on my return ticket for next week. Sorry Dad, but I should be able to pay my own way home when the time comes. It's all happening so fast!

Lxxx

'God!'

Nick looks up from the paper.

'Lori,' I say.

I hand him my phone.

'Another year,' he says. 'It's a fantastic opportunity if she can make a go of it.'

'I know.' I'm still disconcerted, adjusting to the

44

fact that I won't see her for twelve more months.

'And one less mouth,' Nick says.

We share a look. He's received his redundancy notice and has started applying for jobs.

Changing her plans again. Then why shouldn't she? She's not beholden to anyone. It's not as if I was relying on her to come home for any particular practical reason. So why do I feel so let down?

Lori in the Ori-ent

What's in a Name 2?
Posted on 9 March 2014 by Lori

Call me Bird's Net Jasmine. Those of you who landed here before will know I've already posted about my name, Lorelei, and its meaning here. It's a common custom in China for people to work out a Chinese version of their name and likewise for Chinese people who work with Westerners as guides and translators or teachers to take on an English name. Among the Chinese friends I've made are Rosemary (Mo Li) and Oliver (Zhong Pengfei). Looking online, thanks to www.wearyourchinesename.com, I came up with these suggestions for Chinese versions of Lori. Lori is made up of two characters. The first means 'net' or 'bird's net' or 'sieve' or 'twelve dozen', among other things. The second comes from the word 'jasmine'. I could go for Li instead, meaning 'plums' or Lei (pronounced Lee), a 'flower bud'. This might be a slight improvement on 'alluring rock' (see earlier post). My surname is Mad-

45

dox. *This is not a reference to a deranged bull but apparently comes from the Welsh name Madog, meaning 'goodly'. Maybe I should just call myself Manchester or I could double up on the Lei and call myself Lei Lei, or Lilo? Lo means 'dredge'. 'Plum dredge'?*

The jury's still out. All suggestions gratefully received in the comments below.

Lxxx

CHAPTER NINE

From: loreleimx@gmail.com
Date: 11 March 2014 22:19
To: joannamaddox70@hotmail.com
Subject: Hello

Hi Mum,

Tell Nick I hope he gets something soon and that it's way better than his old job. Yep, I'm busy. I have some school-age students, little ones that I teach in the evenings, three different families on different days. Then a graduate who wants to improve his spoken English, and I've just taken on a friend of his too. There's a couple who are learning together (Saturday) and some high-school students – their parents clubbed together. It's quite a big deal here if they can speak English: more opportunity for jobs in tourism and business. I get stopped all the time by people asking me if I can teach them.

I found some lesson plans online. It's hard for us to learn Chinese, the way one word can have so many different meanings, depending on the tones, on how it's pronounced. I'll never get used to that. But English is hard for them too – all the tenses we have and they just don't. Dawn is fine. She is working full time at an English school out near the 3rd Ring Road (more lesson plans for me!) and is looking for an apartment there. It's still cloudy here and it would be nice to get to a beach sometime and catch some rays but she's not sure what holiday she can take. It's pretty restricted.

I've been thinking about a photo project I'd like to do – Chengdu is growing all the time, malls and skyscrapers going up, everyone studying and working and trying to get ahead, get an education, get a good job to buy the shiny things in the shops. Sound familiar? But there's also surprises, hidden bits, weird hobbies people have on the side. One man I know races pigeons. Someone else is restoring a vintage bike. Shona makes jewellery out of waste material, like crisps packets and so on. Anyway, if I can find a few more examples I'll give it a go. Watch this space.

Big hugs to Finn and Isaac.

Lxxx

It occurs to me that while the unemployment situation is still so precarious, especially in the north where we live and even more so for young people, then Lori is better off where she is.

Nick is withdrawing more every day. He's always been a calm, sociable, happy character. I was attracted by his sense of equanimity as well as his looks, and the way he laughed so freely at my jokes. His attitude to Lori, too – she was twelve when she first met him.

47

In the past, when Nick and I had problems, we had at least been able to talk about them, argue even, but now in the wake of his redundancy he is increasingly sullen and tight-lipped.

'How did you get on today?' I say, and he gives an exasperated sigh and shakes his head. Like my even asking is some imposition.

Determined to force some communication, I plough on: 'Did you get any applications in?'

'What does it matter?' he says. 'I could apply for a hundred jobs and hear nothing.' He fetches a beer from the fridge.

Has he given up? 'I know it's hard–'

'Jo, spare me the platitudes, you have no idea.'

Anger spikes through me. 'This is not just about you,' I say. 'It's horrible and depressing but, whatever happens, this affects us all. The least you can do is talk to me about it.'

'Don't lecture me,' he says quietly, and walks away.

Bastard.

Jaws clamped tight, I clear up the kitchen not caring about the noise I'm making even if he is going to bed. We have already agreed that if Nick can find a position with a future outside Manchester we will move, leaving my job, this house, uprooting the boys. Some people thrive on new situations, Tom for example. I am not one of them.

Stacking pots from the dishwasher on the shelves too fast, I knock over Lori's favourite cup, which crashes to the floor and smashes. Bought one Christmas, the sort of huge mug that's great for cocoa, its gold stars have long since faded.

She left it at home when she went to Glasgow. 'It's bound to get broken or nicked there,' she said.

'Fuck!' I blink back tears as I clean up the shards.

'Mummy?' Isaac is in the doorway, blinking at the light. Serves me right. 'What's up, chicken?'

'I heard a noise,' he says.

'That was me clearing up,' I say.

'No, in my room.'

I can't face this, the ritual of checking and re-assurance, the debate about whether Isaac can sleep in our bed 'just tonight.'

'Where's Daddy?' I say.

'I don't know.'

'See if he's in bed. He can–' I hear what I'm doing. 'Never mind, just a sec.' I put the shards of pottery in the bin.

'What's that?' Isaac says.

'Lori's mug.'

'Her star mug.'

'Yes. I knocked it off.'

'Oh.' He glances up, no doubt checking I haven't destroyed his Tiger mug. He gives a little shudder. His feet must be cold and I have a flashback to being that age, to the powerlessness of it, the be-wilderment and sudden heady delights.

'Come on, then.' I scoop him up and take him back to bed.

Finn is asleep in the lower bunk.

Isaac climbs up the ladder. I adjust the night light so it's brighter and he pulls the covers up to his chin. 'Can I have a story?'

All I want to do is sleep. 'One, then I'm going

49

to bed and you go back to sleep. Deal?'

'Deal.'

Leaning against the beds, I rattle off *The Three Bears,* the shortest story in my repertoire. Isaac yawns, which is a good sign.

With the boys safe in their beds, I go to mine. Nick is there, awake. He clears his throat and turns over as I get changed.

We say no more than 'Night.' Drifting off to sleep, I wonder if he's becoming depressed, and if he is, what on earth I can get him to do about it.

Lori in the Ori-ent

Park life
Posted on 18 March 2014 by Lori

Back home our park is used mainly by the following people for the following activities:

a) Parents and kids at the playground

b) The above feeding the ducks

c) Tennis players, whose numbers mushroom every year around the time of Wimbledon, then fade away

d) Bowls players, Wednesday afternoons only, must have a bus pass

e) Footballers, Saturdays and Sundays on the pitches. Little ones with their parents screaming at the ref, big ones screaming at each other and the ref

f) Dog-walkers (plus dogs)

g) Lovers, walking in the rain, lazing in the sun, snogging

h) Teenagers, smoking, drinking, snogging

i) Extreme frisbee players, Saturday only, by arrangement

j) A couple of old men, who share the bench by the rose bed all day long, each with a carrier bag of lager

Today is a typical day in the park near my flat in Chengdu. There are variations of all the above here but there are also

1) Tai chi sessions

2) Ballroom dancing. Really

3) Mah-jong players

4) People doing circus skills – juggling, diabolo

5) Musicians

6) Tea-drinkers at all the teahouses

7) Calligraphers who paint the paving stones with characters using giant brushes and water

8) People selling toffee – it's shaped like filigree cut-outs of the signs of the zodiac, I think

9) Sword dancers

10) Men hitting spinning tops – serious ones, unlike the toys we had. The tops are the size of a large mug, the whips crack

11) People sketching and painting

12) People feeding the carp (with baby bottles, I kid you not) – all the ponds are full of them

The park is heaving. It feels like a carnival or festival but this is just an ordinary day. I am stopped four times by curious people and explain in my atrocious Chinese that I'm from England. I have practised this every day since I arrived. Each time I get a look of total incomprehension. Perhaps I have said, 'Follow that

51

teabag,' or 'How pretty is your camel.' But the word 'Manchester' opens doors. Eyes light up, smiles blossom. Manchester! Manchester United! The Red Devils have paved the way for travellers the world over. Well, those of us from Manchester. I nod and do a little hand cheer, as if we scored a goal. Which we have in a way. Twice people ask to have a photograph taken with me. The last woman pats my arms and chatters away, and I smile and nod and hope I haven't accidentally agreed to anything, like teaching all her grandchildren English every evening. Or marrying one of her sons.

The park is open from six in the morning till nine at night, when lanterns and lights glow among the bamboo plants and trees. And it feels safe. Another difference from the one at home where there's an edginess, the peace shattered by some prat on a mini motorbike churning up the field, or a group of drunk kids getting physical.

Perhaps the biggest difference is that at home we're out in public but we keep ourselves to ourselves – all that British reserve, we stay in our own little cliques. A nod as you pass someone is the height of interaction – apart from the dog-walkers, who like to mingle with their canine friends. In China, everyone is into everyone else's business – there doesn't seem to be any notion of privacy. People stare and interrupt and join in and interfere all the time. A crowd forms at the drop of a hat. It's like a big party where everyone knows everyone else, except they don't, they just act like they do. Lxxx

CHAPTER TEN

Emailing with Lori is sporadic. She usually replies a few days after receiving a message but rarely unprompted. We keep abreast of what she's up to by following her blog. She posted a new one today, about parks. I showed it to the boys and we talked about the pictures.

Isaac kicks off at the tea table. 'I hate macaroni cheese. It looks like sick.'

'Yeuch! Gross!' says Finn.

'It's that or toast,' I say, my voice calm, not wanting a battle.

'Don't want toast.'

'You'll be hungry,' Nick says.

Isaac sets his jaw, scowls, pushes at the pasta with his spoon, moving it to the very edge of his plate. A quick look at me to see if I'll stop him. Another jab and the first of his food spills onto the table. I reach over and remove his plate.

'Isaac,' Nick shouts, 'stop messing.'

Isaac jumps down, runs out and upstairs. I'm disappointed in Nick. If he hadn't risen to the bait...

Nick shoves back his chair, the scrape on the laminate floor shredding my nerves. 'Leave him,' I say.

He hesitates.

'We'll finish tea. No point in him disrupting it for all of us.'

'What's for pudding?' Finn says.

'Apple pie,' I say.

'Yum. Is Isaac getting any?'

'Don't know.' I jump in before Nick lays down any laws. 'We'll see. Are you going to feed Benji?'

Finn nods and starts to move, but I tell him to have his apple pie first.

Nick smiles at Finn but I can still feel the tension in him, almost hear the hum of impatience and irritation just below the surface. I'm getting so tired of his bad mood and resent the fact that I have to mediate between him and Isaac. We've always been good at parenting, well, good enough, presenting a united front. I'll have to tackle him about it. Of course it's the stress of redundancy that's behind this but his refusal to talk to me about it makes it worse. Like he's wallowing in it, savouring it. A martyr.

After another tantrum about toast tasting funny and a crying jag, Isaac is asleep at last. Finn is in bed with his book. He'll drift off soon enough, and when one of us prises the book from his hands, he won't wake.

Downstairs Nick is doing a shopping list, checking the fridge and the cupboards.

'Can we talk?' I say to him.

He makes a noise, noncommittal.

I sit down and pour myself a glass of wine, emptying the bottle. Nick opens another and refills his glass.

Sitting down, I say, 'I'm worried about you.'

'He needs clear boundaries,' Nick says.

'I'm not talking about Isaac,' I say. 'I'm talking

about you. You're shutting me out.'

'I'm doing my best,' he says.

'Maybe you should talk to someone.'

'Jo,' he shakes his head, 'come on.'

'I think you're depressed,' I say.

'This is my problem, I'll deal with it how–'

'But you're not,' I say, more loudly than I mean to. 'You're getting worse. Everything's a problem. You shout at the kids, you freeze me out.'

He glares at me but I don't look away.

'Maybe we need a break, a weekend away. Or you have a get-together with the lads, go cycling, have a laugh. Go to that cottage in Cork.'

'What – just spend the redundancy?' he says.

'Well, a couple of hundred quid isn't going to make much difference.'

He snorts, like I said something stupid.

'You suggest something, then.'

'I suggest you just–' He breaks off. I'm relieved: whatever he was about to say wasn't going to be pleasant.

'Nick?'

He turns away. 'I just need some time.'

'It's been six weeks,' I say. 'It's not your fault but you're punishing yourself and the rest of us.'

'Don't talk crap,' he says.

'Everything is so miserable. The atmosphere–'

'Yes,' he says hotly, 'it's called real life. And having you on my back really isn't helping.'

Stung and defeated, I pick up my wine and leave him to it. But I won't give up because we can't go on like this, not indefinitely. It's bloody horrible.

Lori in the Ori-ent

Weather
Posted on 2 April 2014 by Lori

I'm used to rain, coming from Manchester (rainy city). Sometimes we get several seasons in a day. England has a north–south and east–west split in climate. For the north-west we have the weather coming in from the Atlantic rising up over the Pennines. It's wet and cloudy while the other side of the hills to the east is drier and sunnier. The south is warmer than the north almost always, and that means Manchester (NW) and London (SE) never share the same forecast. So rain I can do. Changeability I can deal with.

But endless, interminable cloud. Chengdu is known as the city where the sun never shines. *Great bumper sticker. Mugs, anyone? Tea towels? It's in the Sichuan basin surrounded by mountains. This traps the cloud. Swampy best describes the summer I am told. Today it is just sticky. Sticky and airless. The cloud seals in the heat and the pollution. Imagine using a wallpaper steamer on a very old doormat in a confined space. That smell. What's not to like? The humidity is about a million per cent. Perfect for mosquitoes. So I am sticky and itchy and STILL having an amazing time. Lxxx*

CHAPTER ELEVEN

I'm in the office, printing off letters and appoint-ment slips for parents' evening, which is the week after next. The staff are up to their eyes writing reports on each child, charting their progress in their key stage and the core subjects. Sheaves of paperwork, much of it to be done at home in their own time.

I break off and check Lori's blog hasn't been updated: it's still the post about the weather. Nine days since she put it up. A week since I sent my last message. Perhaps she's hard at work, keeps mean-ing to reply and hasn't had time. Or she's been away. Or ill. Perhaps she's just being Lori, letting it slide, too caught up in her exciting new life. There could be problems with the Internet – the service is a bit patchy at times. I dither over whether to send a new message, and in the end I do. OK, maybe she'll resent me nagging but I can live with that. She might just need a nudge.

It's raining as we walk home from school. Isaac stops every so often, his attention drawn to a pile of litter or something in the hedge. I hurry him along. Finn walks through the puddles. 'You've not got your wellies on,' I say.

'I don't mind.'

'So your trainers'll be wet.'

'Soon dry,' he says.

The rain is heavier, cold by the time we reach

home. 'I'm soaking,' Isaac says on the doorstep. 'Can I stay here?' Walking Benji is not usually something they can opt out of.

'We won't be long,' I say.

'But if Daddy's here...' Isaac goes on.

'Daddy's busy.'

We get inside. I call, 'Hello.'

Nick answers from the dining room.

'Daddy, I want to stay here,' Isaac says. I motion him to stay in the hall – he's dripping all over the floor. He shudders.

I put my head round the door. Nick's on the computer. 'Is that OK?' I say. 'He looks a bit peaky.'

'Sure.'

Finn has Benji's lead and the dog is jumping up at him, ecstatic.

'Go and get changed,' I tell Isaac, 'put your wet things in the basket and don't bother Daddy.'

'I know,' he says. He gets one bug after another at the moment and most of them make him throw up.

Finn and I walk partway around the park, then retrace our steps. The rain never lets up. My knees are damp, my trousers sticking to them. Blossom on the cherry trees is battered; half of it lies on the ground, a soggy mess already turning brown.

'My nose is wet,' Finn says. There's a drip of water hanging off the end. He sticks his tongue out, shakes his head and catches it.

'Come on,' I say. 'I'm wet inside out – even my knickers are wet.'

He chortles. We walk back, his trainers squelching.

'You take Benji around the back,' I say. 'He can do his shaking dry in the kitchen.'

Inside I am met with the unmistakable acid pong of vomit and Nick is on his hands and knees with a cloth and a bucket.

'Not again,' I say, peeling off my coat.

'He's up in bed.'

'Maybe it's an allergy,' I say.

'Wouldn't he swell up or get a rash?' Nick says.

'Possibly.'

Finn comes squelching out of the kitchen.

'Go back and take your shoes off,' I tell him.

He pulls a face. 'Urgh – that stinks.'

'Off you go... I'll make an appointment,' I say to Nick, 'get him checked out.'

He sits back on his haunches, looks up at me. 'Fine.'

'Any luck?' He has been waiting for a reply from a job application. It's similar work to what he has been doing but down in Walsall in the West Midlands.

'No.' He gets up, lifts the bucket. 'I'd have heard by now. Not even a bloody interview.' He walks away.

The smell lingers. Nick has cleaned the floor but there's a splash against the wall, speckled liquid, that he's missed.

I go upstairs and look in on Isaac. He's awake but seems woozy, eyes bleary.

'You had a drink?' I touch his forehead, definitely hot.

'Yes.'

59

'More?'

He nods. I pass him the water and he shuffles up and takes it, has a sip.

'Poor Isaac. Did you eat your lunch?'

'No,' he says.

'Did you feel sick then?'

'Yes.'

'I think we'll get the doctor to have a look at you and see if you need some medicine.'

He nods solemnly.

'You have a little rest, then.'

In the bathroom I soak a cloth in disinfectant and go to clean the wall in the hall. This way Nick won't see me completing his efforts and have the chance to take my action as criticism. Pussyfooting around each other, that's what we're doing. Skirting hostilities. Somehow no longer on the same side.

Sunday, and we're unloading the car. A trip to B&Q. I've been buying bedding plants and bird food, and he's got all the materials for a DIY project. He's going to move the boys into Lori's room, set up their bunk beds in there, move her bed into the garage for now, then convert the boys' room into a home office. He'll start offering freelance consultancy work. I'm relieved that he's got something constructive to do, something where he can see results, feel he's achieved a goal even if it doesn't mean any paid work yet. He's asked a mate to do him a website design. Nick doesn't particularly want to be a one-man business – he would much rather have the stability of employment and a regular income, along with paid holidays and the like, but needs must. Thanks God he's recognized the need.

'I've still not heard from Lori,' I say to Nick.

'You think she'll complain?' he says, meaning about the room.

'No, I wasn't thinking about that, just that it's over a week since I emailed. And I texted, too. Nothing.'

He puts down the wood he's carrying. 'Try ringing?'

I nod, glad he's not dismissed my concern. It will be seven in the evening in Chengdu. Lori teaches on a Sunday; she might still be at work.

Once we have brought everything in, I try her number. A recorded message tells me that it's not been possible to connect me. Her phone is off.

'Nothing,' I say. 'I'll see if Tom's heard anything.'

'OK.' He gestures upstairs and goes off to begin packing up the boys' things.

Finn is out in the garden, jumping around on the trampoline. Benji is dozing on the ground underneath. It's a dull, warm day, the sky grey chalk. The blackbird is chinking an alarm call, though I can't see any cats about. We've sparrows nesting in the eaves and I can hear them squabbling too.

Tom answers, 'Jo?'

'Hi, how are you?'

'Good. You?'

An urge to tell him the truth, to share, which I squash down. 'Fine, but we've not heard from Lori for over a week now, wondered if you had.'

'No. We Skyped for my birthday.'

The start of the month, April Fool's. It's the

thirteenth now.

'Her last blog was posted on the second,' I say.

'The one about the weather,' Tom says.

'I've tried emailing, calling and texting – nothing,' I say.

'She mentioned the idea of a holiday,' Tom says.

'Yes, to me too. Did she say when or where?'

'There was nothing definite.'

Finn is on his back, arms and legs spread out like a star. Nick moves something heavy upstairs and the whole house shakes with the vibration.

'See if anyone else has heard from her,' Tom suggests. 'Give it a few more days?'

And then what? 'Yes. Do you have a number for Dawn?'

'No,' he says.

'Me neither.'

Someone speaks in the background, a woman, though I can't make out the words, and I realize with a jolt that Tom's not alone.

'OK,' I say. 'Let me know if you hear anything.'

'Yes, of course.'

'Straight away.'

I can tell he's smiling as he says, 'I promise. She'll be fine. You know Lori.'

We say goodbye and hang up. I think of who else she might be in touch with, who else I can contact. The list is small: I've numbers and emails for Jake and Amy, the couple she had been travelling with in Thailand and Vietnam, who should now be back in the UK. And I've a phone number for Erin, the only person from school whom Lori stayed in touch with. We don't have details for any of the friends in China Lori has told us about.

I play down my unease as I talk first to Erin, then to the others. No one has heard from Lori this month. I ask them to spread the word among their social networks, Twitter, Facebook, whatever, and ask anyone who's heard from Lori to please contact me.

Isaac comes into the kitchen and catches me staring into space. The jotter on the table is scored with numbers and notes, some words from the conversations I've just had.

'Where's Finn?' he says.

'On the trampoline. You could go out.'

He shrugs.

'I'm going to come out soon and plant my flowers.'

'Will you twirl me?' he says.

'OK.'

Outside Isaac lies on his stomach on the swing, arms and legs hanging out either side. I twist the swing round, winding the ropes together, he inches higher from the ground. When I let go, the swing unwinds fast, spinning him round, him yelling.

Then Finn wants a go.

They take turns. My stomach feels tense, knotted together like the ropes.

I replay the phone calls I've just made as I tap out the plugs of bedding plants and tamp them down into the troughs we have on two sides of the patio.

'I messaged her on Saturday,' Amy said. 'I thought she might have her phone off if she was teaching. But she didn't get back to me.'

'And she usually would?' I said.

'Most times, eventually.'

The blackbird chinks again, insistent. And Finn sings 'Row, Row, Row Your Boat' at the top of his lungs. I stare at the lobelia, the petunias, the pink and white verbena and the fuchsias, and feel the dread grow in my chest. I set down the watering can, brush the worst of the compost from my hands before going in.

Nick has dismantled Lori's bed and stacked it on the landing. He's taking apart the bunk beds. 'Great,' he says, when he sees me. 'You can give me a hand carrying the double mattress down.'

'Nick,' I say, 'nobody's heard from her. Nothing since the second of April. Eleven days.'

'Right,' he says slowly.

'I'm really worried,' I say, and the words spoken out loud make my legs weak. I take a breath, ignore the way my heart stutters. 'I think something's wrong,' I say. 'I think we should go to the police.'

CHAPTER TWELVE

Penny, a friend I made way back when I used to child-mind her sons, comes to stay with the boys while Nick and I go to the police station. I've rung Tom back and told him I want to report Lori missing.

'Do you really think it's necessary?' he says.

'Yes.'

'Fair enough.' His voice sounds tight. 'I'm in Dublin. I'll be home later.'

I wonder about the woman I heard before. Is she travelling with him? Or has he been to visit her over there? If Lori were here I might know more.

Seeing people out for their weekend walks, pushing buggies, following kids on scooters and roller-blades, others sitting outside the Italian restaurant in their summery clothes as we drive by, feels unreal. A pretty façade plastered over an ugly reality.

The waiting area is small, tidy, half a dozen plastic seats on a rack bolted to the floor, and posters on the wall. There is a receptionist at the front desk. She wears a white shirt, dark skirt and small rectangular glasses perched halfway down her nose. 'Can I help?'

'We want to report a missing person,' I say. My throat is dry and I sound whispery. I speak louder: 'My daughter. She's in China, missing in China.'

'Right.' She nods, as though people pop in every day with this sort of information. Though I suppose her training leads her not to react with shock or surprise to the things she hears. 'Can I take your names?' she says. She looks at me first.

'Joanna Maddox.'

'Date of birth?'

'Eighth of September 1970.'

'And your address?'

I reel it off.

'And you are her mother?'

'Yes.'

'And you, sir?'

'I'm her stepfather,' Nick says, 'Nicolas Myers, twenty-third of August 1968, same address.'

'You're married?' she says to us.

'Yes,' I say. 'I didn't change my name this time.'

'And your daughter's details?' She peers at me over the top of her glasses.

'Lorelei Maddox – shall I spell it?'

'Please.'

I do that and give her the date of birth.

'So she's twenty-three?' she says.

'Yes.'

'And how long is it since you had any contact with your daughter?'

'Eleven days,' I say. 'The second of April she posted a blog. And she Skyped with her dad the day before.' Not even two weeks. Not very long at all, really. Am I being neurotic? Should I have waited? I expect her to send us away, tell us to come back when it's been a month, but she says, 'If you'd like to take a seat, I'll see if there's anyone upstairs can come and talk to you.' She goes out of the door behind the desk.

We sit, not speaking. My toes are curled rigid in my shoes. Outside, wind plays through the trees and the shrubs and flowers along the side of the path; yellow forsythia, purple and white tulips, golden spurge shiver in its wake.

I start at a thump on the window. A bee the size of my thumb careers about and bangs the glass again, then zigzags away.

Perhaps there's no one here, I think. It's a weekend, after all. She'll send us away. Tell us to try normal office hours. I hear the wall clock ticking. Two o'clock. Nine at night in Chengdu.

The receptionist comes back and says, 'Detective Inspector Dooley will be down shortly.' My skin turns to gooseflesh. Nick glances at me, sombre. He rubs his forehead and shifts in his seat.

Another five minutes, then a woman comes in through a door to the side of the waiting area marked 'Staff Only'.

'Mrs Maddox? Mr Myers? I'm Detective Inspector Dooley.' An Irish accent. She holds out her hand. We shake. Her hand is cool and dry, the pressure swift. I catch a trace of tobacco smoke and imagine she's been having a smoke before meeting us. Her hair is dark and curly, salted grey. She is sharp-featured; lines furrow her brow and fan from the corners of her eyes and mouth. Her eyes are a washed-out blue. She carries a plastic folder and pen.

I'd like to pinch myself. But this is no dream.

'I'm very sorry to hear about Lorelei,' she says. 'If you'll come with me I'll take some more details.'

She uses an electronic swipe card to release the door and takes us along a corridor to a small meeting room with four low easy chairs arranged around a coffee table. 'Can I get you a drink?' she offers. 'Only a vending machine, I'm afraid.'

'Some water,' I say. 'That would be great, thanks, just tap water.' *Don't drink the water* – Lori's rule number one.

'Yes, water, please,' Nick says.

'Of course. Please, take a seat.'

67

She's back in no time with two tumblers. Parched, I drink half of mine.

'Let me just check I have all the details correct,' she says, sitting down. She consults her file and goes over what we have told the receptionist. It's all there.

'And Lorelei is in China?' she says.

'In Chengdu,' Nick says. 'Sichuan province, the south-west.'

'What's she doing there?'

'Teaching,' I say. 'English. She went travelling in September and ended up in China.'

'She has a work visa,' Nick says, 'for a year.'

DI Dooley notes it down. 'And when did she acquire the work visa?'

I think. 'That would be February.'

'And you last heard from her on the second of April?'

'Yes,' I say. I explain about the blog. 'And she Skyped with her, father, my ex, the day before.'

'His name?' she says.

'Tom Maddox.'

'And his date of birth?'

'First of April 1969.'

'Is Lorelei good at keeping in touch usually?' DI Dooley says.

'It can be a bit random,' I say.

'Have you spoken to her friends or colleagues in China?' she says.

'We're not in touch with them,' I say. 'She had been talking about a holiday, so it might be that she's gone off somewhere and can't use the Internet or get a mobile-phone signal.'

'A holiday to...'

'She never said.'

'On her own?'

'Possibly,' I say. 'Her friend out there couldn't get the time off.' It all sounds so vague and imprecise.

'Things can be quite last-minute with her,' Nick says.

'We've spoken to her friends here. We've emailed and phoned and texted her...' Faltering, I reach for the water glass and take a sip.

DI Dooley says, 'And while she was still in touch was Lorelei having any problems – health, money, relationships?'

'No.'

'No previous incidents of going missing?' she says.

'No,' I say.

'Any history of mental-health problems?'

I balk at this, recoiling from the scenarios that it makes me think of, but DI Dooley says calmly, 'We have to consider every eventuality.'

'No, nothing like that,' I say.

'Was Lorelei living alone?'

'More recently, yes.'

'And before that?'

'She was sharing with Dawn, a friend she met in Thailand. Dawn's Australian – she's the one who might have been going on holiday with her. They were seeing each other.'

DI Dooley nods and adds to her notes. 'Do you have a surname for Dawn?'

'Sorry, no.'

She lays her pen down, lining it up so it is parallel with the top of the paper. 'There is a limit to what we can do, given this is a foreign juris-diction. At this point I will make some enquiries and see if there's been any recent activity on her phone, for example, any deposits or withdrawals from her UK bank accounts and so on. Depend-ing on the results of that, if we don't have any news, we'll approach the Foreign and Common-wealth Office and ask them to liaise with police in the Chengdu area who would carry out their own missing-person inquiry there. I'm going to give you a list of information I need to get the ball rolling.'

I nod, a bit stunned that she's geared up and ready to act.

She takes a blank page from her file and writes down the things she needs from us. 'You can get these to me some time tomorrow?'

'Lunchtime?' I say.

'Fine. My shift starts at one o'clock. Shall we say half past?'

I'm feeling numb. My brain and my heart feel frozen, as though I'm absent, have slipped away from inhabiting my body.

'There is a charity, Missing Overseas,' DI Dooley says, as we get to our feet. 'They have a website. You might find it useful.'

So that's it. It's official. Lori is missing. Those three words fill me with such anxiety that I have to stop outside and cling to Nick's arm, my heart thumping, wild and irregular, against my ribs, my head buzzing black.

At home, Penny takes one look at us and sends the boys out to get themselves ice creams from the corner shop. She opens a bottle of wine and pours us each a glass. I tell her what the detective said, feel the pressure of tears behind my eyes and force them away.

'Don't tell them yet,' I say, as we hear the boys coming back. I know we can't keep it from them for very long, but I'm hoping DI Dooley might bring us good news and it would be awful to upset Finn and Isaac if we weren't absolutely certain of the situation.

We need to choose a recent picture of Lori. I run through the ones on the computer. Nick points to the snap at the airport. Lori and her backpack.

'Her hair's still pink in that,' I say. I'm worried that people will notice the colour and that's all they will notice so they'll immediately disregard it because they don't recall an English girl with pink hair.

There is one picture from her website, from her blog, that she sent just after arriving in Chengdu. She's seated in a teahouse but there's a clear view of her face. Her hair is an in-between length, without the pink. You can see her eyes are a mid-blue. She's smiling – you can see her dimples. She's wearing a lilac and cherry-red blouse, crinkly material that's good for travel, easy to wash and dries in minutes. 'This one I think.'

The doorbell rings and Tom is here. 'What did they say?' He doesn't bother with any niceties as he steps inside.

'We go back in tomorrow – there's a list of stuff they need, all her details, passport number, bank account, phone, email, when we last heard from her, who we've spoken to. And a photo.' I clear my throat. 'Look.' He follows me through to the computer. 'This one?' I say.

'Fine, and then what?'

I repeat what DI Dooley has said. Tom is agitated: it's visible in the way he holds himself, the set of his shoulders. Nick stares at the floor.

'So we just wait?' Tom interrupts me. 'Why not go straight to the Foreign Office now?'

'The police have to check it all out,' Nick says, 'make sure the information's correct and clear before they involve the Foreign Office or the authorities abroad.'

'You've given them most of the information,' Tom objects, running his hand through his hair, turning away, then back again.

'There are things they can verify that we can't,' I explain, 'like when she last used her bank account or an ATM, where she was then. Like ... I don't know ... phone records. They know what they're doing.'

'Bloody hope so.' His shoulders drop, he exhales noisily. 'I'll come with you tomorrow,' he says.

'One thirty, the station on Elizabeth Slinger Road. Bring anything you have, your laptop, emails, texts, times you Skyped.'

'Why is Tom here?' Isaac has appeared, his face slack with sleep, scratching his belly with one hand, the other clasped at the back of his neck.

No one speaks for a moment. Then Isaac says, 'Is Lori here?' His face alert with excitement.

'No,' I say quickly. 'Tom just popped in. And you need to get back to bed.'

'Come on, Tiger,' says Nick.

'I want Mummy.'

'Go on,' I say. 'Daddy will piggy-back you. I'll be up in a minute.'

Nick crouches and Isaac climbs onto his back.

Once we're alone Tom just stares at me. I don't know what he wants and wait for him to speak. He stuffs his hands into his pockets. 'She could just have taken that holiday,' he says.

'Yes,' I say. But it's more of a prayer than a belief.

Something has shifted. I half hoped that the detective would send us on our way, belittle our concerns, ridicule our fears. The fact that we were taken so seriously, attended to, and that the wheels will be set in motion to investigate, gives a cold, dense weight to my worries.

CHAPTER THIRTEEN

I'm an automaton at work, answering the phone, taking in absence notes and completed parents' evening slips from the most organized families. I deal with little Martha Kentaway, who has a ferocious nosebleed.

At break I am suddenly self-conscious in the staffroom. Pam picks up on my stiffness. She stops her anecdote about a family barbecue and says, 'Jo, are you OK?'

'Not really.' I place one hand over my mug. The steam from the tea is hot, too hot really, but I leave my hand there. 'We've reported Lori missing.'

There is a collective double-take, a one-two punch of surprise, then a ripple of emotion. I see it in Henry's eyes, in the way Zoë's hand flies to her throat, and hear it in the soft exclamation that Sunita makes. Grace and Pam both speak together, asking questions.

'No one's heard from her since the second of April,' I say. 'We have to go back to the police station at half past one.' I glance at Grace.

'Of course,' she says, 'and if there's anything we can do...' Her mouth twists, a shrug, *as if.*

I can feel the rigidity in my neck, in my back, under my skin. Like those pieces of plastic they insert under shirt collars, keeping the thing in shape, invisible until you open the packet and lift the material up to remove it.

I'm back at the police station. Tom is late. *Late for his own funeral.* This trait is not amusing, if it ever was, or endearing. I apologize to DI Dooley, who asks me if I'd like to make a start or if I'd prefer to wait.

It's a simple enough question but I gasp and stutter, not knowing what the right answer is. She puts me out of my misery: 'Let's give him another five minutes.' She checks her watch. The bulky black dial looks too big for her wrist. She leaves me waiting in Reception.

I check my phone again for messages, though I would have heard the notification sound if Tom had texted me.

Last night, after Tom had gone, I looked up the Missing Overseas website, a salutary litany of

74

British people who have disappeared, all ages, in places all over the globe. One had been missing for twenty years. *Good God.* I closed that page and went instead to their guidelines. *Where Do I Start? What Can Missing Overseas Do?* I read them. We were doing the right thing in going to the police here. The website also recommended speaking to the Foreign and Commonwealth Office straight away. I checked and found that they were open only during office hours.

Missing Overseas had a contact form to fill in and a phone number to use in an emergency. Is this an emergency? I wondered. Would I be sitting here with the kids asleep in bed, methodically gathering names and numbers, if it was a real emergency? 'Should we fill this in?' I asked Nick. We decided to wait. The list of how they could help was both reassuring but also unnerving because each bullet point – *Handling All Media; Providing 24-hour Hotlines* – forced me to think that further down the line we might need them to do that. And I didn't want that. I didn't want Lori to be one of those pictures.

Just a mix-up, I keep praying, false alarm, crossed wires.

Now Tom is here, striding up the path, un-shaven and rumpled. 'Sorry,' he says, as he comes in, 'traffic.'

There is always traffic. Any normal person would've allowed for that.

'She'll be down again in a minute,' I say.

'Shit!' He turns to go. 'Laptop.'

'For God's sake!' If he has to drive across town

and back...

'In the car.'

When DI Dooley returns she takes the list I've made and works through it. Lori's passport and national insurance numbers, bank account details. The names and numbers of all the friends I can find. Also an outline of the emails, texts, Skype calls we made in date order.

She holds the pen horizontal below each item as she reads it, occasionally checking things with us.

'Was this an email to all three of you?'

'She has just one account?'

'This is the phone number she's using now?'

'Yes, she got that one in China. It's cheaper to use a local number,' Tom says.

'And you have copies of the emails?'

'Yes.' I've printed out Lori's emails to us and copied our texts from the last few months.

'Screenshots,' Tom says, holding up a pen drive.

'You have her blog address?' I check with the detective.

'Yes. So as of now the last communication was definitely the second of April?'

'That's right,' I say.

'So this is totally out of character?'

'Not exactly,' I say, as Tom says, 'Yes.'

He glares at me.

I look at DI Dooley. 'It's just that Lori doesn't always pick up her messages or maybe she sees them but it can be a few days before she replies. There was a time too...' I feel traitorous raising it but it's been on my mind. I've been turning it over and over, like a set of worry beads, thinking,

If she did that then, well, maybe this is something similar. '...when she was at uni, in Glasgow, we didn't hear from her for a couple of weeks. She didn't respond to an email and then we found out that she'd been on some party trip to Skye, a last-minute invite. And forgot her phone charger. And now ... well, we often don't hear anything for a couple of weeks and she can be slow to reply to things – but for *no one* to have heard, for her to be ignoring us all, something's not right. I spoke to the Foreign Office this morning,' I say. 'I gave them the details and told them we had seen you.'

She nods. 'Who's your contact there?'

'Jeremy Chadwick.'

Tom moves the hair off his face. 'Can't you get the Chinese police to look for her – Interpol or whatever?'

'If necessary, once we've done what we can at this end.'

'Which is what exactly?' he says.

'You're worried,' she says, 'anxious to find Lorelei. I understand that. There are procedures in place that have been built on the experience of previous missing-person investigations. It's the most effective way of working. I do realize how difficult it must be, the sense of being kept waiting, but I need you to give me a couple of days while I carry out my own enquiries.'

'OK,' Tom says, though he doesn't sound convinced. He sits back in the chair.

'Have there been any family arguments between any of you and Lori?' DI Dooley says.

'No,' I say.

77

'Any hint of trouble with her friends or col-leagues?'

'Nothing.'

'Do you have the name and address of her cur-rent employers?'

'Just the name,' Tom says. 'Five Star English.'

'Thank you.' She scans what she's written. Then picks up our printouts and the pen drive. 'And thank you for these.'

'What can we do?' I say. 'There must be some-thing.'

'Carry on as you are, make sure as many people know as possible. I'll be in touch as soon as I can. And if you do find out anything else or hear from anyone, please let me know. You have my direct number.'

Outside it's bright and I have to squint. I left my sunglasses at home, forgotten in the morning's rush.

'We were looking at the Missing Overseas web-site last night,' I say. 'It's useful.'

Tom nods, rubs at the bristles on his cheek. 'You think she knows what she's doing?' He tips his head back towards the building.

'More than we do,' I say.

'Do you want to get a coffee?'

'I've got work,' I say.

An almost imperceptible shake of his head, the release of breath in his nose. I am a disappoint-ment. Dull, hidebound.

'Who's to know?' he says.

And perhaps this isn't Tom wanting to play hookey for the hell of it. I've had Nick to talk to about Lori. Has Tom been able to share it with anyone, the woman in Dublin, say? If he has, then it's not the same as family, as people who know her.

'Half an hour,' I say.

There are plenty of small bars and cafés on Burton Road, among the hairdressers and boutiques. The area is known as 'fashionable West Didsbury' in all the estate-agent blurbs. Tom wants to sit outside to smoke, so we pick the first place that has a pavement table, order two espressos.

'If she'd had an accident...' he says, lighting his cigarette, one eye screwed up against the smoke.

'We'd know, surely. Any hospital, they'd notify someone, notify us.'

'What if she had no ID on her?' he says. 'And they didn't know who she was?'

'They'd get someone to speak English, and ask.'

'And if she was unconscious?'

Couldn't communicate. It's not something I want to think about but it's in my head now, along with all the other unspeakable possibilities. 'They'd put out an appeal, surely,' I say. 'They must have a way of informing the ex-pats. Through the embassies or whatever.'

He smokes, taps ash into the ashtray. 'Or kidnapped?' he says. 'A way of making money.'

'Tom, don't–' My voice shakes.

'You must have thought–'

'Of course. But... Look, there'd have been a ransom demand, wouldn't there?'

'I just feel so bloody helpless,' he mutters.

'Join the club.'

'She's not stupid,' he says, as we part.

'I know. But she can be caught up in the moment...' *Twelve days.*

We leave it hanging. Go our separate ways.

CHAPTER FOURTEEN

Isaac complains that the pictures on Lori's wall are spooky and horrid. He's right about some of them.

'We can move the wardrobe and drawers to that side,' I suggest to Nick. 'That'll cover most of it. And put some of their posters over what still shows.' It feels odd to be reorganizing the rooms when everything with Lori is up in the air. Normal life should be suspended, paused, until we know where she is, but it doesn't work like that.

I've an irrational urge to tell him to move it all back, put everything how it was, as if by re-arranging the furniture we can return to some time before 2 April. Put Lori back in place where she should be posting a new blog about her escapades: *So I am sticky and itchy and STILL having an amazing time. Lxxx*

Finn wants to help but is just getting in the way so I give him the pile of posters and tell him to take them downstairs: he and Isaac can pick three each to go up on the wall.

I empty the wardrobe of the boys' clothes, which are on the shelves at the right-hand side. Neither of them has anything that needs hanging up. Between us, Nick and I lug the wardrobe over to the wall. As we edge it into the corner, I try to see the collage afresh, look for surprises in it, but I'm too familiar with the components: the family wearing gas masks, her landscape photos from Skye, the cityscapes of Glasgow and Manchester, the picture of a skeleton draped with feather boas.

Nick removes the drawers from the chest and puts them on Finn's bunk, then hefts the carcass over and puts it next to the wardrobe. The bedroom door will only open ninety degrees but that will have to do.

There's a wail from downstairs. Finn. I find him standing disconsolate, holding two halves of a poster.

Isaac has a beetle brow, mouth pursed with defiance.

'He tore my picture.'

'I did not,' Isaac yells. 'You snatched it.'

'It's mine,' Finn says.

'I was giving it to you.'

'Isaac–' I say.

'I was! He shouldn't pull.'

'We can fix it,' I say, 'with some tape.'

'It'll still be torn,' Finn says.

'Put it there.' I nod to the table and fetch the Sellotape from the basket on the shelf. The rip is more or less straight so it's easy to repair. When I turn it over, Finn inspects it. 'It's still torn. You can see the mark. I want a new one.'

'OK, but for now we use this. Have you chosen your others?'

'No,' Finn says.

'Two minutes,' I say, 'then if you still haven't I'll pick for you.'

'You tell Isaac off.'

I cannot face this. 'It's a shame the poster got ripped but we will get you a new one.'

'You tell Isaac off.'

I'm saved from having to launch into a reprimand by Nick calling, 'Jo, can you bring up the extension lead from the shed?'

'OK,' I shout, then remind the boys, 'Two minutes.'

Nick shows me the little room. He's not bothered repainting so the wall is scuffed where the bunks used to be and there are stickers here and there, little dinosaurs, dogs, and large round ones from the dentist that say 'Hero!' or 'Champion!' The curtains show cartoon kid astronauts floating among rockets and planets. The computer desk is L-shaped and fits into the corner, giving work space each side. On the shelves where the boys had their toys, Nick's put books and folders from his work.

'You could take those down.' I signal to the curtains. 'Have a blind – or nothing at all. No one can see in.'

'I might,' he says.

'It's fine, though,' I add, wondering if I've struck the wrong tone in implying he could do more.

My phone goes. *DI Dooley.* My stomach drops.

'I've no news,' she says first of all, which helps me stay upright, 'but I've verified there has been no recent activity on Lori's phone or her bank accounts so you should go back to the Foreign and Commonwealth Office, tell them that, and ask them to request the assistance of the Chinese police.' My face freezes as I take this in. Nick stares at me intently. I grimace at him. He moves closer so he can hear.

'Will you let Mr Maddox know or shall I?' DI Dooley says.

'I'll do that. So, erm, what happens now?'

'The Chinese police will do a welfare check on the ground there, then instigate a missing-person investigation. It's not something I'd have any involvement in, other than assisting with forwarding any information we already have. And if Jeremy Chadwick needs anything from me, please tell him to call.'

'Yes. We've been looking at the Missing Overseas site,' I say. 'We could ask them to put Lori's details up there.'

'I think that would be a good idea,' she says. 'If you prepare what you need for that, then liaise with the FCO as to the timing – they may want to make some initial checks over there before going public.'

'Yes.' I look at the helmets and inflatable suits on the astronauts, the perky grins on their faces, the red stain on the flying saucer where Isaac had written *Finn pig* and I'd tried to scrub it off.

'Yes,' I say again.

'I'll be in touch,' she says. 'Get back to me if there's anything you need, anything you want to ask.'

'Thank you.'

Stupefied, I close the cover on my phone.

'Shit,' Nick says.

I feel like I've been hit by a truck. 'We've got to find her,' I say.

'We will,' he says, but I read the flicker of doubt in his eyes.

'Can you ring Tom?' I say.

There's a moment's pause. How can he hesitate? He gets out his own phone. I'm wiping my nose and trying not to beat myself up for crying. What's the point of bottling it all up? Of course I should fucking cry. What sort of mother am I? What mother wouldn't?

I sit on the floor while Nick talks to Tom. From his side of the conversation I can tell Tom's asking a whole lot of questions, none of which Nick can answer. Then Nick covers the phone and says to me, 'He wants to come round.'

The thought exhausts me but who am I to shut him out? We have things to do, things to prepare, like the detective said.

I nod to Nick, blow my nose and wipe my face.

'These ones.' Finn comes up the stairs holding posters. 'And Isaac has four, not three. But I don't mind.'

I can't speak for a moment, still full of tears. Finn watches me. Can he tell I've been crying?

'Get the Blu Tack,' I say, as brightly as I can, 'and we'll put them up now.'

Once he is out of earshot I ask Nick to do it with them. I don't want to. I don't want to cover up her lovely riot of pictures.

CHAPTER FIFTEEN

The GP is new to me. We never seem to see the same one twice. It's a group practice, and although we have a named individual as our primary carer, she only works two days a week and her appointments are like gold dust. So Dr Munir has never met Isaac. He listens while I go over our worries, the run of fevers, the vomiting. Choosing my words carefully, I also talk about his outbursts, the anger and biting.

To his credit the doctor talks directly to Isaac, too, asking him if he has any pains, if anything is worrying him. Isaac shakes his head each time.

'What about school?'

'Sit quietly on the carpet,' Isaac says, 'or Miss gets cross.'

'Do you get cross?'

'Sometimes,' Isaac says.

'Why?'

'If Finn is naughty or Sebastian hits me.'

'Does Sebastian hit you a lot?' Dr Munir says.

A toss of the shoulders. 'Not really.'

Dr Munir asks Isaac to stick his tongue out and say *aaah,* which he does, grinning at the cheek of it. He examines Isaac's ears and feels under his neck. 'Slight swelling of the glands here but nothing to be concerned about. Sometimes an infection presents with vomiting and that would account for the swelling too. Any toilet problems

– constipation, diarrhoea?'

'No,' I say. Isaac screws up his mouth.

Dr Munir listens to Isaac's chest, asks about allergies in the family (none), about Isaac's appetite (picky) and if he's making progress at school (some).

'Would you like a listen?' he says to Isaac.

Isaac does. There's a look of consternation on his face as the doctor puts the earphones in Isaac's ears and places the disc on his breastbone.

Isaac yanks his T-shirt back on. I pull his sweatshirt sleeves the right way out and give it to him.

'There's no obvious cause I can find to explain the sickness,' Dr Munir says. 'It may be that Isaac is simply picking up viruses at school. There has not been any fitting with the fever?'

'No,' I say.

'Any big changes at home?'

'No.'

Isaac doesn't know yet: we're still waiting for *the green light,* as Mr Chadwick from the Foreign Office put it. Yesterday I had a call from him to tell me that one of the consular staff in Chongqing, the nearest consulate to Chengdu, was now liaising with the local authorities on the welfare check. Hospitals were being contacted, the visa departments and immigration authorities. If Lori had left China, it would be documented. Mr Chadwick would let us know the results of those searches as soon as he heard.

I like to think of Lori on some far-flung island having a go at scuba-diving or para-sailing. Or trekking in Nepal, sharing campfire meals under

86

skies dusted with stars, crossing glaciers and sleeping in bags smelling of woodsmoke and moisturizing cream. On top of the world. Alive with excitement.

'I suggest you monitor the situation,' Dr Munir says, 'perhaps keep a chart of any illness. If the situation persists, do come back. We could refer you to a paediatrician or for allergy testing in case there is a dietary trigger. Isaac's not had any respiratory problems?'

'No.'

'Of course, if there is any, worsening of symptoms, fits, for example, or a fever that lasts more than two days, please get emergency help.'

'He was nice,' I say to Isaac, as we walk back to school.

'Yes.'

'And he let you use his stethoscope to listen to your heart.'

His hand finds mine. 'I didn't like it.'

'Why not?'

'Because of the noise it makes.'

'The heartbeat?'

'Like I was scared,' Isaac says, 'boom-boom, boom-boom.'

I try to lighten the mood. 'Babies' hearts beat even faster. They sound like a horse running.' I make a fast clopping sound with my tongue. And I think about hearing Lori's heartbeat for the first time with the midwife's stethoscope. And, like Isaac, hearing fear in the pace of it. 'So fast?' I'd said.

'Completely normal,' the midwife said. 'That's

87

around a hundred and fifty beats per minute. During childhood it will gradually slow until it's like ours.'

The picture when we went for the scan, and all those drawings in the maternity books of the foetus, looking so peaceful, thumb in mouth, eyes closed. But the heart going like the clappers.

There is a missed call on my phone, *Jeremy Chadwick*. As soon as I've left Isaac in class, I go to the staffroom, which is deserted, and try the number.

'Mr Chadwick, this is Mrs Maddox.'

'Hello, I've just spoken to Mr Myers to let you know we've now had word from Peter Dunne at the consulate in Chongqing. There is no report of Lorelei being seen at any of the hospitals and there is no record of her using her passport to leave the country since the trip to Hong Kong in February. That would be when she collected her work visa?'

'Yes.'

'The Chinese PSB, that's the police, have agreed to undertake further enquiries and a visit was made today to her address in Chengdu. The apartment was empty.'

'Right.'

'I've emailed DI Dooley with this information and Peter Dunne will let us know as soon as there are any developments.'

'Thank you. So we can go ahead with the appeal, now?'

'Yes. That's fine.'

We end the call. My arms and the base of my neck are tingling. I sit down and try to clear my head. 'Ring Tom,' I say out loud, 'and Missing Overseas.'

Before I can dial, my phone rings. *Nick.*

'I've just heard,' I say to him. 'If I ring Tom, can you call Missing Overseas and get them to put it up on the site? Talk to them about the press release and...' there was something else we had to do for them but it escapes me '...whatever else.'

'I will. You OK?'

When I don't answer, I hear him draw in a breath. 'See you soon, love.'

It takes me seconds to decide.

Grace is in her office, adding her head-teacher comments to the children's reports.

'Jo?'

'I need to go home. Lori – it's official. The Chinese police are looking for her... I need...'

'Yes, of course, go. Go.' She looks at me, compassion clear in her eyes, her lips parted, as though to say something, but what? What is there to say?

'Finn and Isaac – can you keep them in after-school club? I didn't book?'

'Of course. And anything we can do,' she adds, 'just say.'

I nod, biting my tongue.

And leave.

I speak to Tom as I'm walking home He is at one of his properties, dealing with a contractor, but will join us as soon as he's done.

CHAPTER SIXTEEN

Nick has made a list from his conversation with Edward at Missing Overseas. We divide up the tasks. I begin calling round friends and family so people hear directly from us before it's made public. I find it easier to keep the calls brisk as I tell her friends, Erin, then Amy, that Lori is officially missing, and ask them to spread the word. Jake's voicemail is on so I leave him a message.

There's no one really on my side of the family to notify: I'm an only child, parents both dead now. My mum's brother Norman lives in Oxfordshire but he was too frail to make her funeral. His daughter, my cousin Adrienne, and her brother, Curtis, are still around somewhere but I only have Norman's details. He is very deaf so I won't ring. Instead I type a letter and address it to Adrienne, c/o Norman.

Edward has sent us a template for a press release and Nick is cutting and pasting text into it.

I ask Nick if he'll speak to his parents in Nottingham. They are in sheltered accommodation, still independent but increasingly prone to falling over and the diseases of old age – glaucoma, arthritis, osteoporosis. Nick checks the time. They won't answer the phone before six because of the expense, even though we'd be paying. It doesn't matter whether we've a price plan that includes free or cheap calls to their number, the habit is ingrained. Betty washes and reuses baking foil and darns Ron's socks. One teabag does for two cups.

Nick's brother, Philip, lives near to them and has tea there every Sunday. Philip is a bit of a recluse, never married; he worked on the railways as an engineer for twenty years before going long-term sick with cirrhosis. He has a drink problem. Some insurance policy from his trade union means he can just about manage without having to go on benefits.

I wonder now, as Nick is deliberating over whether to call him first, if Philip is depressed, if that's behind the drinking. Which came first? Then I feel awkward, knowing how much Nick would hate any comparison between himself and Philip, or any pop psychology about genetics and depression.

And this isn't depression, I think, not really. Depression is not being able to get out of bed, literally. It's trudging through one dead grey hour after another; it's complete self-obsession, self-loathing and pain. Isolation. It is grief as deep as the earth. I know these things from stories I've read and documentaries I've seen but also because Tom's mother has been clinically depressed for much of her life. And most of his. Hospitalized for years on end. She couldn't come to our wedding. We took Lori there once, when Daphne was at home. I'd nagged Tom about visiting, letting her meet her grandchild, until he relented. I had seen photographs of her, tall and blonde, like Tom, but very pale-skinned. She did some modelling in the sixties. There are shots of her wrapped in white fur with bare feet and smouldering eyes. When she married Francis, she found herself installed in a crumbling Georgian house, in a Sussex village, expected to take care of the interior design and socializing and, once Tom came along, the childrearing, while Francis spent his weeks in London at his insurance company, living in the flat he kept there.

When Daphne was 'away', Tom was cared for by a nanny until, at the age of seven, he was parcelled off to boarding school. He detested it. When the time came to transfer from prep school to the linked public school, he refused. Clamoured to try for the local grammar instead. Francis wouldn't hear of it. Tom ran away repeatedly until the school recommended he leave. He moved to the grammar school and scraped into university, choosing philosophy because he quite liked the sound of it but, more importantly, because he knew it would annoy his father. Their encounters were always conducted with an icy politeness that would, on occasion, erupt into vicious mud-slinging. When Tom left for Manchester, Francis told him not to bother coming home until he'd graduated and could stand on his own two feet.

The doorbell rings and I let Tom in. He's on his phone, 'Maidstone Avenue house is an inventory check and boiler inspection, and we've a viewing at four for Leybourne Close.' He listens intently, says, 'Five-fifty a month, all inclusive.' Listens again. 'Yeah, well, it's a bit of a shit-hole but demand's high. OK, Moira, catch you later.' He closes his phone. 'So?'

'We've filled in the press release,' I say. 'Missing

92

Overseas said to notify people. I've covered Erin and Jake and Amy. Nick's doing his family...' Tom can fill in the rest.

I point to the kitchen, where Nick has rigged up the family computer. It's the only room with a large table.

'Social media?' Tom says, as he unzips his laptop.

'I asked them to tell their friends on Facebook and so on,' I say.

'Edward says Missing Overseas will use Facebook and Twitter,' Nick says. 'I'm on LinkedIn.'

'That still going?' Tom says. Before either of us can react to the dig, and its juvenile nature, he says, 'You?'

'Why should I be on LinkedIn?' I say. 'I'm a bloody school secretary.'

'OK, the press,' Tom says. 'I know someone on the *Metro*. They should do a feature.'

'*The Big Issue*,' Nick says. 'Edward says he's hopeful they'll do something, talk about Lori as part of a broader piece.'

'What about local news, TV and radio?' Tom says.

The message alert sounds on the computer and Nick reaches over to open it. 'It's up,' he says, and we crowd around the monitor. He clicks the link in the email, which takes us to the Missing Overseas website and Lori's picture appears, with the agreed text:

Lorelei Maddox
Age: 23
Missing since 2 April 2014.

93

Lorelei has been missing in China since 2 April 2014. She was last seen in Chengdu where she was working as a private English teacher. Lorelei is 5'3" tall and of slim build with dark hair and blue eyes.

Do you have any information?

'Daddy and I need to talk to you about something.'

We are at the table and the boys have just eaten. I suggested to Nick we have something later, leftover stew in the freezer that needs using up.

'The holidays?' Finn beams.

'No, Finn, not the holidays.'

'A party?'

Nick touches his arm, mouths, 'Shush.'

Isaac is still, wary.

'You know Lori's gone to China–' Nick says.

'Are we going?' Finn jumps in.

Nick shakes his head. 'Just listen. Well, Lori hasn't Skyped us for a while and her phone's not working and she's not at her house in China, so some people are trying to find her.'

'Is she lost?' Finn says.

'She might be,' I say.

'She should ask a policeman,' Isaac says.

'That's a good idea,' I say. 'Perhaps she will.'

'So,' Nick says, 'we're going to be telling everybody she's missing and asking them to help look for her.'

'There might not be a policeman,' Finn says.

'A grown-up then. Ask a grown-up,' Isaac says.

'Lori is a grown-up,' Finn says.

'Anyway, we hope we find her soon but we

wanted you to know what was happening.' Nick gets to his feet. He pours himself a whisky.

'We've made this,' I say, 'to show people.' I have a copy of the press release. The ink's running out on the printer so the picture is faded, the text striped with white lines.

'Missing,' Isaac says.

I read the rest of it out for them.

'Hmm – like Poncho,' Finn says.

Oh, God. Poncho was Lori's hamster when she was about eight. Finn wasn't even born. But it's a family myth, how Poncho disappeared behind the radiator in the kitchen and was never seen again. How Lori sat up all night keeping vigil, with a saucer full of Poncho treats to tempt him back. How she fell asleep sitting up.

Eager to distract them from the fact that there was no happy reunion with Poncho, I say, 'But Poncho couldn't ask anyone the way home. He couldn't talk, only make noises. What noises do hamsters make?'

Isaac says hamsters don't make any noises – Sebastian has one and it never says anything. Finn says they squeak. They bicker about that for a while and I clear the table.

I stick the 'Missing' sheet up on the cork board. It's as if I'm waiting for it to hit me, as though we've unlocked the floodgates and the water is rushing towards us but we can't hear the roar, can't see the torrent racing our way. There is just the caught breath of a pause, a frozen heartbeat, the unnatural stillness, pinning me in place.

CHAPTER SEVENTEEN

'Mummy, phone!' Finn stands at the kitchen door, waving the handset. I'm fetching the washing in. I dump the clothes in the basket and take it from him. 'Hello?'

'Mrs Maddox?'

'Yes?'

'My name's Dawn Jeffreys. I'm Lori's friend, in Chengdu.'

'Dawn, yes.' My pulse speeds up – there's drumming up my spine. I move to sit on the bench, willing her to say, *Don't worry, she's here, I just spoke to her, everything's OK.*

'I heard about Lori, that she's missing. I'm so sorry.' The line is clear but her Australian twang is unfamiliar so I have to concentrate hard to follow.

'You, haven't seen her? Or heard anything? You don't know where she is?'

The sparrows are fighting over the bird-feeder, jostling for purchase.

'No, I'm sorry.' There's a slight delay between one of us speaking and the other person hearing it.

'When did you see her last?' I say.

'Thursday, the third of April.'

After the blog. Suddenly that seems good. We thought that the Wednesday was her last contact. But Dawn saw her on Thursday. I feel giddy. So it's not twenty-one days now, it's twenty.

'Didn't you think it was odd,' I say, 'that there was no word from her?'

There's a pause and I hear a muffled sound, gulping. Dawn is crying. 'We broke up,' she says, her voice choked, 'that Thursday. I thought she needed some space... I...'

Oh, God. The racket from the sparrows drowns her out, forcing me inside through the kitchen to the stairway, far enough from the kids' television to hear her.

'Everybody here is doing what they can,' she says. 'The police have been talking to us.'

'Was she OK about the break-up?' Could this be the reason for Lori's silence? A broken heart triggering a crisis? I'm shaken, then feel a flicker of anger that Dawn rejected her.

'It was her decision,' Dawn says.

Lori ended the relationship. Why? I struggle to reorient myself. 'Right,' I say.

'And she was around on the Friday – there was a party,' Dawn says.

The Friday. Nineteen days. 'Do you think she might have gone away somewhere?'

'I don't know,' Dawn says. 'No one here has heard anything from her.' She gulps again.

I can't think what else to say, still trying to process the new information. 'Dawn, can I take your number so we can talk again?'

'Of course.'

'I'll just get a pen.'

She reads it out and gives me her email address as well. Our goodbyes are clumsy, speaking over each other, my timing disrupted by all the new questions crowding behind me. And at the core of them, like a heartbeat, driven and relentless: *Where are you, where are you, where are you, Lori?*

'How long do we give them?' Tom is on the phone to Jeremy Chadwick at the Foreign Office, badgering him. 'It's been a week since the Chinese police started work,' he says, 'and we have to hear second-hand from a mate of Lori's, who had the decency to get in touch, that Lori was seen on Friday, the fourth, two days later than we thought. Why are the police not keeping us updated?'

'They may wish to complete their enquiries–'

'No, that's not right,' Tom says. 'We're being kept in the dark. And that means that the information we're using for the appeal is inaccurate. That's not helping anybody. A week, and they've given us nothing. Nothing.'

I can hear the voice, tinny through the handset. 'It isn't very long in the scheme of things. A missing-person inquiry can take many months.'

'Well, we're not going to sit around on our arses any longer.'

I flinch at Tom's rudeness – he sees, and juts out his chin, his eyes hard.

Nick arrives back from taking the kids to school and walking Benji. He stands in the doorway.

'How many people are on the team looking for her? Exactly what are they doing?' Tom says.

'I don't have all those details,' Jeremy Chadwick says, 'but I can assure you that they are taking this situation very seriously. Our relationship with the authorities–'

'I don't want assurances,' Tom says, 'I want action. I want results.'

I'm shaking my head at Tom, signalling with my hands for him to turn it down. Nick watches. I can't read the look on his face – scepticism, disdain?

'As do we all,' says Jeremy Chadwick.

'I want to come out there,' Tom says, 'come and help search.'

Nick looks at me, questioning.

The prospect of travelling to Chengdu has arisen but in a vague way, mentioned as something that might eventually happen, if necessary. But it's not something that's ever been thought through. Now, though, I share Tom's sense of urgency. Inside my fears thrash and churn. Staying put, carrying on as we have been with calls and interviews for the papers, with emails and Twitter, knowing we're five thousand miles away, is no longer bearable. As soon as Tom says it, I know that he's right: we have to act.

I glance away from Nick.

'That's an option,' says Jeremy Chadwick.

'Right. Well, that's what we'll do. Can you let Peter Dunne know, in Chongqing?'

'Certainly. The consulate will need to issue you with letters of invitation for the visa. They can be sent by email.'

When Tom's hung up, he says to me, 'I've got an auction at midday. Can you call Edward and ask for his help arranging flights and hotels?'

I nod.

'What about vaccinations?' Nick asks Tom.

'I should be covered – I was in Thailand, year before last.'

'I'm not,' I say.

Tom stares at me, his light eyes brightening.

'You're not thinking–' Nick stops abruptly.

Silence sings in the air.

'Yes,' I say to him, 'of course.'

His face flushes.

'I know you and I can't both go,' I say to Nick, 'with the boys...'

'But if Tom can...' Nick says.

Tom busies himself, putting his laptop away.

We wait until he's gone, the atmosphere thick with tension. Then I say to Nick, 'I can't stay here – it's driving me mad.'

'But you expect me to?'

'Nick–'

'You just do what you like, don't you? You don't even bother consulting me.'

'It's not what I like,' I shout. 'There's nothing to like about it. For fuck's sake...'

'Maybe I should go. You've got work, the boys–' Nick says.

'You and Tom? That's going to work really well,' I say.

His face darkens. 'I don't have a problem with it. If he does–'

'I'm going. I just think it's best.'

'We don't even get to discuss it,' he says. 'I'm her parent too.'

I don't reply. I walk round the table to get the phone.

'Isn't it a bit premature?' he says.

'I don't know,' I say, 'a week, a month, a year. I

don't know. How can we possibly know if we're being premature, or if it's too late?' The words are loud, raw and dirty. 'Oh, God, I don't mean that,' I say quickly. 'I don't even think that. Oh, God, I don't. But I can't wait any more. At least we'll be doing everything we can.' My mouth is dry and I feel shaky. I fetch myself some water. As I drink it, Nick sits at the table, which is strewn with notes and copies of the press-release flier and typed lists of who has said what to whom. He tidies the papers into piles.

'I have to go,' I say.

There's a pause. Then, 'OK,' he says quietly.

'I'd better ring Edward,' I say. Nick catches my wrist. He gets up and puts his arms around me. I'd like to let go, to weep in his embrace, but I don't because I need to stay in control: I need to walk and talk and get things done. I rest my eyes a moment and breathe steadily until the danger is past. Then I make the phone call. The prospect of going to find her gives me something to cling to, like a guide rail to help me on a swaying bridge over a bottomless gorge.

CHAPTER EIGHTEEN

I've arranged to drop Finn and Isaac off for breakfast club, and Nick has a meeting with the friend who's designing his website. Nick's plans have been shoved aside in the upheaval but the friend has carried on with the work and has mock-ups ready for Nick to consider.

I'm seeing Grace.

She's already in her office and there is a rich smell of coffee from the machine she uses.

'Jo!' She gets up, gives me a quick hug and offers me coffee, which I accept.

'Any news?' she says, pouring it, adding milk.

'No. So we're going out there, Tom and I, to help with the search.'

She nods. Puts the cup in front of me and goes to sit at the other side of the desk.

'We leave Thursday,' I say, 'if everything goes smoothly.'

'Oh, Jo, I'm so sorry. I can't imagine...'

'I know. It still feels unreal.' As if I'm in a play that I never auditioned for and I'm making up my lines as I go along, waiting for somebody to clap their hands together and tell us the performance is done, and we can all go now and resume our real lives. 'And then you read about the girls missing in Nigeria.' Over two hundred of them abducted from a school by a militant group called Boko Haram.

'God, yes,' she says, 'and no one seems to be doing anything about it.'

I take a breath. 'We do know that Lori hasn't left the country. It doesn't narrow it down much, though, the size of the place.'

Grace runs her fingers over the folder on her desk. I drink some coffee. Feel a rush of nausea.

'We've booked for three weeks,' I say.

'As long as it takes, and don't worry. We've sorted out cover – Andrea. A lot to learn but she's quick on the uptake.'

'How's everyone else?' I ask.

She blinks quickly, and her hand stills on the folder.

'What?' I say.

'Zoë,' she says. 'She's just been diagnosed.'

'Oh, no.' *On top of the miscarriage.*

'Bowel cancer,' Grace says. 'She should hear about the treatment plan tomorrow.'

'Oh, God,' I say, 'you should have told me.'

She throws me a look. *Don't be daft.* 'On a brighter note, I'm going to be a grandma. Patsy's pregnant.'

'Really! Brilliant.'

'Twins, actually.'

'No! Grace, how amazing. When are they due?' Suddenly I feel like crying, so I force myself to drink more coffee and concentrate on that.

'November, but they'll probably induce her a few weeks early – it reduces the risks apparently.'

'We didn't make parents' evening,' I say.

'You got their reports?'

'Yes, Finn's was fine but Isaac's...'

'Not found his niche yet,' Grace says. 'Give him time.'

'But the biting, the tantrums.'

'We've a strategy, and I've told Sunita to come to me if she needs more backup. We've dealt with much, much worse,' she says darkly, making me laugh.

It's true. There have been some seriously disturbed children in school over the years, children with challenging behaviour, needing one-to-one care to cope with the school environment.

103

'Me being away won't make things any easier for him,' I say.

'Maybe not, but kids are resilient. He's in a loving home, well cared for. You can't not go.'

We embrace again as I leave and she wishes me luck, adding, 'Please ask Nick to let us know when there's any news.'

'Of course,' I say.

'Lori's a great girl,' Grace says. 'I do hope everything's OK.'

I'm glad she hasn't told me everything will be OK and pretended false hope. I wake each morning and there's a new number in my head, so many days. Today it's twenty-four. I'd be a total idiot to imagine everything is all right.

So we have to fly to China but perhaps, if we're lucky, it will all come right again.

The nurse at the travel clinic checks my destination on the computer and tells me I need hepatitis A and a booster for diphtheria, whooping cough and tetanus.

'Is it a holiday?' she says, as she cleans my skin with a special wipe. 'That's where they have pandas, isn't it? My neighbours went there.'

I swallow. 'No, my daughter's gone missing out there.' It sounds so blunt in the small, neat room.

'Oh, God,' she says. 'I am sorry.'

At this moment all I want is for her to give me the jabs so I can escape. But I have already learned to talk about Lori at each and every opportunity. Word of mouth, the best publicity. So while she prepares the vials and administers the injections, I go through it all and ask her, please,

104

to tell people about it. She gives me the travel medical card, which lists what I've had done, and wishes me luck, her manner subdued.

CHAPTER NINETEEN

It's something I've read online, my eyes skimming over the columns of advice, what to do next, the bullet-pointed lists of *What We Can Do, What We Are Not Able to Do* but I must barely have registered it because when Peter Dunne, from the consulate in Chongqing, speaks to me on the phone, when he says it near to the close of our conversation, adding, 'Just in case,' I feel as though I've been electrocuted. A jolt that sears my heart and sends currents fizzing through my veins to the tips of my fingers and the backs of my thighs.

I grit my teeth and agree I will do as he suggests. After that I put the phone down and rest for a few seconds, arms braced on the table, eyes shut. I stir, pick up a pen and add to the growing list of things we need for our trip to China: *bring something with Lori's DNA on.*

It is macabre, sorting through the boxes that came out of Lori's room for something that will carry strands of her hair or skin cells or whatever else they might use. I'm looking through scarves and belts, bags and necklaces. I stop and say to Nick, 'Does that mean her toothbrush isn't there? At the flat?'

'I don't know,' he says.

'If it were there, we wouldn't need to take any-thing. But if it's not, that would fit with her going on holiday, wouldn't it? She'd take her tooth-brush and her hairbrush.'

'Yes,' he agrees, 'but maybe they're just cover-ing all the bases.' He holds up a joke tiara, black and silver with feathers attached and pointy black ears. Part of a Hallowe'en outfit Lori wore a couple of times. I've a picture of her in my head, like some punk imp, rowdy with her friends, drinking cocktails before setting off to a party.

'That,' I say, 'and this.' I lift up her black beret. 'She's worn this for ever, there must be ... well...' I don't need to spell it out.

Isaac comes in asking for a drink and sees the jumble. He picks up a scarf and Nick tells him to leave it alone.

'It's OK,' I say. 'You can have a play as long as they all go back in these boxes after.'

'And them?' He points to the things I'm holding.

'No, I need them,' I say.

'Why?' he says.

'I just do. Where's Finn?'

He shrugs.

'Isaac?'

'On the trampoline. Why?'

'He might like to dress up, too,' I say.

Isaac drapes Lori's scarf around his head and goes to peer in the hall mirror. I put the beret and the tiara in freezer bags and take them upstairs.

Nick follows me. 'I wish you wouldn't do that,' he says.

106

'What?'

'Undermine me. I just told Isaac to leave stuff alone and you say the opposite.'

'But why should he leave it alone? What harm can it do?'

'That's not the point,' he says.

'So if you say something stupid and illogical I've got to agree to it?' I sound like a bitch so I start to back-pedal. 'Sorry, I just think we have to pick our battles.'

'Don't bother,' he says, and walks away.

I stare at the suitcase I've started to pack and hear Finn's voice drifting up from the garden, some little chant, and realize my hands are aching because I'm gripping the freezer bags so very tightly.

CHAPTER TWENTY

I have the address of the visa office. Tom and I walk up and down Mosley Street among the office buildings trying to find it. I check the street number again and we retrace our steps. The only sign that this building is the right one is the scrap of paper stuck next to the intercom button with *Chinese Visa* scribbled on it. When Tom presses the buzzer, a voice tells us to come to the first floor.

Through the double doors a receptionist is poised at a high desk. She asks our business, then gives us a ticket and tells us to wait our turn. All the twenty or so seats are full, and more people stand around the edges of the room. At the far end there is a row of booths behind glass screens. The room is stuffy, smells of too many people, and I feel queasy as we find a place to stand.

It's a functional space: grey carpeting and chairs, white walls, flashes of red from the large Chinese good-luck charms of knotted string suspended by the booths.

After half an hour we get seats. Tom occupies himself with his phone, answering emails, but I can't shake off the sense of unreality: any minute now I'll get a text from Lori– *So sorry Mum, just bin havin the most awesome time w no internet Lxxx*

Conversation from the brief interviews up at the front washes over me. Two-thirds of the people waiting are European, mostly English. There's a man whose passport has been lost in the post and he's panicking about getting the visa in time to start his job in Beijing, then a young couple, who are sent away because they've not brought proof of their return flights. There's an old woman, who is going to visit her newborn grandson, and a student, who has a place on a master's degree course in Shanghai.

Penny messages me. *Anything I can do? When u go? Thinking of u. Px* I know she means well but I hate that last phrase. Trotted out for bereavement and terminal illness, whenever it's hard to know what to say. It makes Lori's absence and our plans feel more sinister.

Go Thurs, I text back. *Will keep in touch x.*

Our number flashes up on the kiosk at the end to the left. I hand over the visa forms, the letter of invitation from the British consulate, the hotel confirmation, the flight details – all arranged by Edward at Missing Overseas – and our passports. A small sign in the corner of the screen shows the prices for the visa service. Three rates. Rush, Express, Standard. We are Rush, next day pick-up, the fastest possible way to get the documentation. The highest fee. The clerk reads carefully through Tom's application and checks his passport. Then she picks up mine. My mind is dancing about. I need to buy hand wipes and medicines to take, organize after-school club for the boys for the next three weeks, get some Chinese currency.

The clerk looks at my passport and the form, then says, 'The photo here on passport is more than six month old and you have same on visa application. You need more recent one. Less than six month.'

Oh, God. I'd hoped to save time using the spare photo left over from last time I renewed my passport. The whole edifice of plans teeters. The office shuts at three for applications. Coming back tomorrow will mean...

'You can do one here.' She points. At the back of the room is a photo booth. Tom has change. I sit in the booth and follow the instructions on screen. *No smiling, no hair over the face, no glasses obscuring your eyes.* How about crying? I am past caring and choose the first image, even though I look like a serial killer.

The clerk cuts one of the pictures off and places it on my application, giving me the old one. She hands Tom a receipt and clips everything together.

Outside, the wind funnels down the street,

sharp and cold, making my eyes water. I zip my jacket up, stick my hands in the pockets.

'I'll see you Thursday,' Tom says.

'You need to be here before four o'clock tomorrow to collect the visas,' I say.

'Sure.'

'Let me know if there's a problem,' I say.

'It'll be fine,' he says, an edge to his voice. 'See you.' He walks off, the breeze blowing his hair, his coat flying out.

I make for the tram stop and, as I turn the corner, see one pulling in ahead. Running as fast as I can, I dodge shoppers and people in office clothes, the buskers and hawkers who fringe the square. Breathless, a pain behind my breastbone, I reach the platform just as the tram gives a mournful hoot and moves off.

'Shit!' I attract glances from other passengers.

It shouldn't matter that I missed it, there'll be another before long, but it feels like everything is stacking up against me. I stand there, fed up, sweaty and shivery at the same time, and tense with frustration.

CHAPTER TWENTY-ONE

Our flight is from Manchester to Chengdu with a change at Schiphol, Amsterdam. We leave at 17.40 and I've caved in to the boys' pleas to be allowed to come and see me off. Of course they were less than happy when we told them I'd be going. They begged to come as well, and then Isaac, who had been kicking the chair leg harder and harder as we talked, finally kicked me on the shin and told me I was a horrible pig and added, 'I hate you,' as Nick jumped up to remonstrate.

Since then Isaac has stuck to me like a burr. Gazing up at me with a solemn sometimes sullen face while I sort the laundry, holding my hand too tightly when we take Benji out, hovering on the landing while I'm in the shower. I've tried to reassure him, tried to snatch extra time to sit with him while he draws, to watch the latest episode of *Scooby Doo* with him, to read an extra bedtime story, but it is never enough.

And there are endless questions – *What if you can't find Lori? What if the aeroplane goes wrong?* The missing Malaysian plane has been all over the television. We rarely have the news on but they seem to imbibe it from somewhere. *What if it rains?* I'll get wet. *Where will you sleep? How long will you be?* Three weeks, that's all. *What if you get lost?* This is probably the heart of the matter, or a close second to *How can you abandon me?*

So by the time we get to the airport, I'm actually looking forward to five minutes' peace. In comparison, Finn is a piece of cake. Initially sad, but once I'd promised I'd be back in a little while, we'd all have a holiday and go on an aeroplane (all the while ignoring the look of astonished outrage on Nick's face that I hadn't cleared it with him first), he was mollified.

But, of course, as we reach the drop-off zone my stomach churns with apprehension and I feel a visceral urge to stay close to the boys, not to

111

walk away, not to leave them. What was I thinking of? I can't go. Tom could manage on his own, couldn't he?

Squashing my panic, I'm brisk and cheery and we all hug and I tell them in turn, 'I love you and I'll see you very soon.'

Nick says, 'We could park up,' and I say, 'No, you go. I'll be fine. I'll let you know when we land, yes. You both be good for Daddy,' I add. Isaac's eyes are watering. I pretend not to notice. A meltdown now would be horrendous. 'In you get, go on. Bye-bye.'

They climb back into the car and I wait on the pavement with my suitcase. The boys crane their heads round and wave with both hands as Nick toots the horn, parp parp parp-parp parp, and drives away.

I make my way to the check-in desks. There is no sign of Tom but I didn't expect him to be on time and promised myself I would not get wound up about it. What is irritating is that there is no place to sit while I wait. So I wander up and down dragging my case for the next twenty minutes, weaving in and out of travellers, until he appears.

He has a short-sleeved linen shirt on, a yellow colour that might not suit everyone but with Tom's sallow complexion it's perfect, and olive green cargos. Doc Martens too, brown boots. Like father like daughter.

The airport is stifling and I'm too hot with my long-sleeved cotton sweater and jeans. Maybe the plane will be cooler.

We check in our bags. I remember Lori's being

112

overweight but both ours are within the limit. We go through to security. The long queue snakes left and right up to the scanners but it moves quickly enough. We don't make small talk as we shuffle up to the front. I am filmed in sweat. We remove belts and watches, jackets. Place laptops and phones on the tray.

They search me thoroughly. I have to take off my shoes and a woman pats me down, checks my waistband, hairline and around my bra.

Coupled with the heat and the crowds, the overpowering stench of perfume from the duty-free mall that we're forced to walk through makes me want to heave. Imagine working in that every day – the glare of the lights, the lack of pure air, the chemical smells.

'We've an hour,' Tom says. 'I'll use the Wi-Fi.' He points to the desks.

'I'll meet you at the gates,' I say. 'I'm going to get a bite to eat.'

Around me, as I unwrap my sandwich, there are groups of holiday-makers, families and couples, some business types in suits with laptop bags, and a stag party in matching football shirts with rude names on the backs: *Twat*, *Dickhead*, *Arsehole*. Hilarious.

I chew slowly, hoping to settle my stomach, and take small sips of tea.

Two girls come in, backpackers by the look of them, clothes in clashing prints, bracelets, piercings and tattoos. I wonder where they're headed, have a stupid urge to go and make conversation, tell them to be sure to keep in touch with people back home, to pass on the numbers of new friends or lovers, to take care and stick together.

'Look at the state of that,' one of the stag party says. 'You'd have to be desperate.' The girls hear, we all hear, and one of them turns bright red, like she's been scalded. A surge of anger and something like shame flames hot inside me and I turn around and raise my voice to the man, 'Keep your nasty little comments to yourself, you sexist shit.'

This wins me a chorus of boos and jeers and foul language. No one else in earshot says a thing, though they're all aware of the scene playing out: glances fly between groups, people move in their seats or bow to whisper to their neighbours.

I imagine the bride-to-be: what must she be like to accept a proposal from *Fuckwit* or *Knobhead?* I conjure up some girl teetering on high heels with a startling spray tan, false eyelashes and a dress the size of a handkerchief, all feminine incompetence. And then I despise myself for thinking that – isn't the whole point that women should be able to be whoever they want to be, to dress however they like, without any censure?

With my own cheeks burning, I doggedly finish my tea, then find a seat in the concourse and wait until the gate is flagged up on the screens. I text Nick, *Love you, about to board xxx* and he replies, *Safe journey Love you too xxx.* I find my boarding card and walk along the corridor to the far end where a crowd has already gathered, most of them Chinese, and the sound of that unfamiliar language fills the air.

It's only an hour until we land in Schiphol for our connecting flight. We come down in dense fog and cloud. The land is striped with drainage canals and dotted with lakes. The airport is huge. The endless corridors, modulated announcements, glistening walkways and glittering shops remind me of some science-fiction dystopia, where everything is clean, shiny and powered by consumerism, dissent stifled by drugs. Signs advise it's a ten- or fifteen-minute walk between departure piers. There is a second security check. They take away our water and we go through the scanners again. A large group of Chinese people travelling together are laden with shopping bags and gifts.

I imagine Lori here, back in September, striking out on her own, full of excitement, a little on edge, maybe, as she tries to follow procedures.

On board there is a scramble for the overhead luggage space, people squashing in bags, others complaining to the cabin crew that there is no room.

Water is dripping from a panel in the ceiling. The cabin lights go out, come on then fail again, as does the air-con. The television screens on the back of the seats go blank and we are left with only emergency lighting. The captain announces they are attempting a repair and have sent for another onboard power unit in case it is needed. My elbows ache, jammed hard against the arm-rests. I affect resignation but my impatience and worry grow. What if the flight is cancelled, if we can't travel today? All the arrangements will have to change. The start of our search will be delayed.

At last the problem is fixed and we take off.

Tom is restless – no smoking on board. He gets a gin and tonic from the complimentary trolley service and, after a moment's hesitation, I do the same and am given an unidentifiable snack, two small biscuits that taste of fish paste. When the main meal comes, the combination of nausea and hunger makes it hard to know what to eat. I pick at the food. I have wine with it, thinking it might help me sleep, but I just get thirsty.

I've a flashback to a holiday together, Lori and I. Lori was seven and I'd saved enough for a week in the Algarve, a studio apartment on a complex with a pool. We were like little kids together that day, on her first flight, holding hands for take-off, sucking boiled sweets in case our ears popped, taking delight in the smallest things, the plastic cutlery and the tiny packets of salt and sugar.

We've never done this, Tom and I, flown together. The holidays we had as students were a couple of camping trips in the Lakes and, once, down to Cornwall. Then Lori came along and we'd no money. Then Tom left. There had been months of arguments, clashes. The nearest I ever came to understanding it was that he was trapped, confined, reduced by our circumstances. And he would thrash like a wild animal. And me? Wasn't I just the same – not angered but my life suddenly limited by the demands of a child? Were we too young? Or was he too young and me forced to become mature beyond my years? Was Tom simply too shallow, too incomplete with his messy, mean upbringing to rise to the occasion? While I, with my good-enough childhood, a good-enough relationship with my parents, had sturdier

116

foundations to weather the change in lifestyle. I saw my own impending parenthood as a gift, a wonderful experience. Albeit a shock.

Tom was excited at first. Almost manic. Fatherhood seemed to equate with any other life experience – he paid the subscription, was engaged, almost obsessed at first, then lost interest as it became repetitive, boring, relentless, so he let his membership lapse. He loves Lori, but he has hurt her, too. Let-downs and cock-ups. I was probably more upset than she was, all those times he was late or missing and she waited with her bag packed. I tried my best not to project. But who knows?

Tom falls asleep. I give up on rest and scroll through the films. Penny has recommended *Philomena*. I love Judi Dench and start watching before it really sinks in that it's about a mother searching for her child. Just as I am. The performances and the flashes of humour keep me watching, but it makes me cry (there is no happy reunion for Philomena), which doesn't help with the dehydration. The next time the cabin crew come with water, I ask for two, motioning to Tom who sleeps on, his face shrouded by his hair, long legs angled sideways.

We are flying into the light, meeting the dawn, but it's a night flight so the steward asks us to lower the window blinds and use our personal reading lights. Perhaps it's a sign of hope, that endless sunrise. We will land and someone from the consulate will tell us Lori is safe and well, just a little sheepish for all the bother she has caused, that she had a 'bare awesome' time in Nepal or

Hong Kong.

I must've slept because I'm startled awake by a misstep in my dream. Lori's in it and we're Skyping but I can't get the focus right and I try to adjust the screen, pressing buttons on the side. Then she says she has to join the stag do. And she shows me her T-shirt but I can't read the writing. It seems important but I can't understand a single letter of it, and then I'm awake with the endless rushing roar of the air-conditioning, like a thundering weir. My mouth is tacky, my stomach bloated.

We meet the lurch and pitch of turbulence. I feel the bucking of the aircraft, the kick and shift of the whole cabin, the way the panels shudder, as the wind buffets us time and again. I hold fast to the armrests and try to breathe slowly until things calm down.

Then we are closer. Across the aisle, someone raises the blind to blazing sunlight and I see the wrinkle of mountain peaks covered with snow.

We begin our descent.

CHAPTER TWENTY-TWO

As we're coming in to land, I peer out. It's as though everything has been smothered in grey, dusty gauze.

Through Immigration and Baggage Reclaim, we exit and find the car that has been booked to take us to the hotel. The air is warm and humid. People throng the pavements, pulling luggage,

118

talking loudly. Tom lights a cigarette as the driver heaves our cases into the boot, signalling to us to get in. Tom holds up his fag and the driver nods. Tom sits in front and the driver lights his own cigarette. In the back I open the window. There are no seatbelts. Policemen are monitoring the taxi rank, chivvying the drivers, shouting and waving to passengers in the queue to use both lines of cars. There is an air of urgency about it, as though it is imperative to disperse people as quickly as possible.

We speed through miles of high-rise developments along the expressway into town. Trees – palms, ginkgo and feathery ailanthus – line the roadsides. Taxis, coloured bright green, swerve in and out of the lanes, around scooters and bicycles and large SUVs in black or white. I taste dust, brassy, in my mouth. Everything looks strange, foreign.

It's a relief to reach the hotel lobby. The air-conditioning is on. The foyer is spacious, with glinting marble floors and red leather couches and huge Chinese porcelain vases, elaborately decorated. The walls are lined with gold brocade wallpaper.

We are greeted in English by the Chinese receptionist. Behind the desk a wall fresco in 3-D shows tiled pagoda roofs and stands of bamboo. At each end of the desk there are plinths with bonsai trees arranged among miniature landscapes made of pinnacles of limestone rock.

'Welcome to Chengdu,' the receptionist says. She pronounces it *Chungdu*. She is Chinese and wears a badge that reads *Melanie;* her English name. I remember Lori's blog, how her Chinese friends all had English names.

'May I take your names?' Melanie says.

'Maddox,' Tom says.

'And if I could take a copy of a credit card, please.'

Tom gives her his Visa card. He's paid for the rooms – we used some of Nick's redundancy money to cover my flights. I close my eyes. My legs feel wobbly, my head light. It's a quarter to seven in the morning back home, a quarter to two in the afternoon here. She's telling us about breakfast in the restaurants.

Melanie hands Tom a room key. 'Room 608. On the sixth floor,' she says.

'Two rooms,' I say.

'Excuse me?'

'We booked two rooms.'

Tom is grinning. As though there is something amusing about the situation.

Melanie checks on the computer, then asks us to wait a minute and goes through to the offices behind.

'We should get out and walk around,' Tom says. 'Daylight and exercise, for the jet-lag.'

We are meeting Peter Dunne from the consulate here at the hotel tomorrow and he will take us to the police officer in charge of the search for Lori.

Melanie comes back again, with an older man who wears the same uniform of black jacket, peach silk shirt and cream trousers. 'Mr and Mrs Maddox, I'm sorry for any confusion. You wish to book two separate rooms?'

120

'We did book two separate rooms,' I say.

'Very well.' He smiles and speaks to Melanie in Chinese, then leaves her to it.

'Please,' she says, 'the card key?'

We wait another few minutes while she cancels, then re-enters our details and Tom's credit card number, and sorts out two rooms for us.

'Very sorry for the mix-up,' she says. 'You are on the seventh floor, rooms 704 and 715. Enjoy your stay. Lifts are over there.' She gestures to her right.

Outside the lift a TV screen plays an advert for some sort of liquor. Inside, the walls are burnished mirrors and there is another smaller screen above the door – the advert changes to coverage of some film awards, I can't tell what. I recognize some of the stars but the commentary is in Chinese.

We find our rooms, mine on the main corridor, Tom's round the corner.

'Meet up in an hour?' Tom says. 'Get some air.'

'OK.'

'And don't fall asleep,' he warns. 'Worst thing you can do.'

I yawn. 'I know.'

Apart from the fact that the signs in the room are in English and Chinese, and for the water cooler in a corner, I could be in any hotel on any continent on the planet. The same packaged toiletries in the bathroom, fluffy white towels, the cupboard with iron and trouser press, the easy chair and the king-size bed with far too many pillows.

The windows look out over the back of the hotel

to high buildings opposite, their details muted in the mist. Between us is a derelict site, a few long huts, their roofs full of holes. And nearby there are three enormous piles, one of bricks, one of timber, the third of tangled metal. Along the nearest edge of the plot are rows of scooters. Perhaps they're for hire. Chain-link fencing rings the area.

I slide open the double glazing and noise fills the room – the roar of traffic, the shriek and blare of car horns, the clank and rumble of a bulldozer and a truck at work in the lot below. I can hear music, too, and snatches of birdsong, cries, whistles and squeaks in the midst of the thundering sound.

The bed looks so tempting, but instead I unpack my suitcase and have a shower. The body-wash smells of jasmine. I put on light clothes, three-quarter length linen pants and a loose blouse. Find my sunglasses. I text Nick. *Arrived OK. Hot and sticky.* Then I delete the last bit, it seems irrelevant. Add *xxx*.

Studying the map I printed off from Google, I can see that to the east and south of the hotel, in a couple of blocks, there's a park by the river.

When Tom raps on my door, twenty minutes after the 'hour' is up, I suggest it to him.

Outside the heat is fierce, despite the cloud. There's a chemical, metallic taste in the air and my tongue feels gritty. I haven't put sun cream on and wonder whether to go back but can't make a decision, so stop trying.

The streets are busy, the pavements crowded, the roads congested. There's an energy in the rush. I imagine New York must be like this, with the bustle and the constant blast of horns. It's a bit like London, too, except in London there's a melting pot of people. Here everyone is Chinese. As Lori wrote: *it's like another planet, not just another country. And I am the alien.*

Eyes appraise us, sliding over us, then back, double-takes as we pass. Not one but two of us. Tom's height, his hair, attracting interest, the dirty blond, the length of it. All the men have short-cropped hair. The women have contemporary cuts, sometimes long, flowing locks; I see quite a few with coloured hair, burgundy or auburn, but the only blonde woman I see wears Goth make-up and stands out.

From behind they might never guess that Lori is not Chinese: she's slim and short and dark-haired.

Underfoot there is a mishmash of patterned concrete, block paving, textured tiles, slabs and bricks, much of it cracked and uneven. There are sections with raised dots or lines that are less comfortable to walk on. I think these must be for people with visual problems, like at home.

At the junction, the road we meet is six lanes wide, three in each direction, with a smaller cycle lane by the pavement. There are traffic lights and a crowd gathers, waiting to cross. The lights opposite begin to count down 10, 9, 8... People edge and jostle. Then the lights change to green for us and we begin to walk, but there's a blur of movement, loud toots to my left. A stream of cars and scooters and bicycles are riding at us. Tom grabs my arm and pulls me with him. 'They can turn right on red,' he says. We almost collide with a scooter that jinks past us.

As we reach the other side, traffic from the opposite direction is turning right and we have to wait for a gap and run, dodging the scooters and bikes that plait in and out of pedestrians.

On the corner there is a wide plaza and a shopping mall. Outside there's a giant screen playing something. I'm too busy concentrating on not getting run over to look at it for long. Everywhere skyscrapers thrust up, as tall as the ones behind the hotel. We continue threading our way through the crowd until we reach the next block and take a turn to the left.

Along this street there are places to eat, a spicy smell in the air, like star anise, and I catch a faint whiff of sewage as we walk. The small shops have apartments above, clothes hanging on balconies. In some places there are plastic stools and tables out on the pavement and people eating. I see noodles on one table and at another I spot a bowl of rice. Does Lori come here, eat here? *Spiciness is a bit of a euphemism. We're talking chilli at industrial concentrations.*

We stop at a pedestrian crossing, black and white stripes. A boy, about Isaac's age, stares at us. 'Hello,' he says.

'Hello,' I reply. His mother smiles and pats his hand.

'Hello, hello,' he repeats, his face alight with glee.

'Hello,' I say. Tom echoes me and sketches a bow. The woman laughs and the boy skips on the spot. Then a gap opens in the traffic and we cross, among the scooters that glide silently around us. They must be electric.

The trees along the edge of the pavement hang low and we have to stoop to go past the branches. A woman, her face wrinkled like a walnut, sells insoles for shoes, cigarette lighters and hairbands. There is a man on a motorized tricycle, the back piled high with greens.

My body is still travelling, a tremoring in my innards, in the marrow of my bones, droning in my ears. The ground ripples as I walk.

Another crossing, and then we reach the river. There's a promenade with a stone balustrade. Trees provide a canopy of shade – willows I know from home but the others I cannot name.

Construction cranes straddle the skyline and below, far below, the birds that gave them their name glide across the river, dive for fish. The Jinjiang river is a milky green and cuts between pale stone walls. The white cranes gather along the edges, fly up and perch on the parapet, paddle in the weeds. They are smaller, prettier than the herons at home, and each has a few white feathers sprouting from the back of its head, like a scraggly ponytail. Tom says they're storks, then looks them up on his phone and tells me they're little egrets.

My neck aches and I've a dull, thudding pain in my temples. My eyes feel glassy.

A pagoda frames the entrance to the park, richly carved and coloured. At ground level there is a deep wooden cross-bar that we have to step over and another at the far side. Flower displays greet us. Paths split off among bamboo groves. We follow one round and every so often smaller paths lead to different sections; we glimpse teahouses and a waterfall, an area of sculptures made of bamboo.

It's still busy in the park but the cacophony of the traffic is muted and the shade from the trees makes the atmosphere more pleasant. In an open area, a calligrapher draws characters in water on the ground with a brush as tall as he is. A ring of children around him try their hand. The characters are ephemeral, drying in minutes. Gone like the breath of a breeze in the trees.

I think of Lori's post: *Call me Bird's Net Jasmine.*

The bamboo groves have been landscaped with rocks and ground-cover plants and small labels identify each variety. The largest plants have canes as thick as lampposts. 'Graffiti,' Tom says, pointing out where past visitors have scratched their names on them. I spy a sign that admonishes, 'No Scribbling'. At the edge of the path a woman has a stall and is drawing with spun sugar. The filigree signs of the zodiac that Lori mentioned. The boys worked ours out back in January when the school had a Chinese New Year celebration. The fact that Lori was in China and that 2014 was the year of the horse, Lori's sign, made it all the more exciting for them. Finn was delighted to be under the sign of the dog (the same as me). Isaac was born in the year of the rat and Nick the monkey.

People gawk at us and a couple say, 'Hello, where are you from?'

'England,' Tom says.

'Ah! First time in China?'

'Yes.'

In China, everyone is into everyone else's business – there doesn't seem to be any notion of privacy. People stare and interrupt and join in and interfere all the time.

'Our daughter,' I say, 'she is here.'

'University?'

'Teaching English.'

We haven't got the leaflets yet or I would show them. *Missing – please, have you seen her?* Edward at Missing Overseas has arranged for them to be printed here in English and Chinese and delivered to our hotel. I can imagine how these expressions of welcome, the interest in us, would curdle in the light of them.

I need to pee. Luckily there are plenty of public loos, unlike at home. But here the stink is over-powering. The toilets are the squat type, in cubicles. Do I face forwards or backwards? I can't tell. Lori never blogged about toilet etiquette, I balance on the white-tiled footplates undo my drawstring and crouch, pulling my trousers away from my ankles, gagging at the smell of old piss. There's no toilet paper. I read about this but forgot to bring tissues or hand wipes out with me. I wriggle my clothes back up and press the foot pedal for the flush. There is a cold tap near the entrance – I rinse my hands and flap them dry.

In the next clearing there's a teahouse, a large wooden pagoda with seating in front, plastic chairs and square tables. Most are occupied. People are playing mah-jong or cards, eating snacks. Large vacuum flasks are on or beside the tables – perhaps they hold tea or hot water. The noise is dense, percussive, the chatter, and the clatter of tiles. A waiter walks among the patrons clicking metal tongs together.

'We'd better ring the consulate when we get back,' Tom says, 'tell the guy we've arrived.'

'I wish we'd insisted on meeting this afternoon,' I say, 'to get things moving.' But we had been persuaded that it would be wiser to wait until the day after our long journey.

We take a small path that leads onto a hump-back bridge where there is a gazebo above a fish pond.

'Stop a minute?' I say.

I lean on the bamboo bench there, burnished smooth with wear, and peer down. The water is dark, reflecting the delicate tracery of leaves in the canes high above. Large koi, deep orange, some golden, weave and turn. Umbrella plants and ferns, the sort of things we'd keep as houseplants, ring the shore.

'How do you feel?' Tom says.

'Wiped out – like I'm still on the plane.'

He grunts agreement, gets out a cigarette. I drink some water.

Fatigue ripples through me and my legs soften. 'Head back?' I say.

As we follow the path round the outside of the park to the gate, music starts to play though some PA system in the trees, a flute, I think, cool notes that tremble and dip, then climb.

The calligrapher is there still with his brush, the characters on the ground ghosts beneath our feet.

CHAPTER TWENTY-THREE

Retracing our steps, we pick our way among the crowds along the side street, my eyes roaming over all the faces, the dark heads of hair. I ignore the stares I get in return, the expressions of interest and open-mouthed curiosity.

That's her! My stomach falls. 'Lori!' I grasp Tom's arm, clutching tight. Yell her name – 'Lori! Lori!' Ahead of us, walking away.

I let go of him and chase after her, knocking into people, running out into the road when the throng is too busy to get through, my bag bumping against my hip, the dusty air dry in my mouth.

'Lori! Lori!'

I reach the corner where a woman sits, selling orange fruits laid out on a blanket. Panting, I search frantically, right then left, eyes running over heads and faces. Tom is at my side.

'It was her!' I say. My heart is hammering in my chest. 'I can't see her now.' I bend forward, brace my hands on my knees, a stitch stabbing my side.

'Was it?' he says. 'Are you sure?'

I only saw her for a moment, her hair, the back of her head, the right height...

'Jo, are you sure?'

How to answer him? That second, that first glimpse, I was convinced. Every cell in my body sang with recognition. I knew. But now? A few yards down the street a woman throws a bowl of dishwater out onto the pavement. I watch the water flow across the stone into the gutter and feel my certainty drain away.

'I don't know.' I straighten up, push my hands into the small of my back, then look up past the trees and the tangle of overhead wires where the cloud still blankets the sky.

The world keeps turning.

A couple, young and beautiful, arms wrapped about each other, walk past. An elderly woman with a baby in a buggy stops to buy fruit.

My throat aches, so dry it feels as if there are blades in it. I open my bag and get out the water.

'Hello, hello.' Two little girls with, I think, their grandmothers. Tears burn my eyes.

'Hello,' Tom says.

They giggle and one of the women says, 'English?'

I turn away, teeth gritted, trying to breathe through my nose.

'Bye-bye,' Tom says. 'Bye-bye.' He touches my elbow, edges us away and back onto our route to the hotel.

Was it Lori? Already the image I have is fading, like a dream, the detail evaporating, melting away. Wouldn't she have heard me when I shouted? There is a film, *Don't Look Now*, with Donald Sutherland and Julie Christie in it. The couple have lost their child. She is dead and they are in Venice and keep glimpsing her, always in the distance, elusive. A bright shock of colour in her red coat.

We eat in the hotel restaurant, on the top floor with views over the city. The menu includes Asian and European dishes. Tom has steak and chips; I choose pork with noodles. It's all I can do to stay awake.

Back in my room, I call Nick. The boys are still at school. I tell him the flight was OK, the hotel fine. I don't mention my chasing after an apparition. 'I'm going to bed soon. Give my love to the boys. I'll try you tomorrow after we've had the meetings.'

It's dark now. The building opposite is illuminated; changing neon colours cascade in lines down the edges, reminding me of the fairy lights we had on sequence. Lori loved the flashing but I always changed it to a steady glow.

I pour some water but it's tepid and barely touches my thirst. In bed, the mattress is hard, unyielding, and my hips ache. I still feel the thrum of motion, and the drone of the plane engine echoes in my head, and when I sleep, I dream of flying, beating my arms to rise with the egrets up and above the cloud, into the sun.

CHAPTER TWENTY-FOUR

Peter Dunne, the consul, is balding and tanned, with short silver hair and a close-clipped beard. He wears a white chambray shirt, open at the collar, and black trousers. Wire-rimmed glasses. Some citrus type of cologne. His greeting is warm and sympathetic as he shakes hands and checks that everything is OK with our accommodation.

We meet in a private lounge on the ground floor of the hotel. He orders tea, asking if we want black or green. We choose green. It is grassy and refreshing.

He checks his watch and explains we're expected at the police station in an hour.

'There are some things we can sort out now before we meet the police,' Peter Dunne says. 'You've arranged to have posters and leaflets printed?'

'Yes,' Tom says. 'We've draft copies here.' He pats 'the file', the growing sheaf of papers related to Lori's disappearance. 'Just need to email the document to the printer and they'll do them for us overnight.'

'May I see?' Peter Dunne says.

Tom finds a copy and Peter Dunne reads it through. It's similar to the text on the Missing Overseas website, but also gives a number for the PSB, the Chinese police, that Edward at Missing Overseas found for us.

'Good,' Peter Dunne says. 'And you've got an interpreter for yourselves?'

'Yes,' Tom says. 'Missing Overseas have found someone for us. We're meeting him this afternoon.'

'I've brought you a city map,' Peter Dunne says. 'It's in English as well as Mandarin – there are useful numbers and so forth on the back.' He unfolds it and shows us the three ring roads. Points to where we are, near the second.

'Thank you,' I say. 'We want to talk to Lori's

friends. Dawn's getting people together for us this evening.'

'Excellent,' Peter Dunne says. 'My understanding is that the police have already spoken to them and we should hear about that in the meeting. I would like to stress that the police will be in charge of the investigation and they will determine the direction of enquiries. Anything you feel might be relevant, please tell me and I'll pass it on to the investigator.'

'Yes,' I say. 'Also we want to visit Lori's flat.'

'Of course. I'll explain that to the PSB.'

'We've heard nothing from them in all this time,' Tom says, 'apart from the fact that they checked her apartment—'

'Hopefully anything further they do know will be made clear,' Peter Dunne says. 'Had there been any breakthroughs, I can assure you we would have heard and you would have been informed. If you will address any concerns, queries and so on through me, we can ensure things go as smoothly as possible and that nothing gets lost in translation, as it were.' His voice is light, his manner gracious, but there is warning in what he is saying. 'The authorities are understandably cautious in cases like this. Imagine if the situation was reversed and a Chinese family came to the UK looking for their daughter. We would expect them to understand that the police are the investigating authority and have the resources, experience and, most importantly, the legal powers to undertake a comprehensive inquiry. And for the family to be guided by them as to campaigning activities.'

He adjusts his glasses, then tugs at his shirt

cuffs. 'The authorities are committed to resolving the situation. Chengdu is a growing city, a hub of economic development, eager to welcome overseas partnerships, foreign visitors and workers. They bend over backwards to extend hospitality to the international community so they're understandably concerned that Lorelei is missing.'

'What publicity has there been here?' Tom says.

Peter Dunne twists his cup to and fro. 'The consulate has issued an appeal for information.'

'Where?' Tom says.

'On our website, on the Chamber of Commerce site and on English-speaking networking sites.'

'How do people know it's there? They have to visit these sites?' Tom says.

'Yes.'

'Can't we get it on television – in the papers?' Tom says.

'I hope so. That's one of the matters we'll discuss today,' Peter Dunne says. 'It's a sensitive time. The anniversary of the Tiananmen Square massacre is coming up – twenty-five years.'

My first encounter with Tom as I drummed up petition signatures and publicized our vigil. His prediction: 'When the Chinese government have had enough, they'll clear the lot of them out. Water cannon or whatever. None of this will make a bit of difference. Put money on it – the protest is quashed, the Commies carry on and you have a drink with me.'

'You want me to bet on people's lives? Talk about shallow.' Then the horror unfolding. The tank man with his shopping bag. The ruthless slaughter.

Our first date.

'So you're saying we're not free agents?' Tom's

got his knees crossed and swings his foot. It reminds me of a cat waving its tail, a sign of mounting aggression.

'I'd be lying if I told you otherwise,' Peter Dunne says. 'I'm a diplomat, and that's what I'm here for, to make communication, co-operation, work as well as possible. I promise I'll do everything I can to get the action we want from the PSB and the media.'

His phone beeps and he answers, speaks briefly in Chinese, then tells us the car is ready.

The air is almost solid, a thick, steamy heat, as we step outside and walk to where the car waits. The haze remains thick over everything. Inside, the big, black SUV is comfortable and pleasantly cool.

Peter Dunne sits up front with the driver and we are in the back. The journey is, slow, erratic. Short bursts of speed are curtailed by sudden braking and long waits until we lurch forward again. A stop-go, stop-go, stop rhythm. The traffic is bumper-to-bumper and scooters and bikes weave in and out. There are lots of taxis, green saloons. We draw up beside one and I can see, painted on the bonnet, a picture of a panda clutching bamboo. The cab driver is shaving. We race away and then we're flung forward when our driver hits the brakes to avoid a car cutting in from the left. A chorus of horns screams. My hands are gripped in my lap, my stomach tense – I'm not a great back-seat passenger at the best of times. An emergency siren starts up, a lazy chime that rises and falls as though someone had slowed down a British version to 33 revs per minute and channelled it through an ice-cream van.

'This is the second ring road,' says Peter Dunne, pointing to the overhead bridge that crosses the junction. 'It was completed with these new elevated sections last year.'

'Lori posted pictures of it,' I say. 'She can see it from where she lives.'

'That's right,' he says. 'There's a bus service on the ring road – it's a good way of getting about. It connects to the Metro, which is closer to the city centre.'

'How long have you been in China?' I say.

'Fifteen years,' Peter Dunne says.

'It must have changed a lot,' Tom says.

'Beyond recognition,' Peter Dunne says, 'with the explosion in economic growth, construction, infrastructure. Immigration here is mainly Chinese, coming in from the countryside and smaller towns in their thousands. The population's seven million in the city itself, fourteen million in the municipality, and growing.'

An industrial revolution for the twenty-first century. Not unlike what happened in Manchester in the nineteenth but at a far greater pace and on a much bigger scale. Through the window I watch the crowds on the streets and think of the massive changes they're living through, coming from paddy-fields and apple orchards, from rearing pigs and chickens to a world of marble-floored shopping malls and the Metro, to disposable income and the daily commute.

We turn left and the traffic halts again. In the shadow of the flyover, under the ramp, there is a paved area with some planters around the edge and, in the middle, half a dozen people are moving in formation, one arm slowly lifting, elbow bent, hand cupped, head bowed. Tai chi perhaps. Then we sprint forward and they are gone.

CHAPTER TWENTY-FIVE

The car makes its way down a narrow, tree-lined street, with shops at ground level. The buildings here are older, five or six storeys high, clad with coloured tiles. Most of the balconies are hung with laundry. A man with a conical hat is sweeping the pavement with a broom.

We turn into a gap between two buildings leading to a parking area. There is an automatic barrier across the entrance and a guard box at the side. The driver speaks to the guard and the barrier goes up. A row of police cars is parked along one wall; they have white bodywork with a red stripe along the sides and a fancy crest, a bank of red and blue lights on the roof.

The driver parks. We get out and follow Peter Dunne back to the street. The police station, a white-tiled block with a blue sign outside, is smaller than I expected. Inside is the reception area, a white room with a low ceiling and a long fake-marble counter with *Sub Branch of the Chengdu Municipal Public Security Bureau* written across the front. Behind the desk is a row of officers in black uniforms, one in civilian clothes, each at a computer terminal. Peter Dunne speaks to one and shows his ID. The man makes a call.

We wait on computer chairs in front of the counter. Facing us on the back wall is a large crest, like the ones on the cars, a garland of leaves around a silhouette of the Great Wall and five gold stars. There are several blue signs around the room with black and white Chinese writing. I can't read any of them apart from the plaques in English on the doors: *Duty Room, Training Room, Registration Area* and *Offices*. On the end wall there is a colourful poster of the young Mao, surrounded by flowers, no doubt proclaiming some message of exhortation. There's a water cooler in the opposite corner of the room, near to a rotating fan. And a clock on the wall. Three large potted plants provide a little greenery.

One officer has a book open and is copying characters from it onto a pad of paper. He gets up to answer the phone each time it rings, having to undo the plastic buckle on his belt, which is laden with equipment, and adjust it each time. He is too skinny or the belt too heavy.

It is hot, my hair sticking to the back of my neck. The fan doesn't do much more than stir the air around; the breeze, is warm, not cool.

Tom tips his head to the Chairman Mao picture. '"Let a hundred flowers bloom."' I shake my head, I don't know the reference. 'It started out as a way of encouraging criticism,' he says, 'and once people had put their heads above the parapet–'

A man comes through, short, stockily built, wearing smart, pressed trousers and an open-necked white shirt. He speaks to Peter Dunne and they shake hands. Then Peter Dunne introduces us: 'Mr and Mrs Maddox, this is Superintendent Yin.'

The policeman takes my hand. His grip is faint, barely a squeeze.

'Nǐ hǎo,' he says to each of us. Hello. And we reply likewise.

Superintendent Yin takes us through the door marked *Offices* and into a small room. It is bare, functional. There are half a dozen white plastic chairs arranged around a trestle table. A water cooler in one corner, a pedestal in another with a pot of spiky succulents on it, a clock on the wall.

Superintendent Yin sits at the head of the table with Peter Dunne to his right, Tom and I opposite the diplomat. Superintendent Yin has a folder. He flips it open and my heart contracts at the picture of Lori, paper-clipped to a printed form full of Chinese characters.

Superintendent Yin speaks and Peter Dunne translates: 'Superintendent Yin will give you an update of the results of the inquiry to date.'

The policeman refers to the pages in the file as he talks, and it looks to me as if he's reading verbatim what is written there. He pauses and dips his head, signalling to Peter Dunne that he should interpret for us.

'After visa and passport-control checks showed that Lorelei had not left the country, the police visited her apartment and, as you know, found it empty. The door was secure and there was no damage. There was no passport found. Interviews with her friends in Chengdu did not provide any explanation for her disappearance. There has been

139

no response from her mobile phone and attempts to trace that have not yet...' Peter Dunne hesitates, as if he's working out a better way of explaining what's just been said '...yielded results.'

'What about the English school?' I say. 'Five Star. Why didn't they report her missing, if she suddenly wasn't turning up for work?'

Peter Dunne relays the question. There's a long reply from Superintendent Yin. Then Peter Dunne says something else, gesturing to Tom and me. The language is full of vowels, with *sh-shing* and *ch-ching* consonants, the pitch swooping up and down. The two men go back and forth and I try to work out the meaning from their body language. Superintendent Yin looks solemn, a little blank, even, as if he is the reluctant partner in the conversation. Peter Dunne is leaning forward, exerting pressure, perhaps. At last he sits back, places his palms together on the table. 'So,' he says, then turns to look our way, 'here's the thing...' That phrase sounds odd coming from him, one of those picked up from American TV that has now gone global. *We need to talk. Back in the day.*

'...Five Star English is not actually a registered school or an official agency.'

'What?' Tom says.

'It's a shell, a front for making money by getting visas for international workers in return for a fee,' Peter Dunne says.

Tom groans. 'So they don't exist, Five Star?'

'No.'

'And Lori?' I say. 'Does that mean she was working illegally?'

He hesitates, rubs his head with one finger.

140

'Freelance work is not permitted in China. International workers are expected to be employed – if they lose their job the right to remain, to temporary residency, also goes. The type of work Lori was doing, taking on clients herself, making arrangements directly with them, it's all part of the black economy.'

I wonder how she paid for the visa – out of her first wages? Or did she use some of the money Tom sent? Did she understand it was illegal?

'Have they spoken to whoever sold her this visa?' Tom says.

There is more to-ing and fro-ing between Peter Dunne and the policeman. Superintendent Yin's replies are getting terser. He must be pissed off at the situation.

'It is in hand,' Peter Dunne says eventually.

'Which means nothing,' Tom says.

'Exactly,' says Peter Dunne, 'but I don't think we'll get very far pursuing this at present.'

'Could her disappearance have something to do with this – this dodgy visa?' Tom says.

Superintendent Yin thinks this is very unlikely.

The policeman speaks again. Peter Dunne nods in agreement. 'Every year,' he explains to us, 'the police do a sweep of the bars and clubs that are popular with ex-pats, checking that people have the correct visa and are registered with the police. Some people just stay on after their tourist visa or their last work visa expires.'

The policeman speaks again.

'Yes, it is a big problem,' Peter Dunne says.

He says something else in Chinese and Superintendent Yin resumes his report. 'Enquiries continue and the last communication from Miss Maddox was on Monday, the seventh of April...'

Monday. Not Friday when she went to the party. But two days later.

'...at ... twenty past ten in the morning. When she texted a message to...'

Superintendent Yin swings his report round and Peter Dunne examines the entry. They swap words for a bit and then Peter Dunne says, 'Shona Munro.'

'Shona, yes,' I say. One of the friends, Lori mentioned her on the blog and in an email, *Shona makes jewellery out of waste material.*

'An invitation from Lorelei to meet on the Tuesday or Wednesday.'

Superintendent Yin speaks. Peter Dunne listens, then says, 'Shona replied on the Monday afternoon but heard nothing back from Lorelei.'

More from Superintendent Yin, and Peter Dunne says, 'The text message cannot be verified.'

'What does he mean?' I say.

'The message was sent from Lorelei's phone but they cannot be sure that Lorelei sent it.'

My skin goes cold. I shiver in the stuffy room.

Peter Dunne nods to Superintendent Yin and listens to what he says, then tells us, 'Lorelei was last seen in Chengdu on the Sunday evening, the sixth of April, when she taught one of her students at his home. The class finished at seven p.m.'

'Who was the student?' Tom says. 'What did they say?'

We wait for the translation. 'There was nothing unusual about the lesson and nothing out of the

142

ordinary, as far as Lorelei's demeanour or behaviour went. She said she would be there the following week. This is officially the last confirmed sighting of her – Sunday, the sixth of April.'

'We need to change that on the flier,' I say to Tom, 'on the website too.'

He nods. 'Is there anything else?' Tom asks the consul.

That seems to be it.

'What happens now?' I say.

'The search will continue,' Peter Dunne says, 'and Superintendent Yin says he is hopeful that Lori will be found safe and well. That she is travelling in China, perhaps, as she thought of doing.'

'Where are they looking?' Tom says.

An exchange in Chinese, and Peter Dunne says, 'These are operational matters. When any information comes to light you will be informed.'

'What about the gay scene – was Lori part of that?' Tom says. 'Is there a gay bar, a club? Have they talked to people there?'

Peter Dunne speaks to Superintendent Yin, who gives a smile, uneasy. I wonder if he is embarrassed.

'In due course,' Peter Dunne says.

'In due course? It's over two weeks since they were alerted,' Tom says. 'What are they waiting for? He does know she's gay? That she and Dawn were together?'

'He does.'

Superintendent Yin sits stony-faced.

'Is there going to be a problem?' I say to Peter Dunne. 'Will this affect how he does his job?'

143

'Not at all,' Peter Dunne says. 'Homosexuality is not illegal in China any more but is often viewed with suspicion, and there are no civil-rights laws protecting gay people as there are in the UK. But Superintendent Yin is aware of Lorelei's sexuality and her relationship with Dawn.'

Peter Dunne talks some more and finally Superintendent Yin gives a swift nod.

'I told him you will be visiting the apartment and talking to Lorelei's friends,' Peter Dunne says, 'and that the appeal is on the Missing Overseas website and we'll be doing some leafleting where Lorelei lives and where she spends her time to publicize the case. Do you have the draft for the leaflet?'

I find it. 'We need to alter the date,' I say, and pass it to Superintendent Yin who scrutinizes it. He points to the phone number for the police and they seem to be debating it. Then Peter Dunne changes some of the figures.

'Is there CCTV where Lori lives?' Tom says.

They speak, and Peter Dunne says, 'No, but there is a security gate at the entrance, and the guards there have been spoken to.'

'And?' Tom says.

'No help, I'm afraid.'

I swallow. 'I have things of Lori's, for the DNA.' I'd wrapped the freezer bags in brown paper, and now I take the parcel from my bag.

'Thank you.' Peter Dunne gives me a look of sympathy and explains to Superintendent Yin, who takes the bag from me.

The officer closes his folder, placing the bag I have brought on top of it. He speaks, looking from Tom to me.

'Superintendent Yin says that Chengdu is a very safe place,' Peter Dunne translates, 'and the Chinese people very law-abiding. The PSB will do all they can to find Lorelei.'

The policeman adds something.

'He wishes to emphasize that Chengdu is very safe,' Peter Dunne says.

Superintendent Yin gives a nod. 'Chengdu very safe,' he says, in a thick accent.

'Right,' Tom says sarcastically.

'It's true,' Peter Dunne says, unruffled. 'There is very little crime, compared to London, New York or Paris. This is a very safe city.'

'Try telling that to the dissidents,' Tom says.

'You're entitled to your opinions, Mr Maddox, and you're right, critics of the regime are dealt with harshly, but that has little to do with the situation we find ourselves in.' It's a smooth put-down. Tom compresses his lips and looks away.

We are dropped back at the hotel, and as soon as the car has left, I round on Tom. 'What are you playing at? We need the goodwill of that police-man, not to get up his nose making sarky comments.'

'He couldn't understand,' Tom says.

'He probably got the gist,' I say.

'What did we learn?' Tom complains. 'They're keeping stuff from us, Jo, the text to Shona, the lesson on Sunday. We should have been told about that as soon as they found out. They say we can be involved but it's lip service.'

'OK, so we know that now. We've met the man leading the search, we know they don't have CCTV at her place, that she was still here as

145

normal on Sunday. It all matters. Yes, we're here by invitation, on sufferance, if you like, that's just how it is. Just fucking grow up–'

He touches my arm.

'Don't,' I say, rearing back.

He glares at me, then turns away.

'The leaflets?' I break the silence.

'I'll sort it out,' he says. 'I've got all the details.'

'OK. I'll email Nick and Missing Overseas – get them to change that date.'

An enormous coach, full of tourists, pulls up in front of the hotel. I go in to beat the rush. The lobby is hushed and cool, a balm.

I amend the dates in my head: *Missing since 6 April 2014.* Today is 3 May, a Saturday. Lori has been missing for twenty-seven days. Four weeks tomorrow. So very long.

CHAPTER TWENTY-SIX

Anthony, the interpreter with whom Missing Overseas has put us in touch, meets us in the lobby after lunch. He's young, I estimate late twenties, and attractive, with the sort of sculpted cheekbones and even smile that you see on male models. He speaks excellent English with an American tinge. He looks as if he is dressed for business, in a crisp shirt and black trousers. We go over what we want him to do and he seems perfectly at ease, though I imagine it must be very different from most of the work he gets.

He has engaged a driver who, he explains, will want a tip as well as his fee. I give Anthony Lori's address. Dawn is going to show us round the apartment.

The car is a Lexus, slick and white. The driver uses satnav. We wait at lights where workers are erecting hoardings along the edge of the pavement. They wear yellow hard hats and blue boiler suits. The two closest to me are women.

'It's always busy,' I say, as we queue in heavy traffic.

'Yes.' Anthony turns back to us to reply. 'One day a week, each car is banned from driving to help with pollution.' The lights change and we creep forward. At the side, a parade of scooters streams past us.

'See the coats,' I say to Tom. Several of the riders wear their jackets back to front. It must afford them some protection from dust and draughts and the fumes. They remind me of Finn and Isaac dressing up as superheroes.

I see Dawn as we pull in to park. She looks much like her photos – about the same height as Lori but plump with frizzy red-brown hair, her face sprinkled with freckles, a broad nose and large round eyes.

She looks anxious as we meet. I feel the same: nerves grip my stomach. We shake hands, which feels formal, a little awkward. Hers is warm and moist.

We introduce Anthony to her.

'You've still not heard from Lori?' Dawn says.

'Nothing. We've been talking to the police this morning. They didn't give us much idea of where they're looking,' I say.

'Playing their cards close to their chests,' Tom says. 'Not exactly big on sharing. You kept your keys?'

'I never got a chance to give them back.' Dawn reddens, plays with her lip, pulling at it, a nervous tic, I think.

'You know Shona?' I ask her.

'Yes.'

I explain about the text. 'And on the Sunday Lori was teaching, so that's officially the last contact.' A couple carrying shopping bags approach and we shuffle aside to let them pass.

'Do you want to go in?' Dawn says.

There are two blocks, seven storeys high, with a courtyard in between. One building is tiled in cornflower blue, with white bands every other storey and a splurge of foliage on the roof – green shrubs and some climber frothy with purple blossoms. The other block is tiled jade green, almost turquoise. The buildings are remnants from older times, gaudy and shabby now, the grout stained. Rust marks streak down from all the metal balconies. The blocks provide splashes of colour in contrast to the skyscrapers towering round, which are dun and black, grey and brown and silver, a monochrome palette for the new century.

Around the outside at ground level there are shops. Halfway along the roadside, where we are standing, there is a gateway with an automatic barrier for cars and a small security booth.

We file after Dawn through the entryway, past the security box where the guard is eating his

148

lunch, to the blue building. He watches us pass, expressionless.

The lift is an old-fashioned design with an outer door and an inner one like a cage that concertinas. Apprehension makes my jaw and hands tense. I flex my fingers. Every day Lori would be here, in this exact space, travelling out to work, to see her friends, coming back to rest, to sleep.

'Was it a shock, Lori breaking up with you?' I say.

Tom raises his eyebrows at me. Maybe I am being personal but I want to know. It may have something to do with Lori's disappearance a few days later.

'At the time.' Dawn plucks at her lip. 'But things had been up and down. Maybe I should've seen it coming.' She has that rising inflection on everything she says, so it all sounds like she's questioning, like there's some room for doubt.

'Was there any particular reason?' I say.

'Lori, she likes to party, a social life. It's hard for me, out by the third ring road. I wanted to spend more time together, just the two of us. She didn't like coming out there. It got a bit one-sided.'

I've no idea how deeply Dawn felt about Lori. I don't know whether she is heartbroken. They'd been together just a few months.

I watch the numbers change until we reach the fifth floor and Dawn says, 'Here we go.'

Tom pulls back the lift doors in turn and we enter the hallway. It's dim, lit by a weak light recessed in the ceiling. I can smell cigarette smoke and spicy food.

149

'This way.' Dawn takes us to a door halfway along the hallway.

I want to knock, have Lori throw the door wide, laugh that crazy laugh with surprise at our visit, pull me into a hug. I take a breath while Dawn unlocks the door. I have to be strong.

Of course no one's there. But standing in the space, seeing Lori's possessions in turn, each one is like a punch, thumping home the reality of the situation. In her home, her absence is magnified. I say nothing for a few moments, my eyes roving, greedy, hungry.

A kitchen opens into the living room with a balcony at the end, looking out to the high-rises and the ring road alongside. The flat is furnished with orange plastic chairs and blue translucent plastic stools that double as tables. We've seen the same stools outside the snack bars along the streets. Lori's are strewn with bits of litter, paper tissues, food wrappers, empty drinks cans. An old couch has folding tray tables on thin metal legs in front of it. There are marks on the white plaster walls, where other furniture has rubbed off the surface paint, scuff marks on the door jambs, electric wiring loose in the ceiling where the lights once were. Chunks of plaster have come away in the square archway that divides the kitchen from the small living area. Mould speckles the corners. The flooring is vinyl. A Chinese knot, large and red, hangs on the longest wall. Its shape reminds me of a Celtic cross. Pinned to the wall beside it is the photo of us all she took on the weekend before she left for Thailand.

It's stifling. I feel sweat-prick my hairline, trickle

down my sides. 'Is there air-conditioning?' I ask Dawn.

'It doesn't work.'

In the corner beside the fridge there is a water cooler, a red tap and a blue one, like mine at the hotel, the settings read *heat* and *warm* but the lights beside the labels are both off.

'She turned the water off,' I say to Dawn.

'We do. No point in wasting the leccy.'

She blinks rapidly, perhaps worried about whether 'leccy' is acceptable or too frivolous in this situation. To reassure her I leap in, 'Makes sense.'

Above the water cooler, a noticeboard is scrawled with names and addresses, phone numbers, some in Lori's writing, the rest in Dawn's, probably.

Anthony hovers in the living room as we look round.

In the fridge I find tomatoes rotting, oozing liquid in the salad tray. Some beers. The crockery in the kitchen cupboard is all made of plastic or metal. I pick up one of the metal bowls – it's very light, tin, perhaps. I remember breaking Lori's mug. Isaac's expression.

The small bathroom has no bath, just an open shower with a drain in the corner, a washbasin and a toilet. Large plastic wall tiles have cracked and are held, together with lines of thick Sellotape. The sink is chipped around the rim, the chrome on the taps pitted with rust, the acrylic filler at the back of the basin black with mould. The mirror above is tarnished and peppered with white material. Flecks of Lori's toothpaste. No toothbrush.

A double bed with a black tubular steel frame almost fills the bedroom. The duvet cover is patterned with chrysanthemums, perhaps once vibrant yellow and red but now faded to pale lemon and pink. Chrysanthemums are a lucky flower for the Chinese. There was an article in the in-flight magazine. Chrysanthemums and goldfish, the colour red, the numbers six, eight and nine, the Laughing Buddha.

Lori's clothes are on an open rail opposite the end of the bed next to three stacking plastic boxes. Most are things she brought with her.

'Wouldn't she have taken more if it was a holiday?' Tom says.

I look through the boxes: vest tops, pants, T-shirts, shorts, socks and a bra. Under the bed her purple Docs and some Converse.

'Her backpack's not here.' Then I call to Dawn: 'Did she have any other clothes that you can remember?'

Dawn comes in and looks at the rail, frowning. 'Most of them are there. I can't think of anything particular.'

'Shoes?' Tom says, pointing to them.

'Her sandals. She wore them all the time.'

In Lori's bedside drawer I find a small plastic envelope with a photocopy of her passport, a booklet with her vaccinations listed, and a paper with contact numbers. Nick persuaded her to sort this out before she set off.

Two washing lines, made of nylon rope, are strung across the tiny balcony. A small plastic whirligig with pegs hangs from one. On it are

152

Lori's blouse, the crinkly red and lilac one, two camisoles, underwear. All stiff and dusty.

'She'd have taken that blouse,' I say, 'because it's light and dries in no time, if she'd gone on–' My throat catches. I swallow and look across to the taller blocks opposite. Three towers to the left are still concrete shells with a thousand blind eyes to be filled and brought to life, partly wrapped in green mesh and clad in scaffolding, cranes dipping and swinging above. Portakabins, where the migrant construction workers must live, are stacked two or three high around the edges of the site. Shirts and trousers are hanging out to dry. The towers straight ahead are completed, occupied, hundreds of windows, dozens of balconies festooned with laundry and vertical rows of air-conditioning units. To the right, at eye level more or less, runs the elevated ring road, part of the skeleton of the city. Someone is bouncing a ball, a basketball perhaps – it's heavy enough for the sound to travel over the horns, engines and bird calls. I hear a baby crying, a reedy wail.

Fear twists in my veins. Tom touches my shoulder. 'She'd have taken this,' I say again.

Tom and I begin to search the lounge, looking for any valuables, her phone or purse. Her passport, even, in case the police weren't thorough enough.

'Please,' I say to Anthony, 'sit down.'

'It's OK.' He smiles.

I don't know if I should insist, if he's being polite or if he's averse to sitting on the grubby couch, with its threadbare red and green checked cover, mottled with stains. Everything is sanded with dust, despite the frequent rain. Along with the pollution from the traffic, there must be millions of particles of cement and earth and brick dust from all the building work.

Some notes lie on one of the low stools. I sift through them – her plans for teaching. *Apple Balloon Cat Dog Elephant. How are you today? What is your name?* Copies of a weekly timetable. I show it to Dawn.

'Her students,' she says. 'She keeps a record of what they covered. Well, that was the plan.' Dawn's voice goes squeaky and she tugs at her hair with one hand. I have a glimpse into the life the two of them shared, Lori letting her paperwork slide. Did Dawn chide her? Dawn seems more settled, conscientious. I look at the paper: there are names and addresses blocked in with space below each entry to make notes. I work out Lori's routine. 'So, she'd be off Mondays and Tuesdays?'

'That's right.'

I put a copy of the schedule into our file.

A little bamboo bowl holds hair slides and elastic bands, scissors and pens, a friendship bracelet. 'Phone charger,' I say, holding up the cable, 'but no phone.'

I look at the photo on the wall. We're all smiling, even Isaac.

'What about her camera?' I ask Dawn. 'Where does she keep it?'

'There.' Dawn points to the tray table. 'She always has it handy.'

'And her laptop?'

'Usually around here somewhere.'

'The police didn't say they'd taken anything,'

154

Tom says, 'so she must have.'

Clearing my throat, I keep on looking.

Tom is going through all the stuff in the box by the couch. He sits back on his heels, pushing the hair out of his eyes. 'No phone, no passport.'

'Why leave her charger if she was going away?' I say. 'And she's hardly taken any clothes. Left stuff in the fridge to go bad.'

Tom tilts his head, raises an eyebrow.

'OK, maybe that's not so unusual, the food, but the rest...'

'She could have forgotten the charger,' Tom says.

I can hear Dawn on her phone, talking to someone about the meeting tonight.

Stepping back out onto the narrow balcony, I put my hands on the railing, look across to the ring road and gaze at the traffic, silvered in the dull white glare of the day. My fingers are grimy, everything rimed in the fine, gritty dust. What if she walks in now? Comes in breathless from her travels and finds us here, poring over her things, trying to work out where she's gone. Her dad and me, Dawn and Anthony.

'OK, so suppose she forgot the charger,' I say, as I go inside. 'Look what's not here: phone, backpack, laptop, camera, passport – all those things she'd pack for a trip away.' I know the whole holiday explanation, nearly four weeks later, looks a little thin. After so long she should be back in touch with someone, if not here in person. But what else am I to think? Tom looks at me, then leans back, his hair falling away from his face.

Before we leave, I empty the fridge of the perished food and Dawn takes it out with the other rubbish to bins on the landing. Under the sink I see cockroach powder. Two tubs of it and a pack of pink foam sponges. I've chucked the cloth from the sink so I break open the sponges and use one to wash out the fridge.

'We might as well turn it off,' Tom says.

I check the freezer section – if it's choked up it may flood, but there isn't much build-up of ice.

'I'll give you these.' Dawn passes me the key on a fob, a metal goldfish, the body segmented so it appears to wriggle if you shake it.

There is some debate about whether Anthony should accompany us to meet Lori's friends that evening.

'We won't really need a translator,' Dawn says. 'Everyone speaks English.'

'That's good,' I say, 'but I'm not sure we can find our way.'

Dawn says she'll meet us at the hotel and we can get a taxi or even a bus if we walk along to the ring road.

Anthony looks a little disappointed. He offers his services once more and I decline politely. 'Tomorrow, though, we should have the leaflets and posters. We'd like you to help us then, when we hand them out.'

I'm suddenly ravenous as we travel back to the hotel and ask Anthony to drop us at the mini-market nearby. I scour the place for something sweet and starchy, peer at the labels, searching for script I can read, try to decipher photographs. Tom exudes impatience from the doorway. I grab

156

a packet of 'pineapple sandwich cookies'.

Back in my room, the cookies turn out to be like fig rolls with pineapple in the middle, the coating soft, sweet and floury, like undercooked shortbread, cloying. I eat four of them with an instant coffee and feel satisfied for a while. Then queasy again.

CHAPTER TWENTY-SEVEN

When Dawn arrives, I show her the map Peter Dunne gave us and ask her where the bar is. She studies the map for a moment, then points. 'Near here. This road is where we get off the bus so we walk this way.' She traces the route. Her fingernails are bitten to the quick. 'Or we can get a taxi,' she says.

'We'll get the bus,' Tom says, 'be good to orient ourselves.'

'And we're going the other direction from Lori's flat?' I check.

'That's right. You're in between here. It's two stops either way.'

She guides us along the side streets past the park and to the junction where the ring road is. Tom asks about her job. She's teaching at an English training school. 'It's for kids,' she says, 'they come after ordinary school or at the weekends. I asked for the day off today.'

'What age are they?' I say.

'Four to twelve.'

'Did you know that Lori's visa was dodgy?' Tom says.

Dawn stops walking. Her face flames and her fingers pinch her lower lip. 'Kind of,' she says. 'She really wanted to stay and it was the only way she could do it.'

'And the people who arranged it, did she have anything to do with them afterwards?' Tom says.

'No. That was it.' Dawn signals to warn us about a scooter mounting the pavement and we hang back as the man, with a child on his lap, steers past us and parks outside a milk bar. Along this street, tree trunks, the pillars of a building and telegraph poles are all wrapped in a stretchy shiny gold material.

'How did she find people to teach?' I say.

'They found her,' Dawn says. 'Everyone wants to speak English. We get asked all the time.'

'And her other friends, the people we're going to meet, are they all teachers?' I say.

'About half and half. Shona's studying at the university, doing a master's, Bradley does translation for a software company, Rosemary is a teaching assistant at a school like mine, and Oliver teaches at the petroleum university. Rosemary and Oliver are both Chinese.'

'The petroleum university?' I say.

'There are loads of universities in Chengdu,' Dawn says, 'and some of them specialize in certain areas, like science or technology or finance.'

We wait at the lights to cross the road. There's a marquee going up outside the shopping mall. The frame is built and the roof canopy on. I watch a man on top of a stepladder: he has a foot on either side, and he swings the ladders along underneath the tent, like a stilt walker.

Once we've reached the other side, there are steps up to the middle of the ring-road carriage-way, where the bus runs. A woman is sweeping the bridge and a guard in a blue uniform, with a baton hanging from his belt, sits near to the ticket booth.

We offer to pay but Dawn has already slid money under the glass screen and the clerk gives her three counters in return. 'It's two yuan anywhere,' Dawn says.

Twenty pence.

'They can give change here but if you get a bus on the street you have to give the exact money – or pay more,' she adds.

We copy Dawn, swiping the counter on the toll gate at the bottom of the escalator to release the barrier. At the top the platform is enclosed in a transparent shelter with a curved roof. An electronic display shows when the next bus is due. I look at the route map to the side: the names are in Chinese and English. I try to memorize our stop, repeat each syllable silently. Look around for landmarks. There is the mall, and to the side of it two mirrored towers that cast shadows onto each other creating a trompe l'oeil: it appears as though there is a third ghostly black building between them.

The bus pulls in and the automatic gate opens so we can board. We make our way to the back where there are free seats. A television plays adverts for some sort of takeaway food outlet, then tooth-paste.

From this viewpoint I can see the scale of construction work along the route. The base of a huge crater, the size of a city block, has been levelled, its sides banked up, a swathe of red earth. Hoardings at the far side advertise what will come, *Forest Heaven Park,* illustrated with an image of glitzy towers.

I think of that poster, the construction workers in New York, having lunch on a girder halfway to heaven. No safety net, no harnesses or hard hats.

Every so often a ringtone goes off and each passenger answers exactly the same way, shouting, 'Wei?' into their phone.

A recorded voice comes over the speakers, 'The next stop will be...' I can't discern the destination, a string of syllables going up and down, abstract as musical notes.

I'm apprehensive about the meeting to come, these strangers who befriended my daughter, who were part of her new life. It may not be fair but I keep thinking they failed her. Failed to realize she was missing, failed to raise the alarm. The negligence or self-absorption of youth, perhaps. Or did they simply not care for her enough to worry?

The bus pulls in and I can see down a broad road below, lined with skyscrapers, gleaming in the light, choked by traffic. The horizon melts into the haze.

Two young women board. Both wear make-up, orange lipstick and black eyeliner, and gauzy dresses with pleated skirts, one in peach, the other in lemon. On their feet are the most elaborate shoes, tall wedges, jewelled and appliquéd. One pair has buckles around the ankle, the other a zip at the heel. Not the sort of thing you could run in.

Chengdu very safe city.

I look at my own simple leather sandals, blue T-bars, and notice that. Dawn wears flip-flops, with diamanté along the straps. I think of Lori's Docs, her trainers under the bed. She took her sandals so she couldn't have gone trekking or anywhere cold.

'This is us,' Dawn says, just before the recorded announcement, and we pass the two girls standing in the aisle.

Our travel discs go into a slot on the barrier at the bottom of the escalator and then we descend the steps to the street. A few people are waiting on scooters, perhaps collecting friends from the bus.

On the corner, a stall like a tall wheelbarrow has a tray of water full of peeled pineapples on sticks. The man there is diligently coring each one, leaving diamond-shaped holes in the fruit.

Don't drink the water.

It's a ten-minute walk from the bus to the bar. Dawn takes us into the foyer of one of the towers and in the lift up to the twenty-second floor.

'We call it the Ducks,' Dawn says. 'You know – like with bingo calling? Twenty-two – two little ducks. The woman who owns it, she's from London. She married a Chinese fella.'

When we exit the lift, the view from the walkway is astounding. All the towers here are bronze-coloured; they dazzle and shimmer. It's close to sunset and the cloud has thinned so a wash of pink brushes the scene. I grip the edge of the wall; it's chest height for safety, but still I dare not look down.

161

We hear the bar before we see it, music cranked up loud, a gravelly voice. It takes me a moment to recognize it as Paolo Nutini's.

There are four tables out front with a striped canopy over. A group sits at one of them, four young men. Dawn waves hello to them but doesn't stop to talk and we go inside. The room is lit with rope lights and red Chinese lanterns, and furnished with bamboo chairs, stools and tables. The walls are plastered with posters for concerts and festivals. At the far end, there's a table-football game. The place is empty, apart from the young woman behind the bar. She's tapping at her phone but stops when she sees us.

'Nĭ hăo,' Dawn says. 'These are Lori's parents. This is Alice.'

Alice nods quickly, then looks down. 'I'm very sorry,' she says.

'Thanks,' I say. There's a pause that lasts too long.

'Would you like drinks?' Alice says.

We buy beers, fetching them from the fridges along the wall. Tom explains that we're meeting Lori's friends and want to talk to them. Could Alice turn the music down when everyone arrives?

'Of course, no problem,' she says.

We sit outside, at the biggest table. The beer is cold, the bottles sweat. Paolo Nutini gives way to Lana Del Ray. While Tom explains to Dawn how we want to organize the meeting, I catch snippets of conversation from the foursome nearby. Talk of travellers' tales, visa nightmares, accounts of adventures in Vietnam and Korea. A mix of accents, Home Counties, Geordie, Spanish, Australian.

Some are loud, others mostly listen. I catch the smell of weed. They could be kids in any bar, anywhere on the planet, meeting up for drinks and company. Young, apparently confident, hopeful. Like Lori, thrusting themselves into unfamiliar situations, away from all the support they've relied on till now.

A Chinese couple arrive and Dawn fusses about. I can see she's awkward, anxious, as she introduces us to Oliver and Rosemary. Rosemary has waist-length black hair and wears a strapless blue maxi dress. She has butterflies tattooed on her shoulders.

'Rosemary?' I query her name.

'We all choose English names,' she explains, with a warm smile. 'It is easier for everyone. How are you?' Her smile drops and Rosemary looks concerned, a little fearful even, small frown lines puckering her forehead.

'OK,' I say. 'Worried, of course.'

'Yes,' she says. 'I am so sorry. This is very difficult situation.'

Oliver, listening, nods. He has a round face and podgy hands. He wears thick glasses, so his eyes swim in and out of focus when I look at them. He's dressed in a white polo shirt and chino shorts, a bracelet of large wooden prayer beads on his wrist.

Tom glances at his watch.

'We get drink?' Oliver says, as though he is asking my permission.

'Of course.'

While they're at the bar, Bradley arrives. He's come straight from work, he says, and apologizes for being a little late. He has a short-sleeved white

163

shirt and long trousers, proper shoes. 'You do translation?' I ask him, after accepting his expressions of sorrow about Lori going missing.

'That's right, for a software firm, not the most exciting material in the world.' He reminds me of Nick: he has a similar square face, regular features, with light brown hair, cut shorter at the sides. He wears a fine moustache and stubble covers his jaw line. I'm no good on American accents but I can tell his is not the Deep South or the Bronx so I ask him where he's from.

'Midwest,' he says.

'Kansas?' I say.

'Even smaller, the middle of nowhere.'

Oliver and Rosemary come back with bottles and Bradley greets them, then goes inside.

Dawn's been talking on her phone. 'Shona's running late,' she tells us. 'Someone's stolen her scooter. She should be about half an hour.'

'We might as well make a start,' I say.

Dawn nods. Tom goes in to ask Alice to turn the music down, and comes back out with Bradley.

I wonder if we need to explain to the other customers what's going on but the group of lads are already picking up their bags and phones, draining their bottles, ready to move on.

My stomach cramps as everyone waits expectantly, their faces grave, and Tom begins: 'As you know,' he says, 'Lori is officially a missing person and a campaign has been launched to find her. We met with the police yesterday and the guy from the consulate, and we went to Lori's flat today.' He nods at Dawn, who blinks and looks away. 'We're having leaflets done – like this.' Tom

164

spreads out some copies he printed off at the hotel. 'We should get them in the morning and we'll start giving them out tomorrow near her place. We'll have an interpreter with us. If you can tell us any other places that she went to regularly, we'll leaflet there too.'

'Hokey's,' Rosemary says. She looks to her friends to see if they agree.

'Yes,' Dawn says. 'It's a club we go to for birthdays and special occasions – it's popular with expats.' Her face is drawn, pale, and she keeps touching her lip.

'We'd have to go of an evening,' Bradley says.

'Tomorrow night, then,' I say.

'What about online too – the forum on Chengdu Living?' says Bradley.

'And GoChengdu,' Dawn says.

I write it all down. We'll pass the suggestions back to Edward at Missing Overseas, who will co-ordinate all the media appeals.

'The consulate have notified the British Chamber of Commerce,' Tom says.

Most of them look blank at this but Bradley nods. 'The business community network. We have an American one too.'

'Any other physical places?' Tom asks.

'Maybe the university?' Rosemary says. 'Sichuan Normal University, where Shona studies.'

'It's like the main uni for international students,' Dawn says.

'Are there any gay bars she likes?' I say.

Dawn nods. 'Yeah – one we went to a few times. I can show you where it is.'

'The police have told us the last verified sighting

of Lori was on the Sunday evening,' Tom says, 'when she was teaching, and the last communication was a text on the Monday.'

I hate these phrases: *verified sighting, last communication.* They toll in my head, formal and final.

'None of you have heard from her since?' I check.

A general shaking of heads.

My throat's dry and I take a drink. Condensation drips onto my knee. The beer is already warmer. The sky is growing duller, a tangerine sheen to the light.

'It's, like, where can she be?' Dawn says suddenly, tears standing in her eyes. Bradley squeezes her shoulder. Rosemary clasps her hands together and Oliver looks away, his discomfort almost palpable.

Tom clears his throat.

I find the rota and pull it out, put it on the table. 'If anyone can help us leaflet at any time, please put your name down. I know you've all got jobs but even an hour or so – we'd really appreciate it. We hope to arrange a press conference soon. Spreading the word is the most important thing. And we want to make sure we've got everyone's numbers so we can keep in touch. Our numbers are here.' I point to where I've copied them onto the paper. My hand is shaking.

'Sure thing,' Bradley says. He does a late shift, he explains, starts at 2 p.m. so at the end of his day he's able to liaise with the company's American wing, who are just arriving at work. And he has other appointments this coming week, but he can

166

come around with us tomorrow night and Thursday morning.

The others consult their schedules on their phones. Dawn's time is most restricted – she's doing extra hours – and she begins to fret, apologizing. I do my best to reassure her: 'You've already been a great help.'

Oliver can join us on Monday morning. And Rosemary all day Wednesday and Thursday.

'We'd like to talk to you all individually,' Tom says, 'to try to find out as much as we can about what was happening around the time Lori went missing.'

Oliver asks if we can see him first – he has an English lesson to get to. Unlike Rosemary's English, his is hard to follow, heavily accented.

Shona arrives. She's painfully thin, very tall with light blonde hair cut short. She wears a vest top under denim dungaree-shorts. The bones of her clavicle jut out amid strings of beads, all in different materials, sizes and colours. Despite the fair hair, her skin is tanned and she has surprising grass-green eyes. She stoops slightly as she greets us. Her wrists are ringed with bracelets, which clink when she shakes hands.

Dawn goes to buy her a drink and Shona sits down, folding herself into a chair and propping her feet on the crossbar of the table so her knees almost touch her chin.

Tom gives her an update and explains about the rota. She rolls a cigarette, pin thin.

Given we still have the bar to ourselves, I suggest to Tom that we talk to people individually at the spare table opposite, and the friends can have a catch-up while they wait.

'Or we could just do it all together,' Tom says quietly. 'It's only five of them.'

I disagree. 'There may be stuff they don't want to share – like the bust-up with Dawn.'

He shrugs, gathers together the file, and we move over. I fetch fresh drinks and we begin with Oliver. He tells us he missed the party on the Friday. It was his cousin's wedding that weekend so he was busy with that. Oliver does that classic thing of leaving out tenses and pronouns, which aren't used as much in Chinese so when I say, 'When did you last see Lori?' he says, 'See March twenty-eight. Good, happy.'

'Did she talk to you about going away, about holidays?' I say.

'No holidays,' he says. He seems serious, taciturn, and I wonder how he got on with Lori, whether he was a good mate or just hung around the edge of the circle of friends. I can't imagine him having a laugh with her but perhaps the situation, the fact that we're strangers and parents and Lori is missing, is making him stiff and reserved.

We talk to Rosemary next. We don't have much to establish, only whether Lori shared any plans with her when they last spoke and how she seemed then. Rosemary had been at the party on the Friday. She says Lori was a bit quiet early on but she cheered up later. 'I didn't hear from her after that,' Rosemary says.

'Did she talk to you about travelling?' I say.

Rosemary shakes her head. 'No, but the others said she was thinking about it.'

'Can you think of anything else we should do to try to find her?' I say.

She considers this, then says, 'I don't think so.'

'Are you from Chengdu?' Tom says.

'No, a village between here and Leshan,' Rosemary says.

'That must be a big change,' I say.

'Yes, but my father, he works in the city at a factory so I have been here before to visit him.'

'Do you like living here better than the village?' I say.

A sparkle comes into her eyes, a flash of enthusiasm. 'Very much.'

'It's the same in England, for young people,' I say.

'Everywhere, I think,' Rosemary says.

'You didn't try to get in touch with Lori over these last weeks?' Tom says.

Rosemary's expression alters, fretful again. 'I messaged her but there was no reply so I thought she was still away. Maybe she is still away,' she says.

I can't tell if it's a question: her voice is uneven and there's that trace of fear in her look.

The last time Bradley saw or heard from Lori was at the party, the same as Rosemary. 'Lori was OK,' he says, 'maybe a bit down about ending it with Dawn, thinking about a change of scene, having a few days away.'

My pulse picks up at this. 'Did she say where?'

'No. Shona said Lori was thinking about the islands, Hong Kong way or Hainan, but she had to look at the fares,' Bradley says.

'Did the police check whether she'd taken an

internal flight?' I say to Tom.

'Well, I'd hope so,' he says.

'We should ask,' I say.

'If she took a train,' Bradley said, 'she'd show her passport, too. They probably keep a record.'

I jot that down, something to consider.

'Do you remember anything else from the party?' Tom says.

Bradley shrugs. 'Things got sorta crazy after that, a drinking game.'

'Lori played?' I say.

Bradley looks sheepish. 'Lori won.'

I think of newspaper headlines, *TRAGIC DRINKS DEATH*. Those smiling faces of young men or women who'd lost their lives from alcohol poisoning. An image springs to mind: Lori drunk, collapsing, vomiting, choking. The friends unable to rouse her, panicking, desperate to hide the truth. I dig my nails into my palms.

'But she was OK?' I say.

'I think she was sick, you know, after the game but we all left together,' Bradley says.

Besides, I remind myself, she was teaching the next day and on the Sunday, so nothing could have happened to her on the Friday.

When Shona sits down with us and gets out her tin of tobacco and cigarette papers, she begins to talk before we ask anything.

'We had a party on the Friday – it was a bit insane. Then she texted me on that Monday. She was doing this photography project.'

I remember the email back in February: *Chengdu is growing all the time, malls and skyscrapers going up, everyone studying and working and trying to get ahead, get an education, get a good job to buy the shiny things in the shops. Sound familiar? But there's also surprises, hidden bits, weird hobbies people have on the side.*

'She wanted to fix up a time to see me.' Shona's accent is Scottish.

'You make the jewellery?' I nod to the bangles that she's turning round and round on her wrist.

'Yes,' she says, 'from scrap. Lori texted she could visit me Tuesday or Wednesday. I was in lectures so I didn't pick up the message till my break.' She takes a drag on her roll-up.

Tom gets out his cigarettes. I feel a pinprick on the back of my calf and pat at it. A mosquito perhaps.

'And you replied?' Tom says.

'That's what Superintendent Yin told us,' I say.

'Yes, and nothing.' She concentrates on the bracelets, spacing them out at intervals along her forearm, the rollie between her fingers. Only occasionally does she look our way. Is she shy?

'Do you still have the text?' Tom says.

'Yes.' She scowls, seems puzzled by our interest.

'The police say that's her very last communication,' I explain. 'It's when we lose her.' I swallow.

Shona puts the cigarette in her other hand and rummages in her bag. Flips open her phone case, then pulls up the message and turns it so we can see. I read, *Making a start on the project, ur next. Tue or Wed? Lxxx*

I start copying it down but Tom says, 'Can you forward it?'

'Sure.'

He reels off his number and Shona sends it to

171

him. There's a chime as it reaches his phone.

'"Making a start",' I say. 'Who was she making a start with?'

Shona shrugs, puts the phone down, tokes on her rollie, wincing at the last drag.

'What did you know about the project?' Tom says.

'Not much,' Shona says. 'She wanted something a bit … quirky. Challenging stereotypes. Something you'd never associate with China – no wee pandas or chopsticks. The idea of hobbies, obsessions, she talked about that stuff.'

'What about the party? Did she talk about it then?' I say.

Shona gives a small groan. 'God, I'm sorry. I was wrecked. I can't remember much at all.'

'Do you remember anything about her travel plans?' Tom says.

She shakes her head. 'Sorry.'

Bradley told us it was Shona whom Lori talked to about wanting a break and looking at the islands, but Shona's saying she was too pissed to recall it.

'But you think that's where she's gone?' I say.

'Yes,' she says. 'Seems the most likely thing.'

They all assumed Lori was off travelling and none of them thought it was odd that she didn't keep in touch, that she didn't manage to land up at an Internet café every few days. Their complacency, if that's what it is, infuriates me.

There's a burst of laughter, quickly muffled, from the other table where Bradley, Dawn and Rosemary sit. Unbidden, I think of the Meredith Kercher case: her friend, Amanda Knox, and

172

Knox's boyfriend tried for killing her. *Stop it!* I cover my confusion by taking a drink. The bottle is so slippery I lose my grip and it bounces off the edge of the table, drenching my legs. 'Shit!'

Tom gets up. 'Do you want another – do you want to clean up?'

'I'm fine. Sit down.' I've wipes in my bag and do what I can with them. 'Thanks,' I say to Shona, and she rejoins her friends.

'We know Lori was teaching that weekend,' I say to Tom, 'up to the Sunday evening. If she's talking about making a start in that text, perhaps that's where she goes on Monday. And it also sounds like she intends to be in Chengdu until at least the Wednesday.' Another pinch, on my neck this time, and I hear the high-pitched whine for a fraction of a second.

'Making a start's not definitely seeing some-one,' he says.

'No, but she says *you're next* to Shona. That sounds like she has someone else lined up first. And her camera's not at the flat.'

The back of my legs and my torso are sticky with sweat when I stand up and go over to the others.

'Did Lori talk to any of you about a photo pro-ject she wanted to do, on hobbies in Chengdu?'

'She was going to shoot me,' Bradley says. 'I'm doing up a motorbike, an old Chiang Jiang 750.'

'But she didn't?' Tom says, beside me.

'No.' Bradley shakes his head.

'And Oliver too,' says Rosemary. 'He keeps...' She says a word to Bradley.

'Pigeons,' Bradley translates.

'Pigeons, racing pigeons,' Rosemary says.

We try calling Oliver, but his voicemail is on.

We thank them all, confirm arrangements for the leafleting, arrange with Shona to visit the university on Monday afternoon, and get ready to leave.

'Have you eaten?' Shona asks Bradley.

'Not yet. I thought I'd grab something now. What about you guys?' He turns to Tom and me. 'Will you join us?'

We agree. Dawn says she has to get home.

On the walkway, a new group arrives, two boys, two girls. One stops to talk to Bradley and another greets Rosemary: 'How's it going?'

Their conversations flow around me.

'You tired? You look tired.'

'How was Singapore?'

'Cool.'

'You finished?'

'Just my dissertation.'

'No pressure, then.'

Bradley explains who we are and there's a brief gap of silence before the newcomers respond. Only one knew Lori to talk to, the one who's been away.

'We're running a missing-person campaign,' Tom says. 'Anything you can do to spread the word would be great.'

They all agree, eager to help. The young people exchange fist bumps, pats on the shoulder and hugs, and swap promises to meet up, all muted by the spectre of Lori, who should be here with us and is not.

Above, the heavens are fading, violet, no stars or moon, not even the flashing of aeroplane lights in the gloom.

CHAPTER TWENTY-EIGHT

The restaurant is a big, square room on the corner of the block at street level. There are some tables outside, crowding the pavement, and we sit there. It's fully dark now and the sky is a lurid indigo. Across the road I can see a man in shirt, trousers and baseball cap handing out leaflets. I ask Bradley what he's selling.

'Probably mobile-phone contracts or broadband packages,' he says.

'I saw on the map there's a big software park,' I say.

'That's near where Dawn lives,' Shona says. 'It's huge.'

'Twenty per cent of the world's computers are made in Chengdu,' Bradley tells us.

'Seriously?' Tom says.

'Yep.'

'Our new masters,' Tom says.

'Is spicy food OK?' Rosemary says. 'Or we can ask for little spice?'

It would be handy to have some sort of rating system on the menus, sticks of dynamite, maybe, or little bonfires.

We're at a picnic table with bench seats. Tom and Shona are forced to sit sideways, Tom at my left and Shona to my right, as their legs won't fit underneath. In the centre of the table is a large hole and below it a Calor-gas canister. We agree to try the standard hotpot menu. Rosemary and Bradley chatter in Chinese and then Bradley orders.

It's ten at night and the street is still busy. There is a stall opposite us, piled with cherries and lychees and – it takes me a moment to identify them – goldfish in bags. A group of teenagers sit on their scooters, playing with their phones. I watch a couple walking with a toddler. The child holds the string to a shiny gold balloon that bobs above her. She keeps glancing up at it as though she's afraid it will fly away, or burst.

I'm so tired that I wonder if I could just make my apologies and leave. My back feels as though the vertebrae are fused together. My eyes are gritty. Around us the other diners – all Chinese – talk with raised voices to compete with the traffic and each other.

We are served small bowls of pale green tea and provided with chopsticks, bowls and spoons in a cellophane pack. There is a plastic box of tissues at either end of the table and small wastebaskets on the floor. I sip the tea. Beer arrives, and I drink some of that.

'So, your scooter was nicked?' Tom says to Shona.

'Yes.' She pulls a face.

'Nightmare,' Rosemary says.

'Does it happen a lot?' Tom says.

'Yes,' Shona says.

'I wish someone would steal mine,' Bradley jokes. 'I fancy a new one. But there's a garage at my place,' he explains, 'in the basement with a security guy. No one is going to mess with him.'

'You use it for work?' Tom says.

'Yeah – it's an hour by bus; half that on the scooter. No-brainer.'

'Isn't it dangerous?' I say. 'The traffic?'

'You get used to it,' Shona says. 'I've not seen many accidents – people aren't going that fast, really.'

'Are all the scooters electric?' Tom says.

'You can get petrol ones but you don't need a licence for the electric ones so most people use them,' Bradley says.

'Will you report it stolen?' I say to Shona.

She shakes her head. 'No point.'

The waitress brings over a large metal bowl with a lid and places it in the hole. She stoops between Bradley and Rosemary and lights the gas.

The dish is not immediately appealing, a milky grey liquid, reminiscent of washing-up water, with chunks of tomato, bamboo shoots, shredded cabbage, something cream-coloured that I can't identify, and brown meat floating in it. Next comes a large bowl of sticky rice, which Bradley doles out. There is a plate of spice, red chilli and dark green coriander. Shona points her chopsticks at it. 'If you like it really hot, add some of that too.'

Following their lead, Tom and I pick up food from the hotpot, fishing out what we'd like to add to our rice. My first taste, is savoury, salty, a rich stock with a sizzling punch that numbs my lips and catches at the back of my throat. I cough and drink some beer. The steam rises from the pot, my nose runs and sweat breaks across my scalp and face. The tissues are handy for blowing noses but also to wipe my mouth and fingers when things get messy and my attempts to use the chopsticks fail. The cream-coloured food is tofu, unlike any I've had before: silky, with a delicate taste almost like shellfish. The brown meat turns out to be pork, streaked with fat. I lean back from the table and fan my face.

Rosemary smiles. 'We say to eat hot food is good in Sichuan because it is so damp here. This is very good for your health.'

Tom laughs. 'You're bright red, Jo.'

'I'm not the only one.' I snag a sliver of tofu and eat it. The chilli catches again in my throat and I cough.

'These...' Tom points to a burr at the edge of his rice '...these are the peppers?'

'That's right,' Bradley says. 'Sichuan pepper. It numbs the tongue. You feel that?' He reaches for a tissue, wipes his moustache and chin.

'It was Lori who found this place,' Shona says.

Conversation stops.

'Where can she be?' Rosemary says, her eyes pained.

My chest is tight.

No one answers but then Shona says, 'She loves finding new things, exploring.'

They reminisce and I feel an ache in my chest. Wanting her here, wanting her here to share this. I'm not sure that we're any further forward but I'm glad we've met these people, that Lori had their friendship and a sense of belonging in this unfamiliar place.

We get a cab back – I haven't the energy to walk

178

to the bus. We must get in touch with Peter Dunne, our only liaison with the police, and tell him what we've learned. And I still need to call Nick. On the ride, beneath the underpass, I see a figure curled up, sleeping. Homeless, I guess.

I call Peter Dunne from Tom's room, my phone on loudspeaker so we can both hear what's said. It takes the consul a while to answer – it's late, Saturday night: maybe he keeps office hours even with a situation like this, but eventually he's on the line. He listens while I explain the content of the text from Lori to Shona and ask him if he knew about the project. There's a very brief pause, then he says, 'Not as such.'

'We think it might be important, that perhaps she was taking photographs that Monday.' An ugly thought curdles my stomach. I say it aloud: 'Perhaps she was photographing the wrong thing...You said it's a sensitive time.'

'Mrs Maddox–'

'Please, call me Jo.'

'Jo, if the authorities detained Lorelei for any reason, for any length of time, I would have been informed. It happens – visa irregularities, misbehaviour or more serious incidents. I'm called from my bed often enough and together we agree on an appropriate way forward. I can assure you, we would know.'

He sounds so certain.

'But if we can find out where she was,' I say, 'whom she was seeing, that could be important.'

'I agree,' he says.

'Superintendent Yin,' Tom says. 'He never men-

179

tioned the project. Apparently he didn't ask Lori's friends about it. We think it's been overlooked.'

'They may well be carrying out enquiries into it but I'll pass on your thoughts to make sure,' Peter Dunne says.

The boys are in the garden when I get through. I tell Nick all about my day and share my concerns about the investigation. Like me, he's surprised that we weren't told about any of the new information as it was established.

'But we're in their hands,' I say. 'I don't think complaining will get us anywhere.' I tell him I'll Skype the kids another time but will just say a quick hello for now.

Finn says they're going to the museum and wishes I could come too.

'I'm sorry, darling, but we'll do something special when I come back.'

'What?' he says.

'I don't know. You think of something. Bye-bye now, I love you, bye-bye.'

'I don't want to go to the museum,' Isaac says flat out.

I don't want to be having this conversation. I try a bit of reverse psychology, 'OK. You tell Daddy and he'll see if you can stay with Penny or Sebastian. Daddy and Finn can go on their own.'

There is a long pause, then he makes a huffing sound. 'They won't know what to get,' he says.

'What to get where?'

'From the shop,' Isaac says irritably.

Ah. The highlight of any visit. 'That's true – and they've got some cool models there, and pens and stuff.'

'When are you coming home?' he says.

'In a couple of weeks. And we'll do something special then, whatever you like.'

'Bye,' he says, and I hear scuffling. I imagine him thrusting the phone at Nick.

'Tell him I love him,' I say to Nick.

'Will do.'

'And I love you.'

'Love you too,' he says.

As I lie in bed my mind roams over the conversations from the evening. We should talk to Oliver in the morning, see if he was the first subject for her project. But wouldn't he have said so? He was there when we explained about the last sighting and the message to Shona. Then again, his English isn't brilliant. We need to ask him directly. I think of how he slipped away so quickly, of his reticence, the fact that he didn't answer his phone.

It takes for ever to fall asleep.

Waking in the night with a start, I'm wondering what roused me, when a great *whoomph* shakes the building and drives me out of bed. *Earthquake.* There was one here not very long ago, with dreadful loss of life. Another whoomph vibrates through the air, travels though my belly, my chest. My heart bangs hard. Then I hear the clank and grind of construction vehicles. Or, in this case, demolition. From the window, I can see one of the long sheds has been razed to the ground. A cloud of dust hangs over the rubble that is left as a bulldozer backs away. Across the site, two trucks are waiting in position, headlights on, close to the pile of metal, and a grabber with lights on the arm of its scoop swings round, claws filled with a tangle of the stuff. Nothing goes to waste here. I've seen people collecting plastic water bottles and others on scooters piled high with cardboard for recycling.

I watch, sitting in the dark, until my eyes grow heavy and my pulse slows, the trucks have been filled and left in convoy with their loads of scrap. And the lights on the grabber are switched off.

Only the neon still shines, flowing endlessly down the towers, as the city sleeps.

CHAPTER TWENTY-NINE

We are just leaving the dining room after breakfast when the campaign leaflets arrive. A box of five thousand, A5 size, and five hundred A4 posters. Tom takes delivery and pays the man. We check them and everything looks as it should. I feel a moment's dizziness, page after page of Lori's face, the grim fact of us being here – without her.

When Anthony comes we have coffee in the lounge bar and bring him up to date. We try calling Oliver again, hoping to ask him about the photography project, but there's no reply so Anthony leaves a message in Chinese, explaining that we'd like to talk to him as soon as possible.

The car drops us at Lori's street.

'We don't need the driver to wait,' Tom says. 'We can let him know when we're done.'

The three of us call in at each of the units along the street, cafés, a fruit shop, liquor store, mobile-phone shop, tea shop and mini-market, and hand out leaflets. Each time Anthony asks them to display a poster. Outside one of the cafés, the proprietor talks excitedly, nodding, and two of the other staff gather around to join in the conversation.

'Lorelei ate here sometimes,' Anthony says. 'She was a good customer. They can't remember when she last came. Not for a while. I've asked them if she was here in the last month. They don't think she was.'

I look at the trays of raw food set out to entice diners, rows of duck's feet scrawny claws with barely any meat on them – red crayfish, pigs' trotters. Flies circle and land on the meat and one of the girls waves them off.

The older woman leans in close, speaking rapidly, touching her chest.

'She wishes you luck, for your daughter to be safe and back soon,' Anthony says.

The woman talks some more.

'She says you must have good fortune. That luck will come to you.' The woman reaches out and pats my hand. She nods to Tom. My throat tightens.

'Please – say thank you,' I say.

'*Xiè xie*,' Anthony says. *Shay shay.*

I echo him and Tom does too.

We have a similar reception from the women in the mini-market. They even remember what Lori

183

used to buy: honey and orange juice, eggs and nuts and tea and beer. While we're there they put up the poster, on the wall by the till.

Then we start leafleting on the street. We quickly discover that we are ill-prepared. With a break in the cloud and patches of blue sky, the temperature is close to thirty degrees and we have no shade. We have nowhere to keep the leaflets either, nowhere to sit if anyone wants to find out more, no table to rest on if they want to give us any information. There is a low wall next to the entrance to Len's block and the shop beside it is shuttered, so we put our things there. Tom goes across the road with a bundle of leaflets and Anthony and I stay together.

People take the leaflets, expectant at first. As they realize that this is no mobile-phone deal or invitation to a cultural event, their faces crease with incomprehension. Then they see that we are not tourists or university lecturers but here for a darker reason. An inclination of the head, a murmur in the throat, and they back off, continuing their journeys.

Two girls stop and talk to Anthony. I can't follow the conversation, but when they leave, he says, 'They were curious, but they don't know Lorelei. They never saw her.'

The flow of people passing never ends. Men with their T-shirts rolled up to their armpits, exposing their bellies to cool off. Grandparents with kids. Some of the little ones aren't in nappies but wear traditional baby clothing split at the crotch. I wonder how it works, if they have to be toilet-trained first. What if they have an accident?

Listening to Anthony, I learn words that I wish

184

I did not have to: daughter – *nǚ ér;* missing – *shī zōng;* have you seen her? – *nǐ kàn jiàn to le ma?*

After an hour we have a break. Tom asks Anthony if there is anywhere we can get a table with a sunshade for our next stint.

'B&Q,' he says.

'No way!' Tom laughs. 'We could use some stools from the apartment.'

'Yes,' I say. 'I've brought the key.'

Anthony shows us where the store is on the map and we decide to go.

'I can call the car,' Anthony says.

'Be quicker to get a cab.' Tom points to where two taxis are parked further along the road. We collect up the leaflets and walk down that way.

Anthony approaches one car and talks to the driver, who keeps shaking his head. He tries the next, and we watch the scene repeat itself. Then a third taxi drives along and pulls in opposite. Anthony waves to him, a beckoning motion with his palm facing down. The man stays put and Anthony goes up to the car. They talk, Anthony gesturing to us. After some discussion, Anthony waits for a gap in the traffic and crosses back to join us.

'Is it too far?' I ask him.

'It's lunch-hour,' he says. 'They won't take a fare in lunch-hour. I'll call the driver.'

The DIY store is startlingly similar to the ones at home. We find a round plastic table that can collapse flat for storage, and a yellow parasol that will fit into the hole in the middle.

It's crazy: three weeks ago I was on a different continent buying bedding plants in the same outlet, growing anxious about Lori.

'Jo?' Tom touches my elbow. We're at the till and the woman's waiting for me to pay.

'Sorry. Sorry.'

We leave the table in the car while we get some lunch at a place Anthony knows. He guides us through the choices: the menu up on the wall is all in Chinese. We settle for noodle soup, medium-size.

It's spicy but not as hot as last night's food. There are slices of ginger and dark greens in it. Again, it makes me sweat, but it's refreshing in the way that hot tea can be.

On the street corner, a grizzled man sits by a rush mat, which is piled with bunches of herbs that are wilting in the heat, and clips his toenails. Horns punctuate the drone of traffic and Chinese singing comes from somewhere nearby.

Anthony asks about our hotel and I tell him I've been meaning to ask them to fix the water cooler. The water's tepid.

'Tepid?' he says.

'Lukewarm, not really cold.'

'Oh, yes,' Anthony says. 'This is the custom. Very cold drinks are not good in this climate. We don't have it too cold, don't have ice.'

A flock of young people, white shirts, black trousers, ties and lanyards, are milling about outside the shop opposite.

'Estate agents?' Tom turns to check and Anthony agrees.

The boom years.

I don't like going into Lori's flat. It makes me

186

want to weep. That she is still not here, that this is her space with her things, and she is missing.

But I'm brisk, business-like, as I stack the stools for Tom to carry and take the chance to use the toilet and wash my face before we head back out.

The sky is clouding over again, trapping the heat, and the afternoon is sweltering. Not one of the people we approach with leaflets recognizes Lori or can help us.

I tell myself this doesn't matter: all we need is to get them talking, that the ripples will spread and eventually someone somewhere will ring up with those magic words: *I know where she is. I know where you can find her.*

That evening Tom and I manage to retrace our steps to the bus and find our way to the bar. Shona and Bradley meet us there. I'm troubled that there's still no word from Oliver and ask them if they've heard from him today. But they haven't.

'It's just we wanted to talk to him but he's not returned our calls,' I say.

Shona shrugs, looking awkward. Doesn't she understand that this might be important? That we're desperate for leads as to where Lori has gone and Oliver might be able to help?

'Do you want me to try?' Bradley offers.

I say yes, and he calls Oliver, listens, then gives a shake of his head when the voicemail announcement starts. Bradley leaves a message in Chinese. How can Oliver ignore us, given what's happened? Why would he do that?

It's later than the night before – and the bar is

187

busier. We begin handing out leaflets and stop to explain whenever anyone asks questions.

One young woman, with dreadlocks and milky skin, says, 'Oh, my God.' She puts her hand on her chest, just below her neck. 'You must be completely devastated. That is so awful. Not knowing. How would you cope?' She turns to her friends. 'Like with Madeleine, yeah? Not knowing.'

She may be right but I don't need the melodrama, the avid interest that smacks of ghoulishness. She starts asking questions but for once I don't elaborate. 'It's all there,' I say, pointing to the leaflet.

'And that's all you know?' She shakes her head, looking like she might cry.

I walk away without replying.

After our stint at the Ducks, we visit a noodle bar popular with the friends, in the adjacent tower block.

'The food is good,' Shona says. 'Big portions, too, and low prices.'

Bradley checks with the owner if we can put leaflets on the tables and he agrees.

The gay club, known by its street number, 141, is ten minutes' walk away. Like the other places, it's housed in a tower block, this time on the eighth floor. It is dance night and the thump of bass shakes the ground and travels through me as we come out of the lift.

The woman at the door, Kimmie, is happy for us to take leaflets round and tells us to leave some extra with her: she'll put them out during the week. She knows Lori and Dawn. 'I can't imagine,' she says to me. 'Anything else we can do, you just shout.' Her sympathy brings me close to tears.

The dance floor isn't very big and there's a crush of people, arms in the air, filling it. There's no dress code and outfits vary: people in T-shirts and jeans, in stunning frocks, others in leather and PVC. On stage the Chinese DJ is dressed in a white three-piece suit and top hat, which must be unbelievably hot, and has a face painted like an elaborate mask. I can't tell if it's a man or a woman.

The few revellers who aren't dancing sit in the booths around the dance floor drinking, snogging, having conversations, mouth to ear, to be heard. By the time we leave, my ears are ringing. Kimmie wishes us all the best and tells us to take care.

At our next stop, Hokey's, a cocktail bar on a busy street, blue neon characters glow on the sign outside and large black catfish patrol inside a tank bathed in orange light at the entrance. Behind the glass doors it's velvety dark but I can see more of the neon signs. Bradley talks to the doorman, who listens and takes a bundle of leaflets.

The proprietor of the hotpot restaurant we try next waves us away. When Bradley keeps talking, the man all but turns his back. Tom takes one of the leaflets and puts it on the table beside the chits for the diners, the man's ashtray and playing cards.

'He'll probably chuck it,' Tom says, as we leave.

'Why did he say no?' I ask Bradley.

'Bad for business,' Bradley says. 'He's a fucking asshole.'

Shona nudges him. 'What?' Bradley says.

'We don't mind,' I say, thinking she's worried about the language. 'He is a fucking asshole.'

'A fucking arsehole, even,' says Tom, and we laugh.

'We should come later, next weekend,' Bradley says, 'on the Saturday, grab the clubbers.'

Something drops inside me at the thought of still looking in another week's time. Surely we'll have found her by then.

Before I sleep I ring Lori's phone and get the *'It has not been possible to connect you, please try again later'* announcement. I will, I always do. I can't even leave her a message. But I keep hoping. Hope is all there is.

CHAPTER THIRTY

The following morning, we start at eight, to catch the rush-hour commuters. Tom and I get the bus and Anthony is waiting for us when we arrive. For once there is a breeze. It snatches at the dust and sends leaves skittering along the pavement.

The crowds of people heading for work stride past us, dressed in either generic office clothes or this season's casual fashions: sheer fabrics, Breton stripes, cobalt blue, lacy knits and retro prints.

I see two people with surgical face masks on – they must get uncomfortably hot, like when Nick and I sanded the living-room floor before we had the laminate done. Fine sawdust sticking to everything, sweaty and itchy inside the paper mask.

Oliver is on the rota. He still hasn't replied to us and I wonder if we'll see him again. Is he being thoughtless or is he avoiding us? Why come to the bar in the first place, then? There's a knot in my stomach, hard as stone. When he appears, as promised, the lump in my gut burns.

'Hello – sit down a minute.' I point to one of the seats we've brought from Lori's. Anthony is there already and Tom comes to join us. 'We sent you some messages,' I say.

'Oh, yes.' No apology follows. He glances at me through his thick glasses, then down at the table.

'The photography project, hidden hobbies, you were one of the people Lori wanted to photograph?' Does he follow me? I add, 'She wanted to photograph you and your pigeons.' I look at Anthony and he gives us the word, *'Gezi.'*

'Yes,' Oliver smiles, *'gezi.'*

'Did she come? Did she take photographs?' I say.

Oliver shakes his head, serious again.

'On the Monday she texted Shona,' Tom says, 'saying she'd started the project. We think she photographed someone either on the Sunday evening after work or on the Monday.'

I'm not sure Oliver understands so I ask Anthony to translate again. He does and Oliver gives a nod.

'Did she talk to you about the other people? Shona and her jewellery.' I mime bracelets on my arm. 'Bradley and his motorbike.'

'Yes, yes,' Oliver says.

'Anyone else?'

191

'A neighbour with model animal and a student like money.'

I don't know what he means about liking money. He talks to Anthony for a minute.

'Someone who collects banknotes,' Anthony says. 'It is a very popular hobby, like collecting stamps. There are antiques fairs and people trade them.'

'Do you know who this student was, or the neighbour?' I say to Oliver.

'No.' He shakes his head.

'Dawn might,' Tom says.

A man walks along with a radio strapped to his arm, playing music. He's followed by an old couple, tiny in stature, who stop at our table. She wears a traditional cotton top with a mandarin collar, he wears dark clothes and a black Mao cap. Their faces are open, friendly; their smiles show brown teeth, gaps where some are missing.

Anthony explains what we're doing and the couple look shocked. They refuse a leaflet.

'Chinese people,' Anthony says, 'they do not like to get involved.'

'Too risky?' Tom says.

Anthony laughs but he flushes slightly and I sense he is embarrassed.

I think of all the superstitions I've read about – perhaps there is a fear, too, that bad luck is contagious. We come trailing misery, reeking of jeopardy.

I want to ring Dawn so I go to the flat where I can hear without straining. I know she's at work but not when she's actually teaching. She must get breaks, and admin time. I leave a message on her voicemail, then sit for a moment on Lori's couch, letting my eyes roam over the lucky Chinese knot, the photo from home, the bare wires in the ceiling, the plastic basket of bits and bobs, her work folders.

I pick up the files, thumb through them again. I don't know why, except that there's comfort in seeing her writing, even though it's scrappy and hard to read, comfort in imagining her preparing for her students.

I step out onto the balcony. Construction cradles sway up the side of the new buildings. The arrangement of the developments seems to create an echo chamber. I can hear the hammer and whine of drills, and from the occupied towers, the cries and shrieks of children, and the clatter of dishes that sounds different here, as though they're all made of metal, not pottery. Through it all the drone and rumble of the ring road.

My phone rings. It's Dawn. I explain about the neighbour. Does she know who it was?

'Mrs Tang,' she says. 'She's on the second floor. We saw her with this dead bird one day and her son explained she was going to stuff it, for a model. Like taxidermy. Lori did a few conversation classes with her son. I'd no idea she was going to photograph Mrs Tang. But it makes sense.'

'Do you know which flat it is?'

'Number three, I think,' Dawn says.

'Oliver also talked about one of Lori's students,' I say, 'someone who collects banknotes.'

'Oh, that'd be Mr Du. Lori said he was a bit of

a weirdo.'

My stomach twists. 'Weirdo?'

'Lori reckoned he was desperate to get married – he kept asking if she had a boyfriend, that kind of thing.'

'Do the police know about this?' My voice is shaky.

Dawn sounds taken aback, when she says, 'I dunno. Well, they went to see him, didn't they? His lesson was the Sunday evening.'

'Did you tell the police about him being weird?'

'Look, Mrs Maddox, it wasn't anything really heavy – Lori would've sacked him if it had been.' Her voice is doing that singsong rise at the end of each phrase, making it sound like she's pleading with me to agree.

'Did you tell them he had this hobby and Lori wanted to photograph him?'

'No – I didn't know he was part of her project. But the police must have talked to him,' she says.

Maybe they didn't ask the right questions. I think it's unclear whether they knew about the project at all.

'You can check with them, right?' she says, nervousness in her tone.

'Yes,' I say, 'we will.' I end the call, the taste of bile in the back of my throat.

In the kitchen I find a cup, black and white stripes, wonder where Lori got it and pour myself water from the cooler. It's warm and tastes of plastic.

In my head I'm replaying Dawn's words, *a weirdo ... asking if she had a boyfriend ... the Sunday evening.*

The last person to see Lori.

The jittery feeling grows. It sends me hurrying down to Tom, frantic to share what I now know.

'So this guy's hitting on her and the cops weren't told?' Tom jabs at his hair, fingers taut. A line of white edges his lips. 'He was the last person to see her.'

'Ring Peter Dunne,' I say. 'Get him to talk to Superintendent Yin again.'

Oliver looks away, scratches his chest.

'Write down exactly what Dawn said,' Tom tells me.

I close my eyes. It's too hot to think and my throat is dry again already. 'Can we get a drink somewhere?' I say to Anthony. The bottled water we brought is long gone.

'Shop, I go,' Oliver says, pointing to himself.

'You don't mind?' I say.

'Yes, I go,' he says.

'Tonic water, please,' I say. He doesn't understand. Anthony isn't familiar with it either. Tom looks it up on his app and shows Oliver the Chinese translation. 'Cola for me,' Tom says.

'And more water too?' I show Oliver the empties.

They don't sell tonic water but Oliver brings me lemonade. Once we have the drinks I go with Tom back into the flat and he makes the call to the consulate, his phone set so I can hear too. Tom paces as he talks, civil, but his frustration is plain.

'This Mr Du is the last person to see our daughter,' he says, 'and one of the people she wanted to photograph. This could be really important. Has

195

Superintendent Yin come back to you yet?'

'No, not yet. Look, can I suggest that you email over what you've heard?' Peter Dunne says.

'Yes, we will,' Tom says, 'and please emphasize to him that we think this needs looking into straight away.'

When Tom has hung up, I say, 'Could Lori have talked about the project with Mr Du? It was obviously on her mind when she texted Shona.'

'If that text was from Lori,' Tom says.

'I think it was. It was so specific, and if it wasn't Lori it must've been someone who knew her well, knew about the project, knew how she signed off.'

'So we need to find out if she made a start with him during their lesson and, if not, whether she said anything about who she would photograph first,' Tom says.

'We should talk to the neighbour before we leave here,' I say.

'We're meeting Shona to leaflet at the university at three o'clock.'

'I'll fetch Anthony,' Tom says.

But there's no answer from Mrs Tang's flat on the second floor and no one around to ask.

We've put everything away, Anthony has left, and Tom and I are walking to the bus when we are accosted. Three giggling girls approach. They are beautiful, fresh-faced, wearing short-sleeved blouses in pastel colours and miniskirts. They look at us with a mix of delight and fascination. One of them talks to me – I catch the word 'photo' but not the rest. I frown. 'Please, photo?' she says, gesturing to us, then herself and her pals.

I open my mouth to refuse, ready to wave a leaflet at them, look – *nǚ ér, shī zōng* – but Tom gives me a warning look, so I acquiesce. We stand together, Tom and I, a girl on either side, while they take turns with their cameras, counting: *yi, er, san*. Flash. Another. Flash. 'Thank you. Thank you.'

We've made their day.

Bizarre. What will they do with them? Show their parents, their friends? Put them on the mantelpiece? Look – me with the foreigners.

CHAPTER THIRTY-ONE

It's as quick to walk back from the ring road through the park to the hotel and pleasanter away from the traffic so we take that route from the bus stop. A group of children are coming our way, six of them with an adult. They all wear red neckerchiefs.

'Hello, hello.' One starts the chorus.

'Hello,' Tom says, 'hello.' And then as we pass, he calls, 'Bye-bye.'

And there are peals of laughter.

We cross the bridge. The wide grey river gleams, harsh and dull. Men on the promenade are sitting with flywheels big as dinner plates, like fishermen but the lines go up in the air. I'm trying to puzzle this out when Tom points to a kite, up far, far above, the size of a stamp. There are others even higher, tiny black diamonds against the pewter sky.

We built a kite once, Lori and I, from a kit with coloured paper, bamboo dowel and a long plastic tail. And it flew. We took it to the meadows near the Mersey. Lori was delighted.

'The kids OK?' Tom says, as we walk on.

'I think so, missing me. I promised to talk to them tonight. What about you? Anyone waiting to hear from you?'

'Nosy.' His eyes are bright.

'Coy,' I return. 'Or is it a secret? Is she married?'

'Jo.'

'It has been known,' I say.

'Single, as it happens.'

'Moira?' I ask.

'What?' he says.

'There was a Moira,' I say.

He laughs. 'She's a business partner, deals with Liverpool. Why are you so interested?'

'Just making conversation,' I say, sounding defensive, and I don't know why, except I'm tired, my skin feels greasy and there's a blister growing on the back of my heel.

'Aphrodite,' he says.

'Seriously?'

'She's a model,' he says.

'Course she is,' I say.

'A hand model – watches, rings, nail varnish.'

'Is she Greek?' I say.

'Brummie, actually. Lost the accent, thank God.'

I laugh, back on safer ground. Since he left, the longest time we've ever been together was the day of Lori's graduation. We had dinner in Glasgow

198

the night before, Lori and Tom, Nick and I, then went to the ceremony the next afternoon and out for cocktails. No wonder our interactions simmer with antagonism: we don't know how to be with each other any more.

'There's a Cultural Relics bit,' Tom says, looking at the sign near the park entrance. 'We could take a look?'

Sightseeing? Is he mad?

'What?' he says. 'It'll only be a couple of quid.'

'It's not the money.'

'What, then?' He's got his sunglasses on and I can't see his eyes but he sounds annoyed.

'Sightseeing?' I say. It seems wrong, skewed. I'm perilously close to tears. I turn away from him, arms crossed, stare at the rows of scooters in the car park.

'Hey,' Tom says, 'it's just a break. We're not meeting Shona until three. You go back, if you like. Sit in your room for the next couple of hours.'

I shrug. 'I'll come.'

Inside the park, on a small stage, a masked man is dressed in flowing coloured robes, thick with embroidery. Music plays, quick and jangly. The mask, surrounded by a headdress, is stylized, vivid swirls of solid colour, green and white and black and red. He jumps into the air, and twirls, kicks his legs, then strikes a pose. He opens a large fan and swipes it across his face. A clash of cymbals, and the mask disappears, replaced by another, red and black with jagged eyebrows, angry-looking. The man feints to the left, then the right. A scissor kick, another cymbal clash, and a new face.

We buy our tickets for the paying area. I read the leaflet. The park is dedicated to an ancient poet, Xue Tao. There are statues of her among the trees and her grave is here. I shiver in the heat. I don't want to see any graves.

The path leads into an open area ringed with pavilions, landscaped with large stones, statuary and planting. Forest trees provide pools of shade. A standing stone we pass has characters carved into it, painted green. In the borders around the buildings, grasses and flowering shrubs are planted among bonsai pines. Pinnacles of rock remind me of the dribbled sand we would use to make sculptures at the beach.

Signs point to different attractions – the bamboo museum, the brocade-washing pavilion, the river-viewing tower. The tower itself is beautiful, a soaring four-storey pagoda, richly carved from deep red wood. The sculptures and fretwork are decorated with exquisite colours: white and red, green, yellow and blue.

While Tom goes exploring, I find a bench to sit on below a pergola, alongside the river. Across the murk of the water is the cityscape, the bristling ranks of skyscrapers.

The red stone balustrade at the edge of the water is ornately carved with flowers and repeated block patterns. Seed has been left along the tops of the walls and tiny birds with rusty red heads and fantails flit to peck at the grains, and fly away again. White butterflies dance in the grass.

I stretch and relax, wanting to let go of the tension lodged in my shoulders and guts.

Piped music starts coming through speakers hidden in the foliage and then a man's voice reciting something. I pick out numbers *yi, er, san*. Perhaps he is listing the rules of the park, or the attractions to be seen, or some principles of poetry.

I watch the ants running hither and thither around my feet, all the appearance of random panic, though I know they are organized, carefully following trails laid by others, working for the good of the colony. Two ants carry a burden, a grain of rice or perhaps an insect egg, wrestle it to a crack in the paving and release it there.

How much do the police know about Mr Du? Suspicious, half-formed thoughts hover at the edges of my mind, grotesque gargoyles, like the dragons that guard the gates in the park: teeth and claws, leathery scales, sulphurous breath.

Why does everything have to be filtered through Peter Dunne? Can't they give the investigation to someone who can speak English, who can deal with us directly? I think of DI Dooley and the trip to report Lori missing, the enormity of it.

An ant runs over my foot. I dash it away, stand up and walk round the corner where there is a fountain in a circular pool.

Dawn's words echo in my head, *Weirdo ... kept asking if she had a boyfriend. The last person to see her.* Did she go back there? Was Mr Du the subject she was 'making a start' with?

A siren loops from across the water. Then I notice a break in the noise and wonder if the traffic lights have changed because, for two seconds, the roar of engines and the percussion of horns soaks away and birdsong, with the splash of the fountain, comes to the fore. Closing my eyes, I think of home, of clear, clean air and the peace of the garden. There is no way to concentrate with this barrage of sound. It takes so much energy just to shut it out that there's little space left for coherent thought.

On the way back we pass a *tuk-tuk* parked on the pavement, with fruit piled high and a set of old-fashioned scales.

'English?' the vendor says, with a broad smile.

'Yes,' Tom says.

'London?'

'Manchester,' Tom says.

'Manchester?'

'Yes, Manchester,' Tom says.

'You know Jackie?' he says brightly.

We shake our heads.

'Jackie in London. London, yes?'

'No,' I say.

'Chengdu, like?'

I have a spare leaflet in my bag, and show him.

'Aah,' he says sadly.

'Have you seen her?' I say, struggling to remember the Chinese. *'Nǐ kàn jiàn to le ma?'*

He pulls a face, shakes his head slowly. We walk on.

CHAPTER THIRTY-TWO

A cab drops us at the university, at the West Gate. When we meet Shona, she's wearing shorts again, royal blue, patterned with small white angelfish, along with a sleeveless denim top. And the same clashing collection of bracelets and necklaces. I ask her why it's called Sichuan Normal University.

'A normal university is for teacher training,' she says. She tells us it's coming close to the end of the academic year but most courses are still running. There are a lot of courses, like hers, for international students. In her master's class there are people from Italy, Korea, Tibet, France, America, Mexico and Thailand. Classes are taught in Chinese so they all need at least a working knowledge of Mandarin.

'Were you always good at languages?' I ask.

'Sort of. My mum was from Finland so I grew up bilingual.'

At the entrance there's an open-air arcade, three storeys high, with shops selling groceries, DVDs, accessories, then kebab and noodle stalls, a dumpling shop and restaurants. We visit all of these and distribute copies of the fliers.

Further inside the campus, trees line the avenues and provide shade in the courtyards between the buildings – but even here it is stifling. A patina of gritty dust is silted over everything.

We take a broad avenue downhill, lined with busts of famous people: philosophers, musicians, artists, scientists and writers. Their names are in Chinese. One or two I recognize: Charles Darwin, Marie Curie.

Passing a building with rows of large sinks inside, I see ranks of vacuum flasks piled up outside.

'The halls don't have hot water,' Shona says. 'Students fetch it from here for washing.'

The blister on my heel, tight with fluid, stings with each step. My mosquito bites from the first visit to the bar are big red lumps with crusty yellow centres. The need to scratch is intense. I'm able to resist it most of the time but at night I think I do it in my sleep.

We leave leaflets in the library, the gym, the admin offices and the student canteen. Shona takes a bundle to give to her faculty. A couple of times we stop when we run into someone she knows, but neither of them has news of Lori.

Some students are splashing about in the open-air swimming-pool at the bottom of the hill. It's so inviting. I think of Finn, of his prowess in the water. Like a seal, sleek and smooth and fast.

I miss my boys.

'We're in *The Big Issue*.' That's the first thing Nick says when I call. Half nine in the evening my time but it's only half two in the afternoon there. 'I'll scan a copy and email it. Two-page spread. And the *Guardian* have published a small piece, a couple of inches. The *Manchester Evening News* are doing a full page tomorrow. We've a TV crew coming anytime now, BBC, for the local news.'

'I wish there was some sort of coverage here,' I say. 'There's still not been anything.' A press conference seems to be the only way to grab the headlines and we haven't a date for that yet. 'Listen, Nick, we talked to Oliver today. That last lesson Lori did, on the Sunday night, the student was one of the people she was going to use for her photo project. And, according to Dawn, he was a bit odd.'

'Odd in what way?' Nick says.

I tell him.

'Shit.'

'I know. We've told Peter Dunne and insisted that we want the police to look again at this bloke.'

'Yes, they must,' Nick says.

'They have interviewed him,' I'm not sure whether I'm reassuring Nick or myself, 'so he must have checked out all right. There's a neighbour too, whom we haven't seen yet. She was another hobby subject. Look, do you want me to talk to Edward about any of this?'

'No,' Nick says. 'I will.'

'Have there been any calls to the hotline?'

'I don't know. Edward says they check things out first, just to make sure, and pass on anything they judge to be significant.'

I hear our house phone ring.

'I'd better get that,' Nick says.

'I'll Skype the boys later.'

'Great. Bye.'

And he's gone.

When I Skype the boys, I feel as though someone has cut me off at the knees, thinking back to

Christmas when they squabbled and Lori, slightly merry with drink, grinned and blew kisses.

Isaac stares at me reproachfully. 'When are you coming back?' he says.

'Soon.' I am deliberately vague. 'How was the museum?'

His thundercloud lifts for a few moments, light in his eyes, as he gives me an energetic account.

'Brilliant,' I say.

He nods.

'Finn's turn,' Nick says.

Finn is delighted to see me. 'Mummy!'

'Hello.'

He peers closer into the webcam. 'Have you found Lori?'

'I'm still looking for her.'

'Oh. Benji ate my rocket.'

'Ate what?' I say.

'From the museum.'

'His spaceship – he chewed the nose off,' Nick interprets.

'Oh. Naughty dog.'

'It might come out in his poo,' Isaac, off screen, chips in.

Finn laughs. A rich chuckle. They all have different laughs: Finn this throaty chortle, Isaac quieter, almost a titter, breathy. And Lori: Lori's laugh is sudden, abrupt, like a bark, but hilarious and infectious.

'We were on telly,' Finn says.

'Did you see yourselves?' I say.

'Yes, but we were fuzzy,' he says.

'Daddy talked,' Isaac says, 'he talked about Lori–'

'Isaac made too much noise,' Finn says.

'I did not.'

'Did.'

'OK, lads,' Nick interrupts. 'Let me talk to Mum now.'

'What does he mean "fuzzy"?' I say.

'They blurred the boys' faces – privacy rules apparently.'

'Of course,' I say. 'Was it OK – the filming?'

'Bit crazy,' he says, 'but they must be used to all sorts, the team that do it.'

'I'll try to call again tomorrow,' I say.

They all crowd in to wave goodbye and then the screen goes black.

CHAPTER THIRTY-THREE

I'm at breakfast when Tom seeks me out. 'Any word from Peter Dunne?'

'Nothing,' I say, 'but it's only nine o'clock.'

'He had all day yesterday to talk to Super-intendent Yin.' Tom looks tired, in spite of the fact that he's acquired a tan since we got here. His eyes are dull, weary.

'Ring after this, then?' I say. 'Are you not eating?'

'I already did. Give me a knock when you're ready.'

I wish Nick were here. There's a gulf between Tom and me that can't be bridged. The rift when he left me and Lori was so deep, so ragged, that it never really healed. Or not on my side. I've no idea what Tom's perspective is on it. We've never spoken about it in any meaningful way. He was quite ruthless at first, unapologetic almost. I'd be weeping down the phone and he would hang up. As things settled, as it became apparent that the separation was going to be permanent, that I couldn't win him back, I hardened my heart against him. I let all the fire of my love, jealousy and anger crystallize and chill into cold, un-yielding stone. He would never hurt me again. In my own mind I belittled him, a man who couldn't commit, a playboy, a narcissist, his only concern feeding his ego. I bit my tongue in front of Lori as Tom cherry-picked his time with her. I became an expert at tact and diplomacy.

If Nick were here I could share my thoughts and feelings about our search, perhaps even voice the fears I'm working so hard to deny, to ignore. Although Nick and I weren't exactly communi-cating well before I left.

Across the room, a guest drops a glass of juice, making me jump. In the hubbub that follows I leave the table and walk to the lift. I rub at my arms to ease the gooseflesh and the shiver that runs through me.

Tom's window looks down onto a side road and across to the buildings opposite. I think they must be offices – there are no balconies, no ever-present laundry on show.

He's been smoking: the air stinks of tobacco. His bed is a tangled mess, strewn with clothes. Leaflets and notes cover the desk.

208

'Put it on speaker,' I tell him, as he calls the consulate.

A secretary answers and asks Tom to wait while she checks if Mr Dunne is available.

Tom leans against the edge of the desk, a pen in his hand, notepad at the ready.

I look out to where a bus, with a wooden frame like those old half-timbered Morris Minor Travellers, stops and a queue scrambles to board.

'Mr Maddox?' says Peter Dunne. 'I was about to call you. I managed to speak to Superintendent Yin late yesterday afternoon and relayed the information from your email.'

'And what did he say?' Tom asks.

The slightest hiatus, then Peter Dunne says, 'He is not at liberty to disclose details about the ongoing inquiry but the information you provided will be scrutinized.'

Tom grits his teeth.

'They will talk to this student, Mr Du, again, won't they?' I say.

'I'm sure that they will do everything necessary,' Peter Dunne says.

Which is an evasion, not an answer.

'But I was anxious to speak to you both,' he goes on, 'about the press conference. I have good news. We've agreed to a venue in Chengdu, the Rose Hibiscus Hotel for Thursday at ten thirty a.m.' The day after tomorrow. 'That means it should be carried on the news throughout the rest of the day. You're both still willing to be present?'

'Yes,' we answer in unison.

'And be available for follow-up interviews should requests be made?'

'Yes,' Tom says. I echo him.

'Superintendent Yin will give an initial address, outlining the police search and inviting public co-operation. We'll then have one of you making a direct appeal in English. We'll need to approve the wording in advance, so if you could consider that and send me something through? Nothing too long,' he adds.

'Missing Overseas have guidelines,' I say. 'We can talk to them.'

'Excellent. Have you had any response to the leafleting?'

'Not yet,' I say.

'Well, hopefully the press conference will take things to the next level and we'll reach a significant audience.'

'Thank God for that,' I say to Tom, when Peter Dunne has gone. 'I was beginning to think they might be stalling.'

Tom doesn't speak. He takes a cigarette and lights it. 'But they expect us to sit tight, doing fuck-all, while Superintendent Yin decides if talking to the weirdo is worth a punt.'

'What else can we do?'

'Go and see him,' Tom says.

'I don't–'

'Why wait?'

'Maybe we should see what Superintendent Yin–'

'Jo, we waited fuck knows how long to find out about the text to Shona. Now this guy and his–'

Tom's phone rings. Anthony is downstairs. We're leafleting outside Lori's again.

'Change of plan,' Tom tells Anthony. 'We'll be

210

down in a minute.'

I stare at him, wondering whether this is wise.

'We just talk to the guy,' Tom says to me, 'ask if Lori photographed him or talked about filming anyone else. What harm can it do? I'm sick of doing nothing. Every day the chances–'

'Stop!' I say.

He looks away and drags on his cigarette.

Mr Du's address is on Lori's weekly schedule. It takes me a while, and my hand is trembling, but I find the street on the map, and when we go downstairs I show it to Anthony.

'Where does he work?' Anthony says. 'Will he be at home now?'

We don't know.

The weather is muggy today and the cloud is back, an iron sky. I can feel the pressure of it in my skull.

When we reach the right development, Anthony speaks to the guard at the gate, who lets us through without any further discussion.

The complex is built around gardens and fish ponds with a fountain in the centre, where four huge bronze frogs are spouting water. There are a lot of benches in the shade of the trees and most are occupied by people with toddlers and babies in buggies.

A television outside the lift, shows an advert for cosmetic surgery, white coats and beautiful women.

We go up to the flat on the fifteenth floor, but there is no answer.

'What now?' says Tom.

A door opens along the corridor and a young

woman, wearing a smart black dress and gold sandals, comes out from the next flat.

'Nǐ hǎo,' Anthony says. He asks her something, gesturing to the flat we're interested in.

She replies to him, then smiles and says, 'Zài jiàn.' Sci chen, goodbye. She walks to the lift, the slap of her shoes echoing on the concrete floor.

'He comes home for lunch,' Anthony says, 'about one o'clock. He works for a property firm.'

Like half the city, I imagine.

'It's twelve thirty,' Tom says, checking his phone.

'We could sit in the garden and wait,' I say.

So that's what we do.

The garden is planted with red and green acers and glossy palms. A very dark-leafed tree has racemes of shocking pink flowers, their fragrance reminding me of honeysuckle. Finches, with red and white markings, dart in and out of the trees, wiping their beaks on the branches. A bird, the size of a thrush, coloured brown with a white ring around each eye and a tuft on its head, flies down to the path and back.

People come and go, most of them staring at us as they pass. We don't bother looking out for Mr Du: we wouldn't know him.

We chat to Anthony, who wants to visit Scotland. He loves golf and would like to tour all the famous courses. A cousin of his is studying in Seattle and he'd like to visit him too.

At the next bench along a small child, dressed like a princess with net skirts, a shiny pink bodice and a headband with pink rosebuds on it, trots across the path and stumbles. Her mother runs to pick her up, kissing her head and patting her back. It's so much easier to protect them when they're tiny, I think, but once they're grown the parent's role diminishes, even though the sense of responsibility, the propensity for guilt, never goes. Lori's princess days were short-lived: a few months at nursery school, then she switched to witches, superheroes and animals.

I check my phone: quarter to one.

A man walks past and begins to clear his throat noisily, a retching sound, *urk urk urk,* then spits *hack* into the bushes.

Two little boys arrive with, I guess, their grandmas. The kids carry fishing nets and the women stand beside them while they have a go at catching the carp in the pool nearby.

'The press conference will be on Thursday,' Tom says to Anthony. 'We want to get the search on the news, in the papers, kick up a fuss.'

Anthony nods. 'Many girls go missing in China,' he says, 'often in the villages, kidnapped.'

Jesus! Does he think this fate might have befallen Lori?

Tom's eyes narrow. 'Does it happen to foreigners?' he says.

'No, no, not foreigners.' Anthony gives an uneasy smile. 'Only Chinese. To be married.'

Because of the shortage of women, I think, a result of the one-child policy.

'And some for...' Anthony thinks a moment '...trafficking?'

I nod. 'Yes.'

'This is not in the papers,' he says.

'People don't talk about it?' I say.

213

'That is right. But your daughter is an English girl so I think they will put her on the news. Maybe the police will find her first.' He brightens at this. 'Then all will be well. This is often the way. When the police have success then it is public.'

But if Lori's disappearance isn't publicized in the first place, what chance of success is there?

At one o'clock we try the flat again. This time someone's home. Mr Du gives a little start as he opens the door, obviously surprised to find the three of us on his doorstep. He's young-looking, quite tall, with a narrow face and pointed chin. I can smell cooking fat and garlic from inside. Mr Du listens as Anthony talks, only occasionally glancing up at him.

I catch her name, Lorelei, and Anthony gestures to us.

Mr Du makes a sound, a grunt, when Anthony has finished explaining.

'Yes,' Anthony says to us, 'Lorelei came here on the Sunday evening.'

'Ask him about the hobbies project,' I say to Anthony. 'Did Lori photograph him?'

'Bú yào,' Mr Du says, 'bú yào,' and something else I don't catch, then 'zài jiàn'. Goodbye.

'He says no. He's busy now. He wishes you well.'

'For Christ's sake,' Tom says, 'our daughter, is missing. Nǚ ér, shī zōng.' He pushes a leaflet at Mr Du, who waves it away.

'Did she talk to him about photographs?' I say. 'Or tell him who else she was going to photograph?'

Anthony speaks, and Mr Du shakes his head.

214

He flips his hands as though he's brushing us away.

'He doesn't know anything about this,' Anthony says.

Mr Du seems curt, but is that just the sound of the language?

'He has spoken to the police,' Anthony says.

'Did he see Lori on the Monday? The seventh of April?'

Mr Du scowling, speaks rapidly, and Anthony says, 'No, he saw her for the lesson on the Sunday. Now he says he must go.'

'Please, wait,' I say.

But Mr Du shuts the door.

Tom bangs on it.

'Don't,' I say. 'He's told us all he's going to.'

'Fuck,' Tom says. I think he's going to hit the door again, but he just throws his arms up, swearing some more.

In the lift, Tom turns to Anthony. 'Did you believe him?'

Anthony doesn't answer. He looks uncomfortable.

'Why was he so cagey?' Tom says. 'If he is an innocent witness and no more than that, just a student of Lori's, why wouldn't he want to help?'

'Chinese people, they do not like to be close to a big problem like this. They like harmony. Things to be ... smooth.'

'Bad for business?' I say.

'Like this,' Anthony agrees.

Three wise monkeys: see nothing, hear nothing, say nothing. It's not exclusively a Chinese trait, I think. The British have a great capacity for avoiding public confrontation, of acting as though nothing is happening, for turning a blind eye when someone creates a scene. I think of the stag do at the airport.

But is that all it is – reticence, embarrassment – or has Mr Du something to hide?

In the garden the little boys are still fishing; one of the grandmas holds her charge by the straps on his dungarees.

'Oh, great,' Tom mutters, looking ahead.

Striding towards us are two guards. They call to us, in harsh tones, gesturing to the exit.

'They wish us to go,' Anthony says.

The guards follow us to the gates, where Anthony presses the exit button. I feel their eyes on us as we leave.

Across the road there's an open square and a man in a white martial-arts suit is dancing with a sword, whirling it round his head, then posing. The light flashes on the metal and I blink it away. At home you'd be locked up for being out in public with a weapon like that.

Chengdu very safe. Superintendent Yin's words echo in my head.

Oh, really?

Then where the hell is my daughter?

CHAPTER THIRTY-FOUR

Tom suggests we try Lori's neighbour, Mrs Tang, again. I almost wimp out, still smarting from Mr Du's reluctance to talk and the fact the guards escorted us off the premises, but remind myself that this is for Lori, that we have to try everything we can.

As we drive along the length of the block beside her apartment, I can see that the shops all specialize in particular goods. One sells plumbing items, taps and pipes, another soft furnishings, one timber, one Chinese medicine, pet supplies, and window blinds. In front of some shops the proprietor and family are perched on stools, eating noodles and other snacks.

A teenage boy answers the door. Anthony explains who we are and asks if Mrs Tang is at home.

The boy replies and Anthony tells us, 'This is her son, Martin.' Martin nods to us and smiles. '*Nǐ hǎo.*'

'Mrs Tang is at work in Nanchong,' Anthony says.

They talk some more, and Anthony says, 'She travels there every Sunday afternoon. She works Monday to Thursday, then comes home late Thursday night.'

'Lori did some conversation classes with Martin,' I say to Anthony, 'so he'll know her. Can you explain why we're here? And ask him about the photo project.'

The boy looks concerned, then dismayed as Anthony talks. Martin talks quickly back to him.

'She was a very good teacher, a good neighbour,' Anthony says. 'He wishes you well. His mother will want to see you on Friday. His mother was interested in the project but she was shy.'

'Lori hasn't photographed her yet?' I say.

Martin says not.

I pass a leaflet over.

'Thank you,' he says in English, 'thank you very much. Bye-bye.'

We bring the table, the umbrella and the leaflets we left at Lori's flat down in the lift and set up our stall. I'm not sure whether it is the after-effect of Mr Du's reaction but today the passers-by seem more wary, less keen to stop and look, avoiding eye contact and altering their route a little so they don't pass so close to us.

A group of monks, tall and bulky-framed, with shaved heads, all dressed in ochre robes, pause and talk to Anthony. They look at the leaflet, but none of them recognizes Lori.

I call Bradley to let him know we have the press conference on Thursday and won't be leafleting. Rosemary was on the rota for Thursday, too, but she's helping tomorrow so I can tell her then.

Then, as we're packing up, a young woman stops. 'Hello? *Nǐ hǎo.*' She is lovely-looking, a heart-shaped face, dark eyes and hair, flawless skin. She points to Lori's photograph. 'I know her, on bus.' She waves towards the ring road.

218

My pulse jumps. I call to Tom, who's carrying the umbrella away and he comes back.

'When did you last see her?' I say. 'The last time?'

'Last time?' she says.

I glance at Anthony and he translates.

She thinks, looking down. 'Three week, or four week? Sorry. Bad remember.'

The hope fades away.

'Did you talk? Talk to her?' I say, still wanting to gain something useful.

'Little. "Hello, and, how are you?"'

She offers the leaflet back.

'Please, keep it,' I say. 'If you remember anything,' I point to the phone numbers, 'you can phone.'

She nods, tucks the leaflet into her bag and says goodbye.

I imagine them together, Lori and this young woman, recognizing each other, trying to talk in fractured sentences with lots of sign language. Lori on her way to Mr Du's or the bar, thinking up ideas for her next blog.

Where are you? A weariness settles on me. This is so hard.

We are on the bus, almost at our stop, when my phone rings. Peter Dunne.

'Mrs Maddox, I have just taken a call from Superintendent Yin.'

Oh, God. My heart kicks. 'Lori?'

'No, I'm afraid not. He was ringing after receiving an official complaint from Mr Du.' His tone is steely. 'Your actions earlier today were ill-con-

219

ceived and potentially counterproductive.'

My cheeks burn. Tom watches me.

'We simply wanted to find out if Mr Du had any information about Lori's project.'

'Those enquiries will be made by the PSB. I appreciate how difficult the situation must be for you both but this sort of interference is unacceptable. There are protocols in place. I thought I had been clear in that regard when we first met.'

'And we made it clear we wanted to be kept informed,' I say, 'but we're not being, are we?'

Tom gestures to me that he wants the phone. I shake my head. 'Have the police tried to talk to Mr Du again?' I can do steely, too, and people are staring, turning to look. Let them.

'Superintendent Yin is the officer in charge of the investigation into Lori's disappearance. He has the authority to run the investigation however he sees fit. You must accept that. Undermining his jurisdiction by contacting and harassing potential witnesses is less than helpful. The same would hold true if we were in the UK. I have promised Superintendent Yin that I will make sure you understand this and that there will not be any further interference.'

Rage sets my jaw tight, boils in my belly. 'We are trying to find our daughter,' I say.

'We all want the same outcome, Mrs Maddox, but trespassing on the purview of the PSB will only alienate the authorities and risk jeopardizing your cause. I trust I can have your reassurance that there will be no repeat of such conduct. Believe me, Mrs Maddox, you do not want to be regarded as an obstacle to the work of the PSB.

Our best hope rests with them.'

'I understand,' I say. 'Goodbye.' I ring off. 'Arrogant prick.'

My eyes sting.

We get off the bus and I repeat all I can remember to Tom who effs and blinds and throws his arms about in response.

'Why did Mr Du have to complain?' I say. 'Surely he must understand how desperate we are.' I take a breath. 'Perhaps it'll be easier once we've had the press conference. It almost feels like it's being hushed up, you know, her going missing.'

CHAPTER THIRTY-FIVE

When we reach the hotel, Tom says, 'You want to go out and eat?'

I think of the constant noise, of the struggle to decipher a menu, the chaos of it all. 'Not really. I'll just eat here.'

'OK, so let's do that. An hour?' he says.

The hotel is like a cocoon, calm and quiet, reassuring. Bland, perhaps, but bland is, oh, so welcome.

Over dinner, we keep coming back to Mr Du's discomfort, Peter Dunne's reprimand, how much power or influence the consulate actually has, and whether or not Superintendent Yin is any good at what he's doing. We share a bottle of Great Wall Cabernet Sauvignon, made in China,

221

which is surprisingly good. Tom orders a second.

'If Mrs Tang leaves Chengdu on Sunday afternoon and isn't back until Thursday night, she can't have been Lori's first subject,' I say.

'Not your general run-of-the-mill hobby, taxidermy,' Tom says. 'Very popular with the Victorians.' He laughs. 'Lori follows this account on Twitter, Crap Taxidermy. I'd show you but...'

But Twitter is banned.

'All these bizarre creatures,' he says, 'atrocious workmanship. Some of the poses.' He pulls a face, grimacing, exposes his teeth, closes one eye. I smile.

'Sometimes you can't even tell what animal it is. Let's hope Mrs Tang has the knack.'

'Trust Lori to find someone like that on the doorstep,' I say.

'It'll be good for her to keep up her photography,' Tom says. 'She's got a great eye. They don't hand out firsts to just anyone.' He fills our glasses. 'Mind you, these days, everyone's David Bailey.'

'She can write too,' I say. 'The blog's great. It's not like she has to pick one job and stick at it for the next twenty years.'

'Portfolio career,' Tom says.

'Which you had before there was a name for it,' I say.

Believe it was called "mucking about" back then. Playing silly buggers.'

'Your dad's phrase?'

His eyes darken.

'Does he know we're here?' I say.

Tom's mouth twitches. 'I left a message,' he

says. I wait but he doesn't elaborate. Clearly his relationship with Francis has not improved.

'You did all right for yourself,' I say. 'Well, mostly.' I can't name all Tom's enterprises but they included a web start-up, a wine bar, a house-sitting and dog-walking agency, a holiday rental scheme in Portugal and a home-computer repair service.

'We won't mention the guesthouse,' he says.

I groan. Lori worked there as a chambermaid and dogsbody in the summer holidays when she was sixteen. It was in Whitby, on the east coast. Tom bought it cheap with the intention of doing it up after that first season, building the business and selling it on. But once a start was made on the work, structural problems came to light and it was cheaper to condemn the property than fix it.

Tom pours a drink.

'Great summer job for her,' I say, 'but I could never quite see you doling out full English to the guests.'

'It did get a bit Fawlty Towers at times,' he says.

'Will you carry on with the property-business or are you bored?'

'Yes, and yes.' He shrugs. 'I've not come across anything else that grabs me. It's going well so I'll stick at it, put some money aside, travel and see more of the world.'

That plunges me straight back into the present. The glow from the wine fades and there is an ache at my temples. I can feel the weight of something bearing down on me.

'It's good to meet her friends,' I say, 'see where

she's living.' Trying to salvage something, to pre-empt any more considered discussion of our situation. Pollyanna.

Tom's face is serious. The look in his eyes may be pity or criticism but I disregard it. 'You have a fag,' I tell him. 'I'm going to ring home.' He opens his mouth but I keep moving, swing my bag up onto my shoulder, not wanting to hear what he might say about Lori, about what's happened to her, about being realistic, about facing up to things.

'Come to mine when you're finished,' I say, 'and we'll call Edward and do the press-conference statement.'

'If Tom's charging around like a bull at a gate no wonder the cops are pissed off,' Nick says, when I tell him what's happened.

'It's not like that,' I say. 'The guy was really dismissive, then called the guards on us. Anyway, we have the press conference sorted. Tom's going to speak to Edward and work out what to say.'

'You should do it,' Nick says.

'What?'

'You should talk. It'll be more powerful,' he says.

'I don't know, father-daughter?' I say.

'Except you only need one journalist to latch onto the fact that Tom pissed off when Lori was a baby to taint the message.'

I hadn't thought of it like that. Does it matter? Is Nick right or does he resent the fact that Tom is here and he isn't? 'I'll see what Edward says. How is everything?'

He exhales heavily and says, 'Isaac's been sick again.'

'Oh, no.'

'Twice in the night.'

'Is he going to school?' I say.

'Yes, he seemed all right this morning. Ate his Krispies.'

'We can't go on with it like this,' I say. 'The GP told me we could ask for a referral. Maybe we should do that now.'

'Can we do it over the phone?' Nick says.

'I've no idea. You could ring them and ask. Is Finn OK?'

'He's fine.'

'And you?'

'I'm OK,' he says. But he sounds flat. It can't be easy, the pressure of worrying about Lori, the demands of the campaign, holding the fort at home, on top of everything else.

'Two paragraphs max,' Edward says, 'a few sentences. Start with Lori, her personality, her qualities. You want to give her an identity, make people warm to her and see her as an individual. Say something about China or Chengdu and how she liked it – that'll help appeal to Chinese viewers. Next paragraph, keep it simple: if Lori is listening, please get in touch, and appeal to anyone who knows anything, no matter how small, to come forward.'

'Does it matter who says it?' Tom asks.

'Not at all.'

I think of Nick's advice.

'How do we decide?' I say to Tom, when the call

is over.

'You want to do it?' he says.

I think of the pressure, the attention, of trying to get my words straight. I think about breaking down. I think of Lori. 'Yes,' I say.

'OK.'

We compose the text and Tom types it up. 'Lori is a lively, loving girl, a brilliant sister to her two young brothers. She's a photographer and a teacher, who works hard and likes to spend time with her friends. Lori has been keeping a blog about her travels and when she got to China she fell in love with the place. Lori, if you hear this, please get in touch, and if anyone watching has heard from Lori or knows anything that might help us find her, no matter how small, please contact the police or the helpline number.'

Tom checks the spelling, then emails it to Peter Dunne and to Edward.

When Tom has gone, I pull back the double glazing, let in the city noise. It is a still night, the sky a bruised purple. I listen to all the sounds and try to unpick them, to separate them out and name each one. I fight to hear what is beneath, beyond, that wall of sound. If I could just hear her laugh, that joyous, delighted, abrupt laugh. That burst of pleasure. Or the little murmur she makes in her throat when she considers something.

I stand there until I grow stiff, my back aching, then give in.

CHAPTER THIRTY-SIX

We meet Anthony outside Lori's, and when Rosemary arrives, I introduce them. They chat to each other in Chinese. Rosemary's hair is so long and thick I wonder if she finds it uncomfortable with the heat and humidity. She's wearing a maxi dress again, black cheesecloth with a red orchid print. Instead of leafleting on the street I suggest the shopping mall. It's a ten-minute walk – we passed it on the way from our hotel. I check with Rosemary: would Lori have shopped there sometimes?

'Oh, yes, lots of shops. And the big supermarket has Western food.'

We walk in the shadow of the ring road to get there, risking our necks crossing each junction. The cloud chokes the city, thick and dense, impenetrable. Everything is smudged with the haze.

In the plaza, in front of the mall, cheerleaders are performing, boys and girls with red outfits and golden pom-poms. A marching band, also in red, accompanies them, the sound of the bass drum thumping across the square.

Given that both Anthony and Rosemary speak Chinese, we decide to split up. Anthony and I will cover one floor, Tom and Rosemary another, and we will meet up in an hour and a half.

Looking at the signs outside, we could be anywhere in the developed world: Uniqlo, Ted Baker,

Vuitton, H&M, Starbucks and McDonald's.

There's a security guard at the entrance.

'Should we tell him what we're doing?' I say.

Anthony talks to him. The man listens and shakes his head, waves us away.

'He says no,' Anthony says. 'We must get permission.'

'Fuck,' Tom says.

'Probably be the same back home,' I say. 'The Trafford Centre or wherever. We'll stay outside, then, go further along.' We leave Tom and Rosemary at the next doorway. Anthony and I circle the complex until we find a busy spot. A shiny new car, strewn with balloons, revolves on a stage near to a stall. The promoters all wear matching yellow T-shirts and baseball caps.

We intercept people heading towards the mall and hand out leaflets. Most people actually take one, which encourages me. We've been there about ten minutes, when a security guard from the nearest entrance calls out and starts walking over to us. He speaks to Anthony, then into his walkie-talkie. Then he shouts at Anthony again.

Anthony backs away, telling me, 'We have to leave. We are not permitted to be here.'

I'm irritated, but what can I do? 'Let's find the others, then,' I say.

There's no sign of them where we parted so we walk on. The marching band is still parading and a sizeable crowd is watching, but as we skirt around them I realize that a smaller crowd is looking the other way. A police van is on the square and I can see Tom and Rosemary standing beside it and a group of policemen. The police are armed.

I run up. 'What's going on? What's the matter?'

Tom starts to talk but one of the police, a chubby man with a pitted complexion, begins shouting at Rosemary and gestures to me and to Anthony, who has followed me.

The officer comes closer and signals that he wants the leaflets. He snatches the ones we carry and hands them to another cop. All the police are hard-faced, unsmiling.

'They're just leaflets,' I say. 'Tell them,' I say to Anthony. He begins to speak but is cut off. The atmosphere is brittle. The man in charge says something and there's sudden movement as his colleagues grab our hands and bind our wrists with plastic ties.

'What the fuck?' says Tom.

'Please,' Rosemary says, 'be calm and quiet.'

The boss says something to her.

'We are being detained,' Rosemary says, 'for causing a public nuisance and distributing propaganda without authority.'

'It's not propaganda,' I say, 'and Superintendent Yin knows we are leafleting. Please tell him, Anthony, tell him.'

Anthony tries to talk and again the officer shouts over him. He points with his baton to the back of the van. The men who tied us up pull us to the vehicle and make us get in. We sit on the bench seats that run the length of either side, Rosemary and me on one, Tom and Anthony opposite. Our grim-faced escorts get in and sit between us.

'English,' I say, 'British. Superintendent Yin – we have to contact–'

The officer shouts me down, his face contorted. Fear sparks through me, raising the hairs on my arms, making my nerves shriek.

'No talking,' Anthony says. He and Rosemary are ashen-faced. Tom looks furious, his eyes flashing. I shake my head: he mustn't do anything to inflame the situation. The back doors slam. I can still hear the brass band playing. Then, after a moment, the engine starts.

It is hot in the back of the van and it smells of sweat and metal and engine oil. We're jolted about as the driver swings through the traffic.

The men accompanying us look young but sit rigid and aloof, not making eye contact with any of us or each other.

I feel wild with anxiety, my heart thudding and my guts burning. What will they do to us?

It's perhaps twenty minutes later when the van stops. We are taken by our escorts into a police station. Not the one where we met Superintendent Yin. They ferry us through a door at the back and into a holding area where the officer who's done all the shouting is talking to a constable. Our box of leaflets is on a desk. They release our ties and we are made to sit on a steel bench, guarded by the same men.

There are forms to be filled in and they start with Tom. When it is clear that he has no Chinese, they rope Anthony in to translate. Name, place of residence in China, visa details. I hear Anthony say *nǚ ér* and *shī zōng*. He will explain why we're here, I tell myself, and it'll all be cleared up. I'm trying not to cry.

'Give him Peter Dunne's number,' Tom says. 'I've got it here.' He pulls out his phone and the

230

chief starts shouting. The officer at the desk gets a plastic tray out and we are made to empty our pockets, hand over, our bags and remove jewellery and belts. The man in charge picks up my passport and glances through it, does the same with Tom's, a look of disdain on his face.

There is some more discussion with Anthony, and I think I hear the name Yin.

Anthony points to the leaflets. He is silenced with a gesture from the boss.

A woman officer comes in and signals at me to go with her. My knees are weak as I get to my feet.

She takes me along a corridor and down some steps and puts me in a cell. The door is slammed and any sound from beyond is muffled. There's no window, just white-painted concrete walls, a concrete bench and a hole in the floor in the corner. On the ceiling a lamp in a metal cage gives off a sickly yellow light. The stench of sewage is powerful enough to make me heave. The small room is hot, as though the heat has been baked into the concrete. There are marks scratched into the paint, Chinese characters. Names, perhaps, or rude words, complaints, messages of protest.

They can't do this, I think. Which rather flies in the face of the evidence. How's it going to look, though? *CHINESE POLICE ARREST PARENTS OF MISSING GIRL.* But if they just keep it quiet, nobody will know. Like with Lori. Who here knows? The few people we've managed to reach with a leaflet.

The police will contact the consulate, surely. That's what Peter Dunne said: all the times he'd

231

been dragged out of bed when British citizens had fallen foul of the law.

With the sickening smell and the fist of tension gripping my guts, it's hard to breathe. I think of the yoga exercises I once learned but my mind is too panicked to concentrate on anything like that.

What if they deport us? The thought of going home without Lori is unbearable. Of course it's been a storm cloud on the horizon, the possibility that we won't find her, that she will stay missing, but to be sent home early, to be excluded from the search... Would they be that cruel?

I imagine Tom's sarcastic response. I think of Peter Dunne's warning about sensitive times. Of course they would do whatever was deemed necessary to suit the politics of the moment. We're irrelevant. Lori's disappearance is insignificant in the greater scheme of things.

Something moves by the drain: a cockroach, brown and shiny, the size of a plum, skirts the hole. I draw my feet onto the bench and hug my knees. I don't want to watch the insect but I want to lose sight of it even less. Aren't they supposed to favour the dark?

It circles the drain again, then crawls quickly along towards the door. I bite my tongue, resisting the urge to scream. Sweat pricks my skin.

It's important to be calm – calm and co-operative, polite. Show the police that we are harmless. Just ignorant. *Ignorance is no defence* – is that true here too? The bang of a door somewhere sends vibrations through the walls and the bench, then it all goes quiet again. The cockroach parades the width of the door, getting close to my side of the room. I clap my hands to send it away but the fucking thing takes to the air, flying at me, a whirr of shell and wings. They're not supposed to fly. I jerk out of the way, a cry in my throat.

It bumps into the wall and falls, then scuttles, hogging the edge of the wall until it reaches the drain. I press my fist against my mouth. I'm shaking. My heart burns in my chest. All the re-assurances I've given the children – you're much bigger than that is; it's more frightened of you than you are of it; just ignore it and it'll leave you alone – they die on my tongue.

What about Rosemary? She's only young. Will this have her branded a troublemaker, an undesir-able? Could she lose her job for an indiscretion like this? And Anthony? Will their involvement be held against them?

We haven't committed any crime, as far as I can see, we've not been charged. They'd have to charge us, make sure we understood, wouldn't they? They'll try the phone number on the leaflets, speak to Superintendent Yin, won't they?

Perhaps they've already spoken. Perhaps Super-intendent Yin decided our door-stepping Mr Du was beyond the pale and that having us picked up today would teach us a lesson. A flash of anger brings sweat to the back of my neck.

My bladder aches, a band of cramp, deep in my abdomen. The cockroach waves its antennae and edges over the rim of the drain hole. There is no way I can pee with the cockroach there. *Jump, you little bastard.*

There's a sudden shout in the building, a man

I think, but it's blunted by the thick walls. I can't make out the language, whether it's words or just a yell. I don't think it's Tom. I stay stock still, listening, holding my breath until my neck is sore. Nothing.

Then a sudden clattering noise, a whirring as the cockroach jinks through the air, flying drunkenly out of control. I scream and duck, almost wet myself. The insect lands clumsily by the door.

My stomach hurts when I stand but I cross to the drain, pull down my shorts and feel the burning sensation as my bladder empties, leaving the dull ache behind. The cockroach scoots under the bench. I stand by the drain. There's a thumping in the back of my head and my mouth is gummy. They'll have to bring us water, in this heat, surely.

A buzzing, sizzling sound and the light snaps off. I can't see the cockroach. I stifle a sob. The light fizzes back on. The creature hasn't moved: it waits, pressed in the shadow of the bench, antennae twitching.

Isaac hates the dark. He always has his night light on. He won't go into caves or tunnels, not even cupboards, if there's no light. His insecurities leave me feeling helpless as a parent, at times blaming myself or Nick. Why haven't we been able to make him feel safe? What did we do wrong? Did we neglect him in some way? Not enough attention. Not enough cuddles. Should I have nursed him for longer? They say every child has a different role in the family. Is that all it is? Isaac sees Finn as settled, happy, relaxed, so has to claim alternative qualities of his own.

My headache is worse. I try to relax my jaw,

massage my temples. My skin is oily, dirty. The small of my back hurts from standing but the cockroach stays where it is.

What if they do charge us? Send us to prison instead of deporting us. It does happen. Drug smugglers, people charged with corruption, or spying, with offences against the state.

What did we do? A few leaflets, that's all. I try to talk down my panic. Just leaflets asking for help to find Lori. That's all.

Fuck them! Rage surges up my spine into the back of my skull. I cross to the bench and kick at the cockroach. It scurries towards the drain end of the room and I go after it. Kicking out and trying to swipe it into the drain. It lurches up off the ground and crosses the hole to the strip of floor beyond. I twist my foot, kicking with the edge of my sandal and tip it into the hole. I stamp my foot over the space again and again to stop it crawling back up. 'And fucking stay there,' I say out loud, 'just fucking stay there.'

CHAPTER THIRTY-SEVEN

Hours later, I'm lying on my back, on the bench, my knees raised as it's not long enough for me to stretch out, when there's a clanking as the door opens. I swing upright and go dizzy. A woman officer shouts and motions me to come out. I follow her down the corridor and into the same room where we were first held.

She pats her hand at me indicating I should sit.

My mouth is claggy, throat parched. I've had nothing to eat, not even some water since we got here.

Moments after, Tom comes in with an escort.

'You OK?' he says.

'Yes. Your hand...' There is blood on his knuckles.

'Altercation with the wall.'

Our two escorts speak to each other and the woman goes out.

'Where are the others?' I say to Tom.

'Don't know, not seen anyone. Do you speak English?' he says to the policeman. 'English?'

The policeman replies in Chinese. It means nothing to us.

'If they charge us...' I say.

'They're not going to charge us,' Tom says.

'How do you know?'

He says nothing.

The woman comes back in. She has my bag and the tray with our passports and phones on. I feel a wave of relief, a loosening inside. She holds the tray out and we take our things. She has a form, too, which we have to sign. It could say anything but I imagine it must be to show we had our valuables safely returned.

I sign it.

Tom says, 'In English?'

'Tom, just sign it,' I say.

We are taken through the front of the building and left outside the police station. The officers go back inside.

It is dusk; the sky glowers lilac grey. My bottled

water is still in my bag and we share it; it's tepid but I don't care.

I start to call Rosemary but Tom says, 'Let's move along a bit, in case they change their minds.'

We don't know the area but walk down the street, past several bus stops where people are gathered, to a main road. Across the other side is the river. We go and find a bench under the trees along the promenade. The evening is muggy, the heat like warm breath enveloping us.

Rosemary answers straight away. She's fine: she and Anthony were both sent home about an hour ago. The police told them that we were trespassing, that leafleting is not permitted anywhere near the mall without clearance. She sounds shaken – there's none of the usual lightness in her voice. 'I'm so sorry,' I say.

'I'm OK,' she says. 'It is OK now.'

I speak to Anthony, apologize to him, too, and arrange to text him after tomorrow's press conference to make any arrangements for Friday.

My phone goes before I can redial and it's Peter Dunne. 'Mrs Maddox, you've been released?'

'Yes, how did you–'

'We got a call mid-afternoon and I've been talking to people behind the scenes. I understand the local police objected to you leafleting at the mall.'

'We'd have stopped but they didn't give us the chance,' I say.

'You've had your documents returned?'

'Yes,' I say.

'Good. And you were treated reasonably?'

What's reasonable? 'No one explained what was

happening,' I say. 'We didn't get to make a phone call, or have access to a lawyer.' I'm getting angry and there's an edge of hysteria making my voice quiver. 'We weren't given any food or drink.'

'I see. It is very unfortunate but, hopefully, that is the end of the matter. I will be writing in my official capacity to the department responsible to protest their heavy-handed behaviour. Is there anything you or Mr Maddox need from me otherwise?'

'Have you heard from Superintendent Yin?' I say. 'Have they spoken to Mr Du?'

'Not today.' How can he dismiss it like that? 'Thank you for the statement for the press conference. That's excellent. I'll see you tomorrow. If you can be there by half past nine.' And he's gone.

'Nothing from the police,' I say to Tom, 'and he doesn't seem to care. What is taking them so long? Have they even done anything we've asked them to?'

Tom clenches his jaw, gives a shake of his head. 'I wouldn't be surprised if Superintendent Yin was behind our detention.'

'I thought the same,' I say. 'It's like they're boxing us off, keeping us in the dark.'

The air is filled with the roar of traffic, and the Chinese language ebbs and flows, falling and rising. I close my eyes. So tired. My stomach growls. 'I'm starving,' I say.

'Grab something at the hotel,' Tom suggests.

'I need a shower first. I had a cell mate.' I shudder.

He raises an eyebrow.

238

'A bloody great cockroach, this big.' I show him with my fingers.

'You didn't make a pet of it, then?'

'No fear.'

I walk over to check the street sign and peer at the map, then suggest we walk along to a bigger junction where we've a chance of finding a taxi.

Before we get there, I spot strings of lights in the sky. Scarlet and blue, yellow and white, as though someone has taken Christmas lights and draped them high above the city, maybe half a dozen different streams of them. Some flicker on and off, like flashing LED lights.

'What are they?' I say.

'They're on the kites,' says Tom.

I pause. 'How do you know that? How can you know that?'

'Lori mentioned it one time.'

'I don't remember,' I say.

'Maybe in an email,' he says.

We walk on and see people leaning along the stone parapet. Hear a mix of music. On the promenade below two groups of women are dancing. One lot are in pairs doing slow twists and turns, singing along to the song, which is amplified. A couple are in stitches, laughing as they swing gently away from each other then back to clap hands – it's like a languid Chinese jive.

The other group of women all face the river and on the stone wall is a small screen, which shows a figure performing movements that the women copy, stretching and waving one arm, then the other, then both, bending to rub each knee in turn. Keep fit on the waterside.

It's bizarre, like a hallucination. I almost feel like it is being put on for our benefit – see how harmonious our society is, how we cherish our culture, how we share together. Never mind that my being locked in a cell is just a tiny example of the crushing grip of the state.

Just past the dancers, the kite man is surrounded by a group of children. He fixes a ball of light, flickering neon blue, to a line and it soars up the string making the whole length dip and rise in a lazy arc. Above us, bats crisscross and tumble, and all around tiny white moths cloud the air. A few pinpricks sting my calves and neck. I don't know if it's the moths, mosquitoes or some other insects biting me.

I think of Lori standing here, watching the spectacle. Is she out there somewhere, now? Across the river or uptown, glimpsing those glittering strobes in the gloom?

A toddler waddles past, making a squeak with every other step, the sound a baby's squeezy toy might make. Something in his shoe, I think. It feels like everyone is out and about tonight, carrying on this spectacle of communal life. What would they do if we interrupted the placid scene and started talking ugly truths, told them we'd been thrown in a police cell, that Lori is missing, that all over China girls are being kidnapped but their parents aren't heard?

I feel unsafe, untethered, as though I might lose control, start shouting and raving. I gesture to Tom to walk on.

Around the corner a makeshift stall has been laid out in the dark, vegetables and fruits on the

240

pavement and a set of electronic scales. A handful of customers wait their turn. There is a basketball game on in the court by the junction and more music comes from the trees nearby. A man's voice swoops and soars and, as we pass, I can just make out the silhouettes of more dancing couples.

After a long drink of lukewarm water and two painkillers, I shampoo my hair and shower away the grime and sweat and some of the tension.

I don't wait for Tom to arrive in the restaurant but go ahead and order steak, fries and salad. And, on impulse, a beer.

He's only ten minutes late. There's a giddy sense of relief at having come through an unpleasant ordeal unscathed. I wonder if we're right, and if our detention by the police was more than just a coincidence, not simply a case of being in the wrong place at the wrong time. The state flexing its muscle to put us in our place. How can we possibly know?

The beer goes to my head.

We don't linger after we've finished eating and polished off the beer. I can barely string one word in front of another and we have an early start for the press conference.

'Detained?' Nick says. 'What on earth did you do?'

'We were just leafleting, that's all.'

'Christ, Jo!'

He sounds as if he thinks it was my fault. I almost start arguing but I'm exhausted, my eyes

241

prickly and sore, my back throbbing. 'Crossed wires,' I say, 'some jobsworth laying down the law. It's all OK now.' Squashing what I really feel, I give up seeking reassurance and comfort from him. 'Anyway, how are the boys – how's Isaac?'

'Better today – well, not throwing up, but he's being a little shit to Finn. I've sent him upstairs because he won't say sorry. We've only been back half an hour.'

Isaac is stubborn: he'll sit it out all night if he's so inclined. Nick will get more and more wound up. What can I do from so far away?

I put in a plea for Isaac: 'If he's under the weather it always makes him extra cranky. Tell them I love them, both of them. Good night.'

'Good luck tomorrow,' he says. 'I'll see you on the telly.'

'You think so?'

'Edward says they'll all be there: BBC, ITV, Channel 4, Sky.'

'That's great. Night, then.'

I feel lonely, getting ready for bed, homesick. My, boys, I miss them so. I crave the feeling of Isaac's skinny arms about my neck, his whispered secrets. Finn singing and swinging my hand.

And Lori, too, I miss her, oh, how I miss her. The tug of longing, bound in a thread of fear.

CHAPTER THIRTY-EIGHT

A taxi's been booked to take us to the Rose Hibiscus Hotel where the conference will be held. I'm wearing my smartest outfit, a short-sleeved navy shirt-dress.

We find Peter Dunne a little after nine in the lobby. He's travelled on the bullet train, taking just two hours to cover one hundred and sixty-six miles from Chongqing. His greeting is brisk – he seems distracted.

'Can you wait here a moment?' he says. 'I need to speak to one of the managers.'

A few minutes later I see him cross the lobby, talking animatedly on his phone. He watches us all the while. Something's happened, I think. He looks very serious. Is it Lori? Dread sluices through me. I get to my feet. Tom follows my gaze. 'Jo?'

Peter Dunne closes his phone case and walks over to us.

I feel sick. Saliva floods my mouth.

'We need to leave,' he says. He presses the bridge of his glasses with his middle finger.

'What is it?' Tom says.

I can't speak.

'They've cancelled,' Peter Dunne says.

Not Lori then – they've not found Lori? I try to concentrate but I feel dizzy.

'Who has?' Tom says.

243

'Hard to be sure,' Peter Dunne says.

'Can't we just do it anyway?' Tom says.

I become aware of two guards by the door and another at the lift, both watching us.

'I'm afraid that wouldn't be wise. They're saying the adverse publicity would damage the city's image and overshadow the international conventions due in Chengdu this month.'

'Who's saying it?' Tom persists.

'Come on.' Peter Dunne nods to the door where the guards wait, scowling at us.

Peter Dunne is on the phone again as we go through the revolving doors and down the marble steps. 'Veronica? Send an email, high priority, to all the press list for the Lorelei Maddox conference. It's been cancelled. Make sure everybody's informed they will *not* be allowed in.'

A police van squeals to a halt outside the hotel, and a group of men dressed in riot gear pile out. My heart jumps. I've a sense of cold panic. The urge to run. I can't face being locked up again.

'Christ,' Tom says, 'bit over the top, isn't it?'

'It's a show,' Peter Dunne says, 'warning any journalists who ignore our message not to get awkward. Just ignore them and walk with me. This way – there's a teahouse round the corner.'

It's a luxurious one, set in a courtyard garden. 'A hidden gem, popular with ladies who shop,' Peter Dunne says, as the waitress leads us to a table.

I'm trembling, shaken, as I stare at the pool in the centre with water playing over sculpted rocks, the bamboo plants that screen off the tables from one another. It's all so bloody pretty, with chairs and tables carved from a rich red wood and the inlaid table-top depicting a dragon eating its own tail, but we have just been silenced, run off, by the authorities we are relying on for help.

'I can recommend the jasmine tea,' Peter Dunne says.

'I need coffee,' Tom replies.

'They do that, too.' Peter Dunne's phone buzzes and he apologizes. 'Have to get this.' He has a conversation in rapid-fire Chinese. Then the tone seems to shift a little, with Peter Dunne listening more than talking. When it is over he explains that it was Superintendent Yin.

'Did he pull out of the conference?' Tom says, his eyes flashing, 'Is that how it works?'

'No, the decision will have been made by someone higher up in the pecking order. No doubt Superintendent Yin agrees with them. The culture here, the expectation is that the police take full responsibility for investigation and then publicize their success, once results have been achieved.'

Anthony said the same thing.

'Asking for help is regarded as a sign of inadequacy,' Peter Dunne says, 'of weakness. What he did tell me is that they've completed their search through the records for train services and all internal flights. There is no evidence of Lorelei using her passport to travel in either a plane or a train within China.'

'So no holiday,' I say. It's like I've been clinging to a cliff path and have reached the end, where the last part has crumbled. And there is no way forward.

We are interrupted by the waitress who takes

245

our orders.

'So we're being gagged,' Tom says, 'and there's nothing we can do about it.' His voice is rising in volume.

'There may be another option,' Peter Dunne says, 'but I'll need some time to sort it out.'

'What?' I say.

'We host the conference at the consulate in Chongqing. It's sovereign British territory: Chinese law, Chinese authority holds no sway within the consulate. But I'm going to have to ask you to keep that to yourselves for now. If the authorities get wind, there are other measures they can take to make life difficult.'

Tom looks at him, inviting him to expand on that.

Peter Dunne gives a warning look as our drinks arrive. The waitress brings fine china cups and a teapot, Tom's coffee, and a plate of biscuits shaped like lotus flowers.

When she's out of earshot again, Peter Dunne says, 'Journalists might be apprehended. There could be unexpected roadblocks close to the venue. So...' he leans forward and pours our tea '...I'll let you know as soon as I can but we need to be discreet.'

'How long?' Tom says.

'A couple of days, three at the most.'

'Thank you,' I say. 'You won't be popular.'

He gives a thin smile and raises his cup. 'I can't guarantee it will happen but I'll do what I can. I have to speak to the Foreign and Commonwealth Office.'

'Politics?' says Tom.

'Always,' says Peter Dunne.

It's only four in the morning back home so no one there knows yet that the press conference was stopped.

Tom is in a foul mood on the way back to our hotel.

'It's a fucking joke,' he says, getting into the taxi. 'Bastards.'

The driver scowls at him and I think he might chuck us out, too, but then he starts the engine.

'What do you want to do?' I say, as we get dropped off at the hotel. I still feel shaken, my nerves raw. 'We could leaflet at Lori's again?'

'I want a stiff drink,' he says. 'Several.'

'Christ, Tom, it's not even noon. Is that your answer to a set-back? Throw alcohol at it?'

'What are we doing here?' he says. 'This is a fucking joke.'

'Don't say that.'

'It is, Joze.'

I hate it when he calls me that, a pet name from before it all went sour. 'We're looking for Lori,' I say.

'Fourteen million people,' he shouts, spittle on his lips, his eyes blazing. 'Fourteen million. Her friends haven't got a fucking clue, no one else gives a shit, no matter how nicely-nicely they're playing it. We're bad news, Lori missing is bad news. They just want us to shut up and ship out.'

'Fuck you too, then,' I yell.

He grabs my wrist and I yank it away, feel the friction sting as I do. 'Sod off. If you don't care–'

'It's not a competition, Joze.'

247

'Don't call me that.'

He glares, closes his eyes a moment. Looks back at me. 'But realistically–'

'No!' I raise my arms to silence him. My phone rings and I'm too busy shouting to answer it. 'No. We keep looking.'

'How long?' he says.

'I don't know.' I will not cry. *Prick.*

'And Finn? Isaac?' he says.

'They want me to find Lori, bring her home. How could I possibly face them – how could I sleep at night if I hadn't tried everything? If–'

Now he's raising his arms, folding them over the top of his head. His eyes change, flames replaced by liquid. 'OK,' he says.

'Or have you somewhere more important–'

He steps close so quickly I rear back. He places a finger on my mouth. Fury back in his face. I stand there, aware of the heat and pressure of his finger on my lips. It's only momentary but there's the smell of violence in it, an undertow of rage.

Then he wheels away.

I flip him a V-sign

I knew his anger in the past, that awful time when our marriage was falling apart and he would lash out, verbally cruel.

Then the ringing starts again. Whoever it is doesn't want to leave a message.

Nick. 4 a.m. at home. Has he heard somehow?

'Hello?' I say.

'Jo, it's about Isaac.'

'What?'

'He's OK, don't worry, but we're at the hospital, A and E.'

'Nick?' My skin, every inch, freezes. My vision blurs. 'What happened?'

In the second before he answers, possibilities cascade through my mind, outtakes from a gruesome parallel universe: Isaac savaged by the dog; Isaac running away and knocked down by a car; Nick losing his temper and hitting him; Isaac messing with a knife; Isaac in the medicine cupboard; Isaac at the top of the stairs, falling.

'He started screaming, in the middle of the night. I thought it was a nightmare but he collapsed.' Nick's voice wavers. 'I called an ambulance. They're assessing him now.'

'Oh, God.' I should be there. 'Have they said anything?'

'No.'

'Shit. Where's Finn?'

'He's here. I couldn't leave him. He wants to say hello.'

'Yes.' I snatch a breath, sit on the edge of the steps. There are banks of flowers growing at the side, vivid pink cosmos with feathery leaves, showy arum lilies, verbena.

'Mummy?'

'Hello, Finn.'

'We're at the hospital.'

'Isaac's poorly, isn't he?'

'Are you coming home now, Mummy?'

Oh, God. I swallow. 'Not just yet. That's great, you helping Daddy.'

'Yes. I'm going to get some 7-Up now from the machine.'

'OK. Love you. Put Daddy on.'

If I got a flight tonight, I think, it takes thirteen

maybe fifteen hours, depending on connections. With the time difference I could be home tomorrow at noon.

'I can see about flights,' I say to Nick.

'How was the press conference?'

'It didn't happen. We're being jerked about. Peter Dunne's trying to fix up an alternative, in the consulate.'

'When?'

'Soon as he can. We're not to tell anyone yet. But Tom could do the conference. I'll come home if I need to ... if he's not ... if he's...' What am I saying? If he gets worse, if they don't know what's wrong.

'Can you even get a flight?' Nick says.

'I don't know. They must make some sort of provision for emergencies,' I say.

'Wait, let's see what the doctors say. It could be something simple–'

'Like what?' I say.

'I don't know. I'm not a bloody–' He makes an effort to sound reasonable. 'I'm just not sure it makes sense for you to leap on a plane straight away. And if he's better, then what – you leave again?'

I don't know how to respond. A group of Chinese tourists comes out of the hotel. I can feel them glancing at me, sitting on the steps.

What is Nick saying? That if I come home I should stay there?

'He's in the best place,' Nick says.

'How was he, in the ambulance?'

'Finn and I had to go in the car,' Nick says. 'They couldn't take both of us in the ambulance with Isaac.' There's a pause, then he says, 'He wasn't conscious.'

I blink hard. 'I'll look into flights,' I say, 'just in case.' There's a buzzing in my head on top of the edgy percussion of the city.

'Don't book anything,' Nick says. 'I'll ring as soon as there's any word.'

My eyes burn with unshed tears. 'Oh, Nick,' I say.

I can hear Finn calling him, asking him something.

'I'd better go,' Nick says.

'Yes. Fine. You'll ring?'

'Promise. Bye.'

I've only just got to my room when there's thumping at the door.

Tom glares at me, his pale eyes icy. 'I've been trying to call you,' he says, 'Peter Dunne has the go-ahead from his higher-ups. He's thinking Saturday but he needs to confirm a few things. I'll be in the bar. You need to set your bloody phone up so it tells you when there's another call waiting.'

I hit him. I slap at his face and then push his chest with both hands. And then I burst into tears.

CHAPTER THIRTY-NINE

'Fuck. What did I do now?' Tom stares at me.

Through my sobs I tell him about Isaac.

'Shit,' he says. 'Wait there.'

He returns with his laptop and a bottle of some sort of Chinese liquor and insists I drink some. It makes me cough – I feel like it's stripped the lining from my mouth.

'What if he ... what if I can't get there in time?' I feel horrible saying it, thinking it.

'Let's look at flights,' he says. 'At least you'll know what your options are.'

He browses websites. There aren't many to Manchester but we include those to Birmingham, Leeds-Bradford and Liverpool as well. Then he collates the possibilities and emails it to print downstairs.

I am counting the minutes since Nick rang, opening my phone time and again. When it does ring, I leap out of my skin. But it's not Nick, it's Anthony. 'Mrs Maddox, I'm not going to be available tomorrow, I am sorry. I'm going to be out of the city for a while.'

'Right.' I'm not sure what to say.

'There are many other agencies you may contact in Chengdu.'

'Yes.'

A pause. Then he says, 'Goodbye.' And that's it. He's resigned. It's like a slap in the face. I can barely take it in.

'Anthony,' I tell Tom. 'He's not going to be available.'

Tom snorts. 'Really? Couldn't have anything to do with us getting him arrested, could it?'

'Maybe he was warned off,' I say.

'Maybe he just wants a quiet life. Edward will be able to suggest someone else, or Peter Dunne will. There's something about them having a list of translators on the FCO website.'

Tom gets up and stares out of the window. He makes conversation but I'm too distracted to respond. He hovers. 'Come on,' he says eventually.

'What?'

'Let's get out for a bit. You're going to go bat-shit crazy just sat here waiting and I'm going to go crazy watching you.'

I look at my phone.

'You'll still get the call,' he says, 'whether you're here or outside.'

'You go. I'll be fine.'

He looks at me, sceptical.

'I'll be all right. I don't need you ... pacing.'

He's about to argue.

'Tom.' I hold up my hand. 'Please. I'll be OK. I'll let you know.'

I lie on the bed, staring at the ceiling. I close my eyes to rest them but I'm far from sleep.

I think of Isaac, of him being ill, then rallying enough to needle Finn, and of Nick sending him to his room. Did they make up before night time? Before he collapsed?

I ring Peter Dunne. I detect a note of impatience as he starts, 'I still haven't heard back from PSB–'

It's not that,' I say. 'I've had some bad news from home. My son Isaac, my youngest, he's in hospital. He's collapsed and, erm...' I'm out of breath, feeling dizzy, I gulp some air '...they're assessing him now. If he deteriorates I may have to get a flight back.'

'Yes, of course. I'm so sorry. If you do need to travel please let me know and we can arrange a seat for you at short notice.'

'Thank you.'

The phone rings, shrill in the silence of my room.

'Nick?'

'I've just spoken to the doctor. Isaac's being prepped for surgery.'

'Oh, my God.'

'It's his appendix. It's burst. They'll remove it and they said their main concern will be to prevent any infection.'

'Oh, Nick.'

'Try not to worry,' Nick says.

'He's five years old and I'm not there.'

'I am,' Nick says.

But I'm his mum.

'All being well, he'll be in hospital for a few days until he's recuperated enough and then it's bed rest at home. We'll be fine.'

What is he saying? He wants me to trust him to cope with it all? To accept that he is the parent in charge, the one holding things together?

'You've only another week, as it is,' he says, 'and

if there's going to be a press conference, you should stay. Keep looking for Lori.'

He's right: no matter how much I want to be there, to be at Isaac's bedside, it seems the emergency is over and I can't abandon my search for Lori.

'They reckon it'll be about three hours,' Nick says.

'Ring me,' I say.

'I will.'

'How's Finn?' I say.

'Sparked out – and snoring.'

I call Tom and tell him what's happened. 'That's good,' he says. 'They know what's wrong, how to treat it. You haven't eaten?'

'I'm not hungry.'

'Is that a good idea?' he says.

'What?'

'Skipping meals because you're upset. I'm going to one of the snack places. You could come. I won't force-feed you.'

We walk to the row of eateries round the corner from the hotel. Raw food is set out on a table in front of the window of the first establishment and we try to work out what it is. Tom points at a line of thin pink strips of meat and says the word for duck. The vendor frowns. Tom repeats himself. The vendor speaks a stream of words, perhaps thinking we're asking to buy. Tom says 'duck' again and points. The vendor nods.

'Duck's tongues,' Tom says, 'I thought they were.'

'How come?'

'Had them in Chinatown one time.'

Of course he did. Whole swathes of Tom's life I know nothing about, haven't wanted to know anything about. And vice versa, I guess. Though I'd venture his has been more varied and exciting than mine.

The man gestures for us to come inside.

'*Bú yào, xiè xie,*' I say, smiling and shaking my head, 'No, thank you.'

Further down, there's an eatery with a couple of spare tables and laminated pictures on the wall, showing the dishes they offer.

Tom points to the ones he wants. I tell him to get enough to share. He's right – there's no point in keeling over with low blood sugar.

The TV is on in the corner, some sort of soap opera. A girl and two suitors, it looks like. There's a slapstick feel to it. The cook and another woman are sitting on stools, watching it, with a little boy. They're laughing. Perhaps it's a sitcom.

'Peter Dunne called just before we came out,' Tom says.

'He called you?'

'I think he thought you'd rather a lot on.'

'And?' I say.

'The PSB is satisfied that Mr Du had no further contact with Lori after his lesson on Sunday and that she made no arrangements to photograph him. Like he told us.'

'Can they prove it?' I say.

'It seems so, but Peter Dunne wouldn't give me any details. Or couldn't because he's not in the loop.'

Our food arrives. Pork, spring onions, greens and aubergine in chilli sauce with sticky rice. Hot liquid in little glasses, faintly yellow. Water? Or perhaps it's tea, though I can't taste tea. The food is salty and oily and the taste of the Sichuan peppers is strong.

Tom scoops up greens and rice with his chopsticks, dips his head to eat.

'Where does that leave us? Lori hadn't photographed Bradley or Oliver,' I tick off the candidates, 'or Shona. And Mrs Tang was away working.'

'Unless they're lying,' Tom says. 'We've only got their word for it.' He takes another mouthful.

'And Oliver – the way he ignores our messages.'

Tom wipes the juice off his chin with a tissue and puts it in the waste bin. 'But maybe we're getting too fixated on the project,' he says.

'What else have we got, Tom?' I go through it out loud. 'She breaks up with Dawn on Thursday, gets so drunk that she's sick on the Friday. She teaches as normal over the weekend, and on Monday she texts Shona. That's where the trail...' I hear the end of the phrase and almost don't say it but tell myself I'm being ridiculous '...goes dead. There's nothing else and, as far as we can tell, the police haven't come up with anything. There's neither hide nor hair of her. People don't just disappear.'

He looks as if he'll contradict me but I go on, 'They don't. They run away, they have an accident or...' I shiver, feeling feverish, nerves jangling again.

There's a blare of music from the TV, the theme

257

tune. The cook takes the boy off her lap and stands up.

Tableaux flit into my head, an ugly peep show. Dawn in a rage, hurt by Lori, confronting her... Oliver calling Lori up, asking her to the loft where he keeps his pigeons, an argument erupting, he gets angry... Mr Du touching her, Lori pulling away... Some awful mishap with Shona on her scooter. The group of friends sealing an unholy pact to protect one of their number. Lori, with her camera, stumbling upon something hidden, secret and deadly, the triads or government corruption.

I knock them down, shake them off, the scenarios from this catalogue of dread.

'I want to go back,' I say.

'Home? Tonight?' Surprised.

'No, the hotel.'

'Look, if you want to—'

'I'll see you in the morning.'

There's a pressure in the air that makes the back of my skull and my teeth ache. The sky is dark. A gust of wind sends leaves and scraps of litter scurrying down the street. It blows dust in my eyes. I have a sense of hopelessness: we're getting nowhere – people don't want to help, they don't care. Lori is lost and Isaac is sick and I'm floundering. We are scattered, my family, broken.

A text from Nick. *All well. Isaac sleeping. He'll go on to a ward tonight. Finn staying with Penny for a couple of days.*

My room is sweltering. But I prefer the noise of the city to the drone and stale cold of the air-conditioner so I slide open the windows.

In the night thunder breaks. I jolt awake to the sound of a great timpani drum beating above, strike after strike, clanging and jangling in the dark. As if the skin of the sky will split. Outside, sheets of lightning flash over the city; jagged forks stab down among the buildings. The thunder pounds and crackles and roars but no rain comes. There is no respite from the sultry air. The pressure builds even stronger behind my eyes, in my head. I watch until my joints grow stiff.

CHAPTER FORTY

I'm up at dawn. The storm has broken and rain hammers down from the glowering sky.

I dreamed of Isaac. A lovely dream. I arrived home, rushed and anxious, to find him sitting at the top of the stairs in his pyjamas.

As he saw me, he smiled and stood up. 'Look, Mummy, I can fly.' His face full of glee. And he flapped his arms and cycled his legs and was soaring around the hallway, which was a massive dome hung with chandeliers.

It'll be after eleven at home but I text anyway: *All OK?*

Yes, Nick's reply comes. *I'm staying with him. He needs plenty of sleep. Skype when he's up to it?*

Sure.

Penny has emailed to say that Finn is fine:

It must be hard to be so far away when Isaac is poorly but do try not to worry. Nick's with him and Finn is enjoying the novelty of sleeping on a sofa bed in Gav's room with Benji in attendance (Gav's still working in Berlin). We are all thinking of you and hope there will soon be news of Lori. There are some lovely messages for her on Facebook.

In the hotel restaurant I eat some melon, a round of toast, drink tea and return to my room. It is still only seven forty-five. I don't know what to do with myself.

I practise saying my piece for the press conference. Read it over and over until I almost know it off by heart. Then I swipe through the photos on my phone, Isaac and Finn, Lori, Nick. I read Lori's blog again, that first entry.

In my defence I'd like to point out that
a) No one asked me
b) I'm really not the alluring type
c) If I am called after a rock then so are the Jades and Rubys and Ambers out there and maybe my rock has a little bit more character than theirs. Maybe. Granite, anyone? Millstone grit?
d) My singing may drive people to distraction but I have never drowned a soul, mariner or otherwise.

Perhaps people who hear the appeal will look at her blog, get more of an idea of who she is.

By the time Tom comes to my door at nine, I have

showered and tidied up, and I am watching the construction vehicles working in the rain, demolishing the last of the long sheds. The site is pocked with puddles now, some very large. The lorries that are removing the debris drive through them, causing great waves of spray and sending the water streaming across the ground.

I answer Tom's knock.

'How's Isaac?' he says.

'He's sleeping, no problems.'

'OK. I'm going to see Mrs Tang, and then I'll do some leafleting. I'll see you when I get back.'

'Did you get an interpreter?' I say.

He shakes his head. 'No, I forgot. But I'll try to find someone later.'

'And Mrs Tang?'

'Got this.' He holds up his phone. The English–Chinese dictionary app.

'OK.'

He shuts the door. I sit on the bed, feel a swift lurch of misgiving, a flush of heat. What am I doing? It forces me to my feet. I grab my bag and my raincoat from the wardrobe and run to the lift. When I get down to the lobby, I see Tom on the steps outside, his jacket already darkening with the rain. No umbrella.

I race after him. I'd thought the rain would be refreshing and lower the temperature but it's steaming, like being in the shower.

I catch him at the junction.

'Jo?'

'I can't just sit there,' I say, breathless. *And I don't want to be on my own.*

He nods.

We wait for the lights to change.

The park is quiet, everything sodden. We pass life-size models made of bamboo: a yak, a water-wheel, a cottage, a cart.

Tom is drenched by the time we reach the ring road. My top half is dry but my jeans have soaked up the water and stick to my ankles. My sandals are slippery, treacherous.

We buy our tokens for the bus and take the escalator up to the platform. Curtains of rain cloak the city, blurring the view. Once we are on our way, I see a policeman asleep in his car at the side of the ring road. I want to stop the bus, run over and hammer on his windscreen, wake him. 'Find my daughter. Now. Find her. Why aren't you looking? Look now.'

In the grey of the downpour, Lori's building with its vivid blue tiles is a brash slab of colour, smeared with rust marks, like wounds.

Martin answers the door, and smiles. 'Hello. Come, come.' He waves us indoors, takes us through the kitchen into a living room that is divided into two areas: a dining table and chairs and beyond that the lounge area, with two long couches in an L-shape facing a TV. The wallpaper is patterned with tall canes of bamboo, and there is a beautiful fretwork screen concertinaed by the wall next to the dining table. All the furniture is made of rich dark wood, highly polished.

'Mama,' Martin calls, and Mrs Tang comes from the narrow hallway. She welcomes us, shakes hands. She is small, wiry, her hair starting to go grey. She wears a stripy jumper, black slacks and tortoiseshell glasses. There are no signs of her hobby here. We are offered tea several times but say, no, thank you.

Mrs Tang has only a word or two of English. Martin picks up the flier from the dining table and his mother talks to him about it. He says, 'Mama is sad.'

'Lori talked about photos?' I mime a camera, then point at Mrs Tang.

'Yes ... Mama...' He gestures to her and talks in Chinese, clicks his tongue, irritated, I think, that he can't explain.

Tom opens the dictionary app on his phone, shows Martin, who finds the word he wants. 'Reserved,' Tom reads.

'Shy,' I say, remembering what Anthony translated the last time we were here, 'Mrs Tang was shy about doing it?'

'Animals?' Tom says.

'Yes.' Martin understands this: he talks to his mother and Mrs Tang beckons to us. We go along the hall that leads off the dining area to a box room at the end. The walls are covered with stuffed animals, set out on shelves. Two squirrels, various birds, a snake and something I think is a mongoose. Some stand on small plinths and others are under glass cases. In front of the window is a wide desk covered with tools, scraps of material and the body of a rat, which looks crushed.

'Yes,' I say, 'very good.' But the animals with their glass-bead eyes, their curled claws and stiff poses make me uneasy. I don't like to think what Mrs Tang has to do to create her models. The room smells of nothing worse than solvents, glue perhaps, a tang reminiscent of nail-varnish remover.

I daren't catch Tom's eye after his impersonation of the joke taxidermy animals on Twitter.

'Shall we?' I point back to the living room.

We stand around the dining table, but Mrs Tang gestures that we should sit on the sofas.

'When did Mrs Tang last see Lori?' I ask Martin. 'When – what day?'

He speaks to his mother and they seem to agree. Martin gets up, goes through to the kitchen and comes back with a wall calendar. The months are marked on one sheet, no pictures, just the dates in red and black, Chinese and English.

He hands it to Mrs Wang and she points.

'April six,' Martin says.

'Sunday?' Tom says.

Martin checks and Mrs Tang agrees.

'Is she sure?' I say.

Martin doesn't understand me. Tom finds the translation, 'Definite, certain. *Kending.*'

Tom hands the phone to Mrs Tang. '*Kending.*' She nods. She talks for a while to Martin. He thinks for a moment, then explains. 'Sunday six April Ma go Nanchong.'

'To work,' Tom says.

'Work. See Lori,' Martin says.

'See Lori here?' I point to the window, jabbing my fingers down.

'Here,' Martin says. He hums, looks up to the ceiling. His mother says something else and he nods to her.

'Lori talk ... photo.' He mimes a camera, like I did, his fingers forming a rectangle one on top

264

presses the button. 'Photo ... tomorrow, tomorrow, tomorrow.'

I'm confused.

Tom holds out his hand for his phone and Mrs Tang passes it back. Tom looks up 'tomorrow' and shows Martin. Martin pulls a face.

'Photo ... small time,' Martin says.

'Soon?' I guess.

'Soon, soon.' Martin nods. He says something else to Mrs Tang and she smiles in agreement.

I speak in pidgin English: it seems the best way to make myself understood, 'Lori say to Mrs Tang, Lori take Mrs Tang photo soon. Yes?'

'Yes,' Martin says, but he waves his hands as if there's more to come. 'Back Nanchong.'

'Take photo when Mrs Tang back Nanchong?' I say.

'Yes,' Martin says.

I smile and thank them, but I feel deflated. This tells us nothing about Lori's movements on the Monday.

Mrs Tang says something and wiggles her wrists. Martin laughs.

'First photo bike,' Martin says.

'Bike?' Tom says.

Mrs Tang giggles. 'Jumas dee,' she says, 'jumas dee.' As though we might understand. She waggles her hands again.

'James Dee,' Martin says.

'James Dean?' Tom gets it.

'Jumas Dee.' Mrs Tang beams. 'Easy Rider.' She mimes the revving of a motorbike and makes a growling sound. We all laugh. I recall images: Dennis Hopper in his buckskin jacket riding a chopper bike; James Dean, hot young rebel astride his motorbike, fag in his mouth, wearing his leather flying jacket.

Realization slams through me.

First photo bike.

A motorbike. A vintage motorbike.

She was going to shoot me ... an old Chiang Jiang 750. Bradley's words.

It falls through me like slabs of ice. Cold lead weight.

A trap-door opens at my feet.

CHAPTER FORTY-ONE

Back upstairs in Lori's flat, we try to make sense of what we've just heard.

'Bradley said himself that he was going to be involved,' says Tom.

'But he said Lori hadn't filmed him yet. Perhaps her plan fell through,' I suggest. I'm trying to stay rational, not jump to conclusions, but my body is having none of it. A surge of adrenalin has sent my pulse soaring, my guts are knotted, my mouth dry. 'No,' I rebuff my own explanation. 'The text to Shona was sent at twenty past ten. It said *making a start.* Not *made a start* ... as though she was in the middle of working on it.'

'Or about to start it,' Tom says. 'He's lying to us, the little shit.'

Why?

'We need to make sure we've not got our wires

266

crossed,' I say. 'Then we tell the police.'

'Jo, if he is lying, there's a reason. He's not suddenly going to come clean. He'll keep lying. Look, we go round there – it's easier to tell if he's bullshitting us in person.' Tom is already on his feet.

'And say what? Do what?' I look across the balcony, through the veil of rain, to the cranes working on the new buildings.

'Tell him we're double-checking the timeline before Lori disappeared, and ask him again when he last saw her. Depending on what he tells us, we say we've spoken to someone who heard he and Lori were meeting up on the Monday and see how he reacts.'

'And if he just denies it, explains it away?' I say.

'We beat the shit out of him,' Tom says.

I gape.

'I'm joking!'

'How do I know you won't do that?' I say to Tom. 'Lose your temper, attack him.'

'I won't touch him,' Tom says steadily.

'He might freak out, if we just turn up and start asking questions,' I say.

'Where does he live?' Tom says.

'It should be here somewhere.' I check on Lori's noticeboard, find his name scrawled near the top and his address. It takes a while to work out where it is on the map but we do.

'Look,' Tom points, 'there's a tourist attraction here – a monastery – not far from his place. We can tell him we were already in the area and wanted a quick word.'

'Not call him first?' I say.

267

'If he says he's not home we're screwed,' Tom says.

'OK,' I say. 'I just hope he's there.'

'He starts work at two,' Tom says.

'Yes, but he said he had extra meetings some mornings, which is why he's not been able to do much leafleting this week.'

There's some back-and-forth with the cab driver but he finally understands where we want to go.

Bradley's is a gated complex, several towers of black and grey with large red lettering on top that will light up at night, I imagine, like the ones I've seen from the hotel.

'Wait a minute,' Tom says, and we watch the gate from over the road for a few moments. People coming in and out, in a rush, as the rain slaps down.

'They're not all using their key cards,' Tom says.

It's true: people are following each other through and holding the gate open for those coming in behind them. There's a different gate to exit at the other side of the security booth. Three guards are visible, chatting to each other just inside the entrance, umbrellas up against the rain.

I've a sick, fluttery feeling in my stomach.

'Come on,' I say.

We wait for a gap in the traffic and cross. Loiter a minute until a woman carrying bags of groceries makes her way to the entrance. She switches her shopping to one hand and uses the other to swipe her card and release the gate. We follow her through.

The central area is landscaped, like the place where Lori's student, Mr Du, lives. There's no fountain here but pools and streams full of fish, a basketball court and bridges leading to a pavilion. The rain beats down on the water, pitting it like dimpled pewter.

The towers form a horseshoe and noise reverberates between them, the chatter from a television, a burst from a pneumatic drill, someone playing martial music, birds squawking, all amid the susurration of the downpour.

Bradley's block is number five, his flat 1804, the eighteenth floor.

The radio in the lift plays jingles. I feel dizzy. My head is full of vibrations, making it hard to think straight. Are we mad? 'Maybe we should just tell–'

'It's cool, we're here now.' Tom's face is set. 'We're just double-checking in the area, like we said.'

'Wow! Everything OK?' Bradley is bare-chested, barefoot, wears dark chinos. There are scraps of shaving foam on his cheeks either side of his moustache.

'Fine,' Tom says. 'We just wanted a quick word.'

'Aw, I'm going to work.' He grimaces. 'I could catch up with you later?'

'It'll only take a minute.' Tom steps forward, forcing him into the flat.

Bradley laughs, disconcerted. 'Sure. If I'd known you guys were coming we could have–'

'We were just passing,' I say, 'going to the monastery, Wenshu. We're soaked, sorry.' I'm aware that our clothes are dripping on the floor.

269

Tom walks in. The door leads us through the utility area into the kitchen, where sliding-panel doors open onto the living room.

'I really have to be out of here in ten minutes,' Bradley says.

I was expecting something scruffy, like Lori's place, but Bradley's flat is much more upmarket, larger, lighter, and furnished with good-quality pieces. There is a square wooden dining table, four ladder-backed chairs, and a huge settee, upholstered in chocolate brown. A large TV, speakers and games consoles sit on a dark cherry-wood bench. The coffee table is a similar colour, the carved legs shaped like elephants standing upright, their trunks raised.

Several pieces of artwork hang on the walls: a watercolour of mountains in the mist, a night scene in gaudy oils, a calligraphy piece of characters brushed on a bamboo scroll and a framed painting of one of the face-changing masks, like the one we saw performed in the park.

'We're just double-checking some of the facts we've got,' Tom says. He pulls out one of the dining chairs without being invited and I do the same.

Bradley doesn't sit but stands by the table, his knuckles tapping lightly on the edge near to his phone, wallet and keys. 'If you want to call tonight–' he says.

Tom interrupts him: 'You last saw Lori at the party on the Friday?'

Bradley looks at him, mouth agape, as though he can't believe how rude we're being. 'That's right.'

'And you didn't hear anything from her after that?' Tom says.

'No.'

'Did she arrange a date to meet up to photo- graph you and your motorbike?'

Bradley's smile fixes in place. His eyes harden momentarily. 'No. No, she had been talking about it generally but we'd never gotten round to specifics.' He throws up his hands. 'Sorry, I really need to be out of here.'

'You finish off.' I try to smile. 'We'll go down with you.'

'No, really...' He laughs. There is no humour in it.

'I could really do with a minute here,' I say. 'I feel quite faint – everything's so...' I cover my mouth, my emotional incontinence only partly contrived. 'I'm sorry.' I bend down, head between my knees.

Tom puts a hand on my back. 'Deep breaths,' he says.

Bradley hesitates. Politeness? Or maybe he's trying, as we are, to act normally. He slaps the table. 'No sweat.' But he doesn't look at all happy.

He goes into the nearest room, which I assume is the bathroom. The door clicks shut.

Tom reaches over and grabs Bradley's phone. My heart's in my mouth as he opens the case and begins to scan it. I move my chair closer so I can see. Tom enters the messages folder, scrolls through the list of people. The bathroom door opens and we both jump. Tom puts his hand down by his side. Bradley walks away, further along the hall. 'Wenshu is amazing,' he calls over

271

his shoulder. 'There's a great veggie restaurant in there, too.'

'Excellent,' I say. My voice sounds strained.

Bradley goes into a room at the end of the hall and shuts the door.

Tom returns to the phone, rolls back through the message threads until he reaches Lori. 'Fuck!' he mouths. His face darkens. I read her most recent message. *Bit late soz. B there 10.30 Lxxx* It is dated Monday, 7 April.

Bradley's previous message sent the day before. *Can do 10ish? B.* In response to Lori's, *U around tomoz for photos? Lxxx*

It's like a blow to the guts, swift and powerful. She met him. She met him on the Monday. *Oh, Jesus.*

I glance at Tom, see the anger in his eyes. Put my hand on his arm, a reminder, a warning.

There's a sound from Bradley's room: a cupboard door banging, maybe. Tom pulls out his own phone and takes pictures of the message thread. He's putting Bradley's phone back when Bradley comes out, buttoning a shirt. I stand up and move to shield Tom. My legs feel feeble. Hoping to distract Bradley, I walk to the sliding glass doors. He has two white wicker easy chairs outside on the balcony, a palm tree in a brass planter. Eighteen floors up and the city swims below in the teeming rain.

'Lovely flat,' I say.

'Yeah. I was lucky to get it.'

'Lots of space. Time for a tour?' I say.

'Hey, I'm sorry. Like I said, I really have to head out now.' He's sitting down, pulling on shoes.

I ignore him, walk back and turn towards the bedrooms. 'Only take two ticks. Is it two beds or three?'

'Hey.' There's a sharp edge to his voice as he stands up. 'The place is a tip.' He laughs. 'Come another time, we'll do dinner. I'll give you the full tour then. But now...' he claps his hands '...we're outta here.' He picks up his phone and wallet, puts them in a small rucksack and grabs his keys.

'Dinner'd be lovely.' I don't know why I'm not raging. How can I still pretend? My head is buzzing, my face feels brittle – I can't get enough air.

'Still raining?' he says.

'Cats and dogs,' I say.

Tom hasn't spoken. He gets to his feet and we follow Bradley, who picks up a black waterproof cape from hooks by the main door. Bradley locks the door behind us.

There's a burst of noise from along the hallway – it sounds like a pneumatic drill, deafening. Perhaps the one I heard below. It cuts out as we reach the lifts.

I'm desperate to keep the chit-chat going, to stop him getting suspicious. 'Big storm in the night.'

'We get them a lot,' Bradley says. He presses the button for the lift. 'Back home we have twisters.'

'Tornadoes?' I say.

'That's right. Those things can be scary. One time my uncle's car was picked up and thrown right across the yard.'

I watch the lights that indicate the progress of the lift. They change painfully slowly. *Keep talking.*

'You have to stay indoors?'

'Yes, we get warnings and most people know the drill, these days, like staying away from the windows.'

The lift arrives. We get in and Bradley presses buttons for the ground floor, marked as 1 in China, and for the basement.

'So your scooter,' I say, 'it uses a battery?'

'Yeah.'

'How do you charge it?'

'There are charging points in the garage downstairs,' Bradley says.

'How long does it take?' *How can you stand here and lie to me? Lie about my daughter?*

'A few hours'll give me maybe a hundred klicks,' he says. 'If you do want to try the veggie place, just head for the back of the grounds, past all the halls.'

'Thanks.'

Tom still hasn't said a word.

'Dawn said you still might have a press conference,' he says. *Does Dawn know you've been lying?*

'We hope so. The consulate are trying to rearrange.'

'Good.' He nods. 'Hey – I should be around on Sunday for leafleting.'

'Thanks, that'd be great.'

I wait until we reach the second floor, then say, 'Oh, no! I've left my phone upstairs.'

His face falls. 'OK, you wait–'

'No, no,' I say, 'you'll be late. You get your scooter and I'll nip back up. I'll meet you and Tom at the entrance.' I speak briskly, assured, like

274

I'm telling Finn or Isaac what to do. 'I'm so sorry,' I say. 'It's hard to think straight with everything that's going on... Is it just the one key?' I don't dare look at Tom.

The lift stops. The doors open.

'No,' Bradley says. He jabs at the buttons and the lift heads upwards again.

I feel so light-headed I think I might really faint, but I fight to make conversation and fill the silence. 'I'm sorry, my concentration's rubbish. I think it's the stress, you know? I keep losing things, don't I, Tom?'

'Yes,' Tom says.

'And going blank.'

Bradley shifts on the spot.

I fall quiet as we reach the eighteenth floor again and follow him to the flat. My heart is galloping in my chest.

Inside, he glances at the table where we were sitting. 'I can't see it.' An accusation.

My hand is in my pocket, clasping my phone. I've ruined everything, I think. He knows we suspect him – he must do. I'm paralysed. Then the drill starts up nearby, making the floor shake.

'What's the building work?' Tom shouts to be heard.

I seize the chance and scurry to the chair I was sitting on, drop to my knees, arm angled so Bradley can't see. 'On the chair,' I say, turning and lifting my phone. 'These pockets, they're so shallow.'

We go through the pantomime of leaving again.

'So, we head left at the gates?' I say, pointing that way, as we reach the ground floor.

'That's right,' Bradley says. 'About ten minutes,

275

you'll see the signs. Give me a call about dinner.'

'Will do,' I say.

'And I'll see you Sunday.'

The lift doors close behind us and Tom and I walk outside.

'What the fuck was that stunt?' Tom says.

'I thought if I could get up there and leave the door ajar, we could go in. Oh, God, Tom. Thank God it didn't ring,' I say. 'He couldn't wait to get rid of us – he really didn't want me to look around.'

'Fucking lying bastard,' Tom says. 'What the hell is going on?'

'Let's make sure he's really going,' I say, 'and make it look like we are.'

We hurry to the gates – I try not to slip in my sandals. The rain bounces off the floor.

We begin walking to the corner, I keep glancing back to watch the traffic coming up the ramp from the car park. Bradley appears on a black and blue scooter wearing a blue helmet and his waterproof. He closes the mask on his helmet and rolls the bike forward, puts his feet up and joins the traffic. As he passes us he raises a hand and waves. We wave back and walk until he has disappeared from view.

'Come on.' I turn back towards the complex.

I've not thought this through. I'm not sure what I'm doing is the right thing but I'm acting on instinct now. All I know is that Bradley has deceived us. That he is hiding something. That he really did not want us in his flat. And that we are looking for Lori, I tell myself. That's what we're doing. We are looking for Lori.

CHAPTER FORTY-TWO

We tag on behind a young couple, get back into the complex and walk through the gardens to the building. A man waits for the lift, middle-aged, Chinese. I pray he won't try to engage us in conversation: he would surely sense something suspicious. Thankfully, he nods once, then studiously ignores us as we do him, and each other. The lift climbs through the storeys. The drill is thundering away when we reach the apartment.

'We'll have to break in,' I say.

Tom looks at the door. 'That could take some doing.'

'Now – while it's noisy.'

Tom steps back, raises his leg and smashes his heel into the edge of the door near the lock. It bounces but doesn't yield. He does it again and again, as I pray that the drill will keep going. The door shudders from the impact. Then finally, with a squealing sound, the lock gives, shearing through the door frame. The drill stops. Did they hear us?

We push the door open, step inside. I can feel my heart thudding in my throat. Tom is flushed with the exertion, his breath ragged.

The master bedroom has a bed, wardrobe full of clothes, bedside table, desk and chair. There is a laptop on Bradley's bed. The guestroom has a smaller bed, with just a cover over the mattress, a wardrobe and a work area with a desk and chair, a printer, Anglepoise lamp and speakers.

I start to feel foolish: we could be charged with criminal damage, trespass – who knows what laws they have here? But the text messages, I tell myself. Bradley is lying to us. There can't be any good reason for that.

'Maybe there'll be emails on the laptop,' I say, 'messages from Lori.'

Tom is tugging at the wardrobe in the spare room. It's large, old-fashioned, with deep carvings along the top and bottom, two deep drawers beneath the doors, the sort to keep blankets and bedding in.

'Is it stiff?' I say.

'I think it's locked,' Tom says, 'and there's no key.'

We used to have a wardrobe at home when I was little and the door swung open if it wasn't locked so we always kept the key in it. 'There was a little key on Bradley's key ring.' I remember staring at it when it was on the table while we waited for him. 'Gilt, fancy.'

Tom goes to the kitchen and comes back with a knife, broad and sharp. He tries to force it between the doors but can only get the tip in.

'Shit.' He drops it on the bed. Raises his foot and kicks at the wardrobe. A loud crack and a boom reverberate in the room. The drill hasn't started up again and I listen for sounds from the neighbours, footsteps, doors banging, anyone coming. There's nothing.

Tom rears back and kicks again, higher, grunting with the effort. There's a splintering noise as one of the doors cracks, a ragged tear running the length of it, then swings open.

Inside is hanging space to the left, a few jackets above a jumbo-sized, hard-shell suitcase. To the right are shelves, just like the wardrobe in Lori's room at home. A row of five shelves. An assortment of bags and boxes on them and, on the middle shelf, a camera.

A camera exactly like Lori's.

My bowels turn to water. 'Oh, God.'

Tom picks it up, his hand shaking. He tries to turn it on. 'It's dead,' he says. 'Get the laptop.'

I bring it with the cable from the other bedroom. 'We need a USB connector too,' Tom says, as he plugs it in.

I go back to Bradley's room, but can't find any leads. In the desk drawer in the spare bedroom there's a bundle of cables and adapters. And one that fits the camera. Tom powers up the laptop and connects the camera. A few seconds later he is able to turn it on. We can see it's hers. It's all there, Lori's albums. The last-pictures are dated 7 April. Tom runs through them. Nothing of Bradley or a motorbike. Some of a traditional pagoda, one of the river, some close-ups, almost abstract, trees along a street, a couple more. No people in any of them.

Tom starts copying the files onto the laptop. When that's done he disconnects the camera, plugs his phone into the computer and uploads the folder.

'That fucker.' Tom curses under his breath.

'Why are you doing that?' I say.

279

'It's all proof,' he says, 'the camera, the pictures, the text messages. It shows they were in touch. It shows where she was that day.'

'We should get this to the police, now,' I say, 'and get them to pick him up.'

'Yes. Nearly done.' We watch the progress bar as the pictures upload.

Is there anything else of hers? I look through the other shelves, open boxes and bags, searching for Lori's purse or phone. In the big drawers I find pillows, an empty hold-all, an acrylic blanket and beach towels. One of those neck pillows for long flights. 'There's nothing else.' My voice cracks.

I haul out the suitcase. Something shifts and rattles inside.

Tom disconnects his phone and deletes the folder from the laptop.

I lift the case onto the bed and unzip it.

I open the case. The right-hand side is empty, the left is covered with the inner divider. Lumps stick up against the black nylon with its mesh pockets. I unzip the fabric.

A bolt, like lightning, fierce and white-hot explodes inside me. I'm struck dumb. The floor undulates.

I hear Tom's voice. Far away. Indistinct.

I am paralysed.

Petrified.

Stone where there should be muscle. Stone crushing my heart.

Tom is touching me, pulling me, shouting, but all I can do is gaze.

Gaze at the tangle of clean white bones, the

bridge of ribs, the snaking spine, the grinning teeth and gaping dark eye sockets of her lovely skull.

CHAPTER FORTY-THREE

I call Peter Dunne, my teeth chattering, my voice fracturing. His secretary answers. I tell her that we need the police, now, that it is an emergency and I give her the address. 'Now,' I say several times, 'they must come now.' Does she understand?

Waiting is unreal. My legs are rubbery and I sit with Tom in the spare bedroom, staring at the suitcase. Periodically the drilling resumes and it feels as though it will shake me apart.

The police arrive and there is noise and commotion and confusion. Tom gives them one of our leaflets to explain who we are, who we were looking for. He is ashen-faced now, shivering, his wet hair plastered to his head. I feel myself withdrawing as though everything is shrinking away from me, sounds muted, vision blurring, sensations numb.

'Mrs Maddox?' We are back at the hotel, in my room. Peter Dunne is here. And Tom. I blink and try to concentrate. How long have we been here? There aren't enough chairs.

Peter Dunne sits beside me on the bed. 'I am so very sorry,' he says. 'The first thing we need to do is to make sure that these remains definitely are

Lorelei's. I've been in touch with DI Dooley in Manchester and she will get dental records sent for comparison. That shouldn't take long. Lorelei's dentist is still Mr Gargrave?' He glances at Tom, who must have dredged the name up.

'Yes,' I say.

'Not even five weeks,' Tom says. 'How's that ... just bones–' He chokes on the word.

'Until we have all the facts...' Peter Dunne shakes his head, adjusts his glasses. 'We can make arrangements for you to take her home,' he says. 'Would you like me to speak to your husband?'

Nick. The thought brings a fresh wave of dread. 'No. Thank you. I'll do it.'

'Bradley?' Tom says.

'Bradley Carlson has been arrested and is in police custody,' Peter Dunne says.

'Why would he–' I break off. It's not a question anyone here could possibly answer.

'Would you like to see a doctor?' Peter Dunne asks me.

'No.'

'Mr Maddox?'

'No,' Tom says. He looks desolate.

I reach for a tissue, wipe my face, clear my throat. 'What happens now?'

'The police will question Mr Carlson. They will hope to obtain a confession, then hold a trial. There won't now be a press conference but, once Lorelei's identity is confirmed, the news will be made public. Mr Maddox has given me details for your contact Edward at Missing Overseas and I will brief him.'

'What if some hotshot American lawyer finds a

282

way for him to wriggle out of it?' Tom says.

'He won't be allowed to hire a lawyer from the US,' Peter Dunne says. 'He will have to use a local lawyer and here defence lawyers play a much lesser role than we are used to at home. The system is not adversarial in the way ours is. The lawyer will have little to do until the trial, and even then his or her role will be limited, compared to what we're used to.'

'What if Bradley doesn't confess?' I say.

'Ninety-five per cent of suspects in China do confess and then go to trial. That's how they like to do it here. But even if they don't get a confession they will still hold a trial. And the conviction rate is ninety-eight per cent.'

The truth washes over me again. Oh, my sweet girl, my Lori. And I hide my face and weep. Tom comes and pulls me into him and it makes me weep more.

When I stop and pull away, Peter Dunne is still there. His eyes are glistening, the tip of his nose is red. 'I'll be here in Chengdu for the next few days,' he says huskily. 'If you need anything, anything at all, please call. In due course the police will want to speak to you but not until you feel up to it.'

I call Nick. I sit on the edge of my bed, one fist clamped tight.

'Jo?' His voice is hoarse. I must have woken him. It will be early there.

'How's Isaac?' I say, not ready to tell him.

'He's OK. He had a good night. The stitches are a bit tight and he'll be on a drip today, no food, but he's OK, just weak. He needs to sleep as much as possible. So don't worry–'

'Oh, Nick. Oh, Nick.' My breath comes in uneven gulps.

'Jo, what is it?'

I can't just say it straight out. 'It's bad news.'

'Oh, God.'

'We ... erm...' my teeth chatter and I have to force the words out '...we found out that Bradley Carlson had arranged to meet Lori...'

'The American guy?'

'Yes. He'd lied to us about it and ... erm ... we went to his flat...'

'She's dead, isn't she?' Nick says quietly.

I swallow, fight tears. 'We found some remains.'

'Remains?'

'A skeleton.' I sound hoarse. 'They have to do a dental comparison to make sure.'

'So it might not be–' I can hear the hope.

'He had her camera, Nick.'

'Oh, my God. Oh, Jo.'

I sniff hard and blink. 'We should know soon, for definite.'

'Oh, God. I don't know–' He flounders.

'Don't say anything to the boys yet. Not to anyone. Not till we're sure. Peter Dunne, he's speaking to Edward.'

'Right. Oh, good God.' I think he's crying. I keep sniffing. Bite my knuckles hard.

'Oh, Jo.'

There's a few seconds, then I say shakily, 'So if Isaac's all right ... I'll stay here until...'

'Of course, yes, you must. Oh, God,' he says again. 'I wish I could come, we could come–'

'I know, I know. So listen, as soon as we hear I'll

284

ring or text and Peter Dunne, he ... erm ... he said they can arrange everything, getting her home, you know?'

'Yes, right,' he says. 'I can't believe it, I just can't.'

'I know. I love you.'

'Oh, Jo.' His voice is muffled with tears.

'I'll call.'

'Yes. Yes, OK.'

Our goodbyes are clumsy, punctuated by more crying. We can barely speak. And, anyway, words can't suffice. There are no words.

'Should we ring Dawn?' I say to Tom. We're sitting by the Jinjiang river. The dun-coloured water is like dirty brass in the fog that has settled. I can smell the water, a pungent metallic pong, and I can smell the wet stone, too.

I barely remember coming here. Tom wanted to get out and I tagged along.

'No,' Tom says, 'not until it's official.'

Friday, I think. Five weeks ago Lori would have been getting ready for the party, deciding what to wear, when to leave. Perhaps feeling a bit sad after the break-up with Dawn. That's what's Shona said, didn't she? A bit low.

'Lori should never have come here.'

'Don't say that,' Tom says quickly. 'Who could possibly have stopped her?'

'If you hadn't sent the money–'

'Jo.' He groans, rubs his forehead.

'Well, it's true, she couldn't have managed. She'd have had to come home. She'd be safe–'

'It was what she wanted,' he says, 'so I wanted

285

to make it happen for her.'

I shake my head. My eyes ache but they are dry – for now.

A brown dove with a white-tipped tail scours the pavement for food. A little egret chases it away, lands on the stone balustrade a few yards from us. It is slender, elegant, with its long legs and that spike of a beak, the spray of feathers behind its head, like a fascinator. I think of Lori's headband, the antenna. The bag I gave to Superintendent Yin. Then her bones, that shocking jumble, smooth and creamy, grotesque.

'She wanted to explore,' Tom says, 'have fun, see something of the world. What would you have done – locked her away? She's an adult, she wanted an adventure.'

'And you encouraged it.'

'Damn right.' He gets to his feet and the egret takes flight.

Music starts up, tinny, from along the way. A group of women mill about, putting umbrellas and bags down and taking their places. The dance begins.

'I'm proud of her,' Tom says, 'proud of what she's done. I think you are too. And if you're not, you should be.'

I am. Of course I am.

The women dance. They are smiling, all of them smiling, as they turn and wave an arm towards the ground.

'We did OK,' he says, 'really, with Lori, we did OK.'

My face crumples and he moves closer, sits down.

I nod, dash away my tears. 'She's amazing,' I say, 'she's...' I hear the present tense and cling to it '...she's wonderful. Sometimes she drives me mad but, God, I love her so much.'

Before I go to bed, I call Nick. He is at the hospital and Isaac is awake.

'He's very sleepy,' Nick says, 'but they're happy with how he's doing.'

'I'll say hello?'

The sound of Nick passing the phone, then Isaac: 'Hello.' He sounds glum.

'Hello, darling, how are you?'

'I'm in hospital.'

'Daddy says you're getting better.'

Isaac grunts, noncommittal.

'Does it hurt?' I say.

'Loads,' he says.

'Aw.'

I hear him yawn.

'I love you. I'll see you soon.'

Nick comes on the line. 'A ray of sunshine,' he says.

And I smile. And then I want to cry. 'Are you OK?' I ask.

'I don't know,' he says. 'I'm functioning.'

'I just want to come home,' I say.

'It won't be long now,' he says. 'You've not heard any more?'

'No, so...' I sniff hard, '...I'm going to try and rest a bit. It just feels so unreal, you know?'

'Yes, I know.'

I have a shower, a good long shower. Letting the

water drum on my head and my back, eyes closed, until I am as numb on the outside as I am on the inside.

I wake in the dark with a terrible dread. I remember instantly the image of the suitcase, zipping back the lining. Her skull. I switch on the bedside light and sip some water.

I can't stay in bed. At the window I look out onto the demolition site. It is abandoned tonight, silent, dark. The sky is burnt umber; through a ragged tear in the clouds I can see a star. The first star I've seen since we arrived. Lori got a telescope for her tenth birthday. She already had a camera and she'd taken pictures and made scrapbooks; some told little stories. Then she got interested in space after the solar eclipse when she was nine and they did a project at school. Did she miss the stars here? And the sunshine?

PS Mum, send cheese. And baguettes. Now *joke*
PPS Mum, don't worry, I'm fine. Just a lot thinner than you remember. #Notdeadyet.

My breath catches in my throat. I am trembling.

The corridors are hushed. Low safety lights every few yards cast a gentle glow; the carpet is thick under my bare feet.

I knock on Tom's door and hear movement from inside.

He opens it, a towel around his waist, creases on his cheek from the pillow.

'What?'

I don't speak. His eyes search mine. I move forward, he steps aside, closes the door behind us. I reach for him, my hands raised to his face.

'Jo?'

I place a finger on his lips. His eyes are pained, wary.

I want this. I move my hand back to his left cheek, feel the vibration as his muscles tense. Keep my gaze fixed on his, let him read what's there. I watch until I see his expression shift. I see desire bloom in his eyes, see his nostrils widen as he takes a breath. I place a hand on his chest, feel the beat of his heart, the warmth of his skin, the rhythm of blood pulsing through him. The life of him.

I reach up and kiss him.

We make love, and it is as if we are calling her back. Making Lori again.

CHAPTER FORTY-FOUR

I wake with a start. My first thought is Lori. Lori lost. I'm lying on my back, and Tom's arm is across my stomach, heavy and warm. The curtains aren't fully closed and in the pale light I can make out his face, peaceful. Holding his wrist lightly so his arm won't drop and wake him, I edge out of bed.

After putting on my nightdress and finding my room key, I walk along the corridor. I examine my conscience for signs of guilt, for a tell-tale twist in my stomach, a sinking feeling, but there is nothing. Hollow. I am hollow. Calm. Which can't be right. Dazed.

The sky is clear blue. All blue. The medley of horns and music and motors roars on unceasing.

I lie on my bed and scroll through my phone. Lori holding Finn when he was born. Isaac and Finn sleeping cuddled up to Benji. Nick with Isaac on his shoulders. Lori on a horse at the age of thirteen, a few months when it was the only activity she wanted to do. Her graduation day, Tom, Nick and Lori. Her two dads. The three of them beaming.

The skull, its grinning teeth, flashes into my head and I shut my phone. Covered with goose-bumps, I climb under the sheet. Listen to the din of the city, let it fill my head. Every time my thoughts slither back to Bradley Carlson, to the wardrobe, to the suitcase, I change position and focus on the noises outside. Imagine the drivers, irascible in the traffic jams, the women dancing by the underpass, the calligrapher with his giant brush, the licks of water on the stone path, the toddler and his squeaking shoes.

My phone rings and it's Tom. 'I've just had a call from Peter Dunne,' he says. 'He wants to see us – he'll be here in about twenty minutes. There's a meeting room on the ground floor, room four.'

It's unlucky, I think, number four. The character is similar to the one for death so the Chinese avoid using a four when they can. I'm stupid to think this way: how much more bad luck can I get?

'You OK?' he says gently.

290

'Yes.' He's asking about last night.

'Good.'

I shower and dress and make my way to the room.

Tom is there already, with Peter Dunne and a Chinese man I haven't met. All standing.

Peter Dunne introduces the stranger. 'Mrs Maddox, this is Detective Song. He is working with Superintendent Yin.'

Detective Song shakes my hand. He is younger than Superintendent Yin, no sign of grey in his hair. He has a smooth, broad face and one eye is narrower than the other, which makes him look as if he's peering or scrutinizing something.

'Please take a seat,' Peter Dunne says.

Once we're all settled in the easy chairs, he continues, 'We've heard today from the forensic laboratory here in Chengdu.'

My stomach clenches and my mouth goes dry.

'Comparison with dental records proves that the remains found are not Lorelei's.'

'Not?' Tom says.

'Sorry?' I say.

'It is not Lorelei,' Peter Dunne repeats.

Tom makes a noise, like a laugh, incredulous.

I don't understand. I get to my feet. 'How can ... who ... but who...' The room spins.

'Sit down.' Tom reaches for my arm and pulls me back. 'Who is it, then?' he says.

'We don't know yet,' Peter Dunne says. He says something to Detective Song, and gets a reply. 'Detective Song says they're making every effort to determine the identity but they do know the remains are female and either Chinese or Japanese.'

291

I'm trying to disentangle what he's saying. It feels like my brain is stuck, full of fog. 'It's definitely not Lori?' I say.

'Definitely,' Peter Dunne says.

Tom sighs, a great shudder. 'Oh, God.'

'She's still missing, then,' I say. A laugh, twisted, dangerous, flowers in my chest. 'You must tell him,' I point to Detective Song, 'tell Superintendent Yin, her camera, on Lori's camera, there are pictures from the Monday when she was meeting Bradley. They must look at them.'

'Pictures of Bradley Carlson?' Peter Dunne says.

'No. But from that ... it could ... they must–' My words become garbled.

'Thank you.' Peter Dunne exchanges words with Detective Song, who speaks for some time.

'The camera,' I say again.

'Yes,' Peter Dunne says. 'The camera has been taken in as evidence and will be examined. Detective Song has every expectation that Mr Carlson will confess to his crimes and tell them what he knows of Lorelei's disappearance.'

'They are looking?' Tom says. 'They are actively looking for her?'

Peter Dunne speaks and I see a polite smile from Detective Song. Then we wait for a translation.

'Searches are being made of Mr Carlson's place of work, and his current and previous address in Chengdu.'

'They could check his phone, couldn't they?' I say. 'Find out where he was that day. With all the technology they can do that. They do it at home,

292

don't they?'

Detective Song's next statement is that all necessary resources will be used to trace Lorelei.

'Oh, for God's sake,' a rush of anger penetrates my confusion, 'is he just saying what he thinks we want to hear?' I nod towards the policeman.

'This nutter has already killed someone,' Tom says.

'Are they looking?' I say. 'The photos together with Bradley's mobile. They can track where Lori was.'

Detective Song sits unruffled. Peter Dunne talks to him, pressing him, I hope. 'He assures me that they will—'

'When? They should be out there now. My daughter is in danger.' I'm on my feet again. Tom makes no move to restrain me.

'They are also launching a murder investigation,' says Peter Dunne.

'So get Interpol involved, ask for help,' Tom says. 'Whatever the fuck it takes.'

'They wouldn't even know about the murder if we hadn't—' I begin.

'Mrs Maddox—' Peter Dunne sounds like he's cajoling me.

'Don't bother,' I say. 'Don't fucking bother.' And I walk out.

Tom catches up with me in the foyer. I can sense people's eyes on us, the drama unfolding, the Westerners making a fuss.

'We do it ourselves,' I say to him.

'Yes,' he says, his eyes fixed on mine. 'You get the map.'

CHAPTER FORTY-FIVE

Tom opens the window in his room and lights a cigarette. His hand is unsteady. Before we start looking at the photos he copied, I call Nick. His phone goes to voicemail. It is three in the morning at home. I imagine him asleep, on a camp bed beside Isaac.

I'd rather speak to him in person but I want him to know the news the moment he wakes up. So I leave a message: 'Nick, please call me as soon as you can.'

Tom plugs his phone into his laptop so the images are bigger. There are fifteen photographs from Monday, 7 April. Lori hadn't set up any GPS data so they don't give co-ordinates but the technical data includes the time when each image was created.

'Have you any paper?' I ask him.

'Under there,' Tom says, nodding at a room-service menu on the desk.

'I'll do a chart,' I say.

We go through all the pictures, making notes of the exact time they were taken and what they show.

The first six images are of traditional buildings, like the pagodas in the park. Tom thinks one looks familiar. 'Where's the map?'

I pass it to him. He opens it out and turns it over. 'Yes.' He points to a tiny photo of the same

294

pagoda under the detailed list of tourist attractions. *Wenshu Monastery.*

'Which is near Bradley's,' I say.

The six photos were all taken within five minutes of each other. The next one, of the river reflecting the built-up skyline, is some fourteen minutes later. There are then two pictures that we struggle to identify. One is like peeling paint on wood; the other resembles lichen. Next up shows a stencil of a laughing Buddha – the outline is in black and near the bottom of the frame there is a splash of faded red, like spray paint. That was timed sixteen minutes after the river scene. There are three photographs of overhead wires slung between trees and telegraph poles, then a blurry yellow image that looks like a shop sign but is so unfocused that it's impossible to make out the strokes of the characters. It reminds me of those pictures that show streams of car lights at night. I wonder if she took it by mistake.

The last photo is a riot of colour. I think it's wool at first, tangled wool, and then I see glints of metal at the end of some of the pieces. And I realize I'm looking at electrical cables: blue, yellow, white, red, black and grey. No context, just cables. It was taken at two minutes past eleven that morning. If their plan went ahead and Lori had reached Bradley, as she said in her text, she would've been with him by then.

'We start at the monastery,' I say. 'I'll fetch my bag.'

The taxi drops us off close to Wenshu Monastery. The area is milling with visitors, most of them

Chinese but a good few Westerners too. There's building work going on along one side of the complex. The streets around are full of souvenir and gift shops selling jade, brocade, antiques and pottery. I see old stamps and memorabilia, copies of Mao's Little Red Book, toys and games, tea sets and fans, lucky charms hung with red silken tassels. Eateries are thronged with people. And, as always, there is the call and response of car horns. A woman sells double flower buds, cream-coloured – I catch the scent as we pass, sweet and peppery.

We pay and go in through the main entrance, which is a temple hall dominated by a statue of a laughing Buddha, gold and full-bellied, raised up in a glass case. In front of the case are gifts: bunches of flowers, eggs and fruit. Along the sides of the hall, more gold statues wear multi-coloured robes and headdresses. The building is open at the back, leading into a square with another temple straight ahead, and pagodas to either side. A huge cauldron releases clouds of smoke from burning incense.

'They're taken here,' I say to Tom. 'Look.' The first photographs are of the area where we stand. The large pavilion has a single roof with curved eaves and pantiles. In front of the pagoda on the right there is a stall selling flowers and Lori has a photo of that.

I walk over the square to the temple and look inside. Three great statues, all elaborately decorated, and beneath them a sea of offerings: bunches of chrysanthemums and lilies, piles of red apples, black cherries and oranges, votive candles, sweets, seashells.

There are cushions on the floor and I watch a woman approach and prostrate herself, suppli-cant to the Buddhas. Should I do the same? Lie down and beg for help, pray that we find Lori?

'Jo,' Tom says, 'the last of these photos is the tower, the one just outside.'

The cast-iron tower tapers like a chimney, and is designed like a pagoda with roofs all the way up, the eaves hung with bells. Each bell has a metal fish dangling from the tongue.

'So we go to the river from here?' I say.

I check the map: the river is north of us a couple of blocks and Bradley's apartment is to the east. Did she call for him or did they meet somewhere else? At the river? I check the chart. The river photo was taken at ten twenty-eight. Was she waiting for him when she took it?

'Fourteen minutes between the last photo at the monastery and the one at the river. How long to walk there?'

'Let's see,' Tom says.

Stopping to cross the road, I look in one of the shop windows and see a pair of tiny shoes like bootees. Almost a hoof shape, elaborately decor-ated. And then I recoil as I understand what they are: worn by a woman whose feet were bound.

'Look at the shoes,' I say.

Tom realizes too. 'Oh, God.'

The sun blazes down. When I take my sun-glasses off to read the map, the glare is blinding and I duck into the shade of a willow tree where I can see better.

We reach the river after nine minutes and look at

the skyline opposite but it bears no resemblance to the silhouette reflected in the water in Lori's photograph. 'We need two big towers together at the left,' I say to Tom, 'then these four smaller blocks, then another really tall one at the right.'

'If we walk five minutes each way we should find it,' he says.

We go left, to the west, first. A fisherman walks along the centre of the river, thigh deep in the muddy water, dragging a large fan-shaped net. There are cafés and shops across the road. The air smells of pungent spice.

'I've finally worked out what it reminds me of,' Tom says, 'the Sichuan pepper. It's like ouzo.'

I'm catapulted back. A night at university. Someone, I can't remember who, had been on a Greek-island holiday and brought back a bottle of the clear liquor. We poured it into mugs and drank it as well as lager. There was possibly some smoking involved. Certainly cigarettes, if not something stronger. It was just before I found out I was pregnant. I know because when I got morning sickness it was like a flashback to that horrendous hangover, the sort that makes you understand the term 'liver damage'. I was so happy then, giddy at my relationship with Tom and loving my course, and I felt it could only get better.

Now every fifty yards or so we assess the skyline but after ten minutes (to be absolutely sure) we haven't found the one we want. We stop and drink water. My fingers have started to swell in the heat, my ankles too.

'If she got a bus or the Metro,' I say, 'we could be in the wrong place completely.'

We're about to start walking back the way we came when my phone rings. Nick.

'Jo,' he says, his voice thick with sleep.

'Nick, it's not Lori,' I say in a rush, 'the remains – they're not Lori.' I hear a sharp intake of breath. 'They don't know who it is, but it's not Lori.' Relief at that statement tears at my heart anew.

'Oh, Jesus,' he says.

'I know.' I watch the traffic flow across the other side of the river, the taxis and buses, the big fancy cars and bicycles, the phalanx of scooters.

'Jesus,' he says again. 'They're sure?'

'Yes. Definite.'

I give him a few more seconds to take it in, then say, 'How's Isaac?'

'The same, good, sleeping.'

'It's late,' I say.

'Yes,' he says. 'I needed a pee, saw you'd left a message.'

I wonder where he is. Is he on the ward or in some patients' lounge or family room, or the corridor?

'So we keep looking,' I say. 'We just have to keep looking.'

'Yes. Oh, Christ, Jo.' His voice snags and I beat back my own tears.

'Ring me later,' I say.

'I will. Night-night.'

'Night. I love you,' I say.

'Love you too.'

I close my eyes a moment, then look at Tom. He gives a rueful smile, acceptance in his gaze, and I return it. Then he dips his head and we start walking again.

CHAPTER FORTY-SIX

'There!' I point to the bend in the river, to the two towers higher than the others. I'm almost certain, but it's only when we've come closer that we can see the third tall tower that completes the shape we're looking for.

Tom takes a picture, like Lori's, the reflections outlined in the water.

Where did she go next? Where were the pictures of peeling paint and lichen? 'What's the timing for those next two images?' I say, and study the chart. 'Ten forty and ten forty-one.'

There is a bridge just beyond the curve in the river. 'She could've crossed. It'll be like looking for a needle in a haystack,' I complain. 'I think we should forget these two pictures, they're too abstract – they could be anything, anywhere.'

'Same with the Buddha stencil?' Tom says.

'I don't know,' I say. 'People might recognize that – something quirky. It could be graffiti on a wall near here. Though it's hard to tell how big it is.'

We try asking. Tom pulls up the Buddha picture on his phone and we say *Zài nǎli,* where?' and point to the image.

The first woman we ask shakes her head and hurries on. The man we stop next points back south of the river, the way we came. I open the map. He smiles and points. 'Wenshu,' he says. He

300

thinks we want the monastery, to see some Buddhas.

A young couple we talk to have some English but they have not seen the stencil.

We try maybe twenty more people, *zài nǎli, zài nǎli? Xiè xie*, thank you.

A middle-aged woman pushing a child on a tricycle tries her best to help. She nods at the photograph and jabbers away in Chinese. '*Wǒ bù míngbái*,' I say. I don't understand.

She signals for my pen and the map and starts writing Chinese characters down. I shake my head. '*Wǒ bù míngbái.*' She pats my arm and indicates we should go with her. The little boy sings happily as he pedals the trike. Every so often he stops and squeezes the hooter, which parps loudly. We cross the bridge and the woman stops at a café on the corner, apparently conferring with the owner, who waves her arm, signalling up the street.

We carry on and then the woman stops and shows us the shop, smiling. It's a Buddhist gift shop: the window is full of statues of Buddha, packs of incense, prayer flags, saffron-coloured robes and incense burners.

We thank her profusely.

Once she has turned the corner, Tom rolls his eyes. I say, 'We could ask inside.'

The man behind the counter looks at the stencil and shrugs.

Maybe he thinks we want to buy a stencil. '*Zài nǎli?*' I say pointing to the photo, then outside to the street, swinging my arm in a semi-circle.

He shrugs again.

It's useless.

Tom wants cigarettes so we walk to the corner and look up and down for a mini-market. With none in sight we try the next road and find one there.

'Where now?' I say, as he lights up. Though I'm not sure where we are on the map any more.

He takes a drag, blows out a stream of smoke. I flex my fingers – the skin is even tighter and my scalp feels hot from the sun.

Like the previous three pictures, the overhead cables and trees don't include any landmarks, anything to narrow down where they might be. And the streets we're in don't have any overhead wires. The newer parts of the city, the redeveloped areas, have all the utilities underground.

'Maybe it'll be easier to find the neon sign,' I say. I try to hide my mounting sense of futility. We lost the trail, if it actually is one, back at the river. But what else can we do?

I look at the map. 'If we cover these main streets, a block at a time?' I don't let myself dwell on how far we'll have to walk, how huge the city is. We can't stop now. Even though I'm limping, my blister bloody and seeping through the plaster, another coming on my other foot, I promise myself that we will walk all day till it's dark. And again tomorrow and the day after, and the day after that until our flight home. And if we haven't found her by then, we will come back as soon as we can, or Nick will, and we'll keep looking. Because how could we ever stop?

'Yes, OK,' he says. He's not about to give up either.

It seems like every other shop has yellow signage. But we are looking for yellow on a dark blue background, which helps to rule out several as we travel the next few streets. We turn left and it takes me a moment to see it, the clutter of poles and cable in the trees. 'Are these Lori's cables? The overhead wires.'

Tom opens the gallery on his phone and flicks through them. We look and look again. It's impossible to tell if these are the same wires, the same trees and poles. The only background that can be distinguished is part of an air-con unit in the middle snapshot where there's a gap in the foliage. But the buildings are littered with them.

'Keep walking?' I suggest. 'See how many streets have the overhead wires?'

The next block has market stalls in a square selling all sorts, leather goods and huge fancy vases, silk scarves, phone cases, headphones and portable speakers, noodles and patties and toy pandas.

The wires and the trees are all over this neighbourhood. A group of people playing mah-jong outside a café stop their game to stare at us.

I think of Bradley's vintage bike, the one he is restoring, and of the yellow neon sign. Could it be blurred because Lori was travelling at speed? Maybe he gave her a ride and she snapped the picture.

I ask Tom. 'I don't know,' he says. 'There's only a minute between that photo and the last.' He shows me the final photo, the bundle of coloured cables. 'This one isn't blurred.'

Maybe her hand was shaking, then, when she

photographed the yellow sign. Was she scared? Or laughing? Maybe she was laughing. Bradley said something amusing as she took the picture.

If he did take her on the bike, there might have been an accident. That might account for his lies. But not for the bones in the suitcase.

What will they think, Dawn and Shona, Rosemary and Oliver, when they hear that their friend, Bradley has been arrested, the skeleton of a Chinese or Japanese woman found in his apartment? When they learn that he was the last person to have contact with Lori? Does any of them have the slightest idea?

'What time was the yellow sign taken?' I say.

'Eleven oh one,' Tom says.

At a zebra crossing, we let a tricycle go past and two taxis, then a pickup truck, with a gated back, carrying pigs, crammed in on top of each other, every which way. Alive and struggling.

I'm about to step into the road when there's a long blast of a horn and a white van comes at me, the driver yelling furiously. I feel the air displaced, the draught on my forearms as I rear back just in time.

'Shit!' I almost overbalance. I turn to watch the van drive on, tempted to stick two fingers up, and then I see it. On the road to our right, the road we were crossing, a couple of hundred yards along. Yellow characters on a dark blue background.

'Tom, look.'

'I think that's it,' he says. 'It is, that's it.'

CHAPTER FORTY-SEVEN

The shop sells Chinese liquor, and the window has a row of tall plinths. On the top of each is a display bottle beside a matching fancy cardboard case. Gold fabric loops between the plinths. The floor is scattered with white pebbles. On the back wall, behind the counter, there are more bottles.

The shop stands next to an alley, just wide enough to drive down. Across the alley is a fruit and vegetable store, with produce piled up on display outside: melons, oranges and lemons, grapes and pineapples, salad greens and ginger root, turnips and leeks.

Opposite, on the other side of the street, there are more shops with flats above.

'So where did she find the electrical wires?' Tom says. 'Only a minute from here?'

And if we find the site of that picture, I think, we must come back armed with leaflets and make this place the focus for the campaign. It would give us a more accurate time and place for Lori's disappearance. What if Bradley took the pictures? We could be completely off track. We walk up and down each side of the road, looking for an electrician's or any place that might have a large amount of plastic-coated copper wire. No luck.

'Somebody could've been rewiring,' I say. 'Five weeks ago, and it might all be done by now.' I

305

shift my weight trying to relieve the pressure on my new blister. I drink some water – it's unpleasantly warm. The road shimmers in the heat, the sun glancing off the chrome and glass of the cars, dazzling.

Tom swings round, scanning for possibilities.

I watch someone come out of the vegetable shop, put the bags of food in a box strapped to the back of their scooter.

'The alley,' I say. 'We haven't tried the alley.'

The buildings rise up on either side of the narrow lane, shutting out all but a sliver of sunlight. The ground, packed earth, is peppered with puddles from yesterday's rain. Mosquitoes hover in clouds over the dank water.

A row of small units runs along at ground level. People fall silent as we pass. It's off the beaten track: tourists would have no reason to come down this way.

We pass one lock-up, which is full of cardboard, flattened boxes and sheets. Two men in vests are sorting it into piles. Further along a group are playing cards. A baby sleeps in a car seat beside their table. It's hard to tell whether they are running a business or whether they just use the place to store junk. Their eyes follow us.

Ahead, a van is blocking the alley, its bonnet raised, a man hammering at something in the engine.

We edge past and I try to avoid stepping in the pools of water.

A smell of cooking oil comes from the next unit, where a woman hunkers over a small Calor-gas stove. There are several kids in grubby clothes. I glimpse a mattress behind a curtain at the back. Perhaps the poorest people live here, squat here.

'He needs somewhere to fix it,' I say to Tom, 'his bike.'

'A workshop,' Tom says. Then he stops still. 'Jo.'

The woman sits on a low stool; around her stand polypropylene sacks. In front of her a mound of tangled electrical cables. Mountains of the stuff are piled up around the walls. She has pliers in her hands, which are black with grime, and strips the coating from a lead, throws the plastic into a sack and the metal into a plastic tray. Her eyes are sunken, rimmed with deep shadows. She should have gloves, I think. The metal must cut.

I get out a flier. She gives it a brief glance, shakes her head and returns to her task.

'Show her a picture of Bradley,' Tom says.

On my phone, I open the link to Lori's blog and navigate to the entry with the photos of her new friends.

Bradley has better Mandarin than me (hah! everyone has better Mandarin than me).

I enlarge the image so Bradley fills the frame. Tilt it so the woman can see. *Zài nǎli? Zài nǎli?* Where? I point to the building adjacent to hers, which is closed up, step nearer and tap on the shutter. *Zài nǎli?*

But she jerks her chin, as if we need to try further along. The next unit is shuttered too. I gesture to it and she gives a single nod. She picks up a scart cable and cuts off the socket.

I mime a key, point to the padlock at the bottom of the shutters. *Zài nǎli?* The woman ignores me.

The man with the hammer comes to see what's

going on. He glares at us.

We bang on the shutters. I keep miming a key turning. More people gather. I get out the fliers. Some of them recoil. No one actually takes one from me. Are they wary because it's police business? My skin tingles. We are not welcome. There's an atmosphere of suspicion, hostility. The man with the hammer hawks and spits.

Tom checks his phone, finds the word for 'landlord'. Says it, *fang dong,* shows the screen.

No one's willing to help, it seems. They talk to each other in raised voices.

'*Nǚ ér, shī zōng,* daughter missing,' Tom says. He hits the shutter doors once, twice, then kicks as if he'd kick his way in. I think of the suitcase, of the bones and the skull. The Chinese girl. And Lori? My heart bangs against my ribs. Tom is shouting, his hair whipping about as he yells, '*Nǚ ér, shī zōng,* daughter missing.' The man with the hammer grabs hold of Tom by the shoulder, bellowing at him. Tom swings round and throws him off.

The crowd grows, shouting to each other. Then a man comes running. Squat, pot-bellied with puffy jowls, he wears a tatty cap and has a bunch of keys hanging from his belt.

'*Fang dong?*' I say.

He roars at us.

'Hello,' a younger man says to me. 'English?'

'You speak English?' I say.

'Some, English classes, yes,' he says.

'Is this the landlord? Tell him we're looking for our daughter. We want to look in there.'

He speaks to the landlord, who shakes his head, dismissing us with dramatic hand gestures.

'For your trouble.' I hold out a hundred-yuan note to the landlord. The crowd are all shouting. It's impossible to tell if they are for or against us. The man still shakes his head and turns to go.

'We'll fetch the police,' Tom says to the student. 'Does he want that?'

I'm aware of sweat on my back, dust in my mouth, the din from the main road nearby.

'Police,' I say. I point to the word on the leaflet next to the number.

The student repeats the threat.

An older woman, with a wrinkled brown face, wearing black clothes and black pumps, walks forward, wrenches the leaflet from my hand and thrusts it at the man, shrieking.

Someone laughs. Before we can ask what's being said, the landlord flaps his hands towards the crowd and barks some words. People shuffle back a little. A bird squawks. The man unclips his keys, glares at Tom and gives an emphatic nod.

He gets down on one knee and opens the lock, then shoves the roller shutter halfway up. The piercing shriek of metal on metal sets my teeth on edge. We step closer, behind us I sense the bystanders doing the same. The man yells at them, signals them to go away, palms facing the floor, flicking his fingers towards them. He ducks inside and hits a switch. Tom and I follow. A strip light flares blue for a moment, then flickers.

The room is the size of a garage. It smells of damp concrete and motor oil and sewage. There's a trestle table along one wall, strewn with tools and aerosol cans, a socket set, a metal flight case and bits of machinery. At the back a partition juts out four feet high and maybe half the width of the room – a modesty screen, perhaps? Toilet in the corner? Fixed to it is a poster: James Dean astride his motorbike. Opposite the tool bench are boxes and two large oil drums. In the centre of the room a grey tarpaulin covers what I take to be Bradley's vintage bike. Tom throws back an edge to reveal a gleaming wheel, chrome and leather. The overhead light snaps and fizzes, goes off and comes on again.

The landlord barks at us, swings his arm around the room. See? he appears to say. Nothing. He waves us towards the lane. The show is over.

Three or four people have come inside but most are still out there, chattering away. I feel like kicking the stupid bike over. Where is Lori? He brought her here, then what? A spin on the bike to some quieter place, a day trip with only Bradley coming back.

The man is flapping at us again. Tom moves to the back of the room and puts his head round the divider. I see him flinch, his back jerk straighter, his head jolt and hear the intake of breath. By the time he has said my name, I'm at his side, eyes adjusting to the gloom of that corner. The smell is stronger here. An open drain, tap on the wall. A pale lump on the concrete floor, a tangle of stick-like limbs, matted hair. My heart implodes.

'Oh, Lori.'

'Oh, Lori, oh, Lou-Lou.' Tom falls to his knees and I crowd in beside him.

She is curled like a foetus. I reach out a hand and touch her cheek. She is cold.

'Lori? Lori?' He finds her chin and tilts her head

back. Her eyes are closed, crusted with granules that look like brown sugar. Her hair stuck in clumps. Her cheeks sunken. A dark rag is tied around her mouth. The sweet smell is brackish, like baby diarrhoea. She is naked. Insect bites pepper her limbs, angry dots. Her belly is distended – she looks pregnant: a grotesque contrast to the blades of bones in her shins and forearms, the chamber of ribs.

Tom is weeping, his hands cradling her cheeks. Hushing him, I fumble to remove the gag. My fingers slip on the knot – it's a bandanna, I think, black and purple patterns. The rag is stiff and soiled and it reeks of vomit. I wrest the water bottle from my bag, tip a few drops into her mouth. It dribbles out. Putting two fingers between her lips, I meet no resistance. Her tongue is swollen, dry, like a husk, but I feel faint warmth there. I see dark red in the gaps of her teeth. Blood? If she were dead, if her heart had stopped pumping, would there be blood?

'Ambulance!' I call. 'Get an ambulance.'

I shore myself up. More people have come into the workshop. Faces peer round to see us, wary, frozen. I scan them for the student but can't see him. The old woman is there. I wave at her, make the sign for a phone call, finger and thumb at my ear and chin. The landlord is shaking his head over and over. I gesture to him, too, making the phone sign. Scrambling up, I yank the old woman by the arm, show her my daughter, and repeat the phone sign. She rattles off something and one of the other women uses her mobile phone.

Tom is talking to Lori now. 'We're here, baby,

Mum and me. Come to take you home. Lori, you're OK. It's going to be all right. Dad's here, Mum's here.' Her hands and feet, rimed with filth, are bound with plastic ties. A length of plastic rope goes from her ankles to an iron bracket low on the wall. I push through the people and search on the workbench for something to cut her free and find some radio pliers.

'I've got these.' I show Tom. He shuffles her round a little, rests her head on his knee and holds her wrists up so I can work the pliers under the ties and cut. Her arms are like twigs. She makes no response to the snapping sound. Tom catches her arms as they fall apart.

A baby bird, naked, blind, every bone visible through slack skin. Some of the crowd starts melting away.

She is dead. We are trying to wake a corpse.

Angry with myself for the very thought. Her tongue was warm, I'm sure. I free her ankles, put down the pliers. There are puffy, pus-filled wounds around her wrists and ankles where the ties have cut into her flesh. Open sores on her buttocks, her left hip and elbow, around her mouth. We try the water again, the smallest amount possible, half a teaspoonful between her lips. I watch her throat. She does not swallow.

She is dead.

Tom shifts around, bracing his back against the partition and collecting her onto his lap. He kisses the top of her head. I place my palm flat on her chest, feel the bones, her breasts have melted away. There is no heartbeat.

'Tom–' I'm about to tell him that I don't think

she's breathing, that we should try the kiss of life, when Lori makes a sound, a tiny, tiny sound. Some strength in her clinging to a gossamer thread. Behind us, the old woman claps and shouts something and then I hear the ice-cream sing-song of a Chinese siren coming for us.

CHAPTER FORTY-EIGHT

We sit, shell-shocked, in a waiting area outside the emergency room. Paralysed among the bustle of staff, the flurries of activity. Grimy, the muck and oil from the workshop ingrained in our skin. It is sweltering. Even my eyelids feel sweaty.

A doctor who speaks perfect English tells us that Lori is in triage and we will be able to see her once her assessment is completed. When her blood results are back they will know what treatment she needs.

I ask how long that will be.

'An hour, two hours,' the doctor says, 'high priority,' he adds, as he walks away.

Tom is weeping, silently, his eyes red-rimmed, tears making track marks through the dirt on his face.

I go to him, stand and pull his face to my belly until the jerking of his shoulders slows and stops. I move away and he wipes his face, rubbing his nose on his forearm. He turns his ruined eyes to me.

I sit beside him, kiss him.

'She's alive,' I say. 'Yes? She's still alive.'

The same doctor returns. He has charts with him. 'We have blood test results,' he says, 'and X-rays. Your daughter has heart arrhythmia,' he places a finger on his own chest, 'and low blood pressure. This is a result of the lack of nourishment – an electrolyte imbalance. We will need to introduce essential salts, potassium, magnesium, phosphate and so on, as well as rehydrate the patient. Your daughter also has a condition called pneumonitis, in the lung, probably from irritation due to choking on the ... mask?' He signals to his mouth, sketches a line to and fro.

'Gag,' I say.

'Gag,' he agrees. 'She inhaled secretions and these cause inflammation. We will also be treating her for infection with antibiotics. In addition to wounds on her wrists and ankles, she has pressure sores from being immobile for so long. There is some vaginal bruising, which suggests she has been sexually assaulted.'

'Raped?' I need to be clear. I am quivering, all of me, every muscle, and I can't control it.

'Yes. Swabs have been taken for forensic and medical examination and we will test for sexually transmitted infections and HIV. She is being washed now and then will be transferred to intensive care.'

'Can we see her?' I say.

'Soon, maybe one hour for the intensive-care assessment. Please always clean your hands.' He points to a sanitizer-gel dispenser on the wall. 'Every time.'

'Yes. Please – can we see her before she's moved? Just for a moment, please?' My voice shakes. I find it hard to breathe and dots prick my vision.

'I will see if she is still here,' he says.

Five minutes later he is back. 'Come with me.'

We follow. My heart aches. It feels swollen and sore as though it's been crushed.

She is there. On a trolley, covered with a modesty sheet, her hair damp, arms at her sides above the sheet. Her eyes are still closed. The bruises and sores on her face are stark against the pallor of her complexion. There are dressings on her wrists and ankles, on her left elbow. Her feet are swollen, the skin tight and shiny, crazed with fissures. A cannula is fixed to her right hand, connected to a drip.

Something collapses inside me. *Oh, Lori.* I go to touch her and the doctor calls me back, tells me I must wait.

Two women come in and the doctor tells us they have to move her now and someone will fetch us when she is settled in intensive care.

I cannot hold her, soothe her, rock her. All the things my body hungers for.

It is late afternoon. Outside, the sun burns and the city simmers.

Peter Dunne arrives – Tom called him. He helps with the bureaucracy, the fees we have to pay, the forms we have to fill in for Lori's admission. 'Many of the hospital staff speak English,' he says. 'The hospital prides itself on matching international standards – this is a Gold Card facility especially for foreigners. She'll get the best

315

possible care here.'

I ask him if he'll call Nick. I'm dizzy with shock and can't marshal my thoughts. I think if I try to speak to anyone on the phone, even my husband, I'll just seize up. There is a gale in my head, tossing my thoughts about, roaring through and snatching them away before they can be completed.

Peter Dunne magicks up tea and buns and suggests gently that we may want to freshen up.

In the Ladies, I scrub the filth from my face and neck, my forearms. I can't do anything about my clothes but Peter Dunne has arranged to have all our things moved to a hotel nearby so we can walk to the hospital. Later, we can take turns to go and change.

'What was he doing?' Tom asks Peter Dunne. 'Bradley – with the Chinese woman, then Lori – what the hell...'

'The police are still trying to establish all the facts,' Peter Dunne says.

'Why would he ... why?' I say. Vertigo makes my vision swoop, my head spin. Did they know – Shona and Dawn and the others? Were they involved? 'Was it just him?' I daren't say what I'm thinking.

Peter Dunne says, 'Everything so far points to Carlson acting alone. No sign of anyone else being involved.'

We are allowed into the intensive-care unit and told we can see Lori for ten minutes every hour for the rest of the day. She is in a single room. She is covered with wires. A feeding tube goes into her nose, and several different IV lines come from bags suspended by the bed head that lead to the cannula in her hand. A line is inserted near her left elbow and other leads come from large sticky pads, one high up on the right of her chest, and the other on her left-hand side, measuring her heartbeat, I assume. There is a peg on her finger too, trailing a wire. A bag is clipped to the bed frame and the tube from that goes under the sheet. A catheter. Other machines are ranged close by – I've no idea what they are, what they do. A monitor above the bed head records the activity.

The intensive-care nurse says Lori will stay sleeping. She was drugged during her incarceration and can only slowly be weaned off the sedatives – there is a risk of additional complications from withdrawal. The nurse talks on but I barely hear: I'm overwhelmed by the sight of Lori smothered with all the equipment.

The next time we go in, I hear a rattle in her breathing. An alarm beeps fast and high and my heart jumps into my throat. Tom is already on his feet but a nurse comes in, presses something on a machine and replaces one of the bags of fluid. She stands over Lori for a moment, listening, then gestures to Lori's face. 'We clear,' she says. 'Suction.' And she mimes putting something up her own nose. 'Soon, yes.'

'Thank you,' I say.

It seems there is always an alarm shrilling and we can hear different alarms from the other rooms. My heart starts and races with each one. I am drowning in adrenalin. There is no quiet here, no sense of calm.

We are ushered out again when the ten minutes is up and the nurse returns ready to clear Lori's airways.

Nick wants to know everything when I call, and I talk him through finding Lori, then list her injuries, medical problems and the treatment she's receiving. Several times I have to stop and wait, composing myself until I can carry on.

'Jesus,' he says quietly, as I finish. 'Oh, God, Jo.'

'I know. But she's in the best place and they seem to be really good, the doctors and nurses. It's just ... it's just she's so very poorly.'

I hear him sniff hard. 'Right,' he says. He clears his throat. 'OK. Missing Overseas are issuing a press release at lunchtime.'

I think of all the other families who continue to search, to wait. We have found her. The thought makes me giddy. We have found her. And there is a chance she will make it. We are so very, very lucky.

On Sunday morning the doctor tells us Lori is in some pain and because of the trauma to her liver the usual drugs could do more damage. He recommends acupuncture, a common practice here for pain management. Lori is still unable to consent. We agree straight away.

When we ask if we can stay in the room with her now, he says yes, but cautions us that if at any point we are asked to leave we must do so immediately.

318

Tom and I decide to take turns, five-hour shifts.

I walk to the new hotel, numb, unseeing, like a zombie. Twice I collide with people. I cannot remember the Chinese for 'sorry' and just walk on.

CHAPTER FORTY-NINE

'Mummy!' Finn's voice, the joy in it, unseats me.

'Hello, Finn.' Mine squeaks. 'How are you?'

'Fine. Isaac's home. Is Lori coming back now?'

I take a breath. Dare I promise? She's still very sick. Will I jinx things if I say yes? 'Hope so,' I say.

'And you?' Finn says.

'Yes.'

'Then we could get my rocket from the museum.'

'Yes,' I say.

I picture him, sitting on the floor next to the dog, nodding to himself now that everything is sorted out.

'OK, put Daddy on now. Bye-bye. Love you.'

A woman stops me as I'm leaving to go back to the hospital. 'Mrs Maddox?' She says something about press and turns to signal to a man who carries a camera with a microphone attached.

'We'd just like a word with you about your daughter.'

'No, no, I'm sorry.' I veer round her and keep walking.

'Mrs Maddox?' She hurries after me. 'Just a

comment. You must be very happy to have found her, to know she's safe.'

Tears swim in my eyes. 'Yes. But I can't...' I bleat. 'I'm sorry.' I walk on and she leaves me be.

Peter Dunne comes to the hotel early on Monday morning with a copy of the Sichuan daily newspaper. The story is inside, complete with a picture of Superintendent Yin and his team of detectives outside the police station, as well as the photograph of Lori.

Peter Dunne translates for me: 'Chengdu police confirm that Mr Bradley Carlson, a US citizen, has been detained after the remains of a Chinese woman were discovered at his home in the Qingyang area of the city. Carlson is also being questioned about the kidnapping of missing Briton Lorelei Maddox, who was released from captivity on Saturday and is now receiving care at Huaxi hospital. Superintendent Yin said, "These unspeakable crimes have shocked the harmonious community of Chengdu and will not be tolerated. The suspect is now being questioned and justice will be done. The team of detectives have worked very hard on this investigation and their efforts are to be congratulated."'

All hail, Superintendent Yin.

I tell Peter Dunne about the journalist outside the hotel, how I fled.

'It's for the best,' he says. 'The Chinese are going to want to control the story as much as they can. Besides, you've still not made your statements to the police, have you? I understand they want to speak to you both as soon as possible.'

I sigh. It's the last thing I feel like doing.

'You are witnesses,' he says.

'Yes,' I agree. 'I know.'

When I arrive, early afternoon, to relieve Tom, he is on the phone.

'In a few days, maybe, not now, everything's still–'

'Who is it?' I say.

'Dawn. She's with Shona and Oliver – they've just heard. I've told them they can't visit Lori yet but they wanted to see us.'

'Let them come,' I say, 'just for a little while.'

'Here?'

'The hotel. I'll see them,' I say.

He cocks his head – am I sure?

I nod. 'Unless you want...'

'No,' Tom says. 'I'll stay on.'

I nod. He tells Dawn where to go and stresses it can't be for long.

Dawn bursts into tears, inconsolable. 'Mrs Maddox, how could he do that? How could anyone do that?'

I hug her. She's so young, they're all so young, and I hate that Bradley has brought such horror and corruption into their lives. I hate that I ever harboured suspicions about them, about the possibility of a conspiracy, when they were just her friends all along.

We do what we have to, like survivors of an accident or people faced with the sudden shock of betrayal: we pick it over, mining the disbelief, reviewing, rewinding, reiterating all the nuggets of hindsight, the audacity of Bradley's conduct. In our case the lies, the duplicity, the pretence he effected and the stark violence of his actions.

Our own clumsy little inquest.

When I think how close we were to losing her, that if we'd left it to the police we would've been too late, I want to throw up.

Shona seems angry more than anything. 'How could we not know?' she says abruptly, when there's a pause in the conversation. She trembles and says, 'How could we have been so stupid?' She shakes her hands, palms splayed, and the bracelets on her arm chime.

'He's clever,' I say. 'He fooled everyone. All that rubbish about her going on holiday to confuse us.'

Oliver is leaving. I follow him out and say, 'Can I ask? When we left messages you didn't reply. Why not?' I remember thinking Oliver might be hiding something and was avoiding us. I'm also still thinking, Could we have got there any sooner? 'Messages,' I say, holding up my phone. I'm welded to it.

He blinks rapidly, eyes swimming behind the thick lenses, and then looks down. He grasps one of his hands in the other and says, 'I don't like talk phone.' His face flushes.

'You don't like to talk on the phone?' I say.

He nods.

Some phobia, a hang-up. That's all it is. I almost laugh.

'OK. OK,' I say.

'Zài jiàn,' he says.

'Bye-bye.'

I promise to tell Dawn and Shona as soon as Lori is fit for visitors, then walk back to the hospital so Tom can get some rest.

I am bracing myself for when she comes round, determined not to fall apart at the pitiable sight of her.

She smells still, an awful stench, like putrid meat, but the doctor reassures me that there is no sign of blood poisoning, which would almost certainly kill her.

The vigil is terrifying and also profoundly boring. Which seems like sacrilege. The minutes stretch out. Sometimes I doze, or I stare at my phone, wander from website to website. Frustrated time and again to find them censored, not accessible, stuck behind China's great firewall.

CHAPTER FIFTY

I am there, half asleep, when she first stirs. She makes a whimpering sound, no words, her face slack. Her eyelids flutter open, eyes unfocused. And then a whisper, raw: 'Mum?'

My heart tumbles in my chest. My breath stops. 'I'm here, love. It's Mum. I'm here, Lori.' Gently, fearful of hurting her, I put my hand on her shoulder. She winces and I pull it back. 'You're safe now,' I tell her. 'You're in hospital.' I touch her hair. It feels dry and brittle. Leaning in close, I try to ignore the rotten smell. 'You're safe now.' Oh, my sweet girl. She is awake. She is awake. I want to run through the halls calling everyone to see. She is awake!

She makes a sound, a small cry in her chest, but she doesn't speak and I say, 'You rest, and as soon as you're better we're going to get you home.'

Her eyes close and sleep overtakes her.

She knows me, she can speak, she can understand. She is coming back to us. So many fears I've been carrying, like demons on my back. Gone now, lifted and flown away. I ring Tom.

A car picks us up in turn to take us to the police station. I don't know what I expected from them, some recognition, perhaps, that our efforts were instrumental in unmasking Bradley and in saving Lori – but there is nothing. Just bland formalities and tight half-smiles as I go through my statement. At least this time there is a police translator, whose English is good and who takes it all down, a few sentences at a time, before reading the whole thing aloud in Chinese to Superintendent Yin and Detective Song.

I sit in the stifling heat and feel sweat beneath my breasts, at the back of my knees. I see that same file, the picture of Lori: almost unrecognizable from the gaunt-faced waif she is now.

Lori wakes again as Tom gets back from the police station.

Her eyes flutter open and she makes a mewing sound.

'Hello, love,' I say. I reach and touch her shoulder. And again she flinches. My heart drops. Tom walks round to the other side of the bed and she

324

shrinks away from him, her eyes dark pools, haunted. She cannot bear to be touched.

'It's OK, Lori,' I say. 'We're here now. You're in hospital, getting better, and then we will take you home.'

I long to wrap her in my arms and kiss and comfort her. To feel her warmth against mine and sing her to sleep. To fill this empty ache.

'No way,' Tom says, his lips taut, bleached at the edge, when Peter Dunne tells us that the police want to arrange a time to take Lori's statement. 'She nearly died and they want her to dredge it all up. Ain't going to happen.'

'She's not well enough,' I say. 'She's still traumatized.'

'She will need to speak to them before you go home,' Peter Dunne says.

'Or what?' Tom says. 'They'll stop us leaving?'

Peter Dunne's silence is answer enough.

'Jesus!' Tom says. 'She might have died. Left up to them she probably would have.'

'And another woman did,' Peter Dunne says. 'They need Lorelei's account as a victim and a witness. They want to build the strongest possible case against Carlson.'

Lori hasn't spoken about it yet. Tom and I agreed that we would not put pressure on her, not ask any questions, but make it clear that we would be ready to listen whenever she wanted us to. 'Anything you want to tell us,' I had said, smoothing the sheet, longing to touch her, 'anything at all, no matter how bad, we want to hear it. When you're ready. OK?'

325

'Yes,' she said, her brow furrowed, eyes sunken and dim.

Now, accepting that her statement is something that must be done, I say, 'And they must send someone who speaks English. It's going to be difficult as it is.'

Peter Dunne nods.

'And we want to be with her. She'll need support,' Tom says. 'One of us should be with her.'

'I'll pass that on,' Peter Dunne says, 'and nothing will happen until she's well enough.' He takes a breath. 'They have recovered images from Carlson's laptop, photographs of both women.'

My stomach flips over. I think of the Internet, the paedophile rings and the like, people with sick predilections swapping obscene material.

Oh, Lori. 'Was he sharing them?' I say.

'Seems not, though they're still working to confirm that,' Peter Dunne says.

'If he's convicted,' Tom says, 'what will he get?'

'Murder is a capital crime. With the crimes against Lorelei in addition, he would either face life in prison or execution.'

Execution. Something twists inside me. Hanging. The electric chair. Lethal injection. Beheading. I don't agree with capital punishment. Never have. But now... He should be dead, I think. He should be torn into pieces and left for dogs to eat. He should be killed. But some part of me is revolted by the idea. The barbarity.

'I'm not sure we'd want that,' I say. I turn to Tom, enlisting his support.

He moves his head slowly, his mouth tightening a fraction. 'I'd put the rope around his neck myself,' he says.

'It's usually by injection, these days,' says Peter Dunne.

Which is not the point.

I squash my emotions, ignore the impulse to agree with Tom, to indulge the lust for vengeance. If taking a life is wrong, then executing someone is wrong. If we lose all our principles, aren't we as bad as he is? 'If we objected–' I say.

'It's not our call,' Tom says. 'That bastard took a life. People will want him to pay the price. We're a sideshow.'

Peter Dunne reacts: 'I wouldn't describe it–'

Tom cuts across him: 'And Lori needs to understand that,' he says fiercely. 'No guilt trips about compassion and forgiveness and the sanctity of human life. This is not down to us. It's not our country. He probably wouldn't get the chop just for the abduction but he killed someone so he forfeits his life. We have to make her see that.'

'We don't *make* her do anything,' I say.

'The boys want to talk to Lori,' Nick says, when we speak again. He sounds exhausted, as if it's an effort to get the words out.

'Just tell them she's still too poorly.'

We couldn't work out at first how to explain what had happened but my instinct was to stay close to the truth and keep it simple. Lori's story would be all over the papers: it wouldn't be fair to tell them some fairy tale and for them to find out we'd lied.

'A bad man wouldn't let her go home. He kept her in a garage,' I said.

327

'And when they ask why?'

'We're all asking why,' I almost snapped. *Why on earth?* 'Say we don't know. It was a mean thing to do and he shouldn't have done it and now the police have locked him up.'

Now I say, 'She is getting stronger all the time, though.'

'That's good,' Nick says.

'And once she can walk they say we can take her home. They've not found her passport anywhere so we'll have to get an emergency one from the consulate.'

'OK. Give her my love,' Nick says. 'I'd better go.' I can hear Benji barking in the background and Finn calling. I long to be back there with them.

Lori is awake more as the dosage of the sedative is slowly reduced. They alter the position of the bed, raising her head so she is sitting up. And on the fourth day they remove the gastric feeding tube and the nurse tells us they plan to sit her on the edge of the bed for ten minutes at a time. Because of the extreme muscle wastage, such small steps are milestones. She is weak as a kitten.

Each time I see her, it cuts me to the quick: her skeletal frame, the ghastly, savage sores and, most of all, her frailty. But I must hide my pity and sorrow, and adopt the same positive, practical tone that all the medical staff have. She is getting better, I tell myself. She is getting better every day.

'How did you find me?' Lori says, her voice hoarse. The first direct question she has asked.

My mouth goes dry and I stumble over the first few words. 'Mrs Tang told us you were going to photograph Bradley but he said you'd not fixed anything up. We were suspicious. Your dad found messages from you on Bradley's phone and we managed to get into his flat when he went to work. That's where we found your camera. When it seemed like the police weren't doing very much we followed the pictures.'

I have to tell her the rest. I don't want her hearing it from anyone else. 'Lori – Bradley hurt someone else as well.'

Tremors flicker near her mouth. 'Who?' she croaks.

'A Chinese woman.' How do I say it? *He killed her? He kept her skeleton in a suitcase?* 'She died,' I say.

Lori stares, makes a choking noise. 'Who was she?'

'We don't know. The police are trying to find out.'

Tears spring to her eyes. She shuts them. 'Don't go,' she says.

'I'll be here.' She reaches for my hand, hers blackened by the bruising from the cannula. Her skin is hot. It is the first time she has let me touch her properly. I am light-headed. When her grip loosens I keep holding on as long as I can until cramp burns along my forearm and my fingers tingle with pins and needles.

CHAPTER FIFTY-ONE

The nurses get Lori to sit in the chair at the bed-side. She has very little to say. Her only request, 'I want to go home.'

'You will,' I tell her, 'as soon as you can walk a little.'

She is stooped, frail, her eyes huge and wary. Now able to feed herself, she has little appetite and her diet is supplemented with nutritional drinks.

Her hair is dull and ragged, the sores either side of her mouth are two large dark circles, and with her chapped lips joining them she looks like a macabre clown.

But the arrhythmia has cleared up and the in-flammation in her lungs has nearly gone. I'm astonished at the sweep of her recovery, at the work they have done here in the hospital, at her body's capacity to heal.

Her friends are allowed to visit now, two at a time, for short periods. Dawn and Rosemary, then Shona and Oliver. Oliver brings some food his mother has made, little parcels of rice and meat. Lori can't eat it but we thank him all the same.

By Thursday she can take several steps unaided and is transferred to a medical ward. She has a room on her own but the staff recommend she is not left alone so Tom and I sit with her in turn.

'We can arrange for someone from the psychiatric service to speak to you,' the doctor tells Lori, 'about your experience.'

'No,' Lori says.

'You can consider this when you are back in the UK.'

Lori gives a nod, her eyes averted, noncommittal. She is still awkward when we touch her, recoiling or stiffening at a hand on her arm, or the prospect of a hug.

Is it a barrier we need to break through? If we kept touching her, kept our hands on her, while we sit, might we be able to override the fear she has? It's not something I dare try. We have to respect her boundaries. She was always so at ease physically, comfortable in her own skin, generous with hugs and kisses. Has that gone for ever?

The day before we travel home, Peter Dunne meets us at the hotel, bringing Lori's emergency passport and our new tickets. We have a suite, two bedrooms, two baths and a living room. We sit in the living room on the couches with their shot-silk mustard covers, the floor-length drapes drawn back to reveal the vista of the river snaking through the city, olive green today under a clear sky. Tom is still packing but I am nearly done.

Peter Dunne asks after Lori.

'She's gaining weight,' I say, 'and she can walk a little further every day but we will use a wheelchair for the airport.'

'That's good to hear.' He pauses, then, 'I have some news from the PSB.'

331

Tom stops moving, a pile of clothes in his arms.

'We're seeing them today,' I say, 'for Lori's statement.'

'They have identified the other woman,' Peter Dunne says.

Oh, God. A chill settles on me. Tom glances my way, eyes alert.

'Apparently she was a Chinese student, nineteen years old, from Chengdu, studying in Chongqing. She went missing at the end of September, on her way home for National Day.'

Eight months ago. 'What's her name?' I ask.

'Bai Lijuan.'

I remember what Anthony said, how hard it was to publicize cases of missing Chinese girls.

'Do they know how she met him?' Tom says.

'No.' Peter Dunne adjusts his glasses. I sense he has more to say. He draws in a quick breath. 'You saw oil drums in the workshop?'

'Yes,' Tom says.

'The police also found substantial quantities of lye, caustic soda. It's a very powerful alkaline.'

'Jesus.' I see what he is saying. I remember the drain where Lori was tied up, and how the bones we found were so clean.

Tom groans.

'Her parents?' I say.

'They've been notified.'

'Has he confessed?' Tom says.

'No.'

Bradley Carlson has been in custody for a week. He can be held for up to thirty.

I think of Lijuan's parents, how they must have waited like us, anxious, then increasingly desperate. Weeks stretching into months.

'Can we ... I don't know ... send our condolences or something?' I say.

'If you wish to write a note I can get it translated and make sure it reaches them.'

I find hotel stationery. 'Is it Mr and Mrs Bai?' I ask Peter Dunne.

'Mr Bai and Mrs Wen,' he says. 'Chinese women keep their maiden names when they marry.'

I write:

Dear Mr Bai and Mrs Wen,

We are so sorry for the tragic loss of your precious daughter Bai Lijuan and our thoughts are with you now. We hope that your loving memories of her will sustain you at this difficult time and be something to cherish for ever more.

I sign it from Tom, Lori and me, and give it to Peter Dunne.

There are a few moments' silence, then Peter Dunne says, 'Your car's booked for the morning. Is there anything else you need?'

'No. Thanks,' Tom says.

I check the time. We need to leave soon: we are meeting the police in a room at the hospital, then packing Lori's things at the apartment. Lori wants to see it again. Her friends have volunteered to help and I don't know if that's wise. Lori is traumatized – how could she be otherwise – and I worry that this will overwhelm her, but she says she's OK with it. I have to trust her to tell us what she can and can't cope with.

Lori has asked me to sit in with her for the police interview. Three police officers come: Superintendent Yin, Detective Song and Detective Lee. Detective Lee, a woman, speaks good English. She writes down what Lori says and translates it into Chinese for the men as she does so. Her manner is kind, measured and sympathetic.

Lori answers a few questions about Bradley, how long they'd known each other, how often they saw each other, the nature of their relationship, then Detective Lee asks her to describe the events of Monday, 7 April.

Lori remembers meeting Bradley as arranged by the North Street bridge over the river. She had called into Wenshu Monastery on the way – she'd not visited it before but had heard a lot about it. She reached Bradley just before half past ten and from the river they walked to his workshop. She stopped, now and then, to take photographs.

Her delivery is flat, almost monotonous, with lots of pauses. As she talks, she strokes the back of her wrist continually where the wound from the hand tie has scabbed over, like a dark, rust-coloured bracelet.

'We got in the workshop and he gave me a drink, some jasmine tea he'd brought along.' She falters. We wait. 'The next thing I remember it was dark and he had gone. I was tied up on the floor. My... I didn't have any clothes on.'

I sit as still as possible, trying not to react, giving her all the space she needs.

'There was something around my mouth too, in my mouth, so I couldn't call out.'

'How long until you saw him again?' Detective

Lee says.

'I don't know. When he came back–' Lori stops dead and silence fills the room.

Eventually Detective Lee asks, 'What happened when he came back?'

'I was so thirsty,' Lori says, 'he brought me water and I drank it and I was asking what he was doing. I was begging him to let me go and he put the gag on, then I must have fallen asleep again.'

'Did he talk to you?'

'No,' Lori says.

'Nothing at all?' Detective Lee says.

'No,' Lori says.

'When did he come again?'

'I don't know,' Lori says. 'I could never tell how long I slept.'

'Did he come every day?' Detective Lee says.

'I don't know. Sometimes perhaps.'

'Did he bring food?' Detective Lee says.

'No.'

'And when he came, what did he do?'

I press my feet to the floor, grit my teeth.

'He put the lights on,' Lori says, 'and took the gag off, and gave me water. If I ever tried to talk he put the gag back on. Then he would watch me and take pictures on his phone.'

'How long did he stay?' Detective Lee says.

'I don't know. I always fell asleep.'

'He never spoke?'

'No,' Lori says.

'Did he touch you?' Detective Lee says.

'Only to put the gag on, or to help me drink. And sometimes he used the hose when I'd been sick or when I had diarrhoea.'

335

'He hosed you clean?' Detective Lee says.

I bite my cheek.

Lori nods.

'Did he assault you sexually?'

'Not when I was awake,' Lori says.

My throat clenches tight.

'When you were sleeping?' Detective Lee says.

'I think so. It felt like he had. I think he raped me.' Her voice breaks.

I taste bile in my throat, feel a wave of grief and pity for my daughter, a blaze of rage at the man who had inflicted such violence on her.

Thirty-three days, thirty-three nights.

'I am sorry, I know this is very difficult,' Detective Lee says, 'but we are nearly finished.'

Detective Lee adds to the written statement and translates for her colleagues. Then she turns back to Lori. 'When you met Mr Carlson you had your camera with you?'

'Yes,' Lori says.

'Did you carry anything else?'

Lori frowns. 'Sorry – I keep going blank,' she says.

'Did you have your wallet?' I say. 'Or your phone?'

'Yes,' Lori says.

'Did you have a bag?' Detective Lee says.

'Yes, my red canvas one,' Lori says.

'And your keys?'

'Yes,' Lori says.

'Did you have your passport?' Detective Lee says.

'No.'

'Your laptop?'

'No.'

'Your backpack?' Detective Lee says.

'No.' Lori frowns.

'And your toothbrush?' Detective Lee says.

'No.' Lori looks puzzled.

'They were at your apartment?'

'Yes,' Lori says.

All these things are still missing. So Bradley must have been to her apartment and taken her passport and laptop, toothbrush and backpack, making it plausible that she'd gone travelling.

'Did you ever meet a Chinese girl, called Bai Lijuan?' Detective Lee says.

'I don't think so,' Lori says.

Detective Lee shows Lori a photograph. A slender girl with a page-boy haircut and a mischievous smile, she has a pair of over-sized sunglasses pushed up on her head. She wears a pink shift dress and a necklace of daisies that look like they're made of plastic.

'No.' Lori shakes her head. 'Is that her?'

'Yes, this is the other victim,' Detective Lee says.

Lori's eyes are troubled. She lowers her head as if she'll hide. Tears spill down her face, fall onto her arms, into her lap. She makes no sound; she does not move to wipe them away.

'Are we finished?' I ask Detective Lee.

'Yes. Thank you, Lori,' Detective Lee says. 'This is very hard for you and we are very glad for your assistance and co-operation. This will help us make a very successful prosecution. If you remember anything else, please email me.' She has a business card and places it on the table next to Lori.

I know that Detective Lee is right and that Lori's story will be a crucial part of the case against Bradley Carlson but I wish she could have been spared the pain of revisiting her ordeal.

Lori manages to nod and the police scrape back their chairs and prepare to leave. They come to shake hands with me. When it gets to Superintendent Yin's turn I move away, my face burning. I am still infuriated by his incompetence and arrogance, and this petty gesture seems the only power I have to express it.

When they have left, I say, 'Come on.' I touch Lori's upper arm and release the brakes on the wheelchair. Lori looks at me once, eyes clouded with tears, and then into the distance. Lost again.

CHAPTER FIFTY-TWO

Tom wheels Lori into her flat, to the middle of the living room. She looks about and I hear her let go of her breath, a little puff, but I can't tell what she feels about the place, though she's clearly terribly shaken after giving her statement.

We have a new wheeled suitcase that we bought from a shop near the hotel, and a roll of bin bags for rubbish.

'You're going to have to tell us what to pack,' Tom says.

'All your clothes?' I suggest.

'Yes,' she says. I make a start in the bedroom

and before long her friends arrive.

There are greetings and enquiries about how she is today. Lori's replies are brief, muted. I go and say hello to them all.

'Maybe two of you could do the kitchen and two in here?' Tom suggests.

They divide up and I go back into the bedroom. I collect her shoes and put them in the case. I bring the clothes in that she'd left drying on the balcony, among them the shirt that I was sure she would have taken if she had been away on holiday.

There isn't much conversation, but now and again I hear Dawn say, 'Take or leave?' and Lori reply, or Lori say to someone, 'You can chuck that out.'

It doesn't take long. All of the kitchen equipment is left for the next tenant. Her travel guides and work notes, dictionary and other bits and pieces go into the case.

'Nearly done,' I tell them. We will drop the keys at the gatehouse and Dawn will see the landlord to settle the finances. She thinks the deposit will more or less equate to the rent payments Lori missed but will let us know.

Tom takes the photo off the wall and puts it into her case along with the lucky Chinese knot.

I feel a rush of emotion, aware of all the partings that are imminent, but Lori takes it in her stride: telling Oliver to keep in touch; thanking Rosemary for everything and making her promise she'll visit us in Manchester when she comes to the UK. Shona stoops down and gives Lori a small package: inside is a necklace, glass fragments in cobalt blue and bottle green caught in twisted silver.

'It's gorgeous,' Lori says.

'You get well now,' Shona says.

Just Dawn is left. She goes to hug Lori and Lori freezes, then leans forward, her thin arms encircling her friend.

I see Dawn's back judder and hear her sniff. Lori gives a little cry, then releases her arms. Dawn straightens up, saying, 'Sorry,' and blowing her nose. Lori wipes her face with her hands and gives a lopsided smile. '*Zài jiàn*,' she says thickly.

Dawn hiccups a laugh. She turns to Tom, who pats her arm and says, 'All the best.' Tom and I walk her to the door and I give her a quick hug. Her face is working, she's barely holding it together, and I think we both know it'd be best if she didn't go to pieces in front of Lori. She whispers her goodbyes and leaves.

Lori asks me to open the balcony windows and Tom takes her out in the wheelchair. With help she gets to her feet, leaning her arms on the rust-pocked railings.

'It's clear today,' I say.

To the right, we can see across to the second ring road, and beyond that the high-rises stretch to the horizon. The sun glints on the windows in the tower blocks opposite us. A crane at work on the construction site to the left swings a load way up high over the roof. The air is filled with sound, the ubiquitous horns, the drone of machinery, someone whistling, other voices raised, as if in argument, and a dog howling.

'I was so happy here,' she says.

I touch her back, feel the knobs of her spine, a flicker of tension. She doesn't say anything else.

The three of us stand gazing at Chengdu until Lori sits down and it's time to go.

The airport, bright with its shimmering marble floors, is very warm and airless, in spite of banks of air-conditioning vents in the walls. You could look outside, where a thick haze is smothering everything, and think it was a foggy autumn day at home, chilly and damp with the smell of burning leaves and wet wool in the air. It's fifteen days since we arrived in China, but feels so much longer.

Bilingual announcements echo over the PA system. A Chinese group share a picnic, the spicy aroma percolating through the departure lounge.

I buy pandas for the boys.

We have VIP status, will be fast-tracked to our seats, avoid the queues, get extra leg room, considerate attention. But nothing can fast-track the journey. Over fourteen hours until we reach home. It's odd at first to see so many Caucasian faces again, Westerners. No one's staring at us any more. Or not for that reason. Some stare at Lori. Perhaps she is recognizable from the news coverage. Her face and that of Bai Lijuan, along with pictures of Bradley Carlson, have been beamed around the world. A global story for our global village. Or is it simply because she looks so frail? Face still skull-like, no fat on her, shoulders angular, knees sharp, beneath the loose jade silk pyjama-suit she wears.

While we wait at Schiphol for the connecting flight, Tom makes calls, work ones but also to Edward at Missing Overseas – he has been managing the press at this end with Nick. A request has been made for them to respect the family's privacy with the carrot of inducement that some of us may be available to appear at a press conference in due course. It's Lori they want, of course, Lori who survived and emerged from the maw of the monster.

We won't let them do that, we agreed, gawp and preen and pick over her trauma, but as Edward has explained, we wanted the publicity, we courted them when she went missing, invited the press to help us. 'And now it's biting us in the arse,' Tom said.

'We can speak,' I said to Tom, 'you and I can, when we're ready.'

Lori drowsed a lot of the long flight. I had to hold back from fussing, didn't comment when she ignored the food and barely had any of the supplementary drinks she'd been given. Tom and I sat either side of her. He drank steadily, taking full advantage of the complimentary bar service. I didn't dare. I knew I'd suffer with a vicious headache and dehydration. My eyes feel as though they have been peeled.

As we come into the arrivals hall in Manchester, there is a sudden stir: a group of people surge forward, some with cameras, some with microphones, firing questions at us.

'How are you feeling, Lorelei?'

'Will you be testifying?'

'What was your ordeal like?'

'How did the police find you?'

'How is it being home?'

I flinch, stop pushing the wheelchair. Lori cowers, her eyes squeezed shut.

Tom has the luggage trolley. He holds up his hands. 'Wait,' he says loudly. 'We're just glad to be home and we would really appreciate some privacy.' He's on edge – I imagine him taking a swing at someone.

'What's the first thing you want to do, Lorelei?'

'Were you happy with the work of the Chinese authorities?'

They continue to call out. Then, with a lurch of anxiety, I see Nick at the other side of the gangway hurrying towards us. He looks worn out, bloodshot eyes, rumpled clothes, his hair in need of a wash. There's a woman with him and he introduces her as Isabelle – she'll be helping us with the media. I'm just wondering why Isabelle can't start by getting rid of the scrum crowding close by when she speaks up: 'Ladies and gentlemen, I have a statement here from the family.'

Nick nods to me and gestures we should keep moving.

I can hear the beginning of her speech: '"We would like to say that we are very relieved and very thankful to be at home with Lorelei, who is recovering her strength day by day after excellent care from the Huaxi hospital. We would like to thank all those people who were able to help..."'

Out of earshot, Nick stops walking and crouches to greet Lori. 'It's so good to see you,' he says.

She smiles, wan, tired.

We exit the arrivals hall. Tom lugs his case from the trolley. I feel a clutch of panic at the notion of him leaving us now.

'I'll get a cab,' he says. He bends over Lori. 'See you tomorrow.'

'OK, Dad,' she says.

He kisses the top of her head.

As he steps away, I go to him, put my arms around him and hug. There's a fraction of a pause, then he returns the embrace. My eyes shut tight savouring – for the last time, I imagine – the feel of him, his width and height, the heat of his chest, the smell of tobacco and cedar, the prickle of his hair brushing against my cheek.

'Thank you,' I say.

'I'll see you tomorrow.' He draws away, his eyes on mine, clear and calm.

I take the luggage trolley and turn to Nick. 'You'll push Lori?'

'Yes,' he says. He looks at me for a moment too long and my throat closes in panic, but I ignore him and set off across the road to the car park.

CHAPTER FIFTY-THREE

It has been raining and the air is gin clear, everything rinsed bright. The red-brick buildings seem to glow, the trees are a riot of lush vivid greens, the sky a high, aching blue.

And it is so quiet. The streets look empty, only

ever a scattering of pedestrians. I had never thought of Manchester as a peaceful place before. I notice the litter, though, cigarette butts and chewing gum on the ground, plastic bottles and takeaway trays at the edges of fences and walls, carrier bags snagged on bushes. The only street sweepers we have here are little trucks with revolving circular brushes that hoover the pavements and gutters on a seemingly random basis.

'What do you want?' Nick asks us, when we get home. It is four o'clock in the afternoon. 'Shower? Food? Sleep?'

I don't know. I look outside to the garden where the grass has grown long and the bedding plants are thriving, a froth of fuchsia and lavender, red geraniums and blue lobelia.

The air is full of insects, flies and gnats, and I recall the tiny white moths, that night of the kites. Before we knew. Before we found her.

A surge of relief, euphoria, rushes through me. We are back. Home. Safe.

'Lori?' I say. 'What do you fancy?'

She hesitates.

'Tea and toast?' Nick suggests.

'Yes,' she says.

'Me too,' I say.

Nick asks about the flight, the weather in Chengdu. Small talk that we can cope with.

The toast is thick and crunchy, soft in the middle. Homemade white bread. Smothered in salted butter and dark tangy marmalade.

'Penny's bread?' I guess.

'She's done us a few meals too,' Nick says, 'in

the freezer, one in the fridge for tea.'

Benji sits at Lori's side, his eyes on her, ears pricked up, tail thumping, waiting for crumbs.

I drink my tea. It's perfect, strong and full, nothing like the tea I had over there.

Penny brings the boys home.

They are overjoyed to see Lori, both grinning from ear to ear, eager to tell her their news, show her their latest toys.

Isaac looks wiped out. He shows us his scar. I pat my knee and he climbs on.

'I'm so glad you're better.' I hug his shoulders. He relaxes back against me, one hand tracing round and round my knee.

'You look funny,' Isaac says to Lori, when there's a break in the conversation.

'Yes,' she says. She pulls a face, eyes crossed, and the boys laugh.

'Lori's been poorly, too,' I say.

'Did he have a gun?' Isaac says. We all know who he means. Finn stops patting Benji and watches to see what she'll say.

'No,' Lori says.

'A knife, then?' Isaac says.

Lori looks upset, so I say, 'What happened to Lori was pretty scary and she doesn't want to talk about it.'

'Who's hungry?' Nick says, and the boys shout out. Attention turns to the food that Penny left us.

'Shall we eat outside?' I say. 'If we dry the seats, is it warm enough?'

Lori makes it through the meal, then wants to

346

sleep. I carry her case up to the little room. Penny has lent us a single bed – Lori's double might fit into the small room at a pinch but there'd be no space for anything else. Lori has to take the stairs slowly, bent like an old woman, pausing every couple of steps.

'Do you want to sleep downstairs?' I say.

'No,' she says quickly.

Of course not. She doesn't want to feel alone.

Isaac sits with me while Nick clears up and Finn leaps about on the trampoline, calling to us to watch his moves.

I am raw with fatigue, eyes dry, muscles aching, and close to tears of joy at being here.

'Does your tummy hurt now?' I ask Isaac.

'Only if I jump or stretch it.'

'What was it like in hospital?' I say.

'It was really noisy and they kept waking me up.'

'With the noise?'

'And a fermometer.' His voice is growing drowsy, his eyelids drooping.

'I think you're a tired boy.'

'Am not,' he says, but he seems to grow heavier on my lap. I call Nick, who takes him up to bed.

Lori is still awake when I go in to check on her. 'Do you want anything?' I ask.

'My tablets. I think they're in my bag downstairs.'

She's still taking oral antibiotics, she has to finish the course, and she is on the last week of lower-dose sedatives.

I bring them up and she takes them from me.

347

'Leave the door open,' she says, 'and the light on.'

'Yes. Do you want a bedside lamp?' The ceiling light is very bright.

'No, it's OK. And tell Nick, too, about the door,' she adds, a hint of urgency in her voice.

'I will.'

Finn wants me read him a story.

He's on the top bunk. 'Isaac couldn't climb up,' he says. 'We swapped.'

'So, do you want a book or a made-up story?'

'About my panda playing football!' He wiggles the bear at me.

I sit on the chair in the corner, close my eyes and invent a story about a panda who has lost his football, his search in the woods and the stream, and all the creatures he meets who help him look and how he finally finds the football under a giant stork who thought it was an egg and tried to hatch it. I rattle through it but Finn seems happy enough.

'One more?' he says.

'Not tonight, darling. I'm really tired. I've been on an aeroplane for hours and hours.'

'Can we go and get my rocket tomorrow, Mummy?'

'I'm not sure, but soon,' I say.

'What happened to Lori?'

'She was taken away by a nasty man,' I say.

'And you and Tom found her?'

'We did.'

'You went and got her?' His eyes, dark blue with those glints of gold, are wide, fixed on me.

'Yes.'

'And the man's in prison now?'

'He's in the police station, locked up.'

My heart feels swollen, tender, as I answer his questions. I want to shield him from it all but I know that's not possible.

Dizzy with exhaustion, I have a quick shower and find Nick still outside in the last of the daylight. He's drinking wine and offers me some.

'God, yes,' I say, 'and then I'm going to collapse.'

He pours me a glass, tops up his own and joins me on the bench.

'Home,' I say, and touch my glass to his. 'Oh, and before I forget, Lori wants the light on and the door left open.'

I take a sip of wine: it's cold, lemony, delicious.

The sun is setting, brazen, a ball of fire in a wash of peach and rose. I look away, blindsided, and see black discs rimmed green with each blink.

'We need to sort out some follow-up with the GP,' I say. 'Maybe physio too. They suggested counselling.' It is suddenly all too big, too weighty. My head spins. 'I don't know how we do this. How do we help her? I keep thinking, all those days, tied up on the floor. What he did to her...'

'Don't,' Nick says. He puts his hand on my arm.

Sadness pours through me as if a dam has burst. I start to cry and he takes me in his arms and lets me weep until I am spent and his T-shirt is soaked and the dusk has come down.

'There were no stars in Chengdu,' I tell him, making out a few in the darkening sky. 'Too cloudy. Worse than here.'

Something rustles in the shrubs near the wall.

A bird roosting, perhaps, a mouse or a frog. Silence falls, and it's a couple of minutes before the murmur of a car engine interrupts it.

'Finn wants me to take him to the museum to get his rocket.'

'He can forget that,' Nick says.

'I promised ... maybe not tomorrow. But it is Sunday so he'll be off school.'

'We've Isabelle coming at ten. She needs to talk to us about the media strategy,' he says.

I groan. I wanted a normal day, mooching around the house, to the park with the kids, washing clothes, and it strikes me that nothing will be normal again, at least not for the foreseeable future.

'Is she from Missing Overseas?' I say.

'Freelance.'

'So we have to pay her?'

'Yes,' he says.

'Can we afford it?'

'The way they tell it, we can't afford not to,' he says.

The air feels softer, moist, as night sets in. An aeroplane flies overhead, red and white lights winking, and I realize I never saw planes in Chengdu, didn't hear any either. Among that barrage of sound, no jet engines.

'What about you?' I say. 'How are you?'

'I don't know,' Nick says wearily. He gets up, crosses to the picnic table for more wine. 'It's unbelievable. Just seeing her...'

'I know.'

I wish Tom were here to talk to. Everything we shared in our search for Lori, he's the only one who knows what it was like, who understands.

My own bed is blissfully soft after the punishing density of the ones in the hotels. My head is still full of the drone of our plane and I have the sensation that the mattress is vibrating.

My sleep is dark and dense and dreamless. Black velvet.

CHAPTER FIFTY-FOUR

I wake to the *swip swip swip* of the sparrow on the corner of the guttering. *Swip swip swip.* Nick's side of the bed is empty. Even after my sleep, I feel tired.

Lori is still in bed; the boys are glued to games on their tablets. There's no sign of Benji so I assume that Nick has taken him for a walk. After I've eaten, I run Lori a bath, throw in handfuls of salt, to help with the sores, which are almost healed.

Isabelle arrives just after Nick has got back and says she wants to talk to Lori too, about what happens now. Lori is still in the bath so I call her and we fill in the time with coffee and harmless chat about China, the cultural differences, the language barrier. It's a grey day, the breeze pushing clouds overhead. Still – the air is clear.

When Lori comes downstairs she accepts the offer of tea and scrambled eggs.

'You've been through a terrible experience,'

Isabelle says to Lori, 'but you're here, you're a survivor, and people want to hear about that.' Lori doesn't say anything. She doesn't react.

'The last thing anyone wants to do is put any additional pressure on you,' Isabelle says. 'My job is to make sure that this happens at a pace you're comfortable with, that you don't do anything you don't want to do. People want to know about your abduction and about your rescue, but while legal proceedings are under way, my advice is not to discuss that. So, we issue a general statement for now, quotes from all of you, and we release a photograph of you as a family, but we do not go into any details about evidence that may be used in a court case. We wait until the trial is concluded and then we grant exclusives. There's a great deal of human interest in the story.'

It's not a story, I want to say. This is real. It really happened. My daughter was tied up and starved; she was kept naked and drugged and raped. She was hosed down when she was sick. She nearly died.

'What do you mean "exclusives?"' Nick says. 'Like, just one newspaper?'

'That's an example but there are several platforms to consider,' Isabelle says. 'We could be looking at TV, a documentary, say, women's magazines as well as the papers, even a book.'

'A book?' I'm appalled by the idea.

'It's a powerful story. There are ghost-writers and non-fiction writers who have substantial experience of this type of project.'

'Why on earth would we want to see a book about it?' I say.

'Apart from the huge public interest, there is the question of money,' Isabelle says.

'Money?' I say.

'We'd be expecting fees with any of these ventures. If my understanding is right, Lori won't be entitled to any criminal compensation, given that the crimes were committed overseas. And the aftermath of an experience like this can be costly, medical bills, loss of earnings. It may be some time before Lori is back at work.'

'This is all too soon.' I get to my feet.

'It's OK,' Lori says.

'Nothing happens now,' Isabelle says, 'apart from the statement and the photo, if you agree to that. Nothing else is done until the legal side of things is concluded. That will likely be months away. But you need to know your options and I would strongly recommend that you brief me with exploring the route of exclusives.'

'What if we do nothing?' I say.

'You will probably be pestered by the media, some of whom can be unpleasantly intrusive and persistent.' She looks at Nick. 'There have already been people coming to the house, ringing up?'

He nods.

'You all saw the mob at the, airport yesterday,' she says. 'This strategy will be a way to contain and manage the public interest.'

We don't want reporters at the door.

'Lori?' I say.

'Fine.' She shrugs. Nick nods.

'Good,' Isabelle says. 'I suggest we get the photograph done today. I'll show you the draft statement and get it finalized.'

'Today?' I say.

'The sooner the better,' she says.

Two hours later we are posing in front of a photographer. Furniture has been rearranged, special lights, hot and bright, erected, white reflector shields set on the floor and a nearby chair. The stylist has made suggestions for clothing and applied makeup to me. Lori balked at that and I backed her up.

It's a parody of the family snapshot. Tom stands at one side of me, Nick at the other. Lori sits in front of Tom and me, the boys beside her.

The stylist wanted Tom in something smarter but he's no clothes here. He's unshaven too. She asked him if he'd like to shave but he said not, brooking no discussion.

'You could brush your hair,' Lori said. I lent him my brush.

Thank goodness we're not required to smile, though Finn calls, 'Cheese,' the first couple of times, which punctures the tension and has us laughing. I think of all those Victorian portraits, their faces solemn, and wonder when it changed. When smiling came in. Was it due to some technical advance? When people no longer had to sit still for so long? Lori probably knows.

At last it is done. We read through Isabelle's statement and she needs quotes from Tom, from Lori, from Nick and me. The things we come up with are honest enough but clichés too. The sort of thing anyone in our situation would think, would say.

You can't imagine anything like this happening to

someone you know. There really aren't any words to describe what it's like.

We were so lucky to find Lori just in time and the hospital was fantastic. We want to thank all the doctors and nurses there. And the people in Chengdu who helped us in the search for her.

Our thoughts are with the family of Bai Lijuan after their terrible loss.

I'd no idea people were looking for me. I didn't know anything about the outside world. But I'd like to thank everyone who helped and most of all my mum and dad, who wouldn't give up.

It was a complete nightmare but we had such excellent support from Missing Overseas and the Foreign and Commonwealth Office.

You're living on adrenalin, this horrible mix of fear and hope, but you keep hoping... You have to keep hoping.

There's a collective sigh of relief once Isabelle and her crew have gone. Tom sits with Lori in the front room for a while. We heat up some of Penny's food. Tom joins us, and Isaac and Finn chatter through the meal. It's a useful distraction.

'I said I'd visit my folks this afternoon,' Nick says.

'Oh, no!' I complain, not ready for more travel.

'It's OK, I said you'd be too tired,' he says, 'but I've not seen them for ages.'

'We're going to the museum,' Finn says, 'me and Mummy.'

I'm about to disagree, then think, Why not? I'm still feeling displaced – however I spend the rest of the day will be surreal. And Finn deserves some attention.

Lori looks anxious: her eyes dart between Tom and me.

'I can stay here till you're back,' Tom says.

'Yes!' Isaac likes the idea.

There's a flash of something, resentment or irritation, in Nick's face but I say, 'Good,' and it's sorted.

Fatigue, bone deep, hits me as I queue with Finn in the museum gift shop to buy his replacement rocket. He's singing, off key as usual. It takes me a moment to recognize the Bowie song, 'Space Oddity', which the boys got to hear last year when astronaut Commander Hadfield released a version of it from the International Space Station.

On the bus home, it strikes me that I'm invisible again. No longer an object of interest, no longer different.

Lori has gone up to rest, Isaac is drawing in the living room and Tom is smoking in the garden when we arrive back.

Finn stares at Tom's cigarette and pulls a face. But the desire to show off his rocket wins out, and Tom dutifully admires it

'How's she been?' I ask Tom, once we're inside and Finn has gone to watch TV.

'Very quiet,' he says. He runs his hand through his hair. 'I told her I'd call in every other day.'

'OK.'

'And I mentioned the GP,' he says.

'Yes, we'll take her down tomorrow.'

My phone sounds a text message alert.

'I'll head off,' Tom says.

'OK. See you Tuesday.'

He smiles, that crooked grin, and my stomach flips over. I'm aware of the space between us, that we are alone in the room. I duck my head, stuff my hands into the pockets of my jeans. He nods goodbye and leaves. We do not touch.

The text is from Nick. He'll be back later, he's going to eat with his parents.

CHAPTER FIFTY-FIVE

I'm staring into the freezer considering fish fingers and chips as an option when the doorbell goes. Mindful of what Isabelle said this morning, about the press, I look out of the front bay window to see who it is. Penny is there – a large pie in her arms.

'If this gets to be too much,' she says, when I open the door, 'too *Desperate Housewives* or whatever...'

'You've saved the day,' I tell her. 'Come in.'

'I don't want to be in the way.'

'They're all crashed out or hooked up to their consoles,' I say, 'and Nick's gone to his folks. Keep me company.'

'You sure? Not jet-lagged?'

'I am seriously jet-lagged but I want to see you.'

I make coffee and Penny doesn't ask me anything about what happened but I launch into my account. It's jumbled, all out of order, but she's a good listener and a better friend and she lets me tell it my own way. Her eyes fill with tears as I describe finding Lori. I don't tell Penny I slept with Tom. I don't know if I ever will.

'With Isaac on top of everything else,' I say, 'that was so scary.'

'He's doing well,' she says.

'Yes.'

'And Lori?'

I purse my lips, blow out air. 'I don't know. It's so early. I don't know.'

A pause, then I say, 'Tell me about you. How are your boys? What else has been happening here?'

But she bats the question away. 'We're fine, everything's fine.'

'I'm hungry.' Finn comes in, the dog at his heels. His face lights up as he sees Penny.

'Well,' I say, 'you're in luck. Penny's brought our tea.'

I wake Lori to see if she wants to eat but she doesn't. She agrees to a drink. When I get back up there with hot chocolate she's asleep again. Her eyelids flicker and I wonder what she's dreaming about. Are her dreams a respite or a place of horror? Is she back in the lock-up, bound and gagged on the filthy concrete floor? What must it have been like not knowing when Bradley would return, if he would return? Understanding that she would die without the doctored water he let her drink. And that he would rape her when she was completely defenceless. To be so alone.

I force such thoughts away and join Penny and the boys. I distract myself and entertain them with stories of the food we ate, and didn't eat, in China.

They are both in the bath when Penny gets ready to leave.

'Tomorrow we'll be back on track,' I say. 'I'll do a shop. Thanks so much for looking after Finn, for helping out, for everything.'

'Don't be daft,' she says. 'You'd do the same.' She starts to speak again, then stops, closes her mouth.

'What?' I say.

'Nothing.' I know her well enough to smell the lie.

'Penny?'

She gives a weird smile. 'It's probably not the best time... I don't know whether I should say anything.'

'What is it?'

She's embarrassed, her face and neck flushing.

'Penny – what?'

'It's Nick,' she says. 'I'm worried about him.'

I don't know what I was expecting but it certainly wasn't this.

'He's been down,' I say, 'since the redundancy.' Is that what she means?

'Drinking,' she says.

I'm suddenly defensive. 'We've all been drinking. Christ! With everything that's going on...'

'Yes, of course, I know, I'm sorry. But a lot,' she says. 'I'm sorry, Jo, it's not my business. And the house...'

I look around. The house is all right. No worse than when I'm doing most of the chores. 'It's fine,' I say.

'I cleared up,' she says simply.

'Oh.'

'Like you say, it's been such an awful time but ... I don't know.' She puts her hand to her throat. 'I thought I should mention it. Things will probably settle down now.'

'Yes,' I say. I'm stung by the notion of Nick struggling, the house so dirty and messy that Penny had to intervene. But she's probably blowing it out of all proportion. Her house is always tidier than ours, and she hasn't got a dog. Nick must have been completely unmoored, stressed already about work, then Lori missing, me thousands of miles away, Isaac collapsing. Who could blame him for a few glasses of something to get through it?

'Thanks again.' I can't quite keep a measure of reserve out of my voice.

Once the boys are in bed I reheat Lori's chocolate, wake her up and she drinks it.

Then I clear up the kitchen and take the rubbish out. I go to put the empty milk and juice cartons in the recycling bin but the whole thing is full of bottles, not just wine but whisky and brandy too. It looks like the aftermath of a house party.

I think of Nick's eyes when he met us, bloodshot, how I put it down to tiredness. He always did like a drink and, if I'm honest, he was drinking more after the redundancy... Then I chide myself: cut the guy some slack.

I'm woken by the car coming into the drive at half past midnight. There's a thump as Nick shuts the front door, then his feet on the stairs. I hear him in the bathroom, the whine of his toothbrush. He stumbles once in the bedroom changing into his pyjamas.

Fair enough, I think, it's dark, he's tired, he's had a long drive. I'm worn out and being paranoid.

When he climbs in beside me, even the smell of the mouthwash can't mask the reek of alcohol, coming off him in waves.

CHAPTER FIFTY-SIX

Isaac answers the phone, and I hear him say, 'Yes,' a few times. Then he calls to me, 'It's Nanny Betty,' he says. Nick's mum. Nick is still in bed.

'Betty,' I say, 'how are you? Is everything all right?'

'We're all right,' she says. 'I wanted to ring and say hello and send our love to Lori.'

'Thanks.'

'How is she doing?' Betty says.

'Sleeping a lot,' I say, focusing on the physical.

'A terrible thing,' she says, 'terrible.'

I feel the scale of it threatening me anew, so I press on, 'Yes, and with Isaac as well, we don't know what hit us.'

'Isaac? What about Isaac?' Alarm in her voice.

'Didn't Nick say?'

'We've not heard anything from Nick for weeks.'

Shit! My stomach turns cold. He lied to me. 'Oh, I am sorry, Betty, it's been crazy here. Isaac had appendicitis. He had an emergency operation but he's fine now.'

'Oh, my goodness. The poor little lamb. Listen, as soon as you can manage you must all come to see us – it's been far too long.'

'Yes,' I say. 'How's Ron?'

'Oh, not so bad. His legs are going. It's rotten getting old,' she says. 'Don't let anyone tell you any different.'

'And Philip?' I say.

'He's fine.'

I wonder what Betty would say if I broke convention and let on that I knew about Philip's history, if I told her what was really happening to Nick, if I asked for her advice. Has she gained any insight from all the years of dealing with Philip's drink problem?

'And Finn,' she says, 'is he OK?'

'He's great, still winning badges for his swimming.'

'He's a love,' she says. 'Now, I won't keep you but when you get a chance, you will come and see us, won't you?'

'We will, of course we will,' I say.

'Is Nick there?'

I'm tempted to say yes, to wake him and let him try to hide his hangover, and make his excuses to his mother for his neglect, but then she might guess what's going on and he'll know I've caught him in his lie and I'm not ready for that yet.

'He's out,' I say.

'Never mind, then. Bye-bye.'

'Bye.'

A week later I'm at school, talking to Grace about my return to work, when Peter Dunne calls. She must notice the change in my expression, as I see his name onscreen, because she says, 'Take it,' and motions to the door to see if I want her to leave. I shake my head – she can stay.

'Hello?' I say.

There's a slight delay on the line. Then he says, 'Mrs Maddox, how are you all? How's Lorelei?'

'Resting a lot. It's still early days.'

'Of course. Do please pass on my best wishes. Mrs Maddox, I've just been speaking with Superintendent Yin. Carlson confessed this morning and the case has been referred to the procuratorate, who will consider the evidence. As soon as we have a trial date I will let you know.'

Ice water in my stomach. 'We won't have to attend?'

'Most unlikely,' he says.

'And Lori?'

'The same. The statements you all made will be evidence enough.'

It's a blessing. I've read enough about rape trials here to know that many victims describe the court appearance as just as harrowing and demeaning as the attack itself. A second violation.

'Mr Carlson appointed a lawyer,' Peter Dunne says.

'A Chinese lawyer?' I remember him talking about it before.

'That's right. Given he has confessed, the lawyer's role will be to try to minimize any sentence. They really won't be able to do any more than that and, in my opinion, it's already a lost cause.'

'Can he plead insanity or something?' I say.

'No, he's not going down that route.' Peter Dunne goes on. 'With the degree of international interest in this case I predict that the authorities will be bending over backwards to demonstrate that the justice system is fair and transparent. They would lose a lot of face if the US cried foul or the quality of the prosecution evidence was found wanting. It'll be a lead story in the US, once it breaks. They will also want to prove to the home audience that no foreigner kills a Chinese citizen and gets away with it.'

'The evidence is overwhelming, isn't it?' I say.

'Indeed, and that's what counts most.'

'What about motive? Do they know why he did it?'

'There doesn't seem to be any motive, other than self-gratification,' Peter Dunne says. 'As it is, they're much less interested in motive here.'

'Why Lori?' I say.

'I don't know, I'm afraid. But I can tell you we have heard that the FBI is looking into Carlson.'

'What for?' I say.

'I'm told it's very rare for someone to act as he has done, at such an extreme, without some history, prior criminal incidents, escalating over time.'

'There might have been other victims?' I say.

'They think it's worth investigating.'

Oh, God!

'Please give my best wishes to Mr Maddox and to your husband,' he says.

'I will, thank you.'

'And your son, Isaac, how is he?'

'Much better, thank you.'

The call unsettles me. I fill Grace in and she tells me to go. 'We've covered the basics,' she says. 'See you a week on Monday. It'll be great to have you back.'

Walking home, I catch a phrase of music and I'm in Chengdu again. The ethereal rise and fall of a flute cut off by a squeal. Then a crashing sound. Concentrating, I hear the phrase repeat and realize, feeling foolish, that it is the recycling lorry collecting glass. Some fluke of metal and friction producing a tune.

Lori is up but not dressed and Nick is out walking the dog. Which may well mean he is at the pub, or sitting on a bench somewhere with a bottle in his pocket.

I did ask him to wait until I got back from school – Lori still doesn't like to be left alone – but she seems OK so perhaps Isaac's presence, is reassuring enough. He could cope with lessons now but isn't quite ready for the rough and tumble of the playground. Another couple of days and he'll be back at school.

Lori wanders into the kitchen where I'm folding the laundry. She sits down. Isaac's reading book is on the table and she flicks the pages back and forth. Fidgeting.

'I've heard from the consul in Chengdu,' I say. Her hand stills. 'Mr Dunne?'

'That's right. Bradley has confessed to all the charges.'

She flinches at the name and I feel an answering prick in my heart. She gets up. 'I thought you should know,' I say. She walks away.

Would it have helped if I hadn't said his name? It's so hard to know how to behave, what will hurt her and what she can tolerate. The boys are desperate to help. Finn tries singing and chatting. Isaac draws pictures and leaves them on the floor in her room. It's too much. There are times when she withdraws completely, others when she's suddenly angry or frightened.

I hear her climb the stairs, still a slow process. She has been given exercises to help build up her muscles again but I don't think she's been doing them.

My mind plays nasty tricks, conjures up the bleakest scenarios for the future. As if what I've witnessed isn't horrendous enough. I think of Tom's mother, Daphne, in and out of hospitals and clinics. Her inability to manage everyday life. Wounded in her soul and never fully healed. Blighted with a chronic condition. Of parents I know at school with poor mental health. Of lives cut short through acts of desperation. We have brought Lori home, Tom and I, but we cannot make her better. She is still so distressed, and there are days like today when I fear the future. Fear for her.

I have an overwhelming longing to see my mum, to share this burden with her, to be someone's daughter again myself.

It won't always be like this, I think. Surely it won't. Nothing stays the same. And I return to the clothes and the business of folding them into our separate piles.

CHAPTER FIFTY-SEVEN

After Saturday brunch, I'm going to fetch Finn from swimming. Isaac is at Sebastian's leaving party, Nick is out, God knows where. Penny has eaten with us and I leave her and Lori clearing up together. This is engineered so Penny can talk to Lori without me there.

Whenever I've mentioned counselling Lori has dismissed the idea and I've confided in Penny: 'She says she's fine, which she patently isn't. Then she says she doesn't want to think about it, let alone talk to some random stranger about it, which I do understand.'

'She knows what she can deal with,' Penny says, 'but maybe she needs to hear a bit more about what it would involve. How's she acting?'

'She's all over the place. She's showering three or four times a day. She has flashbacks. She's hiding from it but it's not working.'

'Everyone's different,' Penny says. 'Everyone reacts in different ways. I could have a word with her.'

Penny was raped by an ex-boyfriend when she was in her early twenties. It was several months before she confided in a friend. Penny never reported it to the police. She suffered with insomnia and anxiety, and it had a detrimental effect on her work, her friendships and social life. She told me about it a year or so into our friendship, and she described Rape Crisis as a lifeline.

Ten days later Lori asks if I can give her a lift to their counselling service. I wait in the car outside, listening to the radio, and worry about Nick, wondering how to tackle him on the subject of his drinking. He was out till late again last night and the boys found him asleep on the sofa this morning. That's not the first time.

It's a blustery day, unseasonably cold, clouds scudding high and fast. The trees at the edge of the car park whip to and fro. My feet grow numb so I flex my toes and turn my ankles, trying to get the circulation going.

When Lori comes out and gets into the car, her eyes are pink from crying, her nose puffy. She looks completely gutted. All she says is, 'OK,' once she's buckled her seat belt.

Not wanting to intrude, I put a CD on to fill the silence, reggae-dance songs, innocuous enough, I hope.

I've been seeking advice online as to how I can help. Let her take control seems to be the most important thing. Be guided by her. It's easier to say than do.

'Are you going again?' I say, as we reach home.

'Yes,' she says. 'Same time next week.'

'Good.'

The boys run out to meet us. 'Daddy says he'll go for pizza,' Isaac says.

'Does he now?' There's food in the freezer but he wants to splash out on a takeaway. To curry favour, I assume. Or perhaps because it gives him a chance to leave the house and drink in secret.

368

'I want pepperoni,' Finn says.

'Let's get inside and see,' I say.

'I want meatballs,' Isaac says.

Thank God for the children, I think. Their energy, their needs and demands, their zest for life make it impossible to dwell on the dark side for too long. Their presence keeps shifting the perspective.

Nick reaches into the fridge for another bottle of wine, and I say, 'We need to talk about your drinking.'

He pulls a face, mouth open, eyes darting to the side. Like it's the most stupid thing he's ever heard. 'Just leave it,' he says.

'No, listen, it's affecting us all. The boys find you crashed out on the couch, reeking of booze. God knows what Lori thinks.'

'Don't be so melodramatic.' He makes a show of twisting open the wine, pouring a glass, full to the brim.

The boys are in bed and Lori is out with Tom. I can feel the animosity sizzling between us, like static.

'You shouldn't be driving in that state.'

'Fuck off,' he says quietly. His dark eyes are hard, like marbles, as he raises his glass.

There's heat in my face, tension in a ball at the back of my throat. 'You need to do something, Nick.'

'You need to get off my back. Nagging and moaning.'

'It's not about me. You need help.'

He shakes his head, gives a bitter laugh.

'I know things have been difficult,' I say. 'They've been difficult for us all, most of all for Lori. You getting drunk all the time isn't helping. You need to stop. To control it.'

'Don't keep telling me what I need,' he says, his voice low.

'You stop,' I say firmly, 'you get help, whatever, or you leave.'

'I'm going nowhere,' he says. 'This is my house as much as it's yours.' He drinks half the wine.

'Don't you care? Think about the rest of us, think about Lori. The day after we got home, the very next day, you went off on a binge and told us you were going to your parents. We nearly lost her–'

'You slept with him, didn't you?' he says.

My heart thumps. He's staring at me. He drinks more wine.

'Don't be stupid,' I say.

'You fucked him.'

'No, I didn't,' I say. 'Is that what you've been telling yourself? Is that why you've not come near me? Or is it because you're too drunk to get it up?'

'You bitch.'

My anger drains away swiftly to be replaced by sadness. How did we get here? I cover my eyes, elbows on the table. I will not cry. 'I'm sorry,' I say. 'That wasn't fair. But I don't want you here, not acting like this.'

'Well, maybe I don't want to be here.' He hits out at the edge of the table. The wine bottle teeters but doesn't fall.

He goes to the bowl on the side, looking for his

car keys.

'You can't drive,' I say. 'Nick, please, wait a minute. Sit down and talk to me. We can work something out.'

He spins around. 'Where are the car keys?'

'You can't drive.'

'Fucking hell, Jo.' He slams at the table again and the bottle goes over, rolls and smashes on the floor.

'Mummy? Daddy?' Isaac is calling from upstairs.

Nick makes a snarling sound, teeth set, eyes glittering.

'Please?' I say.

He bolts out of the kitchen. I hear the crash of the front door slamming.

'Mummy?'

'I'm coming. It's OK.' I take a deep breath but I can't stop myself shaking. I'm just glad Lori isn't at home.

CHAPTER FIFTY-EIGHT

Bradley Carlson's trial opens in August. Even though he has confessed, the case is still presented to judges in court. Peter Dunne emails the day before to confirm it is happening. He and the US consul general will be attending.

He emails again at the end of the first day, early in the morning our time, summarizing the evidence. No foreign journalists are allowed in but they wait outside the court and we see a fifteen-second piece about the trial opening on the TV broadcast. I feel sick each time there's news. Cold to my stomach. Lori gets messages from Shona, Dawn and Rosemary.

Late afternoon, I find her in tears in the kitchen. 'Oh, Lori.' I sit beside her, tentatively touch her shoulder.

She twists her fingers about her wrist, to and fro, tracing the scars that are now bands of silvery skin. 'I thought it was getting easier but...' she shudders '...it makes me so scared.'

I stroke her back. 'Oh, darling, I'm so sorry.'

She cries some more, then says, 'At least I don't have to be there, see him.'

'That's true. Would it be any better if we asked people not to send any updates?'

'No,' she says. 'I'd only wonder. They don't say much, really, not about the details. There's more online. I'm not going to read all that.'

'That's fine. Of course it is.'

'I just want it to be over.' She looks at me, her lips wobbling. 'Feeling like this – what if it's never over?'

I choose my words with care. 'You said it had been getting easier. And I think it will again. The trial's brought it all back, and of course that's bound to be really, really hard, but once it's finished, things should start to feel different again. You're never going to forget what happened but you won't be thinking about it all the time.'

'Letting it rule my life – everything...'

'I know.'

'I think I'll ring Dad,' she says.

'You'd like to see him?'

'Yes.'

'I'll have a word too,' I say.

After Lori's spoken to Tom, she puts me on the phone and I walk out into the hall. 'Just to warn you, she's finding this really tough. She doesn't want to know all the ins and outs.'

He understands.

Lori seems comforted by Tom's visit and then, perhaps to distract herself, offers to help the boys get ready for bed. Tom has been following the news online. If Lori doesn't want to know any details, he's the polar opposite.

'His confession's backed up with solid forensic evidence,' Tom says.

'Such as?' I say.

'His DNA is everywhere, on the suitcase, inside the suitcase.' Tom looks away. 'On Lori.'

'Oh, God.'

'The pictures on his laptop. And the prosecution can prove he bought the drugs online, the caustic soda, the plastic ties. It's comprehensive. It's completely damning.'

He shows me some of the posts online.

The trial opened today at the Sichuan Chengdu Intermediate People's Court of American Bradley Carlson (28) accused of intentional homicide, kidnapping and rape. The court heard that the defendant had confessed to his crimes. His lawyer, Wang Hongtang, stated that his client accepted his culpability and was co-operating fully with the procuratorate. The prosecution stated that the evidence is abundant and incontrovertible.

Carlson is accused of the intentional murder and rape of Chinese student Bai Lijuan, abducted in 2013. He is also accused of kidnap, rape and intention to murder the British teacher, Lorelei Maddox, abducted on 7 April 2014. Both victims were held by Carlson at a rented unit in the Jinniu district of the city.

In the US Carlson is portrayed as some sort of Tom Ripley character from the Patricia Highsmith novels: a cold, callous, charming psychopath. But Ripley's murders were acts of self-advancement and self-preservation, while Bradley Carlson's come solely from a twisted desire to control and dominate, rape and kill.

Worldwide, there is a fascination with the story and the players: the apparently clean-cut American, the innocent Chinese student, the British backpacker. Lori is variously described as quirky, fun-loving and a party animal. I wonder if 'quirky' is subtext for 'gay'.

Tom tells me what he has gleaned so far. Carlson had encountered Bai Lijuan at the Chengdu North Railway Station, chaotic that day as half the people in the country were travelling to their home villages and towns for the holiday. He asked her for help finding his train, offered her a spiked drink by way of thanks, then got her into a cab. He told the driver she was drunk, that the English class had been celebrating and she had been foolish, that he was her teacher and had to take her to her parents. He spoke Chinese to the comatose girl, pretended concern. The taxi dropped them at the end of the alley. Carlson took her to the workshop. She was petite, like Lori, easy to carry.

The prosecution have described how Carlson kept her chained up like a dog and how, after her death, he disposed of her body, taking the skeletal remains to his flat.

Our statements about finding Bai Lijuan have been read out in court.

I stop Tom talking. I've heard enough. Tears start in my eyes and he puts his hand on mine. 'It'll be OK,' he says. I look at him. His light blue eyes are steady, clear.

I find it hard to speak but I nod my agreement. *It will. It will be OK.*

The trial lasts only two days. As Peter Dunne anticipated, the Chinese authorities have been very careful to conduct proceedings in the spirit of fairness and transparency. No one is accusing them of coercion or heavy-handedness. And they could do with the PR: in Hong Kong pro-democracy activists are staging protests, camping out in the city, disrupting the everyday life of the territory. The ghost of Tiananmen Square hovers in the wings.

Carlson has offered no defence as such, so it is simply a question of laying out all the evidence in turn. His lawyer has emphasized that Carlson has been fully co-operative since making his confession, in an effort to mitigate against the most severe of sentences. The verdict is expected in the coming days.

Lori and I watch the news item about the conclusion of the trial on the computer together. There are pictures of Bai Lijuan, and her parents, the photograph of Lori, one of Bradley Carlson taken outside the court, cuffed to PSB guards, and an aerial shot of the city wreathed in smog.

She moans quietly as she sees him. Pushes back from the table.

'Do you want to talk–' I begin.

'No, Mum, just leave it. Just...' She's agitated, her breath uneven, her hands raised and her head twisting from side to side, as though she's looking to escape. To flee.

'Lori,' I say calmly, 'it's OK.'

'It's not,' she says, tears breaking in her voice. 'It's never going to be OK. How can you say that?' She turns away.

I get up to go after her. 'Lori. I'm sorry. Let's just–'

'No,' she chokes, 'leave me alone.'

I bite my tongue, nod my agreement, watch her go, aching to hug her, to console her.

I wait until I'm on my own and less upset before reading the reports online. There is repeated mention of Bradley Carlson's attitude in court, describing how he appeared to boast about his crimes and relished explaining how he had planned and carried them out.

There's been more coverage of the case in America, lots of discussion on websites. Bradley Carlson is not classed as a serial killer because of his low body count. Serial killers have to murder three or more people over a period of at least a month. Some commentators speculate he will eventually be 'found out', that there will be more victims.

The Chinese police complied with requests

from the authorities in the US to ask Bradley Carlson about any previous victims but he denied any previous rapes or murders. Perhaps in years to come they will match his DNA to unsolved cases. As Peter Dunne said, it's unlikely he'd progressed from a state of innocence to the appalling attack on, first, Bai Lijuan and then Lori.

Some commentators online have tried to answer questions about his psychopathology. Carlson's intelligence, his apparent charm, his successful career, all made him seem like a normal person. He was excellent at manipulating people, to gain their trust and friendship, mimicking appropriate emotions when in fact he would-be incapable of feeling anything. His crimes were organized, carefully planned and coolly enacted. All these are classic attributes of a psychopathic killer. His prime motivation in the crimes was to exercise power through total control. A comatose victim could offer no resistance whatsoever. Some speculate he may have had necrophiliac tendencies. I almost retch when I read that. There was no mention of such behaviour in the trial accounts and, from what I've read, Carlson was frank, arrogant even, in detailing his actions: he bragged about his behaviour. He had no remorse and no shame.

Some transcripts from the trial are made available. The most damning section released by the court demonstrates his total lack of empathy. Carlson was asked why he had kidnapped Bai Lijuan and his reply shocked all present. He wanted to celebrate the holiday in style.

'You went to the North Railway Station with the intention of abducting a woman?'

'Yes.'

'And why did you select Bai Lijuan?'

'She was small,' Carlson said, 'easy to handle.'

'And Lorelei Maddox?'

'The same.'

'Miss Maddox was your friend?'

'Yes.'

'Why would you attack your friend?'

'It wasn't personal,' Carlson said. 'It wasn't about her.'

'It was about you? About your perverted desires?'

'Yes.'

'You took pleasure from this – the kidnaps, the rapes, the murder?'

'Why else would I do it?'

I feel the thrum of hatred for him in the beat of my blood, acid in my heart.

There are short biographies about him online, removed from his birth family for his own safety and adopted as a two-year-old. Raised by a fundamentalist preacher, a strict disciplinarian, and his wife. Bradley Carlson's adoptive mother had died of ovarian cancer when he was eleven years old. He had left the US after graduating in international development. No family members attended the trial and his adoptive father told reporters that Bradley was no longer his son.

Before I close the computer I check for the latest news on the Nigerian schoolgirls who were kidnapped back in April. There's talk of a cease-fire to enable their return but the whole situation sounds chaotic, the government inept. All those families waiting for word, all those girls, those daughters.

CHAPTER FIFTY-NINE

Nick refuses point blank to discuss his drinking with me when he comes back to the house, three days after he walked out.

He's packing a bag.

'We can get through this,' I say. 'Look at everything we've coped with so far. If we stick together, if you get some help–'

'I don't need help,' he says.

'You need to accept you've got a problem.'

He pauses, a pile of T-shirts in his hands, and stares at me, his eyes cold, his face shadowed with stubble. 'I do accept that,' he says, 'and you're the problem.'

'Oh, come on...'

'All this whining at me to stop drinking,' he says, 'it's just a distraction.'

'From what?' I say.

'I'm not the one who's unfaithful,' he says.

I feel a wave of heat and the pinch of anxiety. 'I told you, I did not sleep with Tom.'

'Do you think I'm an idiot?' he says.

'Nick, can we just–'

'No,' he says, throwing the clothes onto the bed, 'we can't *just* do anything.'

'What about Lori?' I say.

He snorts as he opens another drawer. 'That's rich, coming from you. What would she make of it, eh?'

My guts clench. Would he do that? I've no idea how Lori would react but how can he even contemplate hurting her to get back at me when she is so weak and damaged?

'She needs us,' I say, 'and I'm not the one who's pissed all the time.'

He glares at me, a bitter smile on his face. Bends to fill his bag.

'Where are you going?' I say.

'Ivan's.' Ivan is divorced. He lives in Chester, about forty-five miles away.

'What are you going to do?' I say.

'Fuck knows.'

I give up. He's no good to Lori angry and drunk. Or to me.

I can't stay in the room any longer. My throat aches with unshed tears as I leave him to his packing.

He doesn't say goodbye before he goes.

The boys miss Nick. I do, too, the way he was before. It's hard to pinpoint when he started to change but I know we were arguing before I went to China. And the redundancy really didn't help.

He rings every week or so to talk to Isaac and Finn. Lori won't speak to him.

He calls me, too, in the early hours, sometimes drunk and contrite, his words laboured between long pauses, painful and pointless, at other times drunk and abusive. Now I've taken to muting my ring tone when I'm going to bed. Sometimes he leaves rambling messages. It seems clear that, so far, he hasn't addressed the issue, hasn't done anything about it.

The boys think he's gone away to work. Lori knows the situation.

'It's not fair,' she said, when I told her. 'Why is he being so stupid?'

'People say it's a disease. It's complicated,' I try to offer some insight, 'but the only person who can do anything about it is Nick himself and for that to happen he has to admit there's a problem.' And if he did, I'm not sure I'd want him back.

It's the first week in September when we hear from Peter Dunne again. 'We've just come from court,' he says. 'We were called there for the verdict. They've found him guilty on all counts. And they've handed down the death sentence.' My stomach plummets but at the same time there's a rush of dizzying relief. *Guilty. Guilty.* The word we've been waiting for.

'He has the right to appeal, so that process will begin now,' Peter Dunne says. 'Two separate appeals in different courts, the Higher People's Court first and then the Supreme People's Court. His lawyer will be arguing for clemency, to reflect the fact that Carlson made a full confession and co-operated with the police.'

'What happens if he wins the appeal?' I say.

'The death sentence may be commuted to what they call life with two years' reprieve. In effect it's a life sentence in prison. Realistically, that's the best he could hope for. However, Carlson showed no remorse or humility in court. He acted as though it was simply bad luck that he was caught. That won't play well with the appeal judges.'

'I'd like them to lock him up for the rest of his life,' I say. It seems fitting after what he did to Bai Lijuan and Lori. To see him incarcerated, at the mercy of his captors, to have no control over his movements, over any aspect of his life, to be powerless. 'How long will it take? When will we know?'

Peter Dunne can't be sure.

He says goodbye, and I'm aware that the wait for news will go on. The spectre of the case is there all the time at the back of my mind, a shadow, a place of darkness.

The final appeal in the case of American Bradley Carlson, found guilty of intentional homicide, rape and kidnap of Bai Lijuan and the abduction and rape of Briton Lorelei Maddox with intent to kill, has been denied. Wang Hongtang, the defendant's lawyer, argued for clemency on grounds that Carlson had co-operated and made a full confession. However, the procurator-general said, 'We have seen no evidence of contrition or remorse from the defendant. This sentence sends a clear message. These crimes were the most serious. They were planned and carried out with clear intention to murder. There were no extenuating circumstances whatsoever.'

Something buckles in my chest. So he will die. My head fizzes and my vision fractures. The state will kill him. Is he afraid? Surely he must be. I study that notion. See him craven and gibbering, dragged to the place of execution. What if he is indifferent? Or gets some sick thrill at the notoriety this brings. If he is a psychopath, as they say, does he have the capacity to experience terror? Does he understand now what it was like for Lori as he trussed her up, drugged her and raped her? Does he see how monstrous his acts were? I want him to suffer, I acknowledge, but if he is executed next year or the year after then his suffering will end. I would rather he be left alive, rotting slowly, devoid of hope and dignity and freedom.

Still I cannot equate this man, who bought caustic soda and plastic ties, took pictures of his victims unconscious and naked, with the young man who ordered our food at the hotpot restaurant and consoled Dawn when she cried about Lori. The man pictured smiling on Lori's blog, his arm around her shoulders. Had he chosen her then? Marked her out as his next victim?

CHAPTER SIXTY

The phone call comes at seven thirty on a Wednesday morning in mid-November.

'Mr Dunne?'

'Mrs Maddox, we have just been informed that Bradley Carlson was executed this morning.'

A thump in my chest. My legs turn to water. I sit on the edge of the bed. 'Right.' Ringing in my ears. He's dead.

'As you know,' he says, 'it is UK policy to oppose

the death penalty in all circumstances, but the Chinese were eager to make an example of him.'

I think of Carlson strapped to a trolley, IV lines or a needle delivering the fatal dose. Should I be happy about this? Should I feel victorious? Or relieved? I just feel sick.

There's a pause as I try to absorb the news.

'I'll let Mr Maddox know, too,' Peter Dunne says.

'Yes, thank you.' I try to concentrate on the conversation, on responding appropriately, but there's a beating in my head. I'm floundering. 'And thank you for everything you've done.'

'I'm only sorry that your introduction to China was under such terrible circumstances,' he says. 'If you or Lorelei ever need anything in future, please do not hesitate to get in touch.'

I wake Lori and tell her the news. She covers her face with her hands.

Isabelle rings. 'We're going to be asked to comment. Do you want to discuss what you say with Lori, Nick and Tom?'

'Yes, of course,' I say. 'Nick's still away, though.'

'I see. OK.'

'What are we supposed to say?' Lori looks between Tom and me.

'We're glad he was caught, glad he's been convicted,' I say.

'Glad he's dead,' Tom says.

I stare at him.

'I don't feel glad about any of it,' Lori says.

'OK,' I say. 'Maybe that's not the right word.'

384

'We say the absolute minimum.' Tom pulls a piece of paper over and takes a pen.

I have a flashback to his hotel room, those days of leafleting, the list we made about Lori's last photographs.

'"Lorelei and her family are..."' Tom looks at us. Lori shrugs.

'Relieved?' I say.

Tom screws up his mouth but obviously can't think of anything better.

'Isabelle can always tweak it,' I say. '"Lorelei and her family are relieved that the matter has been concluded–"'

'Sounds like a boundary dispute,' Tom says. '"...relieved that justice has been done and now wish to concentrate on looking to the future."'

'That'll do,' Lori says.

There's a ghastly sense of anti-climax to the whole thing. I've no desire to cheer, raise a fist or even sigh with relief at the conclusion of the legal process. Bradley Carlson may be dead but we are still here, swirling in the aftermath of his violence. Still haunted.

We get a letter from Chengdu, addressed to Mr and Mrs Maddox and Miss Maddox. A franking mark tells us it's from the consulate. Inside there is another envelope, thick yellow vellum, embossed with pictures of koi carp. I open it and pull out a note.

Dear Mr and Mrs Maddox and Miss Lorelei Maddox,
I am translating for Mr Bai and Mrs Wen who wish

to thank you for your most kind thoughts. We send you
hope for health and prosperity and happiness and we
thank you for your kindness and assistance.
   Warm regards.

They have signed their names in Chinese characters, delicate pen strokes, in rich black ink.

My eyes fill and the writing swims. I cannot swallow. I look away, out of the window, where dark clouds, huge like galleons, race across the winter sky. And seagulls wheel below them. I think of the Chinese girl with the daisy chain and the large sunglasses, setting out on her life, and how it was stolen from her. So brutally. Of the endless sorrow that her parents must bear. And how in the midst of that grief they could consider us, choose a card, decide what to say and arrange to have it sent. Such human kindness. I think of Lori and her pain, the wounds that may never heal, the invisible ones.

And I weep for us all.

CHAPTER SIXTY-ONE

We are making dough, the four of us, for Christmas decorations to hang on the tree. Reindeer and penguins to be baked, then iced. Benji patrols around the table for bits of raw pastry. Isaac keeps sneaking bits for him.

I had expected Isaac to be even more unsettled in the wake of everything that's happened but he's actually much better. We've gone a whole term without any concerns about his behaviour. Sebastian moved schools and Isaac has a new best friend, Imogen. They spend hours drawing and making things together. He can still be gloomy and petulant, quick to take offence and slow to rally, but I think that's just his personality. I dread his teenage years, especially if I've to deal with him on my own, but that is a way off – God knows what might happen between now and then. Because you never really know what's round the corner, do you?

Lori is back to her normal weight, still skinny, but she has lost that awful gaunt look. In the aftermath of the trial she was interviewed for a feature in the *Guardian* magazine. Isabelle identified other opportunities but Lori was clear she wanted to limit what she did. Lori said the interviewer was really easy to talk to and Lori trusted her not to misrepresent anything. It was hard to read that feature. Lori has never talked to me in any detail about that time: most of what I knew was from the police statement she gave. One thing she's said since then has stuck with me: that the worst thing was the helplessness, the total loss of control.

Finn is singing along to the radio and Isaac clamps his hands over his ears and says, 'Too loud, tell him, Mummy.'

'You've got floury hair, now,' Lori says to Isaac.

'What flowers?' Isaac frowns.

'Not flowers – flour.' Lori pats the bag and a puff of white escapes. 'You're going white, like a ghost.'

'Scooby Doo,' Finn says.

Isaac plunges his hands into the flour and pats it over his head and face. I feel a flash of irritation at the prospect of even more mess to clear up, then Lori laughs, that yelp of pleasure I cherish so, and the mess just doesn't matter any more.

Finn chuckles. 'Make me a ghost, too, then. Go on.'

Isaac obliges, leaving Finn dusted white and sneezing.

'OK, enough,' I say, before they go any further.

'Take a picture,' Isaac says.

'Wait, then.' Lori goes upstairs. She comes back with two bed sheets and her new camera, bought with the money she's been saving up.

She wraps the sheets around the boys and gets them to pose. 'Spooky faces,' she says, and reels off a sequence of snaps.

'Shower,' I say, 'both of you.'

'What about the decorations?' Isaac says.

'They can go in the oven now and we'll do the icing in the morning. Are you at work?' I check with Lori. She's been working for Tom, doing admin for tenancy agreements and filing, and more recently taking viewings, showing people properties in Manchester.

'Yes, ten till four. You two can show me what you've done when I get home,' she says.

The boys trudge off, trailing puffs of flour.

Lori and I put the trays into the oven.

'Aphrodite's moving in with Dad,' Lori says, taking the cookie cutters to the sink.

I feel a pang of dismay but chastise myself. What did I expect? For Tom to carry on rootless, restless, unattached for ever? 'Really?' I say. 'Wow. What's she like?'

'She's nice, actually; really nice. She's doing business studies at Manchester Met.'

'I thought she was a model,' I say. *A hand model.* The time we had in China, Tom and I, seems like a mirage now, rippling in the haze. Unreal. And that night, that precious night, when we found sanctuary together amid the horror, it feels like it happened to other people, in a parallel universe.

Losing Lori, looking for her, threw us together and forced us to move beyond the confines of our past. Brought us to a new understanding. Did I ever wish it might be more than that? At times, if I'm honest. I cannot speak for Tom. He never gave me cause to hope. And, realistically, I think we're still too different, and that those differences would rankle and chafe and soon corrupt any shared future we might have together. Better to cherish the memory: desire in his eyes, the beat of his heart, the warmth of his skin. That love, as if we would call her back to us.

Lori runs the water, squirts in some washing-up liquid. 'Yes,' she says, 'but she wants to do the other stuff and help Dad build his empire.'

I laugh. 'When I met your dad I never for one minute imagined he'd become a property developer.'

Lori closes the tap. She turns. The smile fades from her face. 'Mum?'

'Yes?'

She looks so serious. I don't know what's coming. She rubs at her shoulder. She's had a tattoo done there, a Chinese phoenix.

'I'm going back one day,' she says.

My heart turns over. 'Right.'

'Not yet. I know I'm not ready yet,' she says. 'And I'll need to save up. I could probably stay with Shona. I'm sure I could get a job with one of the English schools eventually, and Rosemary would help me apply. It might be hard, bad days, but that'd be the same wherever I was. And there must be some therapists there.'

'Right,' I say again. A wash of fear and panic laps at the back of my mind but I ignore it, instead cleaving to the burst of elation that swells in my chest. See the set of her jaw, the determination in her eyes. 'You are brilliant, you know that?' I tell her. 'I am so, so proud of you.'

She opens her arms and comes to me. And I bite my teeth together tight and breathe through my nose and blink like mad and hold her, hold her close.

Lori in the Ori-ent

Part 2
Posted on 30 February 2016 by Lori

Nǐ hǎo! I'm back. Apologies for the long absence but I was a bit tied up. (Sorry, sometimes the darkest, weirdest humour helps.)

Most of you will know things got very bad for a while and I've been home in the UK. Please send thoughts and prayers and love to the family of Bai

Lijuan and, if you can possibly manage it, give donations to Missing Overseas. They are an amazing charity who were there for my family at the most difficult time. To those of you who left messages, many, many thanks, you are awesome. If you don't know what I'm on about, or need to know any more, search Bai Lijuan and Lorelei Maddox.

I'm going to draw a line under all that now.

Here is the line.

A little wobbly but unbroken.

So ... what's new in Chengdu?

My building is gone! You turn your back for five minutes... Gobbled up by development. Here are the before and after pics. Mine is the stylish blue block on the left. As you can see in the picture, the new apartments are already occupied. All twenty-eight floors of them.

One place I never got to visit is Flower Town so I'll be making a trip soon and reporting back. I'm pleased to say the hotpot is still as fierce as I remember and the park is as beautiful. Now we just need some of that weather engineering. How about it, guys? Sunny Chengdu, pearl of the Sichuan Riviera!

Klaxon! I'm proud to announce the opening of a new gallery space on the fourteenth of next month. More publicity coming soon but the inaugural exhibition will feature framed photos by me, original pieces of amazing jewellery by Shona Munro, and prints and etchings by Mo Nuwa, one of Chengdu's most inventive emerging artists. Our preview will feature a live DJ and cocktails courtesy of Bar None.

It's sooo good to be back.

391

And I leave you with a few words from Xue Tao's poem, 'West Cliff'.

Raising my wine against the wind, I wave my hand.

Zài jiàn.
Lxxx

ACKNOWLEDGEMENTS

Thank you, *xiè xie*, to everyone who helped me research this book. In England: my partner Tim, Joe, Lynda, Lan and Xi Lei, fellow author Peter May, Detective Superintendent Kevin Duffy (Retd) and Matt Searle at Missing Abroad. In Ireland: my sister Sarah. And in China: my son Dan, Cookie, Stephanie, Cynthia, Jarriane, Mrs Zhou, Joanna from the Bookworm Chengdu, Dawn, Elizabeth and Ricky from Chinese Corner, and Professor He Jiahong – also a crime writer. And I promise – none of you appear in the book, though things you said may well do!

Dreaming In Chinese, by Deborah Fallows, was a great introduction to Chinese language and culture.

Many thanks to my agent Sara, editor Krystyna and all her team at Constable & Robinson, and to my writing group: Mary Sharratt, Sue Stern and Melanie Amri, for invaluable feedback and encouragement.

I have invented the charity Missing Overseas, inspired by the work of Missing Abroad, but I have altered procedures at times to suit my story. I have also taken some liberties with the geography of Chengdu.

The publishers hope that this book has given you enjoyable reading. Large Print Books are especially designed to be as easy to see and hold as possible. If you wish a complete list of our books please ask at your local library or write directly to:

Magna Large Print Books
Magna House, Long Preston,
Skipton, North Yorkshire.
BD23 4ND